A Deadly Cliché

"A very well-written mystery with interesting and surprising characters and a great setting. Readers will feel as if they are in Oyster Bay."
—*The Mystery Reader*

"This series is one I hope to follow for a long time, full of fast-paced mysteries, budding romances, and good friends. An excellent combination!"
—*The Romance Readers Connection*

A Killer Plot

"Ellery Adams's debut novel, *A Killer Plot*, is not only a great read, but a visceral experience. Olivia Limoges's investigation into a friend's murder will have you hearing the waves crash on the North Carolina shore. You might even feel the ocean winds stinging your cheeks. Visit Oyster Bay and you'll long to return again and again."
—Lorna Barrett, *New York Times* bestselling author of the Booktown Mysteries

"Adams's plot is indeed killer, her writing would make her the star of any support group, and her characters—especially Olivia and her standard poodle, Captain Haviland—are a diverse, intelligent bunch. *A Killer Plot* is a perfect excuse to go coastal."
—*Richmond Times-Dispatch*

"A fantastic start to a new series . . . With new friendships, possible romance(s), and promises of great things to come, *A Killer Plot* is one book you don't want to be caught dead missing."
—*The Best Reviews*

"Ellery Adams brings the insight of a Southern, well-funded Miss Marple to the pages. It's a pleasure to see this series under way."
—*Kingdom Books*

Peach Pies and Alibis

Ellery Adams

BERKLEY PRIME CRIME, NEW YORK

THE BERKLEY PUBLISHING GROUP
Published by the Penguin Group
Penguin Group (USA) Inc.
375 Hudson Street, New York, New York 10014, USA

USA / Canada / UK / Ireland / Australia / New Zealand / India / South Africa / China

Penguin Books Ltd., Registered Offices: 80 Strand, London WC2R 0RL, England
For more information about the Penguin Group, visit penguin.com.

PEACH PIES AND ALIBIS

A Berkley Prime Crime Book / published by arrangement with the author

Berkley Prime Crime Books are published by The Berkley Publishing Group.
BERKLEY® PRIME CRIME and the PRIME CRIME logo are trademarks of
Penguin Group (USA) Inc.

For information, address: The Berkley Publishing Group,
a division of Penguin Group (USA) Inc.,
375 Hudson Street, New York, New York 10014.

ISBN: 978-0-425-25199-7

PUBLISHING HISTORY
Berkley Prime Crime mass-market edition / March 2013

PRINTED IN THE UNITED STATES OF AMERICA

10 9 8 7 6 5 4 3 2 1

Cover illustration by Julia Green.
Cover design by Diana Kolsky.
Interior design by Laura K. Corless.

This is a work of fiction. Names, characters, places, and incidents either are the product
of the author's imagination or are used fictitiously, and any resemblance to actual persons,
living or dead, business establishments, events, or locales is entirely coincidental.
The publisher does not have any control over and does not assume any responsibility for
author or third-party websites or their content.

PUBLISHER'S NOTE: The recipes contained in this book are to be followed exactly as
written. The publisher is not responsible for your specific health or allergy needs that may
require medical supervision. The publisher is not responsible for any adverse reactions to
the recipes contained in this book.

ALWAYS LEARNING   PEARSON

In memory of my sister-in-law,
Joceyln Prewitt-Stanley, 1977–2012

The nectarine, and curious peach,
Into my hands themselves do reach;
Stumbling on melons, as I pass,
Ensnared with flowers, I fall on grass.

—Andrew Marvell

Chapter 1

"There's nothing like a wedding to ruin a perfectly good Saturday," Mrs. Dower declared to The Charmed Pie Shoppe's empty dining room. She dropped the newspaper she'd been reading on the table, leaving the radiant faces of new brides to stare at the ceiling.

Ella Mae LeFaye studied her first customer of the morning. Mrs. Dower was gray. Her clothes, her hair, and the cloud above her head were all a shade of dark gray. She sat alone at one of the café tables, rumbling like a thunderhead. With every breath, she seemed to expel an invisible vapor of gloom. It gathered around her and then spread across the pie shop like a low fog, blotting out the light, muting the twang of the country music being piped through the radio, and squelching the pleasant aroma of baking pies.

"Nothin' like a challenge before you've even got your eyes open," said a pixielike woman with nut brown hair. She examined Mrs. Dower through a crack in the swing doors leading from the kitchen into the dining room and shook her head. "It's hopeless, Ella Mae. You'll never make her smile. For half a century, that woman has been swallowin' up all traces of joy like a human bog."

"What's her story?" Ella Mae asked as she moved away from the door to stand behind her worktable.

Reba smirked. "She's been playing the organ at the First Baptist church since before I was born."

Ella Mae pressed a ball of dough flat and picked up her rolling pin. She paused, the flour-dusted pin poised in the air. "You're kidding, right?"

"Of course!" Reba laughed, a sound like the tinkling of tiny bells, and tied her apron strings behind her back. "She only acts like she's older than dirt. Shoot, she's probably younger than I am."

"I don't know what to believe about the people of Haven-wood anymore!" Ella Mae replied heatedly. "*You* try discovering that you're able to transfer emotions into food, thereby directly affecting other people's behavior, and see how muddled your thoughts become."

Waving in surrender, Reba glanced out through the crack again. "I know you've been thrown for a loop, but you'll be all right. The LeFayes are tough." She raised her eyes and steepled her hands. "Wish me luck, I'm goin' out to take her order."

Ella Mae saluted her with the rolling pin and then pressed it into the center of the dough, releasing a burst of buttery scent. She maneuvered the wooden tool up and down, side to side, and up and down again until the dough had been manipulated into a flat circle. Folding it in half, she gently transferred the dough into a glass pie dish.

"She's wants a breakfast pie," Reba announced as she reentered the kitchen, the swing doors flapping in her wake. "But not the one on the menu. Says she doesn't care if she has to wait an hour for her order. She wants what she wants."

Ella Mae pushed a lock of hair out of her face, leaving

behind a streak of flour on her cheek and the edge of her ear. "Then I suppose it's a good thing she showed up before we're officially open. What exactly would she like?"

"I see that twinkle in your eye," Reba said, holding out a warning finger. "You think you're gonna charm her into smilin', but even your mojo isn't that powerful. All jokin' aside, Ella Mae, you don't know how to control your gift just yet. You'd best rein it in for now."

"How am I ever going to control it when no one will give me straight answers about how I got this way!" Ella Mae snapped. "How any of us got this way. What makes me and you and my mother and aunts different?"

Reba shook her head. "I told you, sugar. You have to find your own path to the truth. It's one of the rules."

"Made by whom? Another mystery none of you will explain to me." Gesturing at the pie plate, Ella Mae said, "Forget it. Just tell me what Mrs. Dower wants for breakfast."

Obviously relieved to change the subject, Reba reached into her apron and pulled out a pack of red licorice twists. "Her mama used to make a pie full of cheese, hash browns, bacon, and somethin' crunchy on top. Mrs. D. doesn't remember what made the crunch—probably the bones of small children who lost their way in the woods—but she said if you're as good as folks say, then you'll figure it out."

Ella Mae walked over to the pantry and examined her supplies. She glanced at the tidy jars of dried fruit, passing over the cherries, apricots, cranberries, raisins, prunes, figs, and quince until her gaze rested on the collection of nuts. But she wasn't looking for pecans, almonds, macadamias, walnuts, hazelnuts, pine nuts, pistachios, peanuts, or cashews. What she needed wasn't in her kitchen.

"Just sprinkle a few dead beetles on top," Reba suggested. "She'll think it's some kind of exotic nut."

Ignoring the jumbo tubs of sugar and flour, the canisters of spices, and the clumps of dried herbs hanging from the wire shelves, Ella Mae turned to Reba. "Can you run over to the Piggly Wiggly for a box of corn flakes?"

"Ah-ha." Reba tapped her temple. "You're a clever girl. Be back in two shakes of the devil's tail."

After Reba left, Ella Mae took eggs, bacon, and cheddar cheese out of the walk-in refrigerator. Once the bacon was sizzling on the stovetop, she shredded the cheese and sliced the potato until she had a mound of thin white strips on the worktable. When the bacon was crisp, she removed it from the frying pan and dumped the potatoes in the hot fat, where they jumped and jerked like a child being tickled. By the time Reba returned, Ella Mae had blended all the ingredients together along with a cup of cottage cheese. Seasoning the mixture with salt, pepper, and a pinch of paprika, she poured it into the pie shell and then opened the box of corn flakes.

"You said that Mrs. Dower's an organist. Have you ever heard her perform?"

Reba nodded. "People are so glum when she plays the offertory hymn that they can barely pull out their wallets, let alone pry them open and stick a bunch of cash in the collection plate. And that woman can make a bridal march sound like a funeral procession." She pointed toward the dining room. "You heard what she said. She hates weddings. Hates happiness in general."

"And her mama? The one who made her favorite pie?" Ella Mae shoved her hand into the cereal box, her fingers caressing the small, stiff flakes.

"Passed on years ago. Why?"

Ella Mae scooped up a handful of corn flakes and held them over the pie. "I bet she misses her mother—that she's never gotten over losing her. I need to help her believe that her mother wouldn't want her to spend the rest of her life moping. I need to help her stop feeling so . . . gray."

Reba frowned. "Not blue?"

"Blue doesn't describe loss. Grief robs the world of color.

Turns it heavy and gray." At the mention of grief, Ella Mae thought of her failed marriage and of how she'd left New York before completing her final semester of culinary school. Shoving the memories aside, she glanced at Reba. "Give Mrs. Dower some more coffee, please. I want to add something special to her pie."

"You should save your superpowers for an emergency, like making that hunky UPS man fall madly in love with me. Instead, you're gonna waste them on that sourpuss." With a scowl of disapproval, Reba left the kitchen.

Ella Mae closed her eyes and traveled back in time. In her mind's eye, she was a little girl again. It was summertime and her thin limbs were bronzed and freckled by the sun. There was a kite in her hands. It was shaped like a butterfly and had been made from a rainbow of bright nylon hues. Ella Mae had tied the kite to the basket of her bicycle and sat perched at the top of a steep hill, ready to propel herself forward.

Letting out a holler of anticipation, Ella Mae pushed off with her bare feet, launching the bike into the air. She picked up speed instantly, her whiskey-colored pigtails lifting from her shoulders, the kite shooting into the cerulean sky. She'd looked up at her kite, watching the sunbeams illuminate the reds, blues, yellows, and greens until the fabric seemed to shimmer with life.

Here, in her warm kitchen, Ella Mae relived that moment of light and joy. She saw the colors and felt the wild freedom of her downhill plunge. And she willed those feelings into the cereal flakes as she scattered them over the surface of the pie. "Be happy," she whispered. "Let go of your grief."

By the time the pie was done, Mrs. Dower had finished reading the paper and was glaring at the other customers who'd entered The Charmed Pie Shoppe in search of breakfast. She muttered under her breath and appeared on the verge of complaining to Reba for having to wait so long when the petite waitress burst out of the kitchen carrying her meal.

"Made-to-order 'specially for you, Mrs. Dower." Reba put the plate down with a flourish and then moved to the next table to take the customers' drink orders.

Ella Mae carried a pair of ginger peach tarts through the dining area to the rotating display case in the café's front window. Out of the corner of her eye, she watched Mrs. Dower take a bite of pie. Then another. And another.

The older woman chewed slowly at first, but then her jaw moved with more gusto. Slowly, so slowly that Ella Mae wasn't certain it was there, Mrs. Dower's mouth began to curve upward into the tentative beginnings of a smile. By the time Ella Mae went back into the kitchen and returned with two coconut cream pies for the display, she barely recognized the woman in gray.

Mrs. Dower, who'd been licking the crumbs from her fork, reached out and grabbed Ella Mae as she passed close to her table. "Your pie," she began and then faltered. She touched her cheeks, which had grown flushed and rosy, and lifted a pair of meadow green eyes to Ella Mae. "It was delicious," she whispered, the blush on her face spreading over her neck and arms, infusing her sallow skin with a healthy pink glow.

Ella Mae put a hand on the woman's shoulder and grinned. "Come back again, you hear?"

"I most definitely will," Mrs. Dower promised. She then lifted a sugar packet from the bowl of sweeteners on her table and pivoted it in the light. "What a pretty yellow. Reminds me of buttercups." Looking down at her gray blouse and gray skirt, she frowned. "I like yellow," she told Ella Mae.

"I bet you look lovely in it too," Ella Mae said and couldn't help but giggle as Mrs. Dower shouldered her purse and hustled out of the pie shop, dropping her gray scarf in the trash can bordering the sidewalk.

Reba handed Ella Mae an order ticket. "Where do you reckon she's going?"

"Shopping," Ella Mae replied. "Look out, Havenwood. Mrs. Dower is on the loose."

"Well, at least she'll be dressed like a peacock when she goes into credit card debt." Reba gave Ella Mae a stern look.

Ella Mae held out her hands. "I was just trying to brighten her day. The rest of my pies will be totally normal, I promise. After all, I can't make something special for every customer."

As it turned out, Ella Mae barely had time to think, let alone infuse her food with specific feelings. In the months since she'd opened the pie shop, she'd worked five days a week. Nearly six if she counted Mondays, because even though the shop was closed, Ella Mae used that time to make a week's worth of pie dough.

Her days were long too. She was on her feet for ten hours straight and, after locking the front door at three o'clock each afternoon, she'd say good-bye to Reba, clean the kitchen, and wearily pedal her bike to Canine to Five, Havenwood's doggie day care, to collect her Jack Russell terrier. And yet, no matter how tired she was, her dog's kisses of greeting gave her the energy she needed to manage the uphill ride home.

Charleston Chew, or Chewy, as Ella Mae had taken to calling the impish puppy after he'd succeeded in shredding most of her handbags, belts, and shoes, would perch in her straw bike basket, brown eyes gleaming and tongue lolling, as she made the trek to Partridge Hill, her family's historic house. Ella Mae would dismount in the garage and gratefully step into the lovely and tranquil carriage house. Her cozy refuge from the world.

It still seemed unreal that a only few short months ago, Ella Mae and Chewy had been living in a Manhattan apartment with Sloan Kitteridge, Ella Mae's husband. For seven years Ella Mae had been content as Sloan's wife, but after she'd caught him in flagrante with the redheaded twins from 516C, she grabbed Chewy and took three planes to her hometown of Havenwood, Georgia. She returned to her beloved aunts, her daunting mother, and to Reba, the housekeeper who'd practically raised her. And she'd finally fulfilled her dream of opening her very own pie shop.

"Stop gatherin' wool and plate me some sausage pie," Reba ordered and slapped three more order tickets on the counter. "I sure wish that sweet girl you hired to work the register and handle the takeout side of things didn't have to go back to Georgia Tech. She made my life easier, even though I hated sharin' my tips with her."

"I was hoping to find a nice high school kid to take her place, but no one's responded to my ad." Ella Mae placed a sprig of mint on top of a small bowl of sliced kiwis and fresh strawberries, plated an egg and mushroom tart, and took a bacon and onion quiche out of the oven. She tore off the potholders and quickly filled four more orders, wondering if today would be as busy as yesterday.

The rest of the morning passed by in a blur of baking, plating, and dish washing. The breakfast rush merged into brunch, and before Ella Mae knew it, the lunch crowd had arrived.

With a loud "Yoo-hoo!" Ella Mae's aunt Verena strode into the kitchen, a glass of pomegranate iced tea in hand. Verena, who was clad in a black-and-white-checked dress and a pair of cardinal red pumps, settled onto a stool and drank her tea down in three gulps. Verena was famous for her hearty appetite. As she surveyed the heaps of dirty dishes in the sink and the pies cooling on wire racks, her fingers marched across the worktable and snagged a blueberry from a bowl of fruit salad. "Full house again, I see!" She popped the berry into her mouth.

Ella Mae cut a tomato basil pie into even wedges and wiped a hunk of dried dough from her forehead. "Are you still glad you invested in this place?"

"Of course!" she shouted. Verena didn't have an indoor voice. Whenever she spoke, it was as if she were addressing a large crowd. Her exuberance was as powerful as her appetite. "But we're all worried about you, Ella Mae. You work all day and then you go home, drink some wine, and fall asleep with a book in your hand. That's no way to live! Where's the fun? The adventure?"

"Has my mother been spying on me?" Ella Mae joked, but she didn't really want to hear Verena's answer.

Grabbing another blueberry, Verena shook her head. "No one's peeking in your windows. We only have to look at you to know that you're in over your head!" She scrutinized her only niece. "Your hair's a tumbleweed, you're too skinny, and I bet you can't recall the last time you ate out or went to the movies. You need help!"

Reba entered the kitchen in time to catch Verena's last sentence. "Amen to that. Our girl needs another employee, a car, and a roll in the hay. And not necessarily in that order."

Shooting Reba a dirty look, Ella Mae said, "I'll run another ad in the *Daily*, okay? If I get a break this afternoon, I can check out the auto listings too. As for the roll in the hay? I should get divorced first, don't you think?"

Balancing three plates on her arm, Reba still managed a shrug. "Sloan didn't let his marriage vows get in his way, so why should you?"

"Hush up! She's going about things the right way!" Verena scolded, grabbed the next two orders, and followed Reba through the swing doors. She came back a minute later. "Dining room's stuffed, patio's packed, and there's a line at the counter!"

Groaning, Ella Mae hurriedly plated two lunches, slipped off her apron, and picked up the dishes that needed to be delivered to a patio table.

Verena was right. There wasn't an empty seat in the shop. Reba was busy boxing a key lime pie for a to-go order while the in-house customers eyed her impatiently. Some were waiting for food and others were eager to pay their bill or have their drinks refreshed.

"This place is a train wreck," Ella Mae murmured. Pasting on a smile, she served lunches to the couple seated by a cluster of black-eyed Susans and pink coneflowers, checked to make sure the rest of the patrons were enjoying their meals, and then went back into the dining room to see to her other customers' needs.

By the time she'd walked around the room with pitchers of sweet tea and ice water flavored with paper-thin slices of lemon and lime, the line at the counter had doubled. Without being asked, Verena volunteered to ring customers on the register. Ella Mae blew her aunt a kiss of gratitude and then hustled back out to the patio to tend to people's empty glasses.

Too preoccupied to bring dirty dishes into the kitchen, Reba and Ella Mae piled them on the counter behind the display cases, well out of sight of the customers waiting to buy slices of dessert pies and tarts to take home. Ella Mae had just finished boxing a half-dozen cherry hand pies when Reba thrust a plate containing a piece of blackberry tart into her hands.

"Take this outside to Mr. Burton. He's sitting by the geraniums. And don't get stuck at his table," she warned. "He's a real talker."

Reba was right. Mr. Burton accepted his tart, and before Ella Mae could slip away, asked where the blackberries had come from.

"There's a lovely swimming hole on the way to my house," she explained, momentarily distracted by the image of the deep pool of water in the middle of a copse of old trees. "On a rise above the water, there's a ridge covered by blackberry bushes. They grow plump and juicy all summer long and are the best I've ever tasted." Her eyes grew distant as she pictured the place. "The sun bathes the berries all day, and at night, cool air from the swimming hole drifts upward and coats them in a gentle dew. My mother used to say that fruit and flowers are best picked by moonlight, so that's when I go."

Mr. Burton had yet to sample his tart, but now he lifted a forkful to his mouth. He closed his eyes and chewed slowly, relishing the sweetness of the berries and the flaky, butter-kissed dough. "I taste them both," he said, his eyes filled with delight. "The sunshine and the moon glow. I think it's about the most magical thing I've ever eaten. Could you box a piece for my wife? She's been feeling poorly lately. It's her hip, you see."

Ella Mae did her best to look sympathetic, but she sensed the tale of Mrs. Burton's hip could go on for quite some time, and time was one thing Ella Mae couldn't spare. With an apologetic smile, she interrupted Mr. Burton's narrative and excused herself.

The moment she opened the door leading into the dining room, she was assaulted by an unpleasant aroma. It was strong and acrid—the kind of odor that typically accompanies a fire. Ella Mae stopped and sniffed.

"Something's burning," she murmured and then saw a curl of smoke escape from the crack between the kitchen's swing doors. She began to walk toward the counter, horrified to see another curl and then yet another snake through the tiny opening. The smell intensified.

At first, Ella Mae had found it reminiscent of smoldering

wood, but now it called to mind the image of something blackened and charred. Something like a pie. Half a dozen meat pies to be exact.

"No, no, no!" Ella Mae cried and rushed into the kitchen.

She was met by a wall of gray smoke that obscured the worktable and countertops. As she moved closer to the commercial ovens, the air darkened from pale pewter to dark charcoal. Ella Mae quickly turned the appliances off and opened the top oven door. Smoke burst out like a puff of dragon breath from a cave mouth. Ella Mae waved it away from her face with a potholder. Bubbles of burned cheese and ground beef pooled at the base of six black and unrecognizable shapes. To Ella Mae, the pies looked like charred Frisbees.

"The dinin' room's clearin' out!" Reba shouted, flinging open the back door. "If you wanted a break, you could have just asked. No need for such dramatics."

Ella Mae removed the smoldering pies and dumped them into the garbage can. "I know you're teasing me, but I don't see anything funny about this. By suppertime, everyone in Havenwood will be talking about how I burned an oven full of pies."

Reba slid the window above the sink open. "They didn't exactly stampede out of here. Everybody paid and I gave them a slice of dessert pie to take home for their trouble. I put up the closed sign too. We're done for today, hon."

Sagging against the worktable, Ella Mae watched the smoke race out of her kitchen and rise into the clear August sky. "At least the smoke alarm didn't go off."

Glancing at the ceiling, Reba frowned. "I reckon that's not a good thing. Isn't it supposed to yell and scream when the kitchen is close to burnin' down? And what's that little red blinkin' light mean?"

"A malfunction," a man's voice said.

Ella Mae turned to see Hugh Dylan standing at the other end of the room. He was breathing hard, his chest straining against his navy blue Havenwood Volunteer Fire Department T-shirt. He ran a hand through his molasses brown hair and looked around. "No flames?"

"Not this time," was Ella Mae's foolish reply. She tried to look away from Hugh's startling eyes, but they were as mesmerizing as always. She tried not to be captivated by their brilliant hue—twin pools of blue that made her think of secluded Grecian coves, but she found herself getting lost in them just the same. Eventually, her gaze moved down to his lips, which she had kissed not so long ago, and the strong jawline, which she'd traced with trembling fingertips.

Ella Mae's face grew warm as she recalled the two of them working together in this kitchen. How he'd had his back to her and then had suddenly pivoted until their bodies had been so close that it had felt completely natural to erase the gap between them. She remembered raising her chin and parting her lips, how she'd closed her eyes and slid her hands over his broad shoulders as he'd bent to kiss her.

She remembered the feel of sparks leaping beneath her skin, of the heat coursing through her veins with such force that she thought she was burning from the inside out.

Even now, despite the smoke lingering in the air, she could detect Hugh's scent of dew-covered grass and sun-warmed earth. Just the memory of it filled her senses. But she could also never forget how quickly those seconds of exquisite pleasure had turned to pain. How she and Hugh had broken off their kiss, baffled and frightened. They'd only been alone together once since that day, but they hadn't touched. And as the summer passed, Ella Mae feared that they'd never find a way back to the moment they'd shared in this room.

Reba cleared her throat, forcing Ella Mae back to the present.

"We're okay," she told Hugh. "Just a bit of smoke. There's no damage."

"Speak for yourself," Reba said and put a hand to her forehead, feigning a swoon. "I feel kinda dizzy. You might need to carry me outta here, young man."

Hugh grinned. Along with everyone else in Havenwood, he knew that Reba was an incorrigible flirt.

"How did you find out about my little charbroil incident anyway?" Ella Mae asked.

Hugh focused his blue gaze on her once again. "One of your customers called nine-one-one. The rest of the emergency response crew will be here any—"

The rest of his sentence was cut off by the howl of a siren.

"Oh, no!" Ella Mae shouted and hurried past Hugh and through the dining room. She burst out of the front door onto the wide, rose-covered porch in time to see a neon yellow fire truck turn the corner and head down her street. The wail of its siren cut through the peaceful afternoon.

Ella Mae leapt off the porch. Racing up the flagstone path lined by snapdragons and purple salvia, she frantically tried to wave the truck away.

"They're not going to drive by!" Hugh yelled, clearly amused by her antics. "Someone reported a fire, so they have to investigate now." The smile playing at the corners of his mouth suddenly disappeared. He stared at the fire engine, frowning in confusion. "What the hell?"

Ella Mae followed his gaze. It took a few seconds for her mind to register what she was seeing, but when the image became clear, she began to laugh. For there, clinging to the steel handrail on the back of the fire truck, her canary-colored dress flapping in the wind like a ship's sail, was a middle-aged woman.

She was no firefighter. That much was obvious to both Hugh and Ella Mae. In addition to her bright sundress, the woman also wore a pair of blue Converse sneakers and rhinestone-encrusted sunglasses. As the truck drew closer, Ella Mae could also make out a fuchsia headband in the woman's gray hair.

"Why are you laughing?" Hugh asked. "Do you know that crazy lady?"

"It's Mrs. Dower," Ella Mae replied, delightfully awestruck. "She's the organist at the Havenwood First Baptist church."

Hugh threw out his hands in frustration as the truck drew to a halt and the siren ceased blaring. "I don't care if she's the preacher! She can't just hitch a ride on the back of our engine!"

Ella Mae smiled. "I think she's having a carpe diem moment. It's been a long time coming too, so let her be."

Mrs. Dower hopped off the back of the truck, waved at Ella Mae, and paused by one of the rosebushes marking the far corner of the pie shop's lot. She bent over, drew in a deep lungful of flower-scented air, and then plucked one of the soft purple roses from the bush. Tucking the flower behind her ear, she skipped down the sidewalk in the direction of the church, as agile and carefree as a young girl.

Hugh's shock quickly faded and his eyes twinkled with humor. But then he looked at Ella Mae and his expression changed. She saw longing there. And a reluctant resignation too. "When you first came back to Havenwood and I saw you at your aunt's school, I knew you were going to be trouble." His smile was twisted, as if being this close to her was agonizing. "So why is it I keep ending up here? Why can't I stay away from you?"

And then, without waiting for an answer, Hugh walked off to meet his fellow firefighters.

Hurt and confused, Ella Mae turned back to her pie shop. She noticed how the gray white smoke still hovered over the roof like a pair of wings. She studied their shape, thinking that they didn't resemble the wings of a bird or even an angel. They were wispy and diaphanous, shimmering in the air for a few precious seconds before disappearing completely. Like the wings of a dragonfly. Or a fairy.

Chapter 2

Ella Mae slept late the next morning and awoke thankful that it was Sunday, her one and only day off. The pie shop wasn't open to the public on Mondays, but Ella Mae always went in for a few hours to prepare dough for the upcoming week. She'd also fill the bud vases on every café table with flowers from her mother's garden and spend the afternoon purchasing fresh ingredients from area grocery stores, roadside stands, and farms.

On this particular Sunday, she would have lain dreaming even longer had Chewy not pressed his nose against her cheek and then begun to repeatedly lick her chin.

"Stop." She groaned and tried to hide her face under the quilt, but Chewy thrust both front paws beneath the covers and whined. He was hungry and needed to be let outside, and she knew that he was only going to warn her once before piddling on the shower mat.

Ella Mae reached out a hand and stroked her dog's head. "Okay, boy. I'm up. I'm up."

She trudged downstairs to open the front door for Chewy and was pleased to see that her mother had left a copy of the *Havenwood Daily* on the stoop. After brewing coffee and filling Chewy's bowl with his breakfast kibble, she turned to the classified section and began to search for a used car.

The pickings were slim. Old trucks, ho-hum sedans, high-mileage SUVs, and beat-up minivans—nothing seemed to fit Ella Mae's needs or budget. Then, at the end of the column, was a listing for a retired mail Jeep. She didn't recognize the model number, but the price was right and she liked the description of the sliding driver and passenger doors as well as the roomy rear storage compartment. In the near future, she wanted to deliver pies around town, and her customers had already expressed an interest in hiring her for catering jobs. To do that, she needed one or two additional employees and a roomy and reliable car.

Circling the seller's phone number, she finished her coffee. After breakfasting on Greek yogurt and homemade granola, she slipped on a pair of flip-flops and whistled to Chewy. Together, they walked under an arbor of her mother's periwinkle climbing roses, crossed the back lawn, and down the worn path to the lake's edge.

When she wasn't working, Ella Mae always started her day at the lake. She'd toss a stick into the water for Chewy, wading up to her calves as he swam out again and again to retrieve his quarry. A few mallards or Canadian geese would occasionally borrow Partridge Hill's small dock to preen their feathers, but for the most part it was a solitary place. Ella Mae loved to sit in silence while the sun climbed over the green- and blue-tinged mountains surrounding the lake. She'd stare at the houses dotting the hillside on the opposite shore as the morning sun set their windows aglow with a golden light.

This morning, however, the dock wasn't empty. Ella

Mae's mother stood at the very end, sprinkling rose petals over the surface of the water as if she were preparing a church aisle for a bride.

"Feeding the fish?" Ella Mae asked, and her mother swung around, clearly startled out of a reverie.

Adelaide LeFaye was a handsome woman in her late fifties. Tall and slim, she had long black hair shot through with filaments of silver, and the regal face of a fairy-tale queen. Her hazel eyes were intelligent and oftentimes wary. Ever since Ella Mae could remember, there'd been a hardness to her mother's demeanor. She kept herself slightly removed from everyone, and though Ella Mae knew that her mother would sacrifice anything for her family, she'd never been good at showing affection. Ella Mae could count on her fingers how many times she'd seen her mother hug or kiss one of her three sisters.

As for her own childhood memories, Ella Mae had treasured the moments before sleep when her beautiful mother, clad in a flowing nightgown the same shade as the moonlight, would tiptoe into her room and bestow a butterfly-light kiss on her daughter's cheek. She'd whisper a poem or sing an old lullaby to her only child before saying, "I love you." Then, she'd drift away again, as ethereal as a dream.

"I am feeding the fish," her mother replied with a small smile. "Japanese beetles are hitchhiking on all of those petals. I'm out of the spray I make with cayenne and jalapeño peppers and didn't feel like mixing up another batch, so I'm going after the pests in a slightly more brutal fashion."

As Ella Mae watched, one of the beetles lost its grip on the rose petal and fell into the water. Within seconds, a dark shape emerged from the depths and a white, toothless mouth swallowed the insect so quickly that neither woman actually saw the fish. It was more of an impression of a fish than a genuine sighting. Dozens and dozens of petals drifted away from the dock, coaxed away from the shore by the current.

Everywhere Ella Mae looked, ripples and splashes surrounded the flowers.

"Apparently, the word's spread among the fish population," she said. "Snack time at the Partridge Hill dock."

Her mother smiled and reached down to greet Chewy, who loved her earthy scent and the way her strong, elegant fingers scratched him behind the ears. "What are you up to today?"

"I'm hoping to buy a car," Ella Mae said. "An old mail Jeep, actually. Can I borrow your Suburban to drive to Kennesaw? The sellers told me to swing by anytime."

"Will you bring them a pie?" her mother asked.

Ella Mae hadn't planned to, but it seemed like a good idea. She briefly wondered if she should try to influence the seller's willingness to come down in price, but then hastily discarded the notion. *I will only use my powers for good,* she silently vowed, her mouth curving into a self-effacing grin as she thought about how ridiculous she sounded, even to herself.

"I'll bake them something," she answered her mother. "I have plenty of fresh raspberries. Peaches too. Yes, a peach and raspberry pie with a lattice crust. Thanks for the suggestion."

Adelaide nodded and gazed out over the lake again. "Reba told me about yesterday's fiasco. Are you running a new ad in the paper?"

Irritated by Reba's lack of discretion, Ella Mae sighed. "It's on my to-do list. Buy a car, hire an employee, get a haircut, stop and catch my breath."

"No time for that," her mother teased. "Summer's almost over, but the tourists will be back for leaf peeping and harvest festivals. And September's a popular month for weddings. I heard the Lake Havenwood Hotel has had every Saturday booked for over a year. And though Le Bleu has its own pastry chef, I wouldn't be surprised if a few brides found their way to your shop. Pies are the new cupcakes, you know."

"Wedding pies? Stacked in a tier with a bride and groom stuck into the crust?" With a laugh, Ella Mae threw Chewy's stick onto the grass at the dock's edge. He barked once and leapt after it, his stubby tail wagging madly.

But her mother was serious. "Absolutely. You need to get to the more recent issues of your stack of food magazines. Pies are all the rage. They're even more popular than cupcakes. Many modern brides are looking to have a simpler wedding—a casual, intimate celebration. And others just don't have enough money for a six- or seven-dollar slice of cake."

Nodding absently, Ella Mae thought of her own wedding. Sloan had spent an incredible amount of money on her dress, the flowers, and a luxurious reception at The Ritz-Carlton in New York's Battery Park. Everything had been beautiful, but both the ceremony and reception had passed by in a blur of flashbulbs and the smiling faces of acquaintances and strangers. Ella Mae hadn't told anyone from Havenwood that she was getting married because she knew that her family disapproved of her choice of spouse. As a result, she'd known almost none of the two hundred fifty guests attending what was supposed to have been the most magical day of her life. There'd been a hollow place in Ella Mae's heart as she'd walked up the church aisle without holding on to anyone's arm. It was an emptiness that she hadn't truly been aware of until she'd come back home to the town of her childhood and to women who loved her.

Only then did she know what she'd been missing the whole time she'd lived in New York. She missed being a part of a family, of belonging to others, of being tied to a group that wanted only to see her happy and fulfilled.

"That's what a wedding should be," she quietly told her mother. "The people who matter to the bride and groom should celebrate with them. The day shouldn't be about office politics or couture gowns. It should be about family. It should be about promises and love."

"I blame reality shows," her mother remarked, examining her empty straw basket. "Between the bridezillas and the Kardashians, every girl thinks she needs a diamond tiara and a chocolate fountain in order to say 'I do.'" She shrugged and turned away from the water. "Well, I'm off to collect my next round of victims."

Glancing at her watch, Ella Mae wished her mother luck in her war against the Japanese beetles and returned to her carriage house to bake a peach and raspberry pie. She did her best to keep her feelings neutral during the baking process, focusing on the music on the radio's country music station. The last thing she wanted to think about was Sloan and how he still hadn't mailed her cookbooks or special keepsakes. Instead, he kept sending letters to August Templeton, Ella Mae's attorney, begging her not to proceed with the divorce.

At first, she'd hesitated, wanting to be absolutely sure that she was ready to call it quits, but after the initial shock and the intense pain of her husband's betrayal had eased, Ella Mae realized that she didn't miss Sloan. She missed being a part of a couple, but she didn't miss the man she'd been married to for seven years.

"'Your cheatin' heart will tell on you!'" Ella Mae sang along with Hank Williams and was pleased to discover that the words didn't affect her like they had at the beginning of the summer. She was healing. She was starting to move on.

The scent of the sweet, warm peaches and raspberries coated in sugar, cinnamon, and allspice baking in the oven wafted through the kitchen. Ella Mae sighed in contentment.

"I'll be a divorcée in a few months," she told Chewy. "But I still have a man around the house, right, boy?"

Chewy barked, smiled at her, and sat up on his

haunches—a trick he'd learned at Canine to Five. Ella Mae gave him a treat and tidied the kitchen.

As soon as the pie was cool enough to wrap in foil, Ella Mae loaded Chewy into her mother's Suburban and followed the directions she'd been given by the Jeep's owner to his Kennesaw farm. Because he mentioned the word farm, Ella Mae expected to drive by cows meandering through grassy pastures or crops of summer corn. Instead, she arrived at the address to find a sign with gilt lettering positioned to the left of the driveway. It read, Sherman's Artisan Cheeses.

A gravel road wound gently through the woods until the trees abruptly gave way to a wide, sunny clearing. Ella Mae drove past a meadow populated by a handful of goats. In another pen, a small flock of sheep chewed on sprigs of clover and watched her approach with disinterest.

The Jeep was parked in front of a modest white clapboard house with green shutters. A short distance away was a spacious tobacco barn that had been modernized with automatic lift doors, a row of energy-proficient windows, and solar panels. Groups of daisies, cosmos, and phlox had been planted around both the barn and the house. The bright pink, purple, and white blooms gave the entire scene a picture postcard quality.

A man dressed in khaki overalls and a T-shirt came out of the barn just as Ella Mae turned the Suburban's engine off. Unlike most of the farmers Ella Mae did business with, this man's attire was exceptionally clean. She guessed he was in his early forties. He waved and made his way over to her.

"Vaughn Sherman," he said, offering his hand.

Shaking it, Ella Mae introduced herself. "Your place is beautiful. I had no idea there was an artisan cheese maker so close to Havenwood."

"We've been in business less than a year, but we're loving every minute of it."

Vaughn had the air of someone who'd found his calling. Ella Mae identified with his aura of fulfillment. She'd felt the same way earlier when making the peach and raspberry pie, which she now presented to him. "I bet I could use some of your products in my new pie shop. Here's a little taste of what I do."

Lifting a corner of aluminum foil, Vaughn inhaled deeply. His eyes flew open wide. "Don't tell me! Is The Charmed Pie Shoppe your place?"

Smiling proudly, Ella Mae nodded.

"My wife and I were in last weekend. I hate to admit that I wasn't too keen on eating lunch there. A meal of pie and salad doesn't seem very manly." He puffed out his chest and stuck his thumbs under the straps of his overalls. "Anyway, I ordered the caramelized onion, mushroom, and bacon tart, and you could have asked me to put on a frilly dress then and I would have done it gladly if it meant having another slice of that tart." He laughed and Ella Mae had to laugh with him.

"Did you order dessert?"

"I was too full, but Lynn was dying to try something. She warned me that she wasn't going to split it with me, but she was just bluffing. We've been together since high school and she always shares her dessert with me." After casting an affectionate glance toward the barn, he continued. "I only stole a few bites of her chocolate peanut butter pie, but it was enough to send me to heaven and back."

Blushing with pleasure, Ella Mae thanked Vaughn and then gestured at the Jeep. "So what's her story?"

Vaughn walked to the Jeep and put his hand on the hood. "This gal is a treasure, to be sure, but we've had such a good year that I promised Lynn a new SUV. This Jeep's got some miles on her, but I'm a stickler about neatness and maintenance, and she runs like she just came off the assembly line." He pulled out a key chain shaped like a mouse nibbling on a piece of cheese. "Take her for a spin. See how you feel in the driver's seat."

Ella Mae was about to walk around to the driver's side when Vaughn stopped her. "This used to be a mail truck, remember? The steering wheel is on the right-hand side." He opened what was usually the passenger door and bowed. "Your chariot, milady."

It took Ella Mae a few seconds to acclimate herself to the unusual layout, but as she motored down the driveway, the window cracked and her hair blowing in the late summer breeze, her spirits rose. Unlike the Suburban's ride, she could feel the road more in the Jeep, but she didn't think the amount of bounce would damage her pies. Behind the front seats, there was plenty of storage room, and she envisioned lining coolers along the sides and creating her own little food truck.

"Charmed Pies on the Go," she said, trying out the name. "The Charmed Pie Wagon. Pies on Wheels. The Pie Chariot." She smiled at her own silliness, feeling comfortable and carefree in the old mail Jeep. It was just what she'd been looking for. Pulling over on a grassy shoulder speckled with buttercups, she examined the thick folder Vaughn had left on the passenger seat. It was filled with receipts and a complete record of the vehicle's maintenance history, and Ella Mae could see that Vaughn had taken excellent care of the Jeep.

By the time she returned to the Shermans' farm, another car was parked alongside the Suburban, and Vaughn was nowhere in sight.

Ella Mae heard laughter coming from inside the renovated tobacco barn, so she knocked on the door and then, assuming the Shermans' cheese shop was open to the public, entered.

Vaughn stood behind a counter. He was placing slices of cheese onto small plates while the woman standing next to him showed a young couple a photo album. Three more people wandered deeper in the barn, presumably examining the Shermans' cheese-making equipment.

"You two might want to talk to this lady while you're here," Vaughn said, beckoning Ella Mae closer and then addressing the couple again. "She owns The Charmed Pie Shoppe in Havenwood. All of Northwest Georgia has fallen in love with her baking. Lynn, this is Ella Mae LeFaye. I believe she and your old Jeep had a nice drive."

Lynn Sherman clasped her hands over her heart. "Oh, I hope so! That Jeep has gotten me through rain, snow, sleet, and some seriously deep mud puddles. Come on over and grab a stool. We're sampling our Farmer's Cheese, mozzarella, and herb chèvre."

Ella Mae took a seat next to the pretty brunette and her boyfriend. She instantly noticed the younger woman's diamond engagement ring. It had a vintage look and was more modest than the ostentatious rings featured in most jewelry store ads.

"It was my granny's," the girl said, following Ella Mae's gaze.

"It's beautiful. I love the Art Deco setting."

Spreading her fingers, the brunette admired her ring for what was probably the millionth time. "I still can't believe I'm getting married in a few weeks," she said. "I'm Candis and this is Rudy Lurding, my husband-to-be."

Rudy pointed at his cheek to indicate that his mouth was full and smiled apologetically. Both Candis and Rudy seemed so bright eyed, fresh faced, and innocent. They looked like they'd just graduated high school, and while Ella Mae realized that they were probably in their early twenties, she felt ancient in comparison.

It's because they're just beginning their lives together, she thought. *And at thirty-two, I'm just starting mine over again.*

Candis bit into a cracker covered with the herb chèvre and moaned in delight. "This is amazing, don't you think?" she asked Rudy.

"Totally," he agreed. "We have to get my folks over here to try this."

"We're having a small wedding at my parents' house in three weeks," Candis explained to Ella Mae. "And because we're saving money to buy our own place, we didn't want to spend much on the wedding. We heard about the Shermans' cheeses and decided to do a fruit and cheese bar and dessert bar. With champagne, of course. We have to splurge on something."

Ella Mae swallowed a bite of smooth, creamy mozzarella and nodded. "It sounds lovely," she told Candis. "And I can't imagine you'd find better cheese than this anywhere." She looked at Lynn. "How did you and Vaughn get into this business?"

"It started as a hobby," Lynn said. "I bought a book on making artisan cheese at home and I began experimenting. Vaughn and I were both working as corporate accountants in Atlanta this time last year. We had high-pressure jobs, long commutes, windowless cubicles—you get the idea. So we decided to leave the rat race and take a chance on leading a different kind of life. We decided to buy a farm and give ourselves three years to see if we could make ends meet selling cheese." She reached over and took Vaughn's hand. "So far, we're doing just fine."

After glancing at the Shermans' brochure, Ella Mae said, "I'd love to talk with you about placing an order for my pie shop. I'd especially like to try your ricotta and mascarpone. I'm always using them in my savory pies and I think the freshness of your cheeses would really make those flavors pop."

"Oh, Rudy and I are wild about pie!" Candis exclaimed. "We wanted to have a bunch of different mini pies and tarts at our dessert buffet. Do you cater?"

Ella Mae hesitated. "Honestly, I can barely keep up with the orders at the shop. If I managed to hire the extra employee I need, I might be able to handle a smaller job like yours. When is the wedding?"

"September fourteenth," Candis answered and then plucked her fiancé's sleeve. "Honey, tell Maurelle to come over. I think we're about to see serendipity in action."

Lynn put out three more plates of cheese samples. "We already have. Ella Mae was looking for the perfect used car. She saw our ad and drove up here, just when you and Rudy and the rest of your family arrived to taste our cheese. You need someone to make desserts for your wedding and here's a talented pastry chef. Now if that isn't serendipity, I don't know what is."

"Fate isn't done yet!" Candis declared, grabbing another young woman by the arm and pulling her toward Ella Mae. "This is my friend Maurelle. She's smart, hardworking, polite, and is never late. And she needs a job."

Maurelle, who was petite with silvery blue eyes and close-cropped dark hair, reminded Ella Mae of Sinead O' Connor. However, Maurelle's nose, chin, and ears were pointier than the Irish singer's, giving her an elfish appearance. Maurelle raised her hand in a self-conscious gesture of greeting and managed a little smile. "Yep, that's me. The unemployed maid of honor."

"It's not like you had a choice," Candis stated firmly. "Most people would have a hard time holding down a job in the middle of chemo and radiation treatments." She jerked a thumb at Maurelle. "She had cancer, but she kicked its butt."

Ella Mae wondered how Maurelle felt about having her health issues discussed in front of strangers. Her expression remained neutral, but something flitted across her eyes. A shadow. The briefest flash of anger or maybe anguish that made her appear far older than her twenty-odd years. Perhaps it was the memory of the pain and fear that had ruled her existence during her battle with the disease. And Ella Mae guessed the fight had been recent, judging by the length of Maurelle's hair.

Poor thing, Ella Mae thought. *To have been tested like that at such a young age. She should have been out there taking the world by storm—dating, traveling, being free.*

"It's cool," Maurelle answered as if Ella Mae had spoken aloud. "If I hadn't gone to that Women with the Big C support group, Candis and I wouldn't have met." She smiled at Candis and tugged the cuff of her long-sleeved tee down until it covered her wrist. Seeing that Ella Mae had noticed the movement, Maurelle said, "I had skin cancer, so now I'm super paranoid about being exposed to the sun." Again, there was a flicker of pain in her eyes. "And I have . . . marks on my arms."

Candis grabbed Maurelle's bicep and squeezed. "But, girl, your muscles are rock hard. You could probably whip Rudy at arm wrestling."

"Hey, now!" Rudy protested. "Don't go emasculating me like that. Mama, tell these ladies how strong and manly I am."

A woman in her early fifties drew up alongside Rudy and gave his tummy an affectionate pat. "I don't know, sugar. I'm not feeling any washboard abs like . . ." She turned to the man who'd come up behind her. "Who's that boy, dear? The one from New Jersey who takes off his shirt all the time?"

The man rubbed his salt-and-pepper beard and thought for a moment. "The Situation?" he guessed.

"That's him!" Rudy's mother exclaimed and everyone laughed. "I'm Joyce Lurding and this is my husband, Tom. We can provide Maurelle with a character reference. She really helped us out last week when Tom's mama got sick. If she's half as patient and attentive with your customers as she was with my mother-in-law, then you've found yourself a real treasure."

A blush spread across Maurelle's fair cheeks. "Can we stop talking about me now? I thought we were here to pick out cheese for the wedding."

Everyone focused their attention on the plates of samples, and the Lurdings began to iron out details with Lynn while Vaughn led Ella Mae a short distance away to discuss the original purpose of her visit.

"We'd love to sell you the Jeep," he began. "And we'd also love to become your cheese suppliers. So let me sweeten the car deal by offering you a complete cheese order at no cost. Sample as many kinds as you'd like. We can deliver your selections to your pie shop along with the Jeep. How does that sound?"

Ella Mae didn't hesitate. Holding out her hand, she said, "It's a deal." She handed Vaughn several business cards. "Would you mind giving one of these to Maurelle? If she's serious about finding a job, I'd love to interview her as soon as possible, but I don't want to intrude on your time any more than I already have. The other card is for Candis and Rudy. Please tell them I'd like to help out with their wedding if I can."

"In that case, I hope you have a good interview with Maurelle. I can envision our two businesses stealing a few of the smaller catering gigs away from Le Bleu. I tried to get the chef to buy some of our cheeses, but he shot me down. Wouldn't even taste them. He looked down on Lynn and me like we were pond scum." He lowered his voice. "They say success is the best revenge, and that's what we're shooting for." With an impish wink, Vaughn walked off to rejoin his wife behind the counter.

As Ella Mae drove home, she considered Vaughn's words. She wanted the pie shop to succeed with her whole heart. First and foremost, she needed to know that her passion for baking could translate into a profitable business. She also hoped to make her mother, her aunts, and Reba proud of her. She'd stayed away from Havenwood for her entire seven-year marriage, nursing her anger toward her mother until it became a dark and angry thing that convinced her to keep a tight hold on her grudge, to deny her roots and embrace her life as Mrs. Sloan Kitteridge. And because her mother had been just as stubborn, she and Ella Mae were now practically strangers. Ella Mae regretted that. She wanted to connect with her mother, to move beyond the damage they'd inflicted upon each other. To create new memories.

Those were her reasons for being successful, but Ella Mae knew that she also wanted to prove herself to Sloan and her old nemesis, Loralyn Gaynor. She fantasized about sending her future ex-husband a copy of *Gourmet* magazine featuring The Charmed Pie Shoppe on its cover or imagining Loralyn's expression of shock and envy as she read about Ella Mae's entrepreneurial achievements in the *Wall Street Journal*.

Loralyn had made Ella Mae's school days a living hell, bullying her and spreading lies about her until Ella Mae thought of nothing else but escaping Havenwood forever. The worst blow of all had been when Loralyn had started dating Hugh Dylan, the only boy Ella Mae had ever loved. Now Loralyn used him when it suited her, only to toss him aside to pursue the next in a long line of rich, older men she'd coerce into marrying her. And still, despite how badly Loralyn treated him, Hugh couldn't seem to resist her. He was at her beck and call like a well-trained dog.

Loralyn didn't care who she stepped on to acquire as much wealth as possible, and she'd done little to hide her desire to ruin Ella Mae's business and to scare her into running back to New York. But Ella Mae refused to be cowed.

"We're at war, Loralyn," Ella Mae said as she drove through downtown Havenwood and passed Perfectly

Polished, her enemy's nail salon. "And this time, you don't have all the power. Now I have some of my own."

As she drove on toward Skipper Drive and Partridge Hill, she repeated Vaughn's mantra. "Success is the best revenge." Ella Mae smiled. "And I'm ready for my fair share of both."

Chapter 3

Ella Mae's fingers ached from making so many balls of pie dough. She covered the last one in plastic wrap and put it in the freezer and massaged the sore muscles of her lower back.

Chewy was out on the pie shop's front porch, snoozing under one of the tables, his belly facing the sky and a smile of contentment on his sweet, young face. Ella Mae had put him on a long lead so he could reach the flower bed, but up until this point, he'd spent the morning dreaming away.

After tidying the kitchen, Ella Mae made herself a cappuccino, grabbed the notepad she kept alongside the cash register, and joined her dog outside. Armed with a stack of old cookbooks and a pile of the season's most popular food magazines, she began to create the week's menu using the items she'd bought earlier that morning.

On her way into town, she'd stopped at her favorite fruit and vegetable stand. The farmer, who'd been selling fresh produce at the same location since Ella Mae was a little girl, rarely spoke to his customers, preferring to bury his nose in a paperback. He only accepted cash and refused to bag his customers' purchases until he reached the end of a page. Ella Mae had happily waited for him to finish many a long paragraph over the course of the summer. Unlike most of the impatient tourists, she found his ability to get lost in a book utterly charming.

This morning, he'd been so engrossed in a Harlan Coben thriller that he'd taken Ella Mae's money without bothering to count it. With his eyes fixed on the printed page, the old man folded the bills and shoved them in the pocket of his overalls, grunting a thank-you before resuming his stool and his reading.

Ella Mae was unperturbed by the farmer's distraction, for the taste of his juicy peaches, succulent tomatoes, or crisp lettuce was unrivaled. Today, she'd also come away with an armload of fresh zucchini, a carton of soft, white nectarines, ruby red strawberries, aromatic peppers, and plump, waxy cucumbers. Since Chewy took up all the space in her bike basket, she strapped part of her haul on the bike's grocery carrier and the rest had gone into her backpack. As a result, pedaling to the pie shop had been quite a feat.

"I can't wait until Vaughn brings me my new Jeep," she told Chewy as she struggled up one of Havenwood's many hills. "You're going to love riding in it, boy."

But Chewy didn't seem to mind his cozy bike basket one bit. Tongue lolling, he sniffed the air and grinned, relishing the mixture of honeysuckle, tree sap, and pine needles coming from the woods lining the road.

Now he was surrounded by the scent of the peach and vanilla roses that climbed up the porch columns and onto the roof. Ella Mae had always found the blooms' heady perfume relaxing, and now it had lulled her dog to sleep. Looking away from her cookbooks for a moment, she scratched Chewy's white tummy. She then wrote down the weekly specials, pleased with her selections.

"Here's the lineup," she told the napping terrier. "The savory selections will be zucchini pie and a roasted red pepper and goat cheese tart. For this week's side, I'll offer a cucumber salad. And for dessert, we'll have white nectarine pie topped with a cinnamon sugar lattice crust as well as a strawberry cream cheese tart."

Chewy whined and rolled over, repositioning himself until he resembled a brown and white comma, his black nose inches away from his back paws. He sighed once, almost wistfully, and then fell silent again.

"You're right. Summer's almost over. I should make a pie that says farewell to the heat and humidity. How about a lemon icebox pie with a graham cracker crust?"

Slowly opening his eyes, Chewy yawned and stretched.

Ella Mae made a few more notes and sipped her cappuccino, watching the sky change from a weak blue to a strange yellowish pink. It was the kind of sky that typically foreshadowed a snowstorm. But this was August, and Havenwood was lucky to get a decent rain at the end of summer, let alone snow.

A cool breeze stirred the magnolia tree in the front yard, pulling petals loose and sending them spiraling onto the grass. Without warning, rain began to fall, even though there wasn't a cloud in sight.

Ella Mae closed her notebook and walked to the edge of the porch, confused by the sky's odd hue and the sudden precipitation. She put a hand out and a few drops fell onto her palm. Light as kisses, the sprinkles felt cold as frost on her skin. A mist curled across the ground, carrying tiny sparkles of silver dew.

The shop phone rang and Ella Mae reluctantly withdrew her hand from the peculiar rain and went inside to answer it.

"Are you done with your dough balls?" her aunt Cecilia asked. Known to most as Sissy, she ran the Havenwood School for the Arts. Sissy was prone to wearing pastel-colored tops and skirts made of gauzy, loose materials. She had a flair for the dramatic and often enunciated particular words for no apparent reason. "Because Verena and I would love to take you to lunch. Someone should cook for *you* for a change."

Ella Mae smiled at the thought. "I can't today, Aunt Sissy. I bought a car and the owner's driving it to me within the hour. How about supper?"

Sissy paused. "Okay, but what are your plans for the rest of your day off? You're not going to *work* anymore, are you?"

"No. I was going to take a drive in my new Jeep. Maybe swing by the bookstore. I need to catch up on my reading. The only thing on my nightstand are a stack of *Cook's Illustrated* magazines."

"You don't want your job to define you," Sissy said. "Life is meaningless without art, music, and books—the things that infuse our days with *color.* I like the idea of your getting out on the open road. You could use sun on your face and some wind in your hair, honey."

Ella Mae heard the sound of car doors shutting. "I don't think I'll see much sun today, Aunt Sissy. Not with this weird rain." She walked to the large window containing the rotating display case and peered outside. "I need to run. The couple who sold me the Jeep is here."

"Call me later!" Sissy trilled and hung up.

Vaughn and Lynn Sherman knocked on the pie shop's door. They were each carrying a cooler. Lynn immediately put hers down to pet Chewy. He barked a few times to show her that he was on guard duty, but then quickly changed his tune. Wagging his tail, he jumped up, put his paws on her thighs, and licked her hand.

"Chewy! Down!" Ella Mae scolded the terrier and hurried to invite the Shermans inside. "Sorry about my dog. He's not fully trained yet."

"He's adorable," Lynn said. "And Vaughn's not fully trained yet either, but I still love him."

"Lucky for me," Vaughn said, stepping into the shop. "We have your cheese delivery and the keys and title to your Jeep."

"Wonderful." Ella Mae smiled. "Let me put those coolers in the walk-in."

But Vaughn and Lynn insisted on toting them to the kitchen. After Ella Mae put the cheese away, she offered the Shermans coffee.

"We can't stay," Lynn said with genuine regret. "I'd love nothing more than to spend an hour in this kitchen. It has such a magical feel to it, but we're driving into Atlanta today to have lunch with Vaughn's mother."

Vaughn looked sheepish. "My mama can be a bit of a battle ax. Folks call her General Sherman for good reason."

Laughing, Ella Mae handed him a check and thanked the couple for bringing both the Jeep and the cheese.

"Oh, and I expect you'll be hearing from Maurelle today too," Lynn said on her way out the door. "I hope she works out. She seems like a lovely girl who's been through an awful lot for someone so young. I'd say she's about due for a lucky break."

"I understand that feeling," Ella Mae mumbled to herself as the Shermans drove away. She then jiggled the car keys in her hand and glanced at Chewy. "Wanna go for a drive, boy? We've worked enough for one day."

Chewy performed several high leaps and then chased his tail.

"I'll take that as a yes." Ella Mae locked up the pie shop and untied Chewy's leash. They walked through the rain, Chewy stopping more than once to shake his coat, as if the cold drops bothered him. Once he was settled in the passenger seat, Ella Mae hopped into the Jeep and started the engine. She didn't even have the chance to pull away from the curb when her cell phone rang.

She glanced at the caller ID. It was her aunt Dee.

"Are you busy?" Dee asked in her low and musical voice. Dee crafted metal sculptures for people who'd lost beloved pets. After reviewing photographs and talking to the owners about the character traits of the deceased animal, Dee would create a likeliness so similar to the actual pet that anyone fortunate enough to view one of her pieces half expected the sculpture to spring to life.

"I was just leaving work," Ella Mae said. "I finally got a car and I thought I'd take it for a spin. What are you up to?"

"Well, I wanted to see if you'd like to come with me to drop off my latest sculpture. Melissa Carlisle's rabbit died a few weeks ago, and since she's a friend, I put this project ahead of my others," Dee said. "I thought you might like to meet her because she makes her own honey and you're always on the lookout for fresh, local ingredients. You've probably already seen her at the farmer's market. She has a stall there."

Ella Mae was tempted. "Where does Ms. Carlisle live?"

"Close to Havenwood Mountain Park."

Dee was the most reclusive of the four LeFaye sisters. Valuing her privacy above all else, she lived on the outskirts of town, where she worked in her studio and cared for a dozen rescue cats and dogs. Over the summer, Ella Mae had spied on her aunt while she was finishing one of her sculptures and had seen a wave of shimmering light flowing from Dee's body into the heart of the metal dog. At first, Ella Mae thought it was a hallucination. It winked out so quickly that she doubted it had been there in the first place, but when she examined the dog's eyes later on, the tiniest spark of light was dancing within its steel pupils.

It was an amazing sight, but Ella Mae still felt guilty

about witnessing Dee's gift in action without asking her permission.

"Sure, I'd love to meet you at Ms. Carlisle's," she told her aunt and jotted down directions.

Despite the rain, Ella Mae cracked the Jeep's windows open. She wanted to invite the outside in during her inaugural drive, and as she moved through the downtown business district toward the residential area to the west of the lake, the rain swirled around them in curlicues of glimmering silver.

The Jeep climbed the curvy roads winding through the blue green hills with ease. Chewy stuck his whole head out of the window, his ears perked into eager triangles and his nose quivering in excitement as he tried to capture every new scent. Ella Mae also drew in deep breaths, savoring the rain-infused mountain air.

"How did I grow up here and not realize that Havenwood is so beautiful?" Ella Mae asked Chewy as she turned down a secluded driveway and pulled up in front of a modest cabin.

Chewy ignored her. Having spotted Dee, he barked a chipper greeting and pawed at the window in hopes of escape.

Dee, who'd been sitting in her car, got out and walked to Chewy's side of the Jeep. "Hello, Charleston Chew." She reached in and caressed his head. Normally, Chewy would be leaping like crazy to get more attention, but Dee was always able to calm and soothe him. He sat on his haunches and gave her a gentlemanly kiss on the back of her hand. "Can you be patient for a moment?" she asked the terrier. "After we see Melissa, and if the rain stops, we'll take you to the park. All right?"

Chewy's tail wagged double-time and Dee smiled. "I like your wheels," she told Ella Mae. "Still looks like a mail

truck though. It could use a paint job. A little sign or spot
of color to promote the pie shop."

"You sound like Sissy," Ella Mae said. "But I don't have
the money for a car makeover right now, especially if I'm
going to hire a new employee."

Dee nodded and pointed at a bundle positioned next to
the cabin's front door. "Melissa isn't answering her bell. She
might have forgotten about our appointment or gone into
the woods to tend to her hives, but I hate to just leave Cadbury on the porch. That rabbit was her dearest companion
for over a decade."

"I love the name." Ella Mae grinned and headed up the
slick stairs. "Did you try calling her on the phone?"

"Yes. She didn't pick up."

Ella Mae tried to see inside the house, but the front windows were covered with thick curtains. "Let's walk around
back."

The rain had become featherlight, and Ella Mae didn't
mind its touch on her hair and skin. With Dee close behind,
she made her way around the tiny cabin, their footfalls qui-
eted by the worn dirt path.

The two women gazed at the windowless back door. The
rear wall only had one window, and it was too far off the
ground to peer through. Dee gave a sigh of disappointment.

"If I could find something to stand on, I might get a
glimpse inside." Ella Mae peeked inside the tool shed behind
the house. Seeing a dirty wood crate, she dragged it across
the lawn and positioned it below the window. Turning to her
aunt, she asked, "Do you want me to do this? It makes us
look really nosy."

"Normally, I'd say no," Dee said. "But Melissa is . . ."
she trailed off, her gaze moving nervously over the trees.
"Go ahead. Do it."

Concerned by Dee's obvious anxiety, Ella Mae hopped
onto the crate and stood on her tiptoes. Stretching until her

chin reached past the sill, she looked into the kitchen and saw a pair of legs on the linoleum floor. Only the calves and feet were visible, the toes of a pair of tennis shoes pointing skyward.

"We need to go in," Ella Mae said, jumping off the crate. "Ms. Carlisle must have fallen. She's lying on the floor and isn't moving." Hurrying to the back door, she tried the handle. The door swung inward with a creak of protest.

"Stop!" Dee shouted. Ella Mae was so unaccustomed to hearing her aunt raise her voice that she instantly obeyed. "I should go first," Dee said.

Ella Mae followed her down a short corridor decorated with cherry blossom wallpaper and framed seed packets. Melissa Carlisle had collapsed between the kitchen and the hall. Her upper body rested on a floral rug while her lower half was sprawled on the kitchen's blue linoleum.

"Oh, no," Dee whispered and knelt down by Melissa's head. She felt for a pulse, but Ella Mae knew she wouldn't find any evidence that blood still flowed through the older woman's veins. There was a waxen appearance to Ms. Carlisle's face, and her mouth hung open in a lopsided yawn. Her eyes were closed, but her fingers were stuck in rigid curls. She was gone.

Ella Mae fought the urge to look away. Melissa Carlisle had not had a peaceful death, and the sight of her, frozen on the floor in a state of agony, was terrifying.

"I'll call for help," she told Dee. She pulled her cell phone out of the back pocket of her khaki shorts, dialed 911, and asked that an ambulance be dispatched to Ms. Carlisle's address.

The operator wanted more information. "What's the nature of the emergency?"

Ella Mae hesitated. "Well . . . I guess it's not an emergency anymore. The woman who lives here, Melissa Carlisle, is dead. We just found her, my aunt and I."

"I see," the operator replied emotionlessly and assured her that the paramedics would arrive shortly.

Pocketing the phone, Ella Mae watched her aunt place a hand on Melissa's cheek and whisper a few words over her. They were too low for Ella Mae to hear, but Dee's tone was very tender.

"Were you two close?" Ella Mae asked as gently as possible.

Nodding, Dee touched Melissa's fingers. Clearly troubled by their clawlike shape, her eyes moved up and down her friend's body and then drifted toward the kitchen. She stood up and examined the countertop before peering into the sink. She then opened the refrigerator.

Ella Mae asked, "What are you looking for?"

Dee stared at the cartons of yogurt and eggs, jugs of milk and orange juice, a wedge of white cheese speckled with green mold, and the apples, carrots, and celery stalks visible in the produce drawers. "I don't know," she said after a long pause. "It's just that she was fine when I talked to her and she's always been healthy and robust. It's her face . . . her hands . . . the story they tell."

"She was in pain," Ella Mae murmured.

"Yes," Dee said. "Intense pain. I guess it could have been her heart, but I doubt it." She continued to search the room with her eyes. "It's the timing, you see. The harvest celebration is coming and she would have been chosen to—" Dee abruptly halted. "I can't say anything about this to you. I'm sorry."

Ella Mae was hurt and confused. "Aunt Dee, you're obviously upset. But you can talk to me. You can trust me."

"Please wait outside," Dee whispered, averting her gaze. "I'll be there in a moment."

Though troubled by her aunt's strange behavior, Ella Mae exited through the back door and then made her way around the house to where her Jeep was parked. She decided to let

Chewy out for a bathroom break. After securing his leash, she led him to the edge of the woods. He sniffed and strained against the leash, heading for a break in the trees and a narrow path that Ella Mae hadn't noticed before.

"We can't go far," she cautioned, still trying to process Mrs. Carlisle's death and Dee's strange behavior.

Chewy raced up the hill until the ground leveled out, and then he slowed. The trees fell away, revealing a small meadow of grass and wildflowers. Toward the front of the clearing sat a row of bee boxes. The hives were abuzz, but only a few bees ventured out into the mist. The rain had ceased, leaving a veil of moisture hanging in the air—a gauzy curtain that might have been spun from spiderwebs and dew.

Suddenly, the subtle pink and yellow hues in the sky separated. Deep indigo, bright blue, emerald green, gold, and amber exploded like a firework show overhead. The fragments of color merged, forming a striped ribbon above the trees.

Ella Mae gasped. She'd never seen a rainbow of such brilliance before. And she'd never been this close to one either. It felt as if she could jump up and touch the radiant arc of light.

"I'd like to see the treasure at the end of this rainbow," she whispered to Chewy.

As she watched, the colors pulsed and fluctuated, rippling like waves rolling into the shore. Ella Mae forgot about the approaching ambulance. She forgot about Aunt Dee's fear and Ms. Carlisle's tortured face. She would have forgotten about Chewy too had he not yanked on the leash, eager to keep moving.

Without hesitating, Ella Mae scooped him into her arms and ran back to the Jeep. Above the treetops, the rainbow throbbed in a steady rhythm and Ella Mae could feel her heart beating in time to its cadence. The desire to get closer to it overpowered all rational thought. Gunning the engine, she threw the Jeep in reverse and then pushed the gas pedal to the floor, rocketing down the uneven driveway. On the main highway, she turned north, her mind barely registering the sight of the fire department's EMT truck, which crested the top of the hill and headed down the road she'd just left.

For Ella Mae, nothing existed except for the rainbow. It was calling to her, beckoning her to come closer, to find its source and bathe in its spectrum of glowing colors.

She continued to race north, deeper into the mountains. The entrance for the state park approached, and without slowing down, Ella Mae jerked the wheel to the right, glancing out through the windshield as the Jeep bumped and bounced over the aged asphalt.

"Just wait," she pleaded with the rainbow. "I'm coming."

From the passenger seat, Chewy whined. He was having a hard time keeping his footing with Ella Mae's erratic driving, and though she put her hand out to steady him a time or two, her focus was already divided between the road and sky.

Finally, she reached a parking area several miles away from the main road. She had a vague memory of being there before and was certain that there was a path leading to a lookout directly below where the rainbow appeared to be rising from the ground.

It was vibrating relentlessly now, humming in her mind like a fast, familiar song. Throwing the Jeep into park, she left Chewy inside with a window cracked. She shoved the keys in her pocket and broke into a run. Her hair came loose from its ponytail and streamed out behind her like a horse's mane. She sprinted uphill until her thighs burned and she couldn't draw enough breath into her lungs.

And then, the path came to an end. There was a wall of boulders straight ahead and a steep drop to the right. The path widened into a large circle, and there were several picnic tables positioned near the lookout bordered by a protective steel fence. Ella Mae took in the rounded tops of the blue green hills below and then focused on the boulders again.

The rainbow seemed to originate on the other side of the rock wall. Undaunted, Ella Mae tried to climb the smallest boulder, but her feet refused to find purchase.

"Damn!" she yelled and placed both hands flat against the smooth rock. Instantly, she felt the hum in her head intensify. And then, she felt something blow through her like a hot wind. She shut her eyes, but the sensation was over as quickly as it had begun, and when she opened her eyes again, the boulders were gone.

"Wh-what?" she stammered, gazing around in astonishment. She was in some kind of orchard. Tidy rows of apple trees stood like sentinels. Ella Mae moved past them and found herself in a secluded clearing ringed by more trees. Directly overhead was the rainbow, hovering low in a winter white sky. Ella Mae raised both arms and the colors shifted and scattered. To her amazement, she saw that the entire arc had been made up of thousands of butterflies.

A mass of orange monarchs and eastern tiger swallowtails swooped through the branches of an enormous maple tree, chased by playful ceraunus blues and goatweed leafwings. Yellow skipperlings and red-spotted purple butterflies briefly illuminated the branches of a giant oak before disappearing completely.

Panting from exertion, Ella Mae longed to chase after them, to beg them not to go, but she was too exhausted to move. She felt hot too, as if she were burning with fever. Putting a hand to her forehead, she realized that her skin was fiery to the touch, and yet, her fingertips were ice cold.

Darting a glance over her shoulder, she saw the boulder wall peeking through the line of apple trees. She sensed that she could find her way out by heading for the rocks, but she wasn't ready to leave. She still felt the pull from the rainbow and it led her forward, coaxing her sore and aching legs into carrying her to a wizened ash tree growing on a gentle rise above the clearing.

The tree had an ancient air to it. Stooped like an old woman, its gnarled branches hung down like lank hair. Its bark was scarred and wrinkled and its twisted branches looked like arms. The closer she moved to the tree, the more easily Ella Mae could visualize a female form. She saw the curve of hips, a pair of breasts formed by two knots, and a rounded belly.

"Lady Tree," she said reverently, for there was something powerful about this tree. Bowing her head, Ella Mae placed a hand on the rough bark.

The moment she touched the tree, a jolt of electricity passed through her body. It was so strong that she began to convulse. Unable to stand, she dropped to her knees and gasped for breath as the pain consumed her. It felt like her bones were being burned. Like her blood was on the verge of boiling. The feeling was so extreme, so intensely powerful that she couldn't cry out. She couldn't see either. A searing light filled the field of her vision.

Just when she believed she couldn't take another second of agony, the pain stopped.

And suddenly, supportive hands were holding her upright by the arms. Voices, soothing as caresses, whispered her name.

"You're all right," she heard her mother say. Enveloped in the familiar scent of rosewater, Ella Mae dared to open her eyes.

Her mother grasped her left shoulder while Reba had a firm hold on the right. Verena and Sissy were also close by, hands raised in case Ella Mae should fall.

Ella Mae expected to see alarm in their faces. Or terror. At the very least, concern. But she saw none of these things.

Instead, her mother, Reba, and two of her aunts were gazing at her in unadulterated rapture.

"What happened?" she asked, her words scratchy and raw. Her throat was so dry that she could barely speak. "How did you get here? How did I get here?"

"This is your Awakening," her mother said and held a bottle of water up to her daughter's lips. Ella Mae had never seen such joy in her eyes. "We didn't think it would ever come. When you moved to New York, we believed your time had passed. Most women are Awakened in their teens, but you've always been one to bend the rules."

Reba smiled and squeezed Ella Mae's cheek. "Now we can tell you everythin'! No more hidin' things or talkin' in riddles." Her face grew stern for a moment. "But this also means that your powers are gonna be stronger. Who knows what you could make folks do."

Ella Mae frowned in confusion. She swallowed some water and then looked to Verena and Sissy for help. "Did you all go through this?"

Sissy nodded. "The rainbow called and we came here. This is our sacred grove. It's the place where most of us first discovered our magic. It's where we gather with others of our kind. And once a year, we renew our powers here."

Verena gave Ella Mae's hand a fond pat. "This is the happiest day of our lives, Ella Mae. You, who are like a daughter to us all, have truly come home!"

Ella Mae's mother surveyed the sunny glade. "I hate that Dee is missing this. I can't imagine what could be keeping her. She called and told us to come here, but she didn't say why. She must have known what you saw, and yet, she isn't here."

"I know why," Ella Mae said with a groan. "Oh, poor Dee. I left her without a word of warning. I left her alone. With a dead woman!"

Chapter 4

"A dead woman!" Verena shouted. "Who?"

Adelaide put a hand on her sister's arm. "Let's try to be calm." She looked at Ella Mae, her eyes dark with worry. "Tell us what happened."

Ella Mae did. When she was finished, her mother and her aunts exchanged fearful glances.

"I told you she'd need protectin'," Reba muttered.

Sissy shook her head. "It could have been a heart attack. Melissa wasn't old, but she wasn't *young* either. It's a possibility."

Reba scowled. "She was as fit as a fiddle and you know it. The medical folks might say it was her heart, but I won't believe it. There was ways of scarin' a person to death. Trust me, I know."

This statement caused another quick flurry of anxious looks. The happiness that had illuminated the women's faces a few moments ago was gone. Instead, Ella Mae saw mouths drawn into tight lines and brows creased with worry. "Who was she?" she asked. "Melissa Carlisle? And please don't tell me she was just a nice lady who sold honey at the farmer's market. Tell who she really was and why you're so shaken up by her passing."

"Look at this tree," her mother commanded. "This ash is the source of our power. Every year, she renews our gifts. And she also exacts a price for those gifts."

Sissy gazed up at the tree with an expression of awe. "It's no coincidence that she resembles an old woman. Long ago, she stood straight and tall as a young girl on the verge of womanhood, but her magic is fading. That's why she looks like a crone now."

"Once a century, she is given new life," Verena continued the narrative. "One of us, one of our kind, volunteers to become the next Lady of the Ash. It's a terrible and noble sacrifice!" she cried. "But it's absolutely necessary."

"What are you saying?" Ella Mae couldn't believe what she was hearing. She stared at feminine curves of the ash tree in horror. "Someone's in there? A woman turned into a tree?"

"Not *into* a tree, hon." Reba smoothed Ella Mae's wild hair.

"And it's more of a *joining*," Sissy explained, pressing her graceful hands together. "The woman and the tree become a single entity. For a few years, the tree can gesture by moving her branches. She can use the wind to whisper to people and is even able to speak to a family member telepathically. But over time, she becomes more and more like a tree and less and less like a human. Nature is stronger than us by far. And we're all made up of bits of fire, air, earth, and water."

Reba studied the stooped tree pensively. "This lady's tired. She's ready to let go."

"Melissa Carlisle volunteered to become the next Lady of the Ash," Adelaide said. "The elders had accepted her as the best choice. During the harvest celebration, she would have embraced the tree and it would have embraced her in return. Now she's dead and we have no replacement."

"Who would make that kind of sacrifice?" Ella Mae was astounded. "You'd have to be insane to offer to spend the rest of your life as a tree. Does the Lady of the Ash keep her human memories? Is she conscious inside that skin of bark? What happens if she regrets her choice?"

Sissy made a sympathetic noise. "I've often asked myself the same questions, Ella Mae. And, yes, I believe there are times when the Lady *aches* for the past. I believe she is most lonely right after her transformation. Many of us will visit her. We'll talk to her and play music for her, but you'll see all these things for yourself at the harvest."

Ella Mae reached out to touch the ancient ash, but after recalling how the tree had caused her such pain a few minutes ago, she withdrew her hand. "Did you know this woman? Before she changed?"

"No," her mother answered. "She became the Lady during your grandmother's time. And she has guided us well. She has been firm, but fair. Melissa would have been the same way."

"Do you think she was murdered?" Ella Mae whispered, seeing Melissa Carlisle's open mouth stretched into a crooked yawn.

Reba snorted. "I'm gonna look into it, don't you fret. But for now, we've got to get you back to town. You have to rest after the Awakening and I'm off to find Dee."

"Wait!" Ella Mae grabbed Reba's wrist. "I need to hear the truth first. About all of you. It's time I knew." She looked at her mother. "I know your gift involves growing things. Mostly roses. But what about the times I've seen you with young couples in your garden? Standing in front of the Luna rosebush?"

"I can predict whether or not their love will last," her mother replied. "It only works during full and new moons.

Before taking their marriage vows, people who've heard of my gift will travel to my garden to find out if they're meant to be together."

Ella Mae nodded. She'd seen such a ritual from the window of the guest cottage. At the time, she hadn't known what she was witnessing. Now she did. She turned to Sissy.

"Your gift involves music, right? Are you like a muse?"

Sissy smiled. "I *am* a muse. Music can influence people, so I try to increase its power. At my school, I only accept girls of good character. After they complete their training, these young women will go out into the world and make it a better place through their music. Mind you, they're not all magical, but I treat them as if they were."

Verena put her hand over her heart. "My talent is much more subtle. I know for certain whether or not someone is telling the truth. You cannot lie in my presence! I get a tingling whenever someone does. And I'm a politician's wife. Can you imagine all the tingles I get each day?" She guffawed loudly.

"Dee captures the spirit of animals and preserves them in her sculptures," Ella Mae said. "But what about you, Reba? I've never seen you do anything out of the ordinary."

Reba rolled her eyes. "'Course not! I don't use my superpowers unless there's a fight to be had. When I make a fist, there's nothin' ordinary about me."

"She's our protector," Adelaide said simply. "For years, she's kept an eye on both of us, but now it's her sole task to keep you safe."

Ella Mae was stunned. "So you're like a fairy ninja? One who does housework on the side?"

"More like a pixie assassin," Reba replied matter-of-factly. "And we're not fairies or pixies or jinns or angels or any of those things. Those are just names folks gave us. But I am a different breed than you or your mama or your aunts. My kind serves your kind."

Ella Mae didn't like the sound of that. "Why?"

"Don't get your feathers ruffled on my account," Reba said. "It's an honor to be chosen. A guardian needs to be sharp witted, loyal, and willin' to endure years of intense trainin'. I can take out a threat in a hundred different ways." Her expression softened. "It was always my dream to do this, Ella Mae. I just never counted on how much I'd end up carin' about all of you. We're supposed to keep an emotional distance, but that went out the window the first time I bounced you on my knee."

Ella Mae's mother stood up and brushed a few blades of dried grass from her pants. "This isn't the time to answer all of your questions, Ella Mae. We need to talk to Dee and find out exactly what happened to Melissa Carlisle."

Sissy continued to glance at the ash tree. "And we *must* choose a replacement."

"We should all be especially vigilant until the harvest!" Verena shouted, allowing Adelaide and Reba to pull her to her feet. "Opal and Loralyn Gaynor would like nothing better than to see a woman of their choosing become the next Lady."

"I knew it." Ella Mae groaned. "Always Loralyn. I am never going to escape her, am I?"

"There's no need to run from her, honey. You're about to come into your own. No one's ever gonna bully you again." Reba smiled and put out a hand.

Ella Mae took it and then gasped in surprise as the tiny woman pulled her off the ground in a quick, effortless motion.

"How did you—" she began and then waved off the question. "I guess there are a few things I need to get used to."

"Yes, and there's so little time." Her mother beckoned for her to walk toward the wall of boulders. "Your most important task is to learn to keep our secrets. We can't go over all the rules now, but you mustn't talk about your gifts or this place to anyone. If you do, the pain you felt during your Awakening will feel like a mild pinch in comparison to what happens to an oath breaker."

Reba pulled a licorice twist from her pocket and bit off the end as if to emphasize the point.

"I won't breathe a word," Ella Mae promised. "But people already think I'm a bit odd. It's like they sense I'm different."

"You are different. It's why you've always felt like you never fit it anywhere but here," Verena said. "Wasn't the rainbow's call the first sound that reached right down into your heart and sang inside you like the sweetest song you ever heard? Wasn't it like coming home after a long, long trip?"

Ella Mae nodded. And yet, there was one other thing that made her feel that way, though she wasn't about to mention it aloud. She'd been in grade school the first time she'd heard Hugh Dylan's voice. It had rung through her like church bells, deeply resonant, and uncannily familiar.

"Yes. It was like something I'd been waiting for all my life," she told Verena instead.

Passing between two apple trees, Ella glanced at the boughs, momentarily awestruck by the glistening green, gold, and ruby fruit hanging from every branch. *I bet I could make an amazing pie with those apples,* she thought and then hurried to catch up to the rest of the women.

One by one, they put their hands against the rock wall and the rocks became as transparent as vapor. Suddenly, they were on the other side, standing on the well-worn path in the middle of the blue green hills.

"How does that work?" Ella Mae asked, still feeling a little dizzy.

"We have a few wild places left. Places only our kind may enter. They're usually deep in the woods, but some are underground," her mother said. "We protect our sanctuaries with our lives. Only those with our gifts can find the entrance."

Ella Mae thought about Melissa Carlisle's secluded house. "You all live apart from everyone else. Except for Verena, none of you can see another house, and Verena's blocked her view of her neighbor by growing a hedge row maze between the two properties."

"Our gifts only flourish close to nature," Sissy said.

"And Ms. Carlisle? What was her talent?"

Reba looked grim. "She spoke the language of bees. That meant she was a mighty good seer. The bees would whisper of things to come. They were mostly about crops or weather and such, but they'd also warn her if bad things were afoot."

"And don't go asking about the bad things!" Verena cried. "There's no time to talk about them! We need to get to Melissa's hives and see if they left us a message. Since Dee's undoubtedly busy with the authorities, it's up to us to search for clues."

"Not you, Ella Mae," her mother said firmly. "You need rest."

Ella Mae shook her head. "I'll rest later. I found Ms. Carlisle. I need to know what happened to her."

"Then I'm drivin'." Reba reached for the Jeep keys. "You sit with Chewy, drink down a big Gatorade, and eat the peanut butter and banana sandwich I fixed you. Havin' an Awakenin' is like runnin' two marathons back-to-back. If you don't feel like a complete jellyfish when we get to Ms. Carlisle's, I might let you out of the car."

Knowing that Reba enjoyed fussing over her, Ella Mae smiled wearily. She then wriggled her fingers and said, "Don't boss me around. Now that I've found my mojo, I might bake you into a pie."

Reba stopped and took her by the elbow. "None of this is a joke, ya hear?" She gestured at the mostly empty parking area. "You don't know who's listenin'. You'd best practice that vow of silence startin' right now."

Chastised, Ella Mae got into her Jeep, sank back against the seat, and tried to eat her sandwich with one hand while fending off Chewy's eager tongue with the other. Reba was right. Once she'd finished her food and guzzled down the Gatorade, she closed her eyes, too exhausted to hold them open a second longer. Every inch of her body hurt. Even her bones ached. If the seat belt hadn't been holding her in place, Ella would have slumped over like a top-heavy bag of flour.

When they reached Melissa's cabin, there was no outward sign that a woman had been found dead and taken away via ambulance. All was quiet. Even the birds and squirrels seemed reluctant to chirp or chatter.

"How'd you get in?" Reba asked.

"The back door was unlocked."

Reba nodded. "Stay here with Chewy. I'm going to check out the house. Your mama and aunts might need you to go with them to the hives."

Ella Mae was too tired to argue. While Chewy danced across both front seats, whining to be let out, she kept her eyes shut until she heard cars approaching.

"You're chalk white!" Verena exclaimed after opening the Jeep's passenger door.

"I'm fine," Ella Mae insisted and all but fell out of the car. Luckily, Verena grabbed her before she could. "Melissa's honey will restore you. She made a few jars with each harvest that have healing powers the likes of which I've never seen. And I know where she kept those jars. Come with Aunt Verena, Charleston Chew!"

Like the rest of Ella Mae's family, Verena insisted on calling Chewy by his full name. In truth, he seemed to behave better when they did. Hastening to obey, he pranced over Ella Mae's legs, making her wince in pain, and straight into Verena's strong arms.

"I am not carrying you, you spoiled thing!" Verena declared, hugging him even tighter. That small gesture told Ella Mae how much of an effect Melissa Carlisle's death had on her unflappable aunt.

Too weak to walk, Ella Mae watched her mother and Sissy leave their cars and disappear down the path leading to the beehives. Anxious to join them, she was more than happy to accept the handful of crackers slathered with honey that Verena offered her.

"These will perk you up!" her aunt said and stood back to watch the results of Melissa's golden elixir.

The first thing Ella Mae tasted was sunlight. Following that initial note was a burst of sweetness and warmth. Ella Mae envisioned a field of buttercups, thistles, and rain-drenched grass. She sighed in contentment as a final hint of lavender coated her mouth, and reached for a second cracker.

The honey began to work right away. To Ella Mae, it felt like a salve was coating her muscles and sinking into her flaccid bones. Enveloped in a blanket of gentle, restorative heat, she greedily finished the rest of the crackers.

"There!" Verena cried triumphantly. "Your cheeks look like your mama's roses again!"

Taking a long drink of water from the large bottle Reba had left in the car, Ella Mae jumped out of the Jeep, refreshed and energized. "That honey is amazing. What else can it do? Cure cancer?"

"Sadly, no," Verena said. "But it'll knock out a cold or flu in one punch."

Chewy wriggled out of Verena's arms and headed for the narrow path between the trees. In the clearing, Sissy and Ella Mae's mother were standing in front of one of the hives, their heads close together as they murmured softly to each other.

"The bees are gone," her mother said without turning.

"Was there a message?" Verena asked.

Sissy opened the closest box, revealing a dead spider and cluster of tiny red petals stuck to the honeycombs within.

"I don't know the meaning behind the spider, but the flowers are *Achillea* blossoms," Ella Mae's mother said. "*Achillea* is a symbol of war. The bees gathered these blooms to tell us that Melissa's death was no accident. And then they fled. They don't believe Havenwood is safe anymore." She looked at Verena, the firstborn of the LeFaye sisters, with a question in her eyes.

"We must prepare!" Verena's voice was steely and cold. "Sissy, you and Adelaide find a suitable replacement to become the next Lady of the Ash. We have—"

She stopped and pivoted. Reba had entered the clearing, silent as a breath of air. Striding over to them, she held out her hands in a gesture of helplessness. "Nothin's out of the ordinary inside the house. Did the bees have anythin' to say?"

Sissy pointed at the flowers adhering to the honeycomb. "They've confirmed our greatest fear—that we have enemies who are willing to commit murder to gain control over the Lady."

A guttural snarl rose from Reba's throat. "I'm ready. I dare them to come out from the shadows and into the open." She cracked her knuckles and grinned wickedly. "I've been waitin' for a chance to show off my skills."

Verena's gaze was distant. "Reba, I'd like you to move into Partridge Hill until after the harvest. Once you're settled, you and I will begin the hunt for Melissa's killer."

"What can I do to help?" Ella Mae asked.

Her mother's expression was grave. "Be alert at all times," she said. "And get very good at keeping secrets."

After leaving Melissa Carlisle's place, Ella Mae dropped Reba off at her cottage in the woods. Like Melissa's cabin,

Reba's house was tiny and seemed to have grown up from the forest floor. But while Melissa's home had a simple Puritan style, Reba's was trimmed with gingerbread and looked like a diminutive Alpine chalet.

"When you get home, unlock your daddy's gun closet," Reba ordered. "Pick a weapon small enough to carry in your purse but big enough to do some damage if necessary. Clean and oil your piece. We're goin' shootin' tomorrow after work."

Ella Mae didn't argue. Too overwhelmed to be scared, she simply nodded.

On her way home, she glanced at her phone while at a stoplight and saw that she'd missed a call. She listened to a brief message from Maurelle Ambrose asking if she could come into the pie shop for an interview.

"I'm hanging out at the Cubbyhole bookstore and I think I'll be here for hours. I love this place." She paused. "Um, anyway, if you happen to be in town, I'd love to come over and officially apply for the job."

Ella Mae was so close to The Charmed Pie Shoppe that it made no sense to drive past it and schedule the interview for another time. After her surreal day, she wanted to do something as normal as talk with a potential employee. Just the idea of being in her sunny kitchen among the aromas of buttery dough and fresh herbs made her feel as if her feet were still firmly planted on the ground.

Without further hesitation, she parked in front of the pie shop. After calling Maurelle and inviting her to come over, she tied Chewy's leash to the porch rail, gave him food and water, and then fixed two glasses of sweet tea. Normally, she'd conduct interviews in the main dining area, but today she felt like sitting in the rocking chair on the porch.

Chewy issued a friendly bark when he saw Maurelle heading up the path, and Ella Mae shushed him. The young woman looked especially pale today, but she jogged up the porch stairs with a spry tread that belied the sickly appearance of her skin.

"I thought we'd have an informal chat," Ella Mae said, offering Maurelle a glass of tea. She then went on to describe what she needed from an employee and set out the hours and the salary she was prepared to offer. "And you can take home all the leftover food you want," she added, watching as Chewy's eyelids slid shut. She was always amused by how quickly her young dog dropped off to sleep.

"I have waitressing experience," Maurelle said when Ella Mae was done. "And I've been a line cook too, so I could pitch in around the kitchen whenever you need an extra hand. My energy level is fine, even though my skin's the color of milk." She dropped her silvery blue gaze and tugged the cuffs of her long-sleeved T-shirt. "Do you think how I dress will be a problem? Because I'd really rather not talk about, you know . . ." Swallowing hard, she continued. "I wouldn't want your customers to feel uncomfortable."

"Because you wear long sleeves?" Ella Mae covered Maurelle's hand with her own and was surprised by its coldness. "Fall's on the way, and in two months we'll all be dressing like you. If anyone pries into your personal life, tell them to shove it. I don't care if we end up chasing off rude customers. And if someone bothers you, let Reba know. She'll take care of them."

"Reba?"

"She's . . ." Ella Mae trailed off. It was nearly impossible to describe all that Reba was to her. Surrogate mother, sister, best friend, guide, and protector. "She's our only waitress and a longtime family friend. I'm sure you two will get along great."

A fly buzzed by Chewy's nose and the terrier shifted. Opening his eyes, he rolled on his back and stared at Maurelle.

"I think he's flirting with you," Ella Mae said. "That's his way of asking for a tummy rub."

"Then I can't let him down," Maurelle said with a smile. She reached over and gave Chewy a scratch. His mouth opened and he grinned in canine rapture.

Ella Mae waved at her dog. "Chewy goes to doggie day care, so he won't be able to take advantage of your good nature when the pie shop's open."

Maurelle gazed at Chewy. "You're a ladies' man, aren't you?"

While Maurelle bonded with her dog, Ella Mae rocked in her chair. Gazing out at the lush lawn and the groupings of colorful annuals lining the front walk, she felt some of her tension melt away. The rose-covered cottage and the tidy yard restored an iota of normalcy to her strange and unsettling day. Turning to the young woman beside her, Ella Mae said, "So if you want the job, it's yours."

"I definitely want it," Maurelle answered with a small smile. "Thank you."

"Then I'll see you at seven tomorrow morning. I hope you can get used to going to bed early."

Maurelle looked pensive. "I'm definitely a night person— no sunlight to hide from—but I'm willing to make some changes if it means working here." She stood up. "Um, what should I call you? Ms. LeFaye?"

"Heavens, no! That makes me sound like my mother." Ella Mae laughed. "Ella Mae is fine." She touched Maurelle briefly on the arm. "In no time at all, we'll feel just like family."

"That would be nice," Maurelle said and told Ella Mae she'd see her tomorrow. She moved up the path and to the street in a swift, featherlight tread. It was as if her feet barely touched the ground.

Ella Mae took her time finishing her tea. In a single day she'd bought a car, hired a new employee, and learned that she belonged to a race of magical creatures.

Reluctantly, she pushed herself to her feet and brought the tea glasses inside. Locking the front door, she untied Chewy's leash. "Come on, sweetie. It's time to go home. Mama's got a handgun to clean before supper."

Chapter 5

An hour after Ella Mae hired Maurelle, Reba roared up Partridge Hill's driveway and parked her old Buick in front of the guest cottage. She unloaded a pair of bulging suitcases from the trunk and headed into the main house with a purposeful gait.

Before Melissa Carlisle's death, Reba would have marched straight into the kitchen to prepare a delicious supper. Instead, Ella Mae watched as she checked the locks on all the windows and doors, her sharp eyes running over every inch of the old house in search of weaknesses.

The realization that she'd grown up without really knowing the people she loved had Ella Mae feeling both angry and grief stricken. Now that she'd been Awakened, she expected to be enveloped by a powerful sense of belonging, but she didn't. Staring at her reflection in the mirror, she felt alienated and alone. She wanted to talk to someone about how strange it was to have discovered that she wasn't quite human, but there was no one for her to turn to.

Ella Mae didn't even fit the norms as had been defined by her relatives. According to her mother and aunts, most girls were Awakened in their late teens, like a pack of enchanted debutantes. Ella Mae, on the other hand, hadn't felt a spark of power until this summer. Why was she different?

Desperate to still the flurry of thoughts crowding her head, Ella Mae left Chewy to wander in her mother's garden and set out for the lake. Her mother kept a rowboat tied to their dock, and Ella Mae wanted nothing more than to grasp the oars in her hands and fight against the pull of the water until she could sit in absolute isolation in the middle of the lake. There, with the sun sinking into the trees and the first stars appearing in a saffron and persimmon sky, she could lean back and let the boat lull her into a state of tranquility.

With this image fixed in her mind, Ella Mae untied the boat from its cleat, gripped the oars, and pushed off from the dock. Her first few strokes were awkward and the bow turned too far starboard, setting her on a collision course with the swim platform her mother had had anchored twenty-five yards offshore when Ella Mae was a girl.

As a child, Ella Mae loved to keep track of how long it took her to reach the floating dock from the grassy banks. She started each day of her summer vacation racing against her own best time. With one exception, none of the kids her age had ever beaten her in a freestyle sprint.

"Hugh always won by at least two body lengths," she mused aloud, finally striking a rhythm with the oars. The little craft leapt forward, its prow aligned with the path of the setting sun. Water lapped at the boat's sides, and a gentle spray danced from the oar handles with every pull.

Thinking of Hugh Dylan seemed like an excellent distraction from the day's events, so Ella Mae gave herself leave to indulge in her favorite pastime. How many classroom lessons or conversations had she missed, envisioning Hugh wrapping an arm around her waist, his beautiful eyes fixed on hers as he whispered that she was the only one he wanted? How many years had she dreamed about kissing Hugh Dylan? Now that she had, with such a baffling result, she fell back on her teenage fantasies. In these rosy visions, Hugh's mouth didn't burn her when their lips met.

"Is he like me?" She addressed her question to the hills rising above the lake. Somewhere to the northeast was a dying ash tree awaiting a human sacrifice. Had Hugh been there? Did men have Awakenings?

She thought of the sweltering June day in which she'd come upon Hugh at the swimming hole. Hiding behind the bushes, she'd seen him throw a coin into the deepest part of the water and then dive in after it, staying under far too long. He'd broken through the surface minutes later, his dark hair slick and the muscles of his tan, naked torso gleaming as sunbeams lit the water droplets on his skin. He'd looked like a merman then, painfully alluring and achingly beautiful, and now Ella Mae couldn't help but wonder if he was something more than the owner of Canine to Five and a volunteer fire fighter.

"I'll ask Reba," she said, resting the oars against her thighs and allowing the boat to drift. "She's the one who said Hugh and I weren't right for each other. So he burns me when we kiss. Maybe there's a magical remedy for our little problem. A dose of Ms. Carlisle's reserve honey, maybe?"

Ella Mae realized that not only was she babbling out loud, but her efforts to take her mind off Melissa Carlisle's death were also a complete failure.

Sighing, she picked up the oars, pivoted the boat one hundred and eighty degrees, and began to row for home.

Suddenly, she had the sense that she was being watched. She cast her gaze along the shoreline, but the lake edge was still and quiet. Glancing over her shoulder, she thought she caught a flicker of light on the tiny island in the middle of the lake, but then she blinked and it was gone.

Ella Mae felt foolish for having placed herself in such a vulnerable position after her family had warned her to be cautious. With the approach of nightfall, the atmosphere on the open water had changed. The birdcalls and insect droning had fallen away. Only the haunting hoot of an owl echoed across the lake, raising the tiny hairs on Ella Mae's arms.

She picked up her pace, her back muscles straining in exertion, and the boat shot through the darkening water. A luna moth appeared from nowhere. It hovered above her head for a moment, fluttering its yellow green wings, and then came to rest on the bow. It sat there like a ship's figurehead, its diaphanous body trembling a little in the breeze. Within minutes, more moths alighted on the fiberglass rim, illuminating Ella Mae's way forward.

"Thank you," she told the glowing insects. She closed her eyes, calling forth an image of the butterflies that had formed the rainbow that had led to her Awakening. Butterflies and moths had always been attracted to Ella Mae, and she was especially grateful to have them with her now.

At the dock, she secured the boat and made her way up the path, through her mother's fragrant herb garden, and into the kitchen. Reba was tossing pizza dough into the air like a Frisbee, twirling it around her fingertips. It stretched and grew and stretched and grew again until it had formed a perfect disc.

"The prosciutto and arugula pie is almost done," Reba said, slapping the dough onto a pan. "I thought I'd make an eggplant, green olive, and provolone for Dee. You're havin' the Margherita pizza with a heap of grilled chicken. You could use some extra protein."

"What I need is a drink," Ella Mae said and was delighted when her mother entered the kitchen carrying two bottles of Australian Syrah.

"I thought a full-bodied wine would complement the pizza nicely." She handed Ella Mae one of the bottles to uncork. "I've already had a cocktail. Hard liquor helps me think more clearly."

Reba yanked the oven door open. "Amen. Pour me some of whatever you had." Using a wooden pizza paddle, she removed the prosciutto and arugula pie and then divided it into eight slices with a sharp pizza cutter. Suddenly, she paused and cocked her head. "Your sisters are here."

Ella Mae hadn't heard the sound of an approaching car, but her mother nodded and went off to set the table in the sunroom. Sure enough, by the time Reba finished tossing a salad of field greens with crumbled goat cheese, pecans, and dried cranberries, Ella Mae detected the hum of multiple engines moving down the driveway.

"Have you always been able to do that?" she asked Reba.

"Yep. I could tell if you got out of bed at night before your feet even hit the ground," Reba said with wry a smile.

Ella Mae wondered how many other things Reba had overheard. "Earlier in the summer when that paper boat was shoved into my mail slot, you knew someone had been on the property, didn't you?"

She nodded. "The intruder came out of the woods. I could have gone after them—especially when you told me later that it was Loralyn—but I needed to make sure you were okay first. By the time I started sniffin' around, she was miles away. Definitely female though. I could smell perfume on the pine needles for days afterward."

"We're here!" Verena shouted and strode into the house. She placed a large box of handmade chocolates on the kitchen table and inhaled deeply. "I hope you made more than one pizza, Reba. I'm simply starved!"

"Three pies and a salad," Reba said. "Adelaide's pourin' wine in the sunroom."

Verena told Dee and Sissy to help their sister and then turned to Ella Mae. "How are you, honey?"

"I don't know," Ella Mae answered truthfully. "It's too much to process. All I can say is that I'm glad we're together. It makes everything bearable somehow."

"Good girl!" Verena took Ella Mae's elbow, and together, they joined the other women at the table.

Dee waited for Verena to sit before giving Ella Mae a warm embrace. "I'm so sorry I wasn't there for your Awakening. I'd have liked nothing better than to have been at your side."

"It's not as if you had a *choice*," Sissy pointed out.

"I'm the one who's sorry." Ella Mae sat down and accepted a glass of wine from her mother. "I left Melissa Carlisle's without a word."

Dee waved off the apology. "You couldn't have done anything else but follow the rainbow. Once you hear the call, you have to obey. That's the way it's always been." She raised her glass, her eyes brimming with tears. "To Ella Mae. May your gift bring you nothing but happiness."

"Here! Here!" The women clinked glasses. Sparks flew from the rims, and an orb of white light, as blinding as a supernova, shot out from the center of the ring of hands and crashed through the window screen, leaving a sphere-shaped hole in its wake.

Reba giggled. "Oops. Think someone will call in a report of a UFO tonight?"

"Thank goodness it's still warm out or that would have gone through the glass instead," Sissy said.

Verena frowned. "We need to be more careful! Remember, Ella Mae increases our collective power now." She turned to her niece. "We shouldn't all touch at the same time if we can help it. Our magic binds together whenever we form a joined circle. It must be quickly released or it could incinerate us."

"So we just created a fireball?" Ella Mae asked when she could speak again.

"More like a shooting star," Sissy declared theatrically, gesturing at the sky. "I hope someone makes a wish on that one. It was lovely."

After helping herself to a slice of pizza from each pie, Verena tucked a cloth napkin into the collar of her black-and-white-checkered blouse. She then rolled up her sleeves and said, "I'm going to eat before this gets cold. Dig in, girls!"

The food smelled and looked delicious, but Ella Mae didn't have much of an appetite. She managed to eat a slice of the Margherita pizza, trying her best to savor the blend of Fontina, Parmesan, mozzarella, and feta cheeses as well as the tomato slices and chopped basil from her mother's garden. However, the grilled chicken sat heavy in her belly, so she waved away a second slice and drank her wine down instead.

Once the wine had worked its magic on her frayed nerves, she looked across the table at her aunt. "Dee? What was Ms. Carlisle's official cause of death?"

"No word yet. It'll take days for the coroner's results to come through," Dee said. "I found a bottle of cortisone pills in Melissa's medicine cabinet and gave them to the EMTs. That was the only medication in her house. She didn't even take vitamins."

Reba put down her slice of pizza. "I sure hope you saved me one of those cortisone pills."

Dee nodded and pulled a tiny cardboard box from the pocket of her overalls. Reba opened the box and sniffed the white tablet. "I'll test it after supper, but it doesn't smell funny. Doesn't look tampered with either. Were they all like this?"

"Yes. I checked every pill and before the paramedics arrived, I . . . examined Melissa pretty thoroughly too." The admission seemed to upset Dee. Her cheeks reddened and she dropped her gaze. "I didn't want to. It seemed so disrespectful, but I had to see if there were any marks on her body."

Reba's stare intensified. "And?"

"I noticed a red rash around her elbows and behind her ears. There was another, more severe-looking spot on her right forearm," Dee said. "She might have been taking the cortisone pills to treat the rash. Other than that, there were no bruises, scrapes, bumps, or cuts. She was trim and toned. Melissa's been really fit her entire life."

Sissy sighed. "How did they get to her?"

"Who are *they*?" Ella Mae demanded. "Are the Gaynors all magical? And are they our only enemies or do we have more? I can hardly protect myself if I don't know who to watch out for."

Everyone turned to her mother, who grabbed a wine bottle and stood up. "This is a tale to be told in the library. Bring your glasses, ladies."

The women filed into the wood-paneled room. The walls were lined with floor-to-ceiling shelves stuffed with books, most of which Ella Mae had examined during her girlhood. She couldn't imagine there were secrets in this library she had yet to discover.

Her mother put the wine bottle on the coffee table positioned between a pair of oversized white leather sofas, and moved to the bookshelf to the left of the fireplace. She pulled out a thick tome with a plain brown cover, opened it, and removed a key from a depression carved in the pages.

Moving to the mantel, she inserted the key into the mouth of one of the marble partridges. Ella Mae heard a click and the entire mantelpiece swung away from the wall, revealing a series of cubbyholes.

"Whoa," Ella Mae said, rising to her feet. How had she grown up in this house without having known there was a hidden compartment in the fireplace?

Her mother must have guessed what she was thinking. "There are many secrets about Partridge Hill. Hiding places, escape tunnels, food and weapon stores. After the harvest, I'll show them all to you." She smiled tenderly and lowered her voice to a whisper. "It will be such a pleasure to share everything with you. I never thought . . . I'd given up hope that you'd be Awakened, you see. Reba and my sisters never did. I'm so sorry that I didn't have more faith in you."

Ella Mae was moved by her mother's regret. "You couldn't have known. And I don't care about the mistakes either of us made in the past. I want to focus on the future. I want you to teach me how to be this . . . new person. I feel lost and found at the same time."

"That's completely normal," her mother said, easing a weathered art portfolio case from the secret nook above the fireplace. "It takes time to reconcile how you once saw yourself with who you really are. It's a genuine identity crisis, but the feeling will pass. I promise." She smiled warmly again and then carried the case back to the coffee table and knelt down to untie its leather laces. Carefully, she unfolded the overlapping flaps to reveal a painting.

Ella Mae leaned forward, immediately drawn to the unframed piece of canvas. The painting depicted three figures. Two beautiful women with flowing gowns flanked by a man with black hair and a salt-and-pepper beard. The woman to his right was clothed in a dress of ivory and gold. She had honey-colored hair that fell to her waist and catlike green eyes. The woman on the left had a waterfall of dark brown locks and large hazel eyes. She wore a silver gown trimmed with cobalt. The women held on to the man with one hand, but he seemed indifferent to both of them. Staring straight ahead, his arrogant gaze was so penetrating that Ella Mae was tempted to look away.

"Who are they?" she asked, instinctively disliking the man in the black robe.

"The woman in white is Guinevere," Ella Mae's mother said. "You probably know the man best as Merlin, though we call him by another name, and the woman in silver is Morgan of the Fay, the matriarch of our family."

Ella Mae drew in a quick breath. "But she was a villain, wasn't she?"

"That's what the men who record history would have you believe!" Verena thundered. "Morgan was powerful! Beautiful! She owned her own lands, castle, and army. She was a force to be reckoned with, but her biography has been falsified."

"The true story is shown here, in the painting," Dee said softly. "Two women tried to control King Arthur at the request of Merlin or Myrddin or Aurelius—he had many names."

"Guinevere and Morgan were like us." Sissy picked up the narrative. "They had special powers. And Merlin was their tutor. He'd lived for a long time and had magical gifts no one else had *ever* seen before."

"Morgan knew that the race of men was beginning to increase in number and in strength. By this point in history, fools and religious zealots had hunted our kind until we were no longer plentiful. To protect our future, Morgan sought to make an alliance with the king. But Merlin had other ideas. He wanted to use men like Arthur as puppets to gain control over Britain, and Guinevere agreed." Dee's voice was low and sad. "Tensions escalated, lies were exchanged, and the war that would forever change our fate began."

Ella Mae felt chilled. "We lost, didn't we?"

"Morgan used every bit of magic she had to defeat Merlin, because she knew that as long as he lived, our kind would become weapons, serving his lust for power." Her mother reached out and touched the painting, putting her fingertip on Morgan's belly. "With his dying breath, the sorcerer cursed our line. He channeled the last of his considerable black magic into a spell."

The LeFaye sisters fell silent, as if they couldn't bring themselves to speak the curse aloud. Reba cleared her throat and looked to Verena for permission. She nodded glumly.

"Merlin put his hand over Morgan's womb," Reba said angrily. "Then he whispered that Morgan's children and her children's children would be tainted. The curse said that none of her bloodline would be able to bear a child without a great and terrible sacrifice. He vowed that eventually, the Le Fay line would run dry."

Things began to fall into place in Ella Mae's mind. "That's why my grandmother died in childbirth. It's also the reason none of you have ever had children," she said, glancing from one aunt to the next. She then turned sorrowful eyes on her mother. "And your sacrifice? Was it my dad?"

Reba grabbed her by the hand. "Don't, hon. Don't go there right now."

But Ella Mae knew the answer by the all-too-familiar shadow that crossed her mother's face. "Terran and I agreed that having a child was worth any risk . . ." She brushed a single tear away. "I loved him so much, Ella Mae. I'm sorry you'll never know how wonderful he was."

"Let's focus on this story for the time being." Verena pointed at the painting. "Gaynor is another name for Guinevere. We've been enemies of the Gaynor family since the days of Camelot, but they're not cursed as we are." Ella Mae expected her aunt to sound angry, but she seemed to be saddened by the enmity between the two clans. "Myrddin had many children. They were as wicked and deadly as their sorcerer father. Still are. And they no longer want to use humans. They want to annihilate them—to return to the ancient days when men were few and our kind were plentiful."

"Myrddin's descendants are terrorists, assassins, crime lords, and of course, *politicians*," Sissy said.

Ella Mae looked at the wizard in the painting, repulsed by the maniacal gleam in his dark eyes. Merlin wasn't the bearded, grandfatherly tutor she'd read about in storybooks, but a power-hungry madman. "I can handle the news that the Gaynors are our enemies. I've known that since I was a kid, though I never knew why. But the other group? The dark magic people? Do any of them live in Havenwood? And if they're so strong, how can we fight them?"

Her mother tucked the painting back inside the leather case and placed it in its secret niche. She then tossed a set of keys to Reba, who caught them without taking her eyes off Ella Mae. "Everybody bleeds, darlin'. And there isn't a magic spell that can fix a bullet to the heart."

Ella Mae already had a dozen breakfast pies in the oven when Maurelle showed up for work the next morning. For the first time since she'd opened The Charmed Pie Shoppe, she felt like a complete klutz in the kitchen. Her thoughts were so scattered that she rolled several piecrusts too thin and they tore when she tried to transfer them to the pan.

"Damn, damn, damn!" she shouted, running her flour-encrusted fingers through her hair.

"Girl, you've got to settle down!" Reba scolded, coming into the room with a freshly brewed latte. She perched on her usual stool, her strawberry scent instantly calming Ella Mae. Taking a deep breath, she began to roll out another ball of dough. Reba watched her, sipping her latte and humming along with a Miranda Lambert tune. When the bells attached to the front door jiggled, Reba was off the stool like a shot.

"That's just Maurelle!" Ella Mae called out, but Reba was already gone.

Maurelle entered the kitchen a few seconds later, with Reba following closely on her heels.

Ella Mae made the introductions and then glanced at the oven timer. "Let me give you a quick lesson on the cash register and espresso machine before the breakfast pies are done."

Maurelle turned out to be a quick study. She had an excellent memory and seemed familiar with the café's various machines and appliances. While Ella Mae explained how the pie shop operated, Reba set the dining room tables and shot inquisitive glances at Maurelle.

Eventually, Ella Mae asked her newest employee to write the daily specials on the chalkboard and motioned for Reba to join her in the kitchen.

"What's up with you?" she whispered. "You'll chat with a total stranger at the Piggly Wiggly for an hour, and yet, you're being so reserved toward Maurelle."

Reba crossed her arms over her chest. "I know. I just like bein' in charge of the dinin' room."

"No one's replacing you," Ella Mae said. "No one ever could, but she's a nice girl and we need her, so crank up the Southern hospitality a bit, okay?"

"Have you forgotten about yesterday already? I just wanna get to know her a bit before I get all buddy-buddy," Reba replied. "Why's she wearin' long sleeves anyhow? It's gonna be in the nineties today with a billion percent humidity. The poor girl must be dyin'."

Ella Mae curled her hands around her rolling pin. "It sounds like she almost did. She had skin cancer, and I can only assume that she has some sort of embarrassing scars."

Reba clucked her tongue in sympathy. "I'd best crank up the AC for her then. Any of our customers complain too much about the temperature and I'll stuff them in the oven Hansel and Gretel style."

Glancing at the clock, Ella Mae knew that she needed to

get a move on. "No threatening our patrons," she teased. "Paste on your prettiest smile and go out front. Please?"

Reba produced a frightening grin and dug in her pocket for her licorice twists. A minute later, Ella Mae heard the low murmur of women's voices and knew that Reba was chatting up Maurelle.

In no time at all, she was too busy with breakfast orders to give a second thought to her new server. Reba and Maurelle flew in and out of the kitchen, picking up orders and dropping off dirty dishes until Ella Mae wondered if the swing doors were in danger of coming off their hinges.

"Everything going all right?" she asked Maurelle during a lull between breakfast and lunch.

"Yep," the younger woman said. "The customers are really nice and Reba's been a big help. She's covered me every time I've made a mistake."

Ella Mae smiled. Knowing that her patrons were being taken care of would allow her to relax and concentrate on cooking. She didn't want to taint her pies with feelings of agitation, so she was thrilled that Maurelle had fallen into an easy rhythm so quickly. "Take a break whenever you want," she said. "We're pretty casual about that kind of stuff. And make sure you get something to eat. The lunch rush might be heavy today since it's so hot out, so I'm making lemon icebox pie to cool everyone off."

In fact, she was just about finished with the dessert pies. Having already blended the juice and zest of a handful of sun-ripened lemons with cream cheese, vanilla extract, and sweetened condensed milk, Ella Mae was just about to sprinkle a little sugar into the mixture. However, she wanted Maurelle to leave before adding the last ingredient.

"I'll grab a slice of bacon and mushroom pie," Maurelle said. "I'm not usually hungry at ten in the morning, but I am today." She looked around. "Where should I eat? Out back?"

Ella Mae considered Maurelle's aversion to sunlight. "No, no. Sit at a café table on the front porch. It's nice and shady out there."

Maurelle gave her a thumbs-up sign. "Cool, thanks."

As soon as the kitchen's swing door stopped moving, Ella Mae closed her eyes and began to sprinkle sugar into the stainless steel bowl of her commercial mixer. As she let the granules fall through her fingers, she thought back to December of last year. She was living in Manhattan then and was attending culinary school. She'd just finished her last class of the day, and when she'd stepped outside, it was snowing. The weather forecast had called for clear skies, but the clouds were so thick that Ella Mae could barely see the city's skyline.

Feeling like a little girl, Ella Mae had held out her hand, catching a single flake in her palm. She'd stared at its star shape until it melted, feeling lighthearted and carefree. The snow continued to fall even harder, covering her hair and coat.

Forgoing the subway, she'd walked back to her apartment, reveling in the sight of the newspaper stands and parked cars being blanketed in white. Everything became hushed. Even the taxis stopped their endless honking. Rosy-cheeked businessmen grinned like boys on their way to the sledding hill, and women caught flakes on their tongues, smiling at the simple joy of the season's first snow.

The air had felt crisp and Ella Mae's breath plumed around her face. Half an hour later, the world was white and quiet and breathtakingly beautiful. It was as if the snow had cleansed the city and her people. Everyone felt a jolt of hope, a twinge of childish pleasure, and for a moment, they forgot their adult responsibilities and took a moment to scoop up a handful of snow, delighting in the kiss of cold against their skin.

Now, standing in her toasty kitchen in northwest Georgia,

Ella Mae finished adding the sugar. Opening her eyes, she turned off the mixer, poured the filling over the graham cracker crust, and placed the pies in the walk-in. Two hours later, when she cut into the first of her lemon icebox, a breath of frosty air rushed from the pie and hovered over the wedge like a pair of angel's wings.

Another hour later, all the pies had been devoured.

"What'd you put in those things?" Reba asked as she plated the last piece.

"December snowfall," Ella Mae said.

Reba brought the pie to her eye level and then shrugged. "Sounds as refreshin' as—" She stopped and cocked her head. "What on earth?"

Without another word, Reba disappeared through the swing doors, nearly colliding with Maurelle.

"Um. You should come out front and take a look at something," she said in bewildered amusement.

Curious, Ella Mae followed Maurelle through the dining room and onto the porch. At the end of the block, a crowd of people were clustered around a fire hydrant. Someone had pried off the cap and water was jetting upward into the hazy sky. Lawyers, construction workers, beauticians, bank tellers, shop owners, and the rest of the pie shop patrons were dancing in the spray, laughing and smiling as they kicked off their shoes and hopped up and down in the shallow puddles.

For a few seconds, Ella Mae forgot about her Awakening. She forgot about the Lady of the Ash, her family's enemies, Morgan of the Fay, and the harvest. There was only this scene. This perfect moment.

"Does stuff like this happen often?" Maurelle whispered in awe.

Ella Mae gestured at the sign mounted above the front door. "That's why it's called The Charmed Pie Shoppe. This place is enchanted."

"What do you mean?" Maurelle frowned in confusion.

Ella Mae smiled. "Oh, just that we all seem to find what we need here."

Maurelle glanced at the people in the street. Everyone's clothes were soaked and the women's mascara ran down their cheeks in rivulets of black, but they were too busy enjoying themselves to care.

"What did they need?" she asked.

"I couldn't tell you that," Ella Mae said, recalling her mother's stern warning about discussing magic in front of strangers. "But I think they found it."

Chapter 6

Ella Mae was just about to go back inside the pie shop when a cherry red BMW convertible barreled up the street and screeched to a halt three feet from where she stood.

The driver was a stunning blonde wearing a silk wrap dress, Prada sunglasses, and diamond earrings large enough to be seen from outer space. Easing the sunglasses onto the point of her nose, she called out, "Why, Ella Mae! I do believe you've sprung a leak." The woman smiled, flashing a set of cloud white teeth, and turned to the handsome man in the passenger seat. "It's such a shame that we have to cut our time short because of a silly fire hydrant," she drawled, placing a possessive hand on Hugh Dylan's arm.

Hugh shrugged, clearly not sharing her disappointment. "At least we got to finish lunch. I have so much to do at Canine to Five this afternoon that I couldn't have stayed much longer anyway."

Getting out of the car, he walked around to the back and

waited expectantly. "Loralyn? Can you pop the trunk? I need my tools."

Loralyn Gaynor was no longer smiling. She turned off the engine, slid her sunglasses onto her forehead, and alighted from the sleek sports car with the grace of a Hollywood starlet. Casting an icy glare at Ella Mae, she said, "I suppose this stupidity is your doing. I've been trying to catch up with Hugh for weeks, and the moment I finally have him alone, *this* happens." She gestured at the happy scene at the end of the block with a dismissive flick of her wrist.

"It was just a sandwich at Ham It Up," Hugh said. "We can reminisce about high school anytime."

Loralyn watched Ella Mae's customers splashing in the water, her pretty mouth turned down in a sulk. Then, with an abrupt change of demeanor, she faced Hugh, held the car keys an inch away from her right breast, and gave them a little shake. "If you want these, come and get them."

Ella Mae immediately stiffened. Loralyn's voice sounded different. It was musical; an alluring melody of seductive, honeyed tones. Even Ella Mae was nearly tempted to respond to Loralyn's invitation, but she focused on Hugh instead. He seemed to be struggling to resist Loralyn's voice, but she took a step closer to him and whispered, "Come on, big boy." He relaxed his taut muscles and all the fight left him. With a dazed expression, he moved to Loralyn's side. She pressed her palm flat against his chest and then shot Ella Mae a look of triumph.

"Are you sure you want to mess with that ole hydrant right now?" Her voice was magnetic. It wrapped around Hugh in mellifluous waves until he seemed to forget about the rest of the world. He had eyes only for Loralyn.

"Hey!" Reba shouted, coming up behind Ella Mae. "What are you waiting for, Mr. Fireman?" She clapped her hands. "You wanna see Noah float by before you decide to shut that thing off?"

Hugh snapped out of his stupor. Gently pushing Loralyn away, he reached down next to the steering wheel, pressed the trunk release button, and grabbed his toolbox. Thanking Loralyn for the ride, he strode toward the hydrant, saluting Reba and Ella Mae as he passed by.

"Men," Reba muttered and turned up the path leading to the pie shop. "The show's over." She directed her words at Maurelle, who'd remained in the shadow of the front porch. "Let's clean up so we can all go home."

The two women disappeared inside the shop, leaving Ella Mae and Loralyn alone. Ella Mae was tempted to boast that she'd guessed that Loralyn's power was her voice. She also wanted to warn Loralyn to stop using her enchanted speech on Hugh ever again, but held her tongue. It was better for Loralyn to view Ella Mae as a clueless fool. That way, Ella Mae could quietly find a way to break her enemy's hold over the man she'd been in love with since grade school.

She gestured at Loralyn's left hand. "Don't you have your fifth or sixth husband to snag?"

"Fourth husband, actually." Loralyn examined her reflection in the driver's-side mirror and, pleased with what she saw, smiled at Ella Mae. "And I do have someone in mind. I can't wait to see your reaction when you meet my latest paramour."

"Don't bother introducing me to the poor soul," Ella Mae said. "He's probably old and rich and has a heart condition. He'll be dead within two years and you'll be even wealthier and more depraved than before." She gave Loralyn a look of disgust. "You just buried your last husband a few months ago. Show some respect for his memory."

"Why on earth should I?" Loralyn was genuinely perplexed. "After all, we were terribly mismatched." She scrutinized her manicured nails. "This time, I need a partner who can help me make serious changes around here. I think Havenwood could use a breath of fresh air. A new mayor, for example. The current one could retire. Maybe take up beekeeping."

The reference to Melissa Carlisle was so obvious that Ella Mae had to clench her fists to keep from striking Loralyn. Not only did she allude to Melissa, but Verena's husband, Buddy Hewitt, was the town's current mayor. He was both honest and fair, and Loralyn's insinuation that Buddy needed to be replaced was either a threat or an insult. Ella Mae could feel her rage rising. Moving closer to Loralyn, she spoke in a low, menacing voice. "If you think what happened to Melissa Carlisle will change the course of Havenwood's future, then you're wrong. I'm—" She stopped, sensing that it would be unwise to reveal that she'd been Awakened.

Loralyn threw her head back and laughed. Opening her car door, she eased onto the leather seat and put her sunglasses back on. "You've always been so dramatic, Ella Mae. Instead of baking your bland little pastries, you should have sought a career on the stage. There's still time, you know. And you're already quite familiar with New York City. Why not go back while you still have the chance?"

Tugging on her pale peach apron, which was embroidered with a rolling pin and the phrase, "That's How I Roll," Ella Mae stood as tall as she could. "I'm here to stay, Loralyn. Maybe you should consider stretching your wings. Or is the big, bad, wide world too scary for a small-town beautician?"

Loralyn's lip curled. She owned several businesses, including two nail salons, and was offended by Ella Mae's choice of words. But she recovered quickly, pasted on her phony smile, and fluffed her gorgeous leonine mane. Over the hum of her engine, she called, "Keep an eye on your family, Ella Mae. It'd be a shame if they ended up like Melissa Carlisle."

And with that, she peeled away from the curb, forcing Ella Mae to leap out of the way. Ella Mae watched the convertible zip to the end of the block and then, in a flash of chrome and red, it turned the corner and was gone.

Ella Mae stormed into the pie shop. She wanted to rant and complain to Reba, to blow off steam like she did when she was a girl, but she couldn't vent in front of Maurelle.

"That was the first rude person I've seen in this town," Maurelle said after Ella Mae slammed the door shut, making the bells jangle wildly. "That nasty blonde. Who is she?"

"A julep-guzzlin' socialite," Reba said. "One of them diva types that gets a kick out of causin' trouble for honest, hardworkin' folks. Thinks she's better than everybody."

Frowning, Maurelle said, "I can't stand people like that. But women like her always get the hottest guys. Look at the one she drove here with. Totally hot. Was that her boyfriend?"

The thought of Hugh being manipulated by Loralyn's magic fanned Ella Mae's anger, and she untied her apron and wadded it into a ball. Instead of responding to Maurelle's question, she gestured at the spotless dining room and forced herself to behave normally. "You did a great job today. We're actually done early, so you can head out now." She smiled, hoping it wasn't too obvious that she wanted Maurelle to go home. "Unless you have any questions."

Maurelle shook her head. "No, I'm good. Today was fun. Thanks again for giving me a shot." She took off her apron and folded it into a neat square and then collected her purse from the cabinet under the cash register. "See you tomorrow."

The moment she was gone, Ella Mae released a long sigh, but Reba held out a finger to stop her from speaking.

"Save it for the shootin' range. I need to know that you can still hit a target when you're boilin' mad."

Ella Mae hesitated. She'd rather get Chewy from doggie day care and take him to the swimming hole, but she hadn't practiced firing a handgun for years. She and Sloan had had other hobbies, like attending concerts, plays, art gallery openings, and the occasional opera. And Ella Mae had always felt safe in Manhattan. It was ironic that she was destined to encounter real danger not in a subway station or city alley but in a sleepy town in the Georgia foothills.

The shooting range wasn't far, and when they arrived, Reba unloaded a bagful of weapons from the Buick. After paying the attendant for the rental of two lanes and a pile of paper targets, she motioned for Ella Mae to sign a waiver stating that she'd abide by the range laws at all times.

"That means headphones and eye gear, ladies," the man said, his lower lip stuffed with a fat plug of chewing tobacco.

"You got it, Jessup," Reba said with a charming smile. Satisfied, Jessup returned his attention to his copy of *Guns & Ammo*.

Reba followed Ella Mae into her lane and laid three handguns on the counter. She pointed at an all-black gun. "Smith and Wesson M and P nine compact. Try that one first." She then touched the steel barrel of a slim revolver. "Next, you've got a Smith and Wesson Model Sixty J-Frame with both single and double action." She moved to the third gun, which was black with an attractive wood grip. "This beauty is a Colt Forty-five ACP. Has a nice, light trigger pull and a double safety. A good one to carry in your purse or tuck into the waist of your pants."

Ella Mae accepted a box of bullets and began to load the cartridge of the M&P 9. "Is it that bad?" she asked. "Do I need to carry at all times now? Even in the pie shop?"

Reba nodded. She slid a paper target under a pair of clips and pulled on a chain until the image of a sinister man in a hooded sweatshirt holding a gun was fifteen yards away.

"Think of Loralyn and aim for the ocular zone," Reba ordered. "Do you remember what that is?"

Years of target practice with Reba came back to Ella Mae. "The triangle formed by the nose and eyes. A bullet in the ocular area will stop an attacker instantly. A shot to anywhere else on the head, the heart, stomach, or kneecap might not have the same result. Only the ocular area stops him dead."

Reba grinned proudly. "You can take the girl out of the country but you can't take the country out of the girl."

Ella Mae loaded the cartridge and heard a satisfying click as it locked into place. She then reached for the headphones, but Reba shook her head. "I know what the waiver says, but you won't have head gear or goggles if someone's after you for real. You need to hear the bullets tear through the air without losin' your focus. Go on. Fire away."

Raising her arms straight out in front of her, Ella Mae lined up the sight at the end of the gun's barrel with the target's paper nose and squeezed the trigger.

The force of the bullet exploding from the gun surprised her. She'd forgotten how powerful the sensation was, but her hands were steady and the bullet pierced the paper right between the man's eyes.

"Perfect," Reba said. "Now squeeze 'em off until you're empty. Pretend he won't go down and you need to take him out. NOW! GET HIM!"

The shout served its purpose. Ella Mae took aim and fired twelve shots in a row. She then lowered her weapon and saw that she'd hit the man's chin twice and chest once.

"Not bad. Try the revolver next," Reba said.

Complying, Ella Mae unloaded the gun's five rounds into the paper target. They all hit the two-dimensional assailant in the mouth.

"Doesn't seem to be the best trigger for you," Reba said and handed Ella Mae the magazine for the Colt.

Sliding it into place, Ella Mae ran her fingers over the wooden grip. "Loralyn's voice is enchanted. She can use it to make people do things against their will, like a siren from Greek mythology."

"Her type's been called that and more," Reba said. "And

I'm glad you brought it up, because that's another one of our rules. We can't reveal what kind of abilities other folks have. You guessed Loralyn's, so that's all right, but we don't go around talkin' about these things."

Ella Mae frowned. "What would happen if we did?"

"For starters, the elders would punish you. And if you blabbed about secret stuff to an outsider, then you'd feel terrible pain like you did at your Awakenin'. We don't know how it works, but it's like an invisible energy force that keeps us all in check." Reba tossed a spent shell into the trash can. "Don't go messin' with it, you hear?"

But Ella Mae wasn't listening. She was thinking of how effortlessly Loralyn had been elected class president, homecoming queen, head cheerleader, editor of the student newspaper, and every other lofty position that defined a person's status in school. Ella Mae had always wondered how someone so disingenuous and unpleasant managed to be so universally adored, and now she knew. Though rich and beautiful, Loralyn had had to resort to enchantment to become the most popular girl in school.

A wide smile spread across Ella Mae's face. "She cheated. All along, she had to trick people in order to get what she wanted. She was never better than me."

Reba pulled the paper target in and replaced it with a female silhouette. "What are you gonna do about it?"

Ella Mae barely waited for the target to be reeled back out before she started firing. The Colt felt good in her hands. She thought of Hugh and how Loralyn must have been enchanting him since they were children.

A cloud of smoke billowed across her face as she lowered the pistol. She felt strong and confident. "This is the gun," she told Reba, and then looked up to see that all nine bullets had pierced the ocular window.

"Hell, yes, it is." Reba nodded happily. "That's at twenty

yards too. You've still got it, girl. Now move that target out to fifty yards. I'm going to show you a few of *my* tricks."

The next morning, Reba duct-taped a loaded rifle to the underside of Ella Mae's worktable in the pie shop's kitchen. She hid another beneath the display case in the dining area. Patting the holster concealed under her loose T-shirt, she said, "Not very flatterin', I know. I prefer to wear tight tops, giving the menfolk a clear picture of my assets, but my sexy clothes will have to stay in the closet until after the harvest."

Ella Mae touched the oven mitt she'd put on the counter next to the commercial mixer. "The Colt's inside. I can't work with it stuck in my waistband. It's too distracting and I can grab it like this just as quickly."

Reba looked unconvinced. "Show me." Without warning, she pulled a knife from her pink cowboy boot and rushed Ella Mae.

Fingers curling around the Colt's grip, Ella Mae yanked the pistol free and aimed. She could have put a bullet between Reba's eyes, but only a second or two before her wicked little knife would have punctured her lung.

"Shave a second off that draw and I'll be satisfied," Reba said, sliding the knife back into her boot.

"What's in your other boot? A grenade?" Ella Mae teased. Despite the fact that she'd come into the pie shop an hour earlier than usual to make a group of tarts for Candis and Rudy to taste later that afternoon, she was in a good mood.

The discovery that Loralyn had used enchantment to achieve her goals had Ella Mae looking at her own life through new eyes. For the first time, she felt superior to her nemesis. After all, she'd never bent the rules to acquire anything, and now here she was, running a successful business.

And then there was Hugh. Last night, in the moments before sleep, with Chewy snoring at her feet and ribbons of moonbeams sneaking between the bedroom curtains, Ella Mae knew that she had to find a way to free Hugh from Loralyn's spell. Fantasizing about this while she melted chocolate over a double boiler had her feeling tingly with hope and excitement.

"Glad to hear you hummin'," Reba said. She stood at the sink, washing fresh fruit, a licorice twist tucked behind her ear. "I thought you'd hit me with a billion questions this mornin'."

"Believe me, I have plenty." Ella Mae poured the chocolate into four miniature tart pans lined with Oreo cookie crusts. "But I want these tarts to taste like a bright and happy future. Candis and Rudy don't need to sample forkfuls of confusion or worry."

Reba nodded. "Makes sense. Well, you get back to your daydream and I'll let the radio keep me company. That Keith Urban can sing me a love song anytime he wants."

By the time Maurelle arrived, Reba was dancing to a Taylor Swift song and the oven was filled with breakfast pies and dessert tarts. Ella Mae was careful not to add unnecessary emotions to any of the pies, tarts, quiches, or salads she prepared, and the three women worked with such an easy rhythm that the hours passed in a pleasant blur of food, music, and chatter.

"Candis is coming in at two thirty," Ella Mae told Maurelle when the younger woman came into the kitchen, balancing an armload of dirty dishes. "She and Rudy are going to sample a selection of mini tarts."

Maurelle smiled. "I haven't talked to Candis for days. With the wedding only weeks away, she's been super busy. She's no bridezilla or anything, but she and her stepmom still have to organize the seating, the flowers, the dress, the food, and the booze." She wiped her forehead with the edge of her apron. "A glass of chilled champagne sounds really good right about now. I am so ready for summer to be over."

Ella Mae thought of the harvest and of the stooped ash tree in the secret grove in the mountains. Would she have more of an understanding of her own abilities by the first official day of autumn? Would the mystery behind Melissa Carlisle's death be solved? Would Verena and the other elders find a replacement in time? Suddenly, she realized that Maurelle was still talking.

"Sorry. I drifted off there for a second. What did you say?"

"Oh, just that Candis asked me to be her maid of honor and I have no idea what to wear." She touched the sleeve of her shirt. "And I don't want to ask her to go shopping with me when she has so much to do." She hesitated. "Can you recommend a store that isn't too expensive?"

Ella Mae felt a rush of sympathy for Maurelle. Didn't this quiet, hard-working young woman have any other friends who could take her dress shopping?

With a prick of guilt, Ella Mae realized that she hadn't made much of an effort to get to know her new employee. Sure, she was aware of her medical history and had read the facts written on her application, but she hadn't asked Maurelle any personal questions. She knew nothing of her family, where she came from, or even where she lived. "Listen, I'd love to show you some of my favorite shops after work this week. After closing, we could each go home, get cleaned up, and then spend a few hours finding you something pretty and hip to wear." She babbled on. "We could grab a bite to eat afterward. What do you say?"

"That would be great." Maurelle's smile illuminated her whole face. The bells on the front door tinkled, and she smoothed her apron and said, "They're playing my song."

That's exactly how I feel every time I hear those sweet silver bells, Ella Mae thought.

An hour later, Candis and Rudy arrived accompanied by a tall, Rubenesque woman with strawberry blond hair. "I'm Freda Shaw," she said, shaking Ella Mae's hand with gusto.

"Freda's my stepmom, but she's more like my fairy godmother," Candis explained, giving Freda's waist an affectionate squeeze. "If I didn't love her as much as I do, I wouldn't have invited her to taste the goodies before the wedding. But here we are, and all three of us skipped lunch so we'd be good and hungry."

"Don't worry, I've made more than enough," Ella Mae said. "I wasn't sure if your folks were coming too, Rudy."

He shook his head. "No, they had some mysterious wedding surprise to plan." Glancing at Candis, he shrugged. "They can't get into too much trouble, right?"

She laughed and nudged Freda playfully. "We're trying to keep everything low-key, despite our parents. We're both only children, and I think they want to pull out all the stops, but as long as we're together and have tasty things to eat, it'll be perfect."

"Tasty things to eat? That's my cue." Ella Mae led them over to a café table. "I've put out water, but would anyone like coffee as well?"

"Oh, I would," Freda said. "I've been in court all day and I'm worn out."

Ella Mae thought she looked as fresh as one of her mother's roses. Freda was probably only a couple of years older than Ella Mae, but her smooth skin and intelligent gaze gave her an air of ageless authority. She reminded Ella Mae of a younger version of Verena.

Just then, Maurelle came out of the kitchen and, after receiving a big hug from Candis, poured Freda's coffee. Reba appeared a moment later bearing a tray laden with miniature tarts.

"Because the wedding's in September, I wanted to

include apples, so your first sample is a caramel apple cream cheese tart," Ella Mae explained.

Reba served Freda, greeting her with a reverent, "Nice to see you, Your Honor."

As the trio took bites of the apple tart, Ella Mae introduced the second offering. "This is a white chocolate tart with a garnish of raspberries, blueberries, and kiwi. It's very colorful, creamy, and refreshing."

"Yum," Rudy said. "This is how I'd like to get my daily serving of fruit."

Ella Mae looked at Candis. "Do any of your guests have nut allergies?"

"I don't think so," she said. "We've shared meals with almost everyone who's coming, and I've never heard anyone mention an allergy."

"Except for your daddy," Freda interjected. "He's got issues with penicillin."

Candis nodded solemnly and turned to Ella Mae. "I'm afraid we'll have to skip the penicillin tart."

Playing along, Ella Mae feigned disappointment. "In that case, your guests will have to settle for this almond toffee tart. I like to pair creamy tarts with something crunchy so that your guests can enjoy a variety of textures."

After suggesting that they all cleanse their palettes with water, she signaled for Maurelle to bring out the next round of samples.

"This one's the richest of our selections." Ella Mae indicated a trio of dark chocolate tarts garnished with a white chocolate dove. "I can use white chocolate shavings if you'd rather not have the dove."

"No, I love it!" Candis exclaimed, plucking the bird garnish from the tart. She held it up to the light. "It's so thin. How did you make this?"

"I pipe the chocolate onto wax paper and then chill it.

No two doves will look exactly the same, but I like the contrast of dark brown and white."

"Me too," Freda agreed. "One doesn't quite stand out without the other." She stared at her with such intensity that Ella Mae wondered if she'd done something to reveal her magical abilities.

Breaking eye contact with the judge, Ella Mae pointed at the next tart. "This is lemon mascarpone with a garnish of honey-glazed strawberries. The mascarpone was made by Lynn and Vaughn Sherman." She gestured at the samples. "In fact, all of the herbs, fruits, and cheesees are locally grown. The honey too."

A shadow crossed Freda's face, and in that moment, Ella Mae knew that Freda was one of her kind. She couldn't say exactly how she knew with such certainty, but she did. It was a powerful feeling arising from the depths of her being, like the instant bond between a mother and her newborn child. She recognized a fellow creature who shared her origins, and it felt good because she sensed Freda was good.

"Next up is a bourbon molasses pecan tart," Ella Mae continued, trying to redirect her focus. "You can't have a Southern wedding without bourbon."

"Unless we're talking about Uncle Hoyt," Rudy mumbled around a bite of tart. "He gets his hands on bourbon and he'll start serenading the lawn gnomes again."

They all laughed. Maurelle refilled the water glasses and then Ella Mae told her to join her friend at the table. "I've saved the best for last. Because you're as sweet and pretty as a Georgia peach, Candis, the centerpiece will be filled with mini peach meringue tarts with a garnish of candied ginger curls. Except for the one on top. That one will have a pair of caramelized sugar hearts so that you two have something to feed each other. Your families would never forgive me if you didn't give them that Kodak moment."

"Wow!" Candis breathed after swallowing a piece of peach tart. "This is delicious! They all are! Everything tastes so amazing! How do you do it?"

Ella Mae's heart swelled with pride. "Using fresh, seasonal ingredients is key." She held out her hands, indicating the remaining tarts. "So which ones would you like to include on your dessert buffet?"

Candis and Rudy exchanged smiles. "All of them!" they said in unison.

Freda chuckled. "I couldn't agree more. And the desserts for the wedding are my treat," she told the couple, and then held up a finger to stop them from arguing. "I won't take no for an answer. Candis, your daddy gets to pay for the flowers and the dress, so let me take care of the food. It would mean the world to me if I could contribute."

Candis leaned over and hugged her stepmother. Freda held her tightly, her eyes growing moist with unshed tears.

"Oh, don't cry!" Candis scolded with a tremble in her voice. "I'm not going anywhere. Rudy and I will always be close by."

"I know," Freda whispered, sniffing. "I can't help it. I'm just so proud of what a lovely young woman you've become." She smiled warmly at Rudy. "And what a fine choice of husband you've made."

Reba cleared her throat. "I'm gonna blubber all over this tablecloth in a minute. How about I fix you all a glass of cold lemonade? You can sit out on the front porch and rock away some of those tarts."

"You're spoiling us," Candis said, but she and Rudy pushed back their chairs and stood up. Since there were no more customers in the pie shop, Ella Mae told Maurelle to join her friends on the porch.

"I'll be along shortly," Freda told Candis. "Ella Mae and I need to hash out the numbers first."

"Are you okay?" Ella Mae asked Freda when they were alone. "You looked really sad a minute ago."

Freda watched Reba carry a pitcher of lemonade and three clean glasses outside. Her face became etched with sorrow. "That's because I'm going to miss her so much."

Ella Mae put her hand on Freda's. "You heard Candis. She'll always be nearby."

"I know," Freda said. "It's me who won't be there. I won't see her first house or hold her children. I won't be able to meet her for lunch or give her advice. I love that girl as if she were my own flesh and blood, and it's breaking my heart to think that I can't even say good-bye to her."

"I don't understand." Ella Mae felt the stirrings of alarm. "Why can't you tell Candis where you're going?"

"Because I've volunteered." Freda spoke very softly. "I'm to become the next Lady of the Ash."

Chapter 7

Ella Mae sank onto a kitchen stool and cradled a mug of coffee in her hands. She and Reba were the only ones left in the pie shop.

"Poor Candis," she murmured, feeling no comfort from the warm ceramic against her palms.

"It's a huge sacrifice, to be sure," Reba said, untying her apron and unstrapping the holster from beneath her T-shirt. "Lord, that feels good! I was sweatin' like a fat man in the sauna!"

Ella Mae wasn't listening. "Freda seems like a great choice."

Reba nodded. "Sure is. She's smart and tough and fair. That's what makes her such a good judge. Her courtroom experience will make her a great Lady of the Ash. And, yes, her husband and Candis are gonna be hurt, but Freda's doin' something bigger than herself. Without her, it'd be the end of our sacred grove."

"I can't believe there isn't another way to preserve our magic."

Reba set her gun down on the worktable. "We pay a price for being what we are. I don't know why, but it's been this way for a thousand years. Freda was always meant to serve her people. Her name comes from Elfreda or Aelfthrynth." She pronounced the latter as "elf-thrith." "Means counselor to the elves."

Ella Mae took a sip of coffee. "Over the summer, I remember you saying that there's power in a person's name and I looked up everyone in one of those baby name books. Verena means truth, my mother's first and middle names combine to mean ruler of the moon, Delia is named after the birthplace of Artemis, the goddess of wild animals, Sissy comes from Cecilia, or patron of music, and your name, Rebekah, means to tie, bind, or protect."

"That's right. I'm bound to protect the LeFaye family. Specifically you and your mama. I was born to do it." She studied Ella Mae. "Is somethin' else troublin' you besides Freda's announcement?"

"Yes, there is. All of you were given names that helped define your role in life," Ella Mae said, feeling tired and confused. "But Ella just means 'enchanted' or 'beautiful fairy.' That, paired with the month of May, has no significance. How does being named Ella Mae explain my purpose?"

Sliding the pistol into her purse, Reba shrugged. "I don't have all the answers, sugar. Nothin' about you fits the standard operatin' procedure. You're the child of two magical parents. That's not supposed to be possible. You had an Awakenin' in your thirties. Unheard of. My girl, there's somethin' mighty special about you, but you have to figure out what that means." She touched Ella Mae's cheek. "Maybe it's time for you to start readin' the books in your

mama's library. And I'm not talkin' about *Pride and Preju-
dice*. I'm talkin' about the hidden ones."

"That's an excellent idea." Ella Mae perked up as she
recalled the secret niche behind in the mantel. "I'll start
tonight."

"Just don't try to take in too much at once," Reba said.
"You could go crazy lookin' for the whys and hows of things
that can't be explained. Don't forget to walk through the
garden when the stars are first comin' out or do a cannonball
into the lake durin' a pink and orange sunrise. You've got a
life to live, Ella Mae. Even though you can't see where your
path is leadin', you still need to walk it."

Ella Mae grinned. "That's a serious dose of fortune
cookie philosophy. And speaking of stopping to smell the
roses, what are you doing tonight?"

"Remember Jessup from the shooting range?"

"The guy with the wad of chewing tobacco?" Ella Mae
grimaced. "Don't tell me . . ."

"Lord have mercy, no!" Reba exclaimed. "He's got an
older brother. Wayne's a fine-lookin' man who promised me
a big steak dinner and a good bottle of wine if I can outshoot
him at fifty yards."

Ella Mae laughed. "I feel sorry for this Wayne guy. I hope
he keeps plenty of cash in his wallet."

"Don't you fret, darlin'. I'll make losin' worth his while."
Reba gave Ella Mae a saucy wink and left the pie shop.

Ella Mae spent that evening and many more like it in the
library at Partridge Hill. She drank wine and read while
Chewy ran in and out of the room or kept company with
Reba or her mother, who showered him with treats and
attention.

Ella Mae quickly became obsessed with the fantastical

tales and illustrations of the magical men and women she'd always believed were the stuff of legend. Fairy tales, tall tales, myths, fables, folklore—they all turned out to contain fragments of truth. The real versions of these stories were recorded in the leather tomes and parchment scrolls in her mother's library, and they were utterly fascinating.

The first story she read was about a girl with golden locks who'd been raised by bears. In this adaptation, thieves kill the girl's parents as they traveled through a forest, and a female bear discovers the tiny child shivering in the cold and carries her home to the den. Ella Mae then read an unusual interpretation penned by the British poet in the early eighteen hundreds. He described the main character not as a naïve and curious girl but a foul-mouthed, ugly hag. It took many years and many versions for the girl be known as a precocious child named Goldilocks.

The truth was a combination of both. When the magical, golden-haired girl was with the bears, she was young and beautiful, but whenever she entered the world of men, she became old again. Speaking in the only tongue she knew, the growling language of the bears, she'd enter their villages and beg for a bowl of porridge. The people thought she was crazy. They drove her from their streets by throwing stones at her. One day, she was struck on the head by a rock and died before she could return to the safety of the den. The bears woke to find her gone.

To her horror, Ella Mae found that most of the versions of the traditional tales she'd heard since childhood were filled with similar tragedies. The magical beings, her ancestors, were often treated very badly. Over the centuries, her kind had been ostracized, persecuted, and hunted as witches. As a result, they learned to conceal their gifts. They hid in plain sight among the normal humans and survived because they abided by a list of rules Ella Mae had yet to discover.

One September afternoon, with the last of the summer

heat clinging to Havenwood, Ella Mae decided she needed a night free of research.

"No more books," she told Chewy and lifted him into her bike basket. "We're going to have a picnic, a swim, and then we'll watch the lightning bugs dance through the trees. How does that sound?"

Chewy barked, his tail thumping in anticipation. Standing on his front paws, he tried to climb out of the basket, his nose quivering feverishly as he detected the scent of fried chicken.

"I'll give you some as soon as we get there. Promise."

Ella Mae pedaled slowly. With the heavy, cloying air pressing down, she couldn't wait to hit the downhill stretch, to let the wind pry the damp strands of hair off her sticky cheeks. It was nearly six o'clock and yet the sun still beat down on her. The entire town seemed parched and wilted, and though a cold front was due to arrive any day now, it seemed impossible to believe that fall would ever arrive.

At the sandy bank alongside the swimming hole, Ella Mae laid out a picnic supper on a large, flat rock. She gave Chewy some of Reba's buttermilk fried chicken but shooed him away when he began to sniff her container of Caprese salad. Too full to eat the strawberries she'd brought for dessert, Ella Mae stepped out of her white denim cutoffs and drew her lavender T-shirt over her head. After straightening a twisted strap on her silver tankini, she glanced around the placid swimming hole and smiled.

"Come on, boy!" she called out to Chewy, racing into the water with a laugh.

The terrier didn't need any encouragement. With a yip of delight, he launched himself after her, his feet paddling ferociously as he strove to catch up.

Ella Mae caught hold of a stray twig that had fallen from one of the many trees leaning over the swimming hole, and tossed it onto a spit of dry land. Chewy pivoted in the water and swam to fetch it. They played catch for a while and then Chewy settled down on the picnic blanket to rest. Ella Mae lay back in the refreshingly cool water, stretching out her arms and legs until her body looked like a star. Closing her eyes, she floated for several minutes, her hair fanning around her head as she bobbed in the subtle current.

For the first time in weeks, she felt utterly relaxed. In this place, she was able to empty her mind of the harvest, the strange and convoluted history of her people, and the fact that her inaugural catering job was coming up in a few days. Concentrating instead on the gurgling and lapping noises of the water, she focused on the soothing melody as the sun began to sink behind the hills and the shadows stretched and lengthened around the swimming hole.

In her trancelike state, it took Ella Mae several moments to realize that the barking she heard from the ridge of trees near the picnic blankets didn't sound like Chewy. It was the deep bark of a much bigger dog.

Slightly disoriented, Ella Mae began to tread water, turning this way and that as she looked around for her terrier.

"Chewy!" she shouted. "Chewy! Where are you, boy?"

Two sets of dog barks erupted from a break in the trees where a path wound up through the woods and to where the blackberry bushes grew in a wild tangle of thorny branches.

Ella Mae had left her bike in the cover of those bushes, a few feet from Skipper Drive. The road wasn't a busy one, but she didn't want Chewy anywhere near it. And who was the other dog? Was he a threat to her little Jack Russell?

"Chewy!" she yelled again, swimming toward the sandy bank.

Suddenly, she heard a splash from behind her. It wasn't loud, but she could tell that something had just entered the water from the rocks jutting out over the center of the swimming hole. Whatever it was, the thing was big enough to have sent waves rippling wildly along the surface.

Ella Mae felt terribly vulnerable. Quickening her pace, she'd almost reached dry land when a hand clamped around her ankle. She screamed.

"Whoa, whoa!" a man said with laughter in his voice. "It's just me!"

Swinging around, Ella Mae lost her balance on the slick stones underfoot. She fell back into the shallows with an angry, unintelligible shout.

Hugh snaked his arms under her thighs and upper back and raised her to the surface in a single, effortless motion.

"I didn't mean to scare you. I'm sorry." The corners of his mouth twitched with amusement.

Ella Mae slapped him on the chest. "I could kill you! I thought you were some monster who wanted to tear me into pieces!" Too angry to move, she glared at Hugh, but it was difficult to hold on to her ire with him cradling her so tenderly. Water trickled down his jawline and dripped from his chin. Droplets shone on his wide shoulders and along his muscular arms. The last rays of the setting sun cast a golden sheen over his skin and tinged his dark, wet locks with filaments of copper. He looked her over with his bright blue eyes, surveying her tight, silver swimsuit and her tanned limbs.

"You're beautiful," he whispered.

Ella Mae was unaccustomed to being touched by a man other than Sloan. She knew she should wriggle out of Hugh's arms, but it felt so right to be nestled against him. It didn't matter that she was still legally married or that Hugh was a captive of Loralyn's power—no one else existed beyond this moment, beyond this circle of cool water.

Glancing up at the outcrop from which Hugh had jumped, Ella Mae realized that there was so much she didn't know about this man. She wanted him and he wanted her, but that wasn't enough. And yet, considering all that she'd had to digest over the past few weeks, she didn't want to think tonight. She didn't want to analyze her feelings or worry about the future. She wanted only to lose herself with Hugh, to surrender to his eyes and lips and hands in the indigo twilight.

"Why do we keep ending up like this?" she asked. She'd meant to sound playful, but the huskiness of her voice betrayed her desire. "This close to each other."

He drew her even nearer, so that her hip rested against his waist and her face was inches from his. "You're my mermaid," he answered, running his thumb and forefinger down the length of a lock of her hair. "Silver and beautiful as moonlight."

The image reminded Ella Mae of Loralyn.

I'm not a mermaid. Or a siren, she thought, feeling her hatred for Loralyn taint the moment.

Hugh must have noticed the shift in mood, for he released her legs, letting them sink gently to the bottom. He kept hold of her shoulders though, refusing to let her pull away. She was glad of that. Her anger was meant for Loralyn, not Hugh.

"I've been in love with you for as long as I can remember, but you've never been free," she said. "Loralyn's always been in the picture, hasn't she?"

He dropped his gaze, and Ella Mae was tempted to kiss his sweep of long, damp lashes. "I know that she doesn't really care about me. She never did. I'm just someone she reaches for in between husbands, but I couldn't see that about her—or about myself—until you showed up earlier this summer." He looked at her, and in his eyes she saw a reflection of her own yearning.

They were silent for a few seconds, and then Hugh spoke again. "I'm not looking for a fling. I want something real. Something life changing." His fingertips traced Ella Mae's cheek and then traveled down the curve of her neck. "All those years ago, the most amazing girl of all was right in front of me. For some reason, I couldn't see that. I couldn't see *you*. And then you left. You got married. It was too late to win you."

Ella Mae's heart was booming like thunder inside her chest. "But I'm back now," she said. "To stay."

His eyes turned glum. "But you're not free."

"I will be. In just a few months." She brought her lips close enough to breathe her next words into his ear. "And I'm worth waiting for."

Hugh's arms slid around her waist and tightened. "I know you are." His fingers dug into the flesh of her lower back and she felt his need in his touch. It pulsed through her like a second heartbeat. "I've watched you at the pie shop," he said. "I see how hard you work and how great you are with people. How you cherish your family. I see the way your smile lights up a room, and every time you laugh, I hear music." He traced a pattern on her skin, an infinity symbol stretching from one hip to the center of her back and out to the other hip. "Are you worth waiting for? Hell, yes. You are."

"Then prove it, Hugh Dylan." Ella Mae pulled back in order to look him full in the face. "If we both want this, if we both *really* want to be together, then nothing should stand in our way. Prove it by kissing me. Kiss me like you'll never let me go."

She expected him to mention that the last time they'd kissed the heat between them had become too intense, causing genuine pain, but he didn't say a word. He closed his eyes and put his mouth on hers.

Ella Mae waited for the tingling feeling to start, but it didn't. There was no sensation of being burned. No crackles of electricity. There was only Hugh. His mouth, his tongue, his hands moving up the slope of her back, pressing her closer and then closer still.

Their kiss was slow and tender at first and then rapidly became deeper and greedier. As she clung to Hugh, Ella Mae felt as if her body were floating again, adrift on currents of heat and need. Kissing Sloan had never felt like this. This kiss was like being pulled underwater. It was like drowning in a dream, and Ella Mae sensed that Hugh Dylan was not like other men. But was he one of her kind? Is that why they'd hurt each other when they kissed before?

As if reading her mind, Hugh gently broke away. "I don't know why this isn't like the time at the pie shop, but I am so glad to be able to touch you without . . ."

She put a finger to his lips. "Nothing from before matters. We have lots of things to figure out and that's okay. I just need to know that you're willing to do whatever it takes to make this work."

"I am," he said solemnly. "And I don't intend to start off by assaulting you at the local swimming hole." His hands moved over the rise of her shoulders and slid down her arms, making her shiver all over. "Though I don't know how I'll ever force myself to stop touching you."

She reached for him, but he grabbed her hand and kissed her chastely on the palm. "I want to do this the right way. You deserve to be courted, Ella Mae. You should have flowers and candlelit dinners. I want to hold your hand at the movie theater and go on hikes to places where there are no other people. Just you, me, and the dogs," he added with a smile.

"I like the sound of that," Ella Mae said.

"So we'll take it slow until after the divorce. After that, look out. You'll be mine. Every inch of you."

At that moment, Hugh's Harlequin Dane, Dante, burst through the trees and ran to the lake's edge, Chewy following close behind. The dogs were all toothy smiles, lolling tongues, and wagging tails.

Hugh and Ella Mae laughed and then exchanged a brief

look of agreement. It was time for them to get out, to break the water's magic spell.

"I'd like to see you on Saturday," Hugh said as they moved apart. "I know you're doing the desserts at Rudy and Candis's wedding, but I'm going to be there too because Freda Shaw's my cousin. Twice removed or something, but we're related somehow. Anyway, you and I could spend time together after it's over."

If Hugh's related to Freda, he might be an Other. He might be like me, Ella Mae thought excitedly.

They reached the bank, and she wrapped herself in a towel and sat on the rock where she'd had her picnic. "We'll already be dressed to the nines, won't we?"

"I'll take you dancing," Hugh said. "There's a live band playing at the resort."

"Sounds like heaven," Ella said, already imagining Hugh in a tux, his hand around her waist as they spun slowly across the dance floor. She could see the two of them pausing between songs to drink sparkling wine or a cold beer, chatting and laughing as starlight filtered into the waterside pergola, making the surface of the lake sparkle like glitter.

Ella Mae and Hugh sat on the rock by the swimming hole and talked for the next two hours. They ate sweet strawberries and reminisced about old classmates while the night air dried their hair and wrapped them in a state of drowsy contentment.

Eventually, Ella Mae sighed and said, "I'd better go."

"Let me give you a ride." Hugh collected her picnic things.

She gestured at the bright moon. "I'll be fine. Besides, Partridge Hill is totally out of your way."

"It gives me five more minutes with you." He turned to his snoozing Dane. "To the truck, boy."

Dante rose and yawned. He then nudged Chewy with his

big black nose and loped up the path. Chewy looked at Ella Mae expectantly.

"Go on!" She told her dog and then grinned at Hugh. "Your Canine to Five staff is teaching him such excellent manners. I feel guilty leaving him there all day, but I don't even think he misses me."

"Sure he does," Hugh said. "There's a bond between the two of you. You got him from a shelter, right?"

Ella Mae nodded.

"Animals know when they've been rescued. Dante knows it. Chewy knows it." He cast her a shy glance. "People can be rescued too."

Hugh's words stayed with her long after he'd unloaded her bike and given her a parting kiss on the cheek. She drifted upstairs and got ready for bed in a dreamlike state, replaying every second of the evening over and over again, wrapping the fresh memories around her like a blanket.

Opening her bedroom windows, she inhaled the perfume of her mother's roses. Tonight, they smelled of dew-covered strawberries and promises.

"Those wedding tarts are going to be amazing," she whispered to the silent garden. "Just one bite and folks will know exactly what love tastes like."

The next afternoon, Ella Mae went with Maurelle to pick up her bridesmaid dress. Candis had told her that she'd gladly pay for whatever her friend wanted to wear, but Maurelle had refused the offer. Ella Mae had been there when she first tried on a merlot-colored dress with a form-fitting jacket of the same hue. With her pale skin and dark hair, the color had suited Maurelle perfectly.

"I'll probably never wear this again," she'd said with a sigh when the boutique owner offered to take the waist in at no extra charge.

"Pretty thing like you?" The woman had been incredulous. "Come on, the boys must be lining up to take you out!"

Maurelle had smirked. "Not exactly."

"It's only because she's new in town," Ella Mae had said quickly.

"Well, that explains it! Maybe you'll meet a nice boy at the wedding." The woman studied Maurelle kindly. "Where are you from, honey?"

Shrugging, Maurelle had said, "My folks live in Arizona, but it's too hot and sunny for me there. I moved to Atlanta a few years ago and that's where I met Candis. She was in her nursing school."

"A nurse? How wonderful!" The woman had acted unduly impressed. "Were you two in school together?"

Fidgeting with the hem of her sleeve, Maurelle murmured, "No. I was a patient."

That had shut the boutique owner up. After giving Maurelle a sympathetic pat on the arm, she'd rung up the dress and a pair of silver heels. Maurelle paid with what had to have been all of her tip money, since the pile of cash was mostly made up of wrinkled five- and one-dollar bills.

Afterward, Maurelle had been quiet during dinner and Ella Mae hadn't had the heart to ply her with questions. Her new employee had withdrawn since their visit to the boutique, and Ella Mae was relieved when the waiter arrived with the check and the two women had called it a night.

By Saturday, Maurelle was her pleasant self again. She worked her regular shift at the pie shop and then helped Reba and Ella Mae pack up all the tarts for the dessert buffet.

"I'm glad you got this gig," Reba said as she and Ella Mae sat in the shade garden at Partridge Hill later that afternoon. The two women were drinking iced coffee and relaxing before they had to shower, change, and head back to the pie shop to fill Ella Mae's Jeep with the wedding treats. "It'll be a sweet sight when those darlin' young folks walk down the aisle. Lord knows we could use a life-affirmin' moment like that."

Ella Mae nodded. "No news on Melissa's lab results yet?"

Reba shook her head. "I thought for sure we'd hear somethin' this week. Judge Freda was gonna put pressure on the coroner's office. The authorities are still statin' that the cause of death is unknown, and Freda wants answers even more than we do."

"In case the killer comes after her."

"Exactly." Reba patted Ella Mae's arm. "But you have enough on your mind, so don't fret about Melissa or Freda tonight. Wait 'til you see Freda's place. It's set high up on the hills above the lake and backs up to a big stretch of woods. It's a whole lot better than some stuffy wedding hall."

Reba couldn't have been more right. Freda Shaw's house was a low country jewel with an enormous wraparound porch. Magnolia branches with gold satin bows were tied around every porch column, and a path made up of pink, yellow, and coral rose petals invited guests to the back of the house. There, on a gentle slope of lawn overlooking the lake, Candis and Rudy would exchange vows. The scene was breathtakingly beautiful.

Neat rows of rental chairs were positioned on the grass, and vines of clematis with blush-colored blooms covered its wooden arch. The center aisle between the chairs was made entirely of a thick carpet of flower petals. Rose blossoms mingled with merry daisies, star-shaped asters, bright coreopsis, and wild chrysanthemums.

"This is the most romantic setting I've ever seen," Ella Mae said.

She and Reba had already set up the tarts on the buffet table on the back porch and were now watching the guests mingle on the lawn. Everyone was waiting for the bride and groom to arrive.

"Your mama and aunts are here," Reba said, though none of the LeFaye women were in sight. "I can hear Verena clear as a bell. I'd better go make sure she doesn't steal a hunk of cheese on the sly. Vaughn and Lynn don't realize they're gonna have to stand guard over the food."

"That's because they don't know Verena." Ella Mae laughed. She then focused on the gorgeous vista and indulged in a fantasy in which the wedding guests were all gone and she was alone with Hugh. She longed to kiss him under the flower-covered arch.

"Aren't you supposed to be working?" said a woman.

Ella Mae swung around to find Loralyn standing in the middle of the aisle, scattering the perfect arrangement of petals with the toe of her shoe.

"That's for Candis to walk on, not you!" Ella Mae snapped. "You've had three weddings already. Get off."

Loralyn looked down at her feet in mock innocence. She slowly made her way back onto the grass, leaving a trail of trampled flowers in her wake. "I might have my fourth ceremony outdoors. It's rather rustic. Perhaps more appropriate for a farmhand or a baker, but not without its charms."

Ella Mae wanted to slap the sneer right off Loralyn's face. "Who invited you?"

"The Gaynors are always included in these provincial events. After all, we give the best gifts." She put her hand over her mouth as if regretting her words. "Oh, but you didn't have to bring anything because you're the *help*." She examined Ella Mae. "Pretty fancy dress for a baker."

It was true. Dee had invited her to pick and choose from any of the items in her closet, and Ella Mae had discovered a treasure trove of vintage coats, dresses, and gowns. Before she'd adopted a uniform of overalls and T-shirts, Dee had worn clothes that would have made Audrey Hepburn jealous.

Tonight, Ella Mae was clad in a chocolate brown cocktail dress with a form-fitting bodice. Made of silk, taffeta, and tulle, the hourglass shape flattered Ella Mae's curves, and the full skirt was perfect for dancing. She'd pinned her whiskey-colored hair into a messy bun, leaving strands to frame her face and curl at the nape of her neck. Her skin glowed, her hazel eyes glimmered with flecks of gold, and she had never felt so beautiful.

"I have a date after the wedding," Ella Mae said.

"Really?" Loralyn seemed absurdly pleased. "I doubt he can measure up to the man I'll have on my arm." She turned back toward the house. "Ah, here he is now, bringing me champagne. He's a keeper, I tell you. Total husband material."

Ella Mae couldn't speak. She couldn't move. All she could do was gape, dumbfounded, as Loralyn's date crossed the lawn, his familiar mouth curving into a smile. He drew up next to Loralyn, and Ella Mae caught a whiff of his aftershave. She stared at him, wondering how she'd been able to forget how handsome he was.

"Seeing as I don't need to introduce the two of you, I think I'll go inside and powder my nose." Loralyn accepted her glass of champagne and took a dainty sip. "Feel free to catch up. You must have lots to talk about." With a wicked grin, she sashayed back toward the house.

Waiting until Loralyn was out of earshot, Ella Mae grabbed the second glass of champagne from the man's hand and downed it in one swallow. "Jesus," she muttered, wishing she could chase the champagne with a fifth of whiskey. She then locked eyes with her husband and said, "What the hell are you doing here, Sloan?"

Chapter 8

Sloan Kitteridge looked her over with appreciative eyes. "Gorgeous. You're like one of the flowers in the bride's bouquet. This place"—he waved his hand to encompass all of Havenwood—"suits you."

Ella Mae didn't answer. She crossed her arms over her chest and glared at him.

"Sorry," Sloan said. "It's just that I haven't seen you in months and now here you are. As breathtaking as the day we were married." He exhaled and took a step closer. "Honey, I know I screwed up. What we had was really special and I don't want to let it go. I knew I had to do something big to prove that I'm a changed man and that's why I'm here. Didn't you say that if I came to you that you'd be willing to give us a chance?"

She had made him that offer, but that had been months ago.

"You told me that you were staying in New York," she

said. "Your life was there. You belonged there. That's what you said."

He shook his head. "I was wrong. My life is wherever you are."

Wishing that Sloan's words didn't move her, Ella Mae fixed her gaze on the lake below. The sight of the familiar water instantly steadied her. Knowing that Partridge Hill's dock was there on the opposite shore, obscured by the small island in the middle of the lake, gave her strength. This was her home. The vast lake, the lush grass, the unblemished sky. She fit here.

Sloan was from a different world. A different life. In her mind, he had already taken a place in her past, fading from the present like a ghost. After only a few weeks in Havenwood, she forgot how penetrating his dark eyes were, what his laughter sounded like, or how it felt to hold his hand. And yet, now that he was here, all of those things came rushing back to her.

She couldn't help but remember how often she'd met his gaze and seen sparks of amusement or affection in his eyes. Once, she would have found it hard to look away, but that was before he'd made a fool of her. "I don't think I understand what point you're trying to make. Showing up at a stranger's wedding with Loralyn Gaynor on your arm is your way of showing me love and devotion?"

Sloan frowned. "I'm not *with* her. I just rode with her. My big statement is that I moved to Atlanta. For us, Ella Mae. I applied for a transfer and I'm working for the firm's Georgia branch. The Gaynors were my first important clients. When Mrs. Gaynor told me where they lived, I asked about you." He smiled. "I thought it was a miracle that I'd found someone who could help me work my way back to you. Opal and Loralyn have been really gracious. And I wouldn't be a very good investment banker if I didn't take advantage of every opportunity that came my way."

"So it was Loralyn's idea to bring you here?"

"Yes." Sloan touched the rose tucked into his buttonhole. "She thought the romantic setting would remind you of how much we loved each other when we exchanged our vows."

Feeling dazed, Ella Mae noticed that the wedding guests were beginning to take their seats. A group of musicians positioned themselves to one side of the wooden arch and a preacher carrying a Bible joined them. As the members of the string quartet tuned their instruments, the preacher greeted the couple seated in the front row. Ella Mae recognized Rudy's parents. Rudy's father looked proud and cheerful while Rudy's mother alternated between beaming and dabbing at her eyes with a tissue.

"We need to move," Ella Mae whispered urgently to Sloan and, without waiting for him to answer, turned and strode up the lawn in the direction of the back porch. She saw Reba waiting for her, her mouth drawn in a tight line of anger.

"I'm all right," Ella Mae said. "I just need a drink and a moment to wake up from this nightmare."

Reba dug a small flask out of her sequined handbag. "Let Mr. Jack Daniel settle your nerves. As for the nightmare, I can take care of *him*."

Ella Mae grabbed Reba's arm before she rushed off. "Don't. The wedding's going to start any second now. I don't want to ruin it with my own drama. I'll deal with Sloan later."

When her husband stepped onto the porch, Ella Mae held out a hand for him to stop. She swallowed the contents of Reba's flask, grimacing as the strong, bitter taste of the whiskey coated her tongue and sent a rush of fire down her throat. "This isn't the time or place for this, Sloan. Give me your number and I'll call you."

"No way." His voice was soft, but firm. "I've waited so long to be near you. I know this setting is suboptimal and that you're working." He gestured at the buffet table. "By the way, the desserts look unbelievable, Ella Mae. I'm so proud of you."

"Thanks," she murmured, unable to conceal her pleasure over the compliment. Behind Sloan, Reba scowled and Ella Mae couldn't help but wonder if Reba had hidden a holster somewhere beneath her form-fitting, emerald-colored dress.

The string quartet began to play "Air" from Handel's *Water Music* and the guests stopped chatting and took their seats. There was no more time to argue with Sloan. The wedding had begun.

"Sloan. *Please.*" Ella Mae felt the stirrings of panic. How could she focus on her job if he wouldn't leave? And what about Hugh? How was she going to explain her husband's presence to him?

"You heard the lady," Reba growled over the music that floated over the lawn, the notes featherlight and breezy. Ella Mae imagined them spiraling down the hillside and skipping over the surface of the lake like a water strider.

Reba didn't seem to notice the music. All of her senses were honed in on Sloan. "This is her first gig," she hissed at him. "Do you wanna ruin her professional reputation or, for once in your self-absorbed life, act like a gentleman and hightail it outta here?"

A shadow of annoyance entered Sloan's eyes but he ignored Reba. "I don't want to do anything to hurt you, Ella Mae. Not ever again," he said sincerely. "I'll go sit with the other guests, and when the reception is over, we can talk. Until then, I promise to keep my distance. You won't even know I'm here."

Ella Mae was about to protest when the string quartet started to play the "Allegro" movement from *Water Music* and an aura of delightful anticipation surrounded the guests. The time had come. The bride was on her way.

Sloan hurried to a vacant chair and managed to sit down

seconds before Rudy and another young man took their places under the wooden arch. The preacher stood in the center, cradling his Bible against his chest, and smiled as the bride appeared from around the side of the house.

"Lord have mercy!" Reba cried in amazement. "Have you ever seen anythin' like her?"

"No," Ella Mae said breathlessly. "Never."

There was Candis, resplendent as a princess, seated on the back of a tall horse with a gleaming red coat and a lightning-strike-shaped blaze on his forehead. Satin ribbons and clusters of Queen Anne's lace had been woven through his blond mane and tail. The name "Flash" was embroidered on his bridle. Candis's father, Peter Shaw, walked on one side of Flash's head while Freda was on the other, looking lovely in a tea-length dress made of cranberry chiffon.

Like Rudy, Peter wore a tux and a pale orange rose boutonniere. And though Ella Mae noticed Peter, Freda, and the horse, she was utterly transfixed by Candis.

Perched astride Flash, Candis radiated happiness. The train of her soft white gown billowed over the horse's flank and hindquarters, reminding Ella Mae of the meringue topping on some of her dessert tarts. The fitted bodice had a sweetheart neckline with knife pleating on the edge, drawing attention to Candis's slim figure. The skirt had a beaded waistband that wrapped around her hips, and there was a lustrous, chocolate-colored satin sash tied around her waist. Her hair was swept up in the front and cascaded down her back in loose, touchable curls. Like Flash's mane, delicate flowers had been threaded into her shiny locks. She wore no veil and very little makeup. Her only accessories were a pair of pearl drop earrings and the ivory ballet slippers that peeked out from beneath the gown's hem.

Freda caught Ella Mae's eye and smiled. It was a brief, bittersweet smile, and Ella Mae felt her eyes growing moist. "Candis is the most beautiful bride I've ever seen," she whispered to Reba, watching as Peter Shaw held out his hand. Candis slid off Flash's back and wove her arm through her father's. Freda handed the horse to one of the ushers and then took Candis's free arm. Together, the family marched up the aisle of flower petals.

"Check out Rudy," Reba said gleefully. "Now that's what real magic looks like."

Ella Mae couldn't agree more. Rudy's eyes were glittering with joy and it was clear that, for him, the rest of the world had faded away. There was only Candis. It was as if the young couple were completely alone—that's how intently they were staring at one another.

"Did you feel that way?" Reba asked, shooting Ella Mae a curious glance.

"Not like that," Ella Mae said. "I was happy. And hopeful. But I also remember wondering if I really knew the man waiting for me at the end of the aisle. He always kept parts of himself hidden from me." She paused. "And if I'm being honest, I did too. I never talked about Havenwood. It was like I put all those memories on a shelf for another time, like my past would have interfered with our relationship."

Reba nodded. "I suspect if you'd let those memories out, they'd have taken root. You'd have felt a pull to come home. By leaving them in the dark, you cut yourself off from the light, honey. You can see now that you and this place are linked, can't you?"

Ella Mae took Reba's hand, just as Peter Shaw placed his daughter's hand in Rudy's. "I'll never leave again, Reba. I can only be myself in Havenwood."

The Shaws took their seats in the front row, and at that moment, Hugh Dylan turned in his chair and smiled at her. When she saw the shining promise of his gaze, her heart thumped with joy. Then she darted a quick look at Sloan and her hands grew clammy. How was she going to handle this situation? Sighing, Ella Mae knew that unlike Candis and Rudy, her evening was unlikely to end with a champagne toast and a long, deep kiss beneath a canopy of stars.

"Take a breath," Reba said and muttered, "neither of them are right for you anyhow."

Ignoring her, Ella Mae did her best to focus on the couple standing beneath the arch. A light wind had sprung up from the surrounding hills and was tickling the tree branches and the ends of Candis's hair. The scattered flower petals from the aisle twirled in the air, forming little dervishes of color and scent.

After Rudy and Candis exchanged vows, three of the musicians lifted their instruments and the sweet, subtle notes of Marc Cohn's "True Companion" drifted from the strings of the two violins and the viola. The cellist rested the fingerboard of his instrument against his body, and then, with his the bow tucked under one arm, he began to sing. His voice was gravely and raw and entrancing. The song penetrated the heart of every guest, reminding them of old loves, lost loves, and in the case of the lucky few, a love that had stood the test of time. Ella Mae saw Peter Shaw put an arm around Freda's shoulders. As he drew her in close, Ella Mae thought of how little time Freda had left to be held by her husband. At the thought, she couldn't stop the tears from coming.

"It makes everything seem more beautiful, doesn't it?" Reba said softly. Her eyes were glistening with unshed tears. "Knowing it'll all be gone soon."

"There's so much beauty here that it hurts," Ella Mae said, her throat tight with sadness. "Why do love and pain always have to walk side by side?"

Reba didn't say anything. The two women listened to the rest of the song, captivated by the lyrics and the hauntingly romantic melody.

When it was over, the preacher blessed the couple and, after smiling tenderly at each other, Rudy and Candis shared their first kiss as man and wife.

More music burst into the evening air and the wind suddenly grew more purposeful. Without warning, rose petals of yellow, white, and pale orange were raining into the open palms of the spellbound guests.

"Did my mother . . . ?" Ella Mae began and Reba nodded before she had the chance to finish her sentence.

Rudy and Candis faced their friends and family, and the preacher introduced them as Mr. and Mrs. Lurding. The guests clapped and cheered.

"I wish I could be like them," Ella Mae said. "Normal. I don't see the benefit of being one of our kind. Look at you and my mother and aunts. Except for Verena, you're all alone. None of you have ever had what Rudy and Candis have, right? Freda seemed to have found someone special, but she has to throw her life away to save our sacred grove. I hate this. I don't want to be different."

Reba watched the newlyweds move down the aisle, hugging their loved ones and posing for pictures. "Think of what you did for Mrs. Dower with a single piece of pie. You put color in her gray world. You released her from guilt and grief. She's going to laugh and sing and *live*, all because of you. It is a gift, Ella Mae. As much as it's a burden."

Ella Mae wasn't able to respond, because as soon as the recessional music ended, Peter Shaw stood under the arch and invited the guests to gather on the back porch for refreshments. "I don't know about you," he said. "But I can't wait to see my daughter and new son-in-law feed each other some wedding pie."

"All hands on deck," Reba said and took her place at the head of the buffet table. She removed a pair of peach meringue mini tarts garnished with delicate caramelized sugar hearts from the small cooler under the table and plated them. These had been made especially for the bride and groom.

Candis swept onto the porch, hugging and kissing Ella Mae and Reba like they were family.

"Rudy and I want everybody to meet the woman responsible for creating this amazing dessert display!" Candis said, beaming at Ella Mae. "If you haven't been to The Charmed Pie Shoppe yet, then you're missing out on a totally life-altering experience."

Blushing, Ella Mae handed Candis the plate with the peach tarts and laughed as Rudy smeared meringue on his bride's nose. Candis returned the favor by pressing her whole pie into his face. He then grabbed her and kissed her, leaving them both covered in meringue.

"Your turn!" Candis taunted Freda, pursing her white, meringue-coated lips.

"Oh, no, you don't!" Her stepmother giggled. "Lay one on your daddy!"

Peter Shaw stepped forward with open arms and Candis gave him a light kiss on his chin. He then wiped off her face with his handkerchief, his movements so sweet and tender that the guests clasped their hands and sighed. Suddenly, they were distracted by the *pop, pop, pop* of multiple champagne bottles being opened at once. As if on cue, the string quartet broke into a lively performance of Dvořák's *Slavonic Dance*. The music, laughter, and chatter entwined, forming the jaunty sounds of celebration.

Once the bubbly began to flow, the guests crowded around the two buffet tables. The majority headed to Vaughn and Lynn's table first, piling their plates high with creamy goat cheese spread over whole grain crackers, cubes of herb cheese served on bamboo skewers along with cherry tomatoes and green olives, and wedges of soft, white Farmer's Cheese paired with hunks of fresh bread.

At the end of the table, two watermelons had been hulled and filled with ripe fruit. The guests sipped champagne, talked, and ate. And when they'd finished their cheese course, they began to drift over to the dessert buffet.

Ella Mae and Reba described the various tarts and encouraged people to sample more than one treat. When Verena got in line, she turned to her husband, Buddy, and said, "Take two of everything! I'll eat anything you don't want!"

"I know you will, darling," he said, giving her round hip a fond pat.

"There'll just be more of me to love after this evening!" She laughed heartily.

The guests moaned with pleasure as they took bites of Ella Mae's tarts. They nibbled buttery crusts with their front teeth, licked meringue from their fingers, and laid candied ginger curls onto their tongues, savoring a host of textures and flavors. It wasn't long before the effects of the tiny pies began to influence them and they set their empty plates down haphazardly in order to dance with their spouses or dates on the lawn. Though they couldn't explain why, they were compelled to hold another person, to move as one body over the soft grass.

By this time, the sun had set and Freda and Peter lit candles all around the porch. The moon wasn't quite full, but it hung low enough in the sky to bathe the ground with a wash of ivory light.

Sensing the shift in mood, the string quartet began to play a slow waltz and Peter led his daughter to the center of the ring of wedding guests and took her in his arms, his face aglow with pride and love.

Freda looked on with a wistful expression until Candis pulled her onto the lawn and the trio formed a tight family circle. They swayed together until the song ended and then Rudy led his mother into the center of the group of dancers.

"See what you can do," Reba whispered. "No one will ever forget this moment." She then trotted down the steps and into the arms of a middle-aged gentleman with a bald head and an impish grin.

Ella Mae glanced around. The porch had nearly emptied. Every guest had claimed a dance partner, surrendering to the enchantment created by Ella Mae's pies. Even Vaughn and Lynn had abandoned their stations behind the buffet table. Ella Mae's mother and aunts had all accepted invitations to waltz, leaving very few unattached women on the fringes of the makeshift dance floor.

One of them was Loralyn. She was staring daggers at Sloan, who was threading his way through the guests toward the porch. Toward Ella Mae.

"Is Cinderella ready to join the ball?" a voice asked from behind her.

Ella Mae turned to find Hugh standing in the garden bed, a rose in his hand. He offered it to her with a smile that pierced her heart like an arrow.

"I can't . . ." she began and then trailed off. How was she going to explain Sloan's presence?

"They've eaten all of your pies," Hugh pointed out. "I don't think you have to stand guard over an empty table. Come on. Put this rose in your hair and dance with me. I've been thinking about nothing else for days."

A shadow fell between them, and Ella Mae pivoted to find Sloan beside her, blocking the soft candlelight.

"Sorry, friend," he said to Hugh, though his voice made it clear that he wasn't the least bit apologetic. "I've been waiting a long time to talk to her."

Hugh frowned and searched Ella Mae's face. "Who is this guy?" he asked, clearly taking an immediate dislike to Sloan.

Again, Ella Mae hesitated. What could she say?

He's the man who cheated on me with a set of redhead twins? she thought ruefully. *This is Sloan Kitteridge, my soon-to-be ex-husband? The person I thought I'd spend the rest of my life with? The man who's trying to win me back?*

And that's when it hit her. The hurt she'd pushed aside all summer long welled up inside and she looked at Sloan. She really looked at him, seeing the man he used to be. The man she'd once loved. He was still her husband, and she couldn't deny that she felt something for him. She just wasn't sure what that something was. They'd been together for seven years. He was familiar. And yet, he was a stranger too.

Suddenly, Loralyn appeared from around the corner of the house. She quickly took in the situation and grinned with satisfaction. "Hugh," she purred. "Aren't you dancing?" She glanced up at Ella Mae. "If the pie girl's busy, you could always ask me."

Ella Mae heard the enchantment woven in Loralyn's voice. Invisible threads of magic shot through the air, and Ella Mae saw the glimmer vanish from Hugh's eyes. His jaw went a little slack and he seemed befuddled.

He tried to resist Loralyn's charms. With a shake of his head, he reached forward with the rose once more, silently imploring Ella Mae to accept it. She did, nearly weeping as she breathed in its scent of moonlight and champagne.

"We need to leave these lovebirds alone," Loralyn said, injecting her voice with more magic. The unseen threads tightened, binding Hugh in their power.

He furrowed his brow. "Why? Who is that guy?" He looked to Loralyn for an answer and she was more than happy to oblige.

"Hugh Dylan, may I present Mr. Sloan Kitteridge?" She swept her arm in Sloan's direction. "This is Ella Mae's husband. I believe he's here in Havenwood to make things right with his estranged wife. I don't think it would be very courteous of us to interrupt, do you?"

Taking hold of Hugh's elbow, she began to pull him toward the dancers. No longer able to fight against her, he blinked in confusion and then followed Loralyn like an obedient dog.

"It seems I have competition," Sloan said, his dark eyes fixed on Hugh's back.

At that moment, Ella Mae could feel the sparkle vanishing from the evening. It was as if a black hole had opened in the sky above and was sucking all the light into its core. The music sounded flat, the stars were dull, and joy no longer perfumed the air. Instead of feeling beautiful in her dress and heels, Ella Mae felt sad and tired. She'd had her chance. She'd had her wedding day with Sloan all those years ago, and now the night belonged to Candis and Rudy. To their guests. To everyone but her.

"I'm going to fight for you," Sloan said, taking her gently by the hand.

Sighing, Ella Mae pulled her hand away and retrieved her purse from under the buffet table. "Don't go all gladiator on me. Please. Can we just have a cup of coffee and a conversation?"

"Sure." Sloan smiled. "Where to?"

"My pie shop," Ella Mae said, collecting her serving utensils and cooler. "It's the only place I truly belong."

Stepping away from Sloan, she spotted Hugh spinning Loralyn around in a graceful twirl. She sighed again, and the sound of her heartache drifted, unheard, into the night.

Chapter 9

Ella Mae didn't get far. She'd barely collected her things when Freda Shaw stumbled up the porch steps. Her face was pale and a sheen of sweat glistened on her brow. Gripping the railing, she paused on the top step, and then abruptly bent at the waist as though she'd just been assaulted by a terrible pain. Letting out a groan, she leaned over and retched into the garden bed below.

"Is she drunk?" Sloan whispered as Freda sank to her knees, wincing.

"Freda!" Ella Mae raced to her side. "Are you okay? Do you need help?"

Freda shook her head. "It's nothing." She was practically panting. "I just need to sit down for a minute."

Ella Mae took hold of Freda's left arm. Her skin was hot to the touch. "Sloan, help me get Mrs. Shaw inside."

Sloan put an arm around Freda's waist. "Lean on me." His voice was strong and calm. He'd always been cool in a crisis, and for this moment in time, Ella Mae was grateful to have him with her.

Once they'd gotten Freda to the living room sofa, Ella Mae examined her flushed face and listened to her shallow breaths. Acting on impulse, she put a palm on Freda's cheek. "You're burning up," she said, half expecting steam to rise from the sick woman's flesh. "How long have you felt like this?"

Sloan headed to the kitchen to fetch a glass of water while Freda slumped against the cushions. "I started running a fever two nights ago, but I figured it was just wedding-related stress. I haven't been sleeping well lately either. My neck hurts, my head hurts." She brushed her temples with shaky fingertips. When she spoke again, her voice was a weak whisper. "To tell the truth, every muscle in my body aches. This feels like the flu, but it's only September. I need to get back out there, Ella Mae. Candis and Rudy are going to ride off on Flash pretty soon and I have to be there. I have to say good-bye to her."

As if on cue, the music of the string quartet suddenly ceased, followed by a burst of joyous applause. The noise was muted inside the empty house, but its meaning was clear.

"It's time," Freda murmured weakly and tried to stand up, but she could barely lift her head off the throw pillow. "She's going!" she croaked, her eyes filling with tears.

Sloan helped her sit upright and pressed her to take a sip of water, but she waved the glass away. "I need to see her. Please. Help me to the front door. They'll come around this way before galloping down the driveway and . . ." Her voice trailed off, and without warning, her body went completely limp. She sagged back onto the sofa without another word.

Ella Mae reached out to touch her on the shoulder when Freda's torso began to shake. At first, it was a mild tremor, but within the space of a few seconds, her entire body started to buck violently. It looked like she was being struck by lightning over and over again.

"She's having a seizure," Sloan said with unearthly calm. "Is she an epileptic?"

"Call for help!" Ella Mae cried, rolling Freda onto her side to keep her airway clear. "And see if there's a doctor among the wedding guests!"

Not knowing what else to do, Ella Mae slipped onto the sofa and gently lifted Freda's head onto her lap. She stroked Freda's hair and whispered, "It's all right. It's all right."

The sight of the taut cords in Freda's neck and the flash of white as her eyes rolled back in their sockets filled Ella Mae with dread, but she repeatedly promised Freda that help was on the way. Silently begging her to hang on, Ella Mae prayed for someone to come to her rescue.

That someone was Hugh Dylan. He barreled into the room carrying a first-aid kit and peppered Ella Mae with questions. With his attention firmly fixed on Freda, who had abruptly stopped convulsing and was now lying deathly still, he listened to Ella Mae's account of Freda's symptoms and then pulled a stethoscope from his kit.

"Her heart rate's accelerated," he said and then tore open a pack of smelling salts. Waving the powerful aroma under Freda's nostrils, he spoke her name and asked if she could hear him.

Slowly, Freda appeared to return to her senses. The improvement was only physical, however. Her eyes regained focus, but she stared at both Hugh and Ella Mae without recognition. Even when Peter came flying to her side, she looked at him with a blank expression. Blinking in confusion, she hugged a throw pillow to her chest and whimpered. She looked incredibly vulnerable, like a lost child.

"Freda?" Peter's voice quavered with fear. He held out

his hands, palms up, as though begging her to see him, to know him. "It's me. Peter."

She shrank back from his touch, her frightened gaze traveling from one face to another.

"Give her some space!" Verena barked from the doorway. "Come on, folks! Nothing we can do but make matters worse by crowding the lady!"

Ella Mae had been silent during Hugh's examination, but when Freda leaned her head against her shoulder, she took the other woman's hand and lightly rubbed her hot skin. "It'll be all right," she repeated softly while tracing circles over the back of Freda's palm.

Freda gave her a feeble smile and then closed her eyes.

By the time the paramedics arrived, she had lost consciousness.

"Good thing Candis left before this happened," Reba said after the ambulance disappeared down the driveway. She offered her flask to Ella Mae. "No bride wants to see flashin' lights on her wedding day unless they're comin' from a camera."

Ella Mae glanced at the flask and shook her head. She felt drained by the shock of Freda's collapse, especially since it had fallen on the heels of Sloan's unexpected appearance. All she wanted to do was go home. Gone was any notion of sitting down with her husband and having a calm and civil conversation over a cup of coffee. He would just have to wait a little longer to talk with her.

Suddenly wanting to escape the living room and its overstuffed couches and floral pillows, Ella Mae stepped out onto the back porch. Most of the guests were gone and the musicians were snapping their instrument cases closed and making their way across the lawn, heads bent as if they were leaving a funeral, not a wedding. Lynn and Vaughn gathered the last of their serving platters, said their good-byes to Ella

Mae and to Rudy's parents, and practically tiptoed to their SUV.

Sissy, Dee, and Verena joined Ella Mae's mother near the wooden arch where Candis and Rudy had exchanged their vows. In wordless synchronicity, the four women blew out the flames of the lawn torches. They then collected all the stray champagne glasses and dessert plates from the backyard and made their way onto the porch.

"Was it my imagination or were you talking to Sloan before Freda . . . became ill?" Ella Mae's mother asked, her hazel eyes dark with disapproval.

Ella Mae nodded unhappily. "He showed up with Loralyn. And believe me, this is the last place on the planet I want him to be. However, I'll have to deal with him now that's he's here. But not tonight. Tomorrow." She gestured at Reba and her aunts. "Forget about Sloan and tell me what's going on. You all seem stricken."

"We're worried about Freda," Dee whispered quietly.

"She'll be okay," Ella Mae said with more confidence than she felt. "It's just the flu or a virus or something."

Reba's eyebrows shot up. "Last time I had the flu, I felt like I'd been hit by a Mack truck, but I didn't have the fits or wake up not knowin' what was goin' on. We're thinkin' that this might not be the kind of thing that a handful of Advil and a bowl of chicken soup can fix."

"Oh no." Ella Mae felt a chill pass through her. "Do you think someone got to Freda? That someone's trying to stop her from volunteering—like they stopped Melissa Carlisle?"

Sissy shrugged. "We shouldn't jump to conclusions, but we are *very* concerned. Right before the wedding started, Verena learned that Melissa Carlisle died from food poisoning, and while that sounds *somewhat* accidental—"

"What type of food poisoning?" Ella Mae interrupted. She'd studied the subject at culinary school and was familiar with the signs and symptoms of many types of harmful bacteria. Anyone who worked with raw food knew to take precautions when handling, preparing, storing, or cooking it. Melissa Carlisle would have known all about these precautions. After all, she'd been producing her own honey for two decades.

"Listeria," her mother said. "And before you ask any more questions, I don't have any more details than that. Verena is friends with the medical examiner and received a voice mail message from the ME's office minutes before the wedding ceremony began. So we now know what killed Melissa, and none of us believe that it was an accident."

Ella Mae glanced over the back lawn and lifted her eyes to the dark sky as if the answers were written in the stars. Her mind churned as she searched her memory for facts about *Listeria.* "I remember a half-dozen cases from a few years ago. There was a crop of infected cantaloupe," she said. "The melon came from a single source—a farm with contaminated soil. The bacteria can be transferred into raw fruits and vegetables through the soil or the water supply, and I believe both were tainted at the farm producing those cantaloupes."

Dee shook her head. "How would that apply in Melissa's case? She bought her fruits and vegetables at the Havenwood farmer's market, so it doesn't make sense that she was the only person to be infected. Wouldn't other people come down with symptoms? Wouldn't a few of them get as sick as she did?"

"That's why the whole thing stinks to high heaven," Reba said with quiet anger. "Why would one woman die from this bug? A woman who was the front-runner to become the next Lady of the Ash?"

"It's like Snow White's poisoned apple," Ella Mae murmured and involuntarily imagined the pristine, white pulp of a juicy apple squirming with wormlike bacteria. She could almost see the parasites swimming through Melissa's veins, a million microscopic invaders bent on destroying their host.

Verena grimaced and then cleared her throat, instantly transforming into the eldest sister and the leader of their band of women. "Sissy, you and I will go to the hospital. We need to tell the doctors to check Freda for signs of *Listeria* poisoning. Adelaide, will you and Dee keep the Lurdings company? Calm them down and then talk them into going home. I'd like the house to be empty so Reba can do a thorough search."

"I saw a computer in the Shaws' study," Ella Mae said. "Why don't I try to log on and research the symptoms as well as possible sources for this type of food poisoning?"

Her mother gestured at the house. "You'd better get rid of your future ex-husband first. We don't need any outsiders snooping around, especially now." She sighed heavily and looked at her sisters. "I thought Freda was safe—that we were all alert to danger and that surely, this time, we'd see it coming. The harvest is a week away. This isn't the flu. This is an attack on the next Lady."

Verena straightened to her full height, squaring her shoulders and narrowing her eyes. "We won't fail Freda! Let's go, Sissy. The rest of you, take care of things on this end."

Once her two aunts had left and Dee and her mother went off in search of Rudy's parents, Reba cracked her knuckles and inhaled a deep gulp of night air. "You get on the computer. I'll send Sloan packin'."

Ella Mae was about to protest when Reba held out her hand. "No one gets close to you right now, you hear? There's a bona fide threat in Havenwood, girl, and you heard your mama. This isn't the time or place for an outsider. I'm afraid things are gonna get worse before they get better." She flashed a wicked, little smile. "Don't you worry. I'll use my best manners with Sloan."

"Your best manners might include kicking in his teeth," Ella Mae pointed out.

"That's not where I kick men I don't like," was Reba's bland retort before she jogged down the porch steps and disappeared around the side of the house.

Ella Mae knew she should be talking to Sloan herself, but she was too worn out to argue with him. And while he was obviously trying to impress her, he'd chosen the wrong place and time to insert himself into her life, and so she reasoned that there was nothing wrong with letting Reba chase him off like a farmer shooing a hawk from the hen house.

It was a relief to enter the quiet solitude of the Shaws' study. The room was a blend of masculine and feminine, and it was clear to Ella Mae that both Freda and Peter shared this space. For one thing, there were two desks. Peter's was extremely cluttered. Along with a scattering of papers and manila file folders, it was covered with framed photographs of Freda and Candis, as well as a pair of golf tournament trophies. His desktop computer was turned off.

Freda's desk was tidy. A laptop sat squarely in the middle of the polished wood, and a brass lamp rested in one corner while a bronze statue of a woman wearing a toga and holding a set of scales took up the other. The sculpture of Lady Justice was the only ornament.

No distractions for the judge, Ella Mae thought as she took a seat in Freda's chair. She opened the laptop and was relieved to find that someone, most likely Freda, had obviously been browsing an Internet site on wedding etiquette, saving Ella Mae from having to deal with passwords. The page showed a beaming father of the bride dancing with his beautiful daughter as the guests looked on in delight. Several of the links on responsibilities of the mother of the bride had been clicked, including one called, "If You're the Bride's Stepmother."

"You loved Candis as well as any biological mother loved her daughter," Ella Mae whispered to the quiet air as if Freda's spirit were already haunting the room.

Realizing that she'd spoken in the past tense, Ella Mae swore under her breath, angry with herself for assuming the worst. She shook her head, banishing the morose thought that Freda was fatally ill, and typed "Listeria" into Google's search box.

The results didn't make her feel hopeful. Freda's symptoms matched those for listeriosis as listed on the Center for Disease Control website.

"Headaches, stiff neck, fever, convulsions, confusion," she read aloud, a sickening feeling growing in her belly. "But it shouldn't be that bad for a healthy adult. Freda wasn't elderly, she wasn't pregnant, and she didn't have a weakened immune system." Ella Mae paused to consider her last statement. Freda had been both stressed and sleep deprived. Would those issues have been enough to compromise her immune system?

The question caused Ella Mae to initiate another search. By the time Reba entered the study, her sharp gaze sweeping the room as she approached Freda's desk, Ella Mae was staring at the screen in dismay.

"What'd you find?" Reba asked.

"Nothing good. Freda's immune system wasn't functioning at its best. She was stressed over the wedding, and undoubtedly, over her decision to become the Lady of the Ash too. She mentioned that she hadn't been sleeping well, and all of her symptoms match the ones for listeriosis." Ella Mae passed her hands over her face, wishing she could wipe away the anxiety. "What about your search?"

Reba frowned. "Nothin' jumped out at me. I went through the fridge and the pantry, but that isn't gonna tell us what Freda's eaten over the past few days." She pointed at the computer. "Does that say how long it takes for this bug to show itself?"

Ella Mae scrutinized the Department of Health's website. "Its incubation period is anywhere from three to seventy days, but most people will show signs of being infected within a month of eating tainted food."

"How the hell am I supposed to track thirty to sixty days' worth of meals?" Reba began to pace about in a tight square, looking like a caged tiger. "She could have been given poisoned food anywhere. I keep goin' back to what you said about Snow White. Someone could have had a beautiful red apple prepared just for Freda. Or a ripe, juicy cantaloupe."

Ella Mae scrolled farther down the web page until she reached the list of foods documented as having previously been contaminated by *Listeria*. She'd just finished reading the examples of tainted raw fruits and vegetables and was about to start on the list of ready-to-eat chilled foods when her mother entered the study.

"Freda's condition is grave," she said in a leaden voice. She had her cell phone in hand and was holding it so tightly that her knuckles were white. "She's slipped into a coma. Verena and Sissy called from the hospital. They told Peter to have Freda's blood checked for *Listeria,* and he insisted that the test be done right away. Maybe the doctors can give her the right antibiotic or whatever she needs to fight this thing in time."

"I hope so," Ella Mae said. She turned off Freda's computer and looked out the window. The darkness had taken over, painting the tree limbs black and casting deep, impenetrable shadows over the plants and grass. Like the night itself, a dark thing had come, uninvited, to the wedding, to a place of joy and light. It had taken Freda away and left the rest of them wondering what to do next. Ella Mae shuddered.

"Rudy's parents went home," her mother continued.

"Sissy's with them. I doubt they're in danger, but she wanted to see them safely to their house."

"If someone did this to Freda, and I'd bet my Buick that it was no accident, then the deed was done days ago," Reba said. "Tell your mama how this bug works."

Ella Mae shared the details she'd read on the Internet, and then a thought struck her. "Melissa and Freda could have been infected at the same time. The incubation period varies from person to person. So the question is, where could they have eaten the same contaminated food? Who could have offered them something to eat without raising suspicion? You know these two women. I don't. When did their paths cross?" she asked her mother. "Are there other festivals like the harvest? Was there a meeting of our kind where they could have been given tainted food?"

Her mother looked at Reba. "The Midsummer Rites?"

"No." Reba dismissed the notion. "This was done in secret. In private. And with stealth. There were too many guardians at the summer solstice. We would have known somethin' was wrong. And no one came to this weddin' with ill intent. I didn't sense a threat and I haven't taken my eyes off Freda for more than a few seconds. Trust me, the evil had already been done long before today. I think you're right about someone gettin' to Melissa and Freda at the same time."

"But who?" Ella Mae demanded. "What about Loralyn? If she and her mother and the rest of the Gaynors want to choose their own Lady of the Ash, couldn't she be involved?"

Reba snorted. "As sure as the river flows, but that girl had another kind of mischief in mind tonight, and I believe she did exactly what she came here to do."

Ruining my date with Hugh, was Ella Mae's anguished thought.

"Indeed." Her mother looked at her with an uncharacteristic expression of sympathy. "I'll have Verena talk to Peter about Freda's diet—see if she tried a new restaurant or received a gift of food that he didn't eat. Other than that, I don't know what else we can do."

The three women fell silent.

"Poor Candis," Ella Mae whispered. "She's going to wake up tomorrow morning filled with a rosy glow of happiness. And just like that"—she snapped her fingers—"it'll be swept away like a winter wind."

She saw her mother absently touch the thin, gold wedding band glinting on the ring finger of her left hand. Her face was unreadable, but the involuntary movement told Ella Mae that her mother still grieved for the man she'd loved, married, and lost.

Pushing Freda's desk chair back into place, she crossed the room to where her mother stood. "Let's go home. We won't be much good to anyone if we're all half dead."

Her mother nodded. "You're right. And we only have a handful of days to find a murderer. It's up to us, ladies. The authorities can't help. Melissa's death has been ruled an accident and they'd call us crazy if we told them that we believe Freda was deliberately infected with *Listeria*."

"We don't need them," Reba said. She reached under the hem of her dress and pulled a twenty-two pistol from the diminutive holster strapped to her thigh. She dropped her eyes to the gun. "I won't fail again, Adelaide."

Ella Mae expected her mother to tell Reba that none of this was her fault, but she didn't. "We need to know our enemy's identity. Nothing else matters."

Reba nodded solemnly and left the room.

"How is she supposed to find out?" Ella Mae asked, feeling angry on Reba's behalf. "No one else has any clue what's going on? Why should she?"

"Because that's what she does. It's who she is." Her mother studied her. "My gifts are of no use. Neither are my sisters' talents. We're depending on Reba."

Ella Mae picked up her purse, feeling the weight of her father's Colt inside. "We have other weapons. Me, for instance."

"What can you do? You don't even know the extent of your abilities."

"I can get people to talk," Ella Mae said, her voice steely with determination. "I'll make enough pies to get the whole town talking. Someone must know something!"

Her mother smiled wryly. "What do you have in mind? Are you going to invite the Gaynors to lunch?"

Ella Mae didn't return the smile. "Yes. That's exactly what I'm going to do."

Chapter 10

The next morning, Ella Mae woke to a leaden sky. Her limbs were as heavy as the knot of gloomy clouds obscuring the horizon, and her eyes felt puffy and sore, but she knew this was not the time to wallow under the covers. There were only six days left until the harvest. Six days to find a killer and restore the Lady of the Ash.

Unlike Ella Mae, Chewy was raring to go. He danced in tight circles over her floral comforter, delighted to find that she was finally stirring. She rubbed his belly and caressed his soft ears until he leapt to the ground, barking for her to follow.

After a cup of strong coffee, Ella Mae threw on a robe and went outside. She found her mother in the herb garden, murmuring to a rosemary bush the size of a Christmas tree. Ella Mae pressed one of its needlelike leaves between her fingers, releasing a burst of fragrance. The scent of the mint, basil, and lavender curled around her, cocooning her with comfort.

"Any news of Freda?" she asked.

Her mother shook her head and clipped a stalk of thyme as tall as Ella Mae's shoulder. "Her condition's unchanged. Verena and Sissy stayed all night. Reba relieved them this morning. None of us want Freda to be alone, and Peter needs to rest. What are your plans?"

"I'm going to church and after that to the farmer's market," Ella Mae said. "I'm hoping to chat with the vendors and see if anything strikes me as unusual. I haven't noticed any new products since I started shopping there, but maybe the farmers have seen something I haven't." She shrugged. "I don't really know what else to do to help until the pie shop opens for business on Tuesday."

Clipping several sprigs of oregano, her mother placed them in a basket on top of an aromatic pile of dill, sage, and several varieties of parsley. "I think that's a good idea. I wish I could tell you that Peter had some notion of where Freda's tainted food came from, but he didn't. We're all in the dark."

Ella Mae took in the pewter sky and the thick line of gull gray clouds. "It's a full moon tonight, isn't it? Will you still perform your ritual?"

"Yes," her mother said. "If the Luna rose blooms for a couple beneath a harvest moon, their lives will be doubly blessed. They'll have love and riches. Not a bad combination."

"And if they're not blessed?" Ella Mae asked, glancing at the brown and twisted Luna rose bush and the tight, colorless bud waiting in its center. The bud looked like a heart trapped in a tangle of thorns, but she knew that if tonight's couple had fortune on their side, the rose would burst into life with the brilliance of a hundred moons.

Tucking a pair of clippers into the pocket of her garden apron, her mother plucked a spent bloom from the lavender bush. She crushed it and let its pieces fall to the ground.

"They'll either break up and search for a more suitable partner or they'll ignore the signs and stay together, determined to change their destiny."

"Is that possible?"

"No, but not many people are willing to give up on a dream. Very few can simply walk away from the person they've fallen for, but some do."

Ella Mae thought of her own marriage. What if she and Sloan had stood before the Luna rose? Would it have remained dark and still? Would she have stayed in Havenwood even if the ritual had predicted that her future marriage was doomed from the start? She knew the answer. She would have run off to New York anyway, hoping against hope for a different fate.

"I know how hard it is give up on a relationship," she said. "When you first fall in love, you feel invulnerable. Sometimes, it takes years for the cracks to show—to see that it's not going to work. Maybe it's better to have had that time together than nothing at all."

Her mother touched Ella Mae on the cheek. Her fingers smelled of lavender and honey-scented roses. "A few years of happiness? That's not what I want for you. Most mothers want a good man for their daughter. A decent man. For you, for *my* daughter, I want a great man. Someone strong, true, smart, and brave. A fortress of a man. A champion. A sanctuary."

"I guess I thought I had that when I left here with Sloan," Ella Mae said. "And we had a good marriage until the end."

"*Good* is not enough. You should settle for nothing less than extraordinary. I didn't." Her mother's smile was wistful as she bent over to pick up her basket. "I'm going to hang these for drying and then head over to the hospital. If Freda's condition changes, I'll call you."

Ella Mae felt the spot on her cheek where her mother's cool fingers had lovingly brushed the skin. Such maternal gestures were rare, and Ella Mae treasured both the touch and the words.

Leaving Chewy at Partridge Hill, Ella Mae attended the early church service. She prayed for Freda to be restored to health, for Candis and Peter to find strength and comfort, and for justice to prevail over the wicked person who'd infected Melissa and Freda with *Listeria*. Her final prayer was for help in sorting out her feelings for both Hugh and Sloan.

"At times like these, I could really use a friend," she whispered to the polished wood pew in front of her. As much as she loved Reba, her aunts, and her mother, she knew that none of them were unbiased listeners when it came to her ex-husband. And because Hugh could fall victim to Loralyn's power at any given time, they disapproved of him as a suitor as well.

Ella Mae thought of all the casual friendships she'd formed at culinary school, of the dozens of times she'd gone out for coffee, to Broadway plays, or shopping with a group of women her own age. She'd been so busy working that she forgot how wonderful it was to have a girlfriend.

She raised her eyes and listened as the preacher invoked his benediction and then joined the other worshippers as they filed outside. The church bells pealed and the sound resonated through Ella Mae's body, its triumphant notes making her blood quicken and her feet move with a lighter step.

Uplifted, she drove to the farmer's market held every weekend in the park adjacent to the town hall. While she sniffed and squeezed fruits and vegetables, sampled fresh baked bread smeared with homemade berry preserves, and loaded her hemp shopping bags with items for the pie shop, she kept her eye out for suspicious behavior or new and unusual food items. She saw neither.

In fact, by the time her bags were laden with local produce, the sun had burned the gray from the skies and was gilding the leaves on the oak trees standing guard over the square.

By noon, most of the church services were over and the streets of downtown Havenwood were full of townsfolk searching for their midday meal. Because everyone was on the lookout for parking spots, Ella Mae decided to leave her Jeep in the town hall lot and walk to the pie shop. As she passed the little boutiques and gift shops that would either stay closed or open after one o'clock, she began to replay yesterday's events in her mind. She was so wrapped up in her own thoughts that she didn't notice a large white dog barreling toward her.

"Jasmine!" a woman called out. "Jasmine!"

Ella Mae paid no attention to the shouting. "Could it be?" she murmured to herself as she stared at the framed poster hanging in the window of the town's wine shop. The print was of a hunk of yellow cheese sitting on a cutting board alongside a bunch of plump, red grapes. "Could that be the source of the *Listeria*?" Just as she pressed her finger against the glass, she heard a frantic cry of, "JASMINE! *NO!*" before a blur of white knocked her right off her feet.

Grunting in surprise, Ella Mae landed hard on her backside.

A woman with hair the color of summer honey and meadow green eyes grabbed the end of the dog's leash with one hand and Ella Mae's elbow with the other. "I am so sorry!"

Ella Mae recognized her as Suzy Bacchus, the owner of the Cubbyhole, Havenwood's only bookstore.

"Jasmine is usually obedient," Suzy said in dismay. "But she saw a squirrel dart across the road, and before I knew it, the leash was out of my hand and she was off like a rocket. Oh, your shirt!"

Looking down, Ella Mae saw a dark purple stain growing in the center of her blouse like a bleeding wound.

"Smells like plum jam," she said, trying to show Suzy that she wasn't the least bit upset.

Suzy bit her lower lip and picked up the shattered jar of preserves. "Are you hurt? She ran into you pretty hard."

"I'm fine. Really." Ella Mae gestured at the wine store's window display. "I wasn't paying attention. If I had been, I could have stepped out of her way." She smiled at Suzy, wanting to ease the other woman's guilt. "But if I ever need a bouncer at the pie shop, can I borrow your poodle?"

Suzy's shoulders sagged in relief. "On one condition. My store is right up the street. Let me make you a cup of coffee and give you a Cubbyhole T-shirt to wear." She indicated Ella Mae's soiled blouse with her eyes. "If you go anywhere looking like that, people will think you've been shot."

"You're probably right," Ella Mae agreed with a laugh.

The two women collected the spilled fruits and vegetables, tossing several bruised apples and flattened bananas into a nearby trash can. Suzy then gave Jasmine a stern scolding and the trio headed off to the bookstore.

Ella Mae had shopped at the Cubbyhole several times, but she hadn't had much of an opportunity to chat with Suzy. As they walked past tourists out for a Sunday stroll, she learned that Suzy was thirty-one, unmarried, and had relocated to Havenwood from Ocean Isle, North Carolina.

"How could you leave the beach?" Ella Mae asked as Suzy unlocked the shop's front door. "I've always thought it would be like paradise to live by the ocean."

Suzy let Jasmine trot inside the store and then turned to Ella Mae, her expression forlorn. "I had man trouble."

"I can relate to that," Ella Mae said, and by the time she and Suzy had shared half a pot of coffee, Suzy knew all about Sloan, and Ella Mae had listened to a story very similar to her own featuring a louse named Rob. As it turned out, Suzy was only a year younger than Ella Mae and had chosen to relocate to Havenwood because her grandparents, who lived nearby, suggested she sell her bookstore in Ocean Isle and open up her own place in the mountains of Georgia.

"And I'm happy that I listened to them," Suzy said. "I love it here. People are fun, friendly, and they love to read. The area's beautiful. Where else could you be surrounded by these blue green hills and a huge expanse of water? The lake is so big that I sometimes forget that it doesn't stretch all the way to France." She glanced into her empty cup. "I have been a bit lonely, though. I've been on a few dates, but I'm not ready for anything serious, and you're the first woman I've had a real girl talk with in ages! Can I say how much I miss doing this? Just sitting with another chick and having a royal gabfest?"

Ella Mae laughed. "Believe me, I'm with you. This has been one of the best afternoons I've had in ages. We need to make this a regular thing."

Suzy clinked the rim of her coffee cup against Ella Mae's. "Amen. How about this weekend? We could go out to eat or catch a movie."

An image of the stooped and gnarled ash tree in the hidden grove beyond the wall of boulders appeared in Ella Mae's mind. The harvest was only six days away. There would be no movies or dinners with her new friend until peace returned to Havenwood. "I can't," she told Suzy with genuine regret. "How about the weekend after? I could also drop by after work and bring you a piece of pie. We could make it a weekly tradition." She grinned. "You make a mean cup of joe for a bookseller."

Smiling, Suzy took the dirty cups into the back room. Ella Mae started to follow, but when she walked past a display shelf showcasing regional cookbooks, she froze. "Listen, I know the store's officially closed right now, but I was wondering if you carried any books on cheese making."

Suzy thought for a moment. "Like an at-home type thing? Or a large-scale operation?"

"Definitely at home."

"I've got a great book on artisan cheese making," she said, waving for Ella Mae to join her in the Do-It-Yourself section. "It has gorgeous photographs, and I like how the author explains how to make each particular cheese. He uses really detailed diagrams and presents everything in a cookbook format. Not only that, but the last twenty-five pages are filled with the most amazing recipes." She reached for an oversized book with a red and yellow spine. "I'm biased though, because I love cheese. I'd rather have a hunk of Gouda than a cupcake."

Ella Mae feigned offense. "I hope you don't feel the same way about pie."

Suzy handed her the book. Its cover featured a large wheel of milky white cheese set on a wooden cutting board with a kitchen sink and a window covered by gingham curtains in the background. "I particularly like American cheese on my apple pie," she said and wiggled her eyebrows. "So if you're going to drop by next week . . ."

"Say no more." Ella Mae winked and turned her attention to the book. She was pleased to find an entire chapter on how to properly sanitize equipment and maintain the highest standards of food safety. "This is exactly what I was looking for." She flipped through several more chapters. "And you described it in such perfect detail. Do you know your entire stock this well or is this book special?"

Suzy shrugged. "Let's just say that I have a really good memory when it comes to books. If I've seen a book once and held it in my hands and flipped through its pages, then I'll never forget it. I can even remember subtle differences between editions." She smiled self-effacingly. "Ask me to call ten of my regular customers by name and I'll be hopelessly lost. Ask me where my car keys are and I'll admit that I have no clue. But books? Those I remember."

Ella Mae briefly wondered if Suzy had a magical gift,

but realized that she'd find out soon enough. If Suzy showed up at the harvest, then she could truly be the special friend Ella Mae had prayed for earlier that day. Even if she wasn't enchanted, Ella Mae knew that she'd found a kindred spirit in Suzy Bacchus. "Can I pay for this book?" she asked Suzy. "I know you're closed, but I'm dying to read it."

"Register's turned off, so I guess it's on the house," Suzy said in a firm tone that brooked no argument. "I'm sure Jasmine ruined more than the cost of that book in clothes and produce. If you can forgive a ditsy woman and her squirrel-crazed dog, then we'll call ourselves even."

"But you already gave me a Cubbyhole T-shirt," Ella Mae protested.

Suzy snorted. "And no one's ever worn it so well. If you walk around town in that, I'm sure to get dozens of new customers. Just take the book and come back soon with a piece of pie. Deal?"

"Deal." Smiling, Ella Mae slipped the cheese-making book into one of her shopping bags and stepped outside into what had turned into a glorious fall afternoon. The air held a refreshing hint of coolness and smelled slightly of wood smoke and crisp apples. Unlike the overbearing summer sun, the autumn sun had a gentle touch. It turned the world gold and crimson, coaxing the leaves on the Japanese maples lining the sidewalk to shine like garnets.

Ella Mae walked briskly to the pie shop, put away her purchases, and sat on a kitchen stool to read the first few chapters of the cheese-making book. She pictured the renovated tobacco barn where Vaughn and Lynn Sherman made their cheese. It had appeared spotlessly clean to Ella Mae, but had that always been the case? Could there have been a time in which the soil or water of their farm was tainted by *Listeria*?

After taking several notes on sanitizing procedures, Ella Mae compared the book's recipes of homemade cheese with the Shermans'. They were nearly identical. The only cheese that Lynn and Vaughn produced that the book didn't include was a queso fresco with chives. Ella Mae didn't remember Vaughn serving that cheese to Candis and Rudy, and the Shermans hadn't brought her any when they'd delivered her Jeep and a sampling of their product line to the pie shop.

However, Ella Mae couldn't stop thinking of the hunk of cheese in Melissa Carlisle's refrigerator—the half wheel of soft white cheese with a slightly grainy texture. It had been embedded with flecks of green, and at the time, Ella Mae had assumed that the surface of the cheese was riddled with small patches of mold.

"What if it wasn't mold?" she said to the silent kitchen. "But chives."

She sat there for a moment, frowning. She didn't want to believe that the Vaughns had deliberately poisoned two women. The very thought of it put a sour taste in her mouth.

"It's ridiculous," she said dismissively and crossed to the sink to fill a tumbler with cold water. "Why would they do such a thing? They're not even from Havenwood. They probably know nothing about the Lady of the Ash."

Staring out at the empty parking lot, Ella Mae drank her water and tried to dismiss her own theory, but the idea had taken root in her mind and would not let go.

Ella Mae took out her cell phone and called her mother.

"Are you still at the hospital?" she asked without saying hello.

"I am," her mother said. "And there hasn't been any change. The blood tests came back and Freda has been infected by *Listeria*. She's been given an antibiotic, and we're waiting to see if the medicine has any effect on her condition."

She didn't sound very hopeful.

"Is Mr. Shaw with you?"

"He went to the cafeteria for more of their terrible coffee.

I offered to go out and get him something decent, but he said he needed to stretch his legs. I think he just wanted to be alone so he could have a good cry. Men aren't good at this kind of thing, Ella Mae. Peter's coming apart at the seams and he refuses to tell Candis what's happened. He wants her first day as a bride to be a happy one."

Ella Mae was surprised to hear this. "She's going to be angry with him when she finds out."

"Maybe, but it's none of my business. Ah, he's coming down the hall now. I should go."

"Can you ask him if Freda's ever been to the Shermans' farm? Vaughn and Lynn made all the cheese for the wedding."

Her mother was quiet for a moment. "I met them yesterday. They seemed like a lovely couple. Is there something I should know?"

"Not at this point. I'm just trying to examine every angle."

"I'll ask Peter. What are you up to?"

Glancing around the sunny kitchen, Ella Mae could feel a tingle in her fingertips, as if her body was fueled and ready to put her magical abilities to the test. "I'm going to invite the Shermans to lunch on Tuesday. And Opal and Loralyn Gaynor too. I can't force them to accept, but if they do, I'll get them to talk."

"Make sure Reba is made aware of your plans. I want her on guard in case something goes awry."

"Don't worry, I'm calling her now."

Reba was on her way back to Partridge Hill, and Ella Mae hesitated to start a conversation with her while she was driving. She was reckless enough without distractions, so Ella Mae made her pull over to the shoulder before saying another word.

"If I get chiggers from standin' in this tall grass, you're gonna be the one paintin' my thighs and butt cheeks with clear nail polish. You hear me?" Reba grumbled.

"Loud and clear." Ella Mae couldn't help but grin, but the humor faded quickly. "Listen, Reba. When you searched Melissa's house, did you go through her fridge?"

"Of course." Reba sounded offended. "I'm very thorough. Slim pickin's, if I recall correctly. Looked like the inside of a college boy's dorm fridge. Without the beer," she added.

Not wanting to know how Reba had acquired her knowledge about college boys and the contents of their refrigerators, Ella Mae continued. "What happened to the cheese Melissa had in there?"

"That awful stuff! I suppose it's still sittin' on the middle shelf. Why?" Then the pieces fell together and Reba sucked in a sharp breath. "You think the bugs were in that hunk of cheese?"

"I don't know, but we should have it tested. And I need to see if there was a label on it—if it was store-bought or homemade."

She could hear Reba slam her car door shut and the roar of the Buick's engine as she hit the gas pedal. "I'm on my way."

Ella Mae's next call was to Sloan. To her relief, he didn't answer, so she left him a voice mail requesting his presence at The Charmed Pie Shoppe at noon on Tuesday. "I'll be working," she told him. "But I promise to set aside some time to talk."

After hanging up, Ella Mae walked over to her shelf of dried herbs and spices, mulling over what to bake for what was certain to be a memorable luncheon. She unscrewed the lids from glass jars of cinnamon and paprika, dry mustard and ginger root, cayenne pepper and cardamom. Closing her eyes, she considered the weather forecast for Tuesday. Havenwood could expect persistent rains with plenty of thunder and lightning. According to the *Daily*, there would be localized flooding and possible power outages—a nasty storm was barreling toward the northwest as a result of a major hurricane that had just made landfall along Georgia's coastline.

Normally, Ella Mae would be dismayed by such a forecast, but she knew that only a handful of diehard customers would brave the tempest in order to dine at the pie shop. That meant fewer people could accidentally be served one of her enchanted dishes. To protect them further, she planned to create a menu for the walk-in patrons and another for her invited guests. The only question remaining was what to cook for the Vaughns, Gaynors, and Sloan.

"Rain calls for something warm and comforting," Ella Mae mused aloud. "The savory pie should be as warm and soothing as a mother's hug. It should loosen the tongue and make people want to talk. And the entrée is just the beginning." Her fingers ran over bulk bags of sugar and baking chocolate. "By the time they get to the dessert, the diners will have an unquenchable desire to confess something. A fierce and desperate need to share a secret. Their secret will burn inside them like the lightning piercing the sky outside the shop's windows. They'll want to tell someone, anyone. And I'll be there in the privacy of my kitchen. Waiting."

She breathed in the scents of basil and nutmeg, cumin and anise, and then opened a canister of pine nuts and rolled a few of them around on her palm. Within minutes, she knew which pies would appear on the special menu.

Ella Mae's last phone call of the afternoon was to Verena. "Are you busy Tuesday?"

"Not if you need me!" Verena's voice boomed through the speaker. "I have an American Legion Ladies Auxiliary meeting at ten, but I can scoot out early. What do you have in mind?"

"I need your gift," Ella Mae said. "I might be able to draw things out of people, but I won't know if what they're saying is true or not. Sometimes, people can lie to themselves so effectively that they can't recognize the truth anymore."

Verena made a clicking noise with her tongue. "It won't be an easy task to feel all those people out at once! I have to make eye contact to be able to work my magic."

"Don't worry, I'm planning my own brand of kitchen confidential. I just want you out in the dining room in case someone talks about Melissa or Freda or anything hinting at the harvest," Ella Mae said.

"Sounds lovely. Plenty of intrigue and drama. But will there be chocolate?" The word was infused with longing.

Ella Mae smiled into the phone. "Naturally."

"Excellent! Then I'll see you Tuesday. And Ella Mae? My gift functions best on a full stomach, so count on seeing me at eleven thirty instead of twelve!" And with a loud guffaw, Verena was gone.

Chapter 11

Normally, Ella Mae would have set her alarm for midnight in order to watch her mother's Luna rose ceremony from her bedroom window, but she was too tired to do anything other than slide under the covers, kiss Chewy on the nose, and close her eyes.

The next morning, she woke wondering if the couple who'd paid for the privilege of standing beneath a harvest moon in her mother's garden had received the answer they'd been looking for. Had the fireflies gathered en masse around the single rosebud, setting it afire with an ethereal glow? Had they seen the breathtakingly beautiful flower and known that they were meant to live a charmed life together?

"I hope so," she told Chewy as he was gulping down his breakfast. "*Someone* should be happy around here."

After dressing in jeans and a T-shirt, Ella Mae slipped on a pair of tennis shoes and carried her second cup of coffee and a copy of the *Daily* into the garden. Chewy darted in the opposite direction, setting his sights on the woods bordering Partridge Hill. He streaked over the grass, his dark eyes glimmering with anticipation as he launched himself from the lawn onto the carpet of pine needles. Startled mourning doves and chipmunks scattered at his approach. Within seconds, Ella Mae could no longer see him, but she knew where he was by the sound of his zealous barking.

Sipping her coffee, Ella Mae strolled past a tall hedge and a row of camellias, following the path of pale blue stones deeper into the garden. When she reached a marble bench near one of the perennial beds, she was surprised to find Noel, the husband of her mother's pretty young housekeeper, kneeling on the ground. He was busy removing the spent buds from a massive, ochre-hued chrysanthemum, but looked up when he heard the sound of her footfalls on the gravel.

"Good morning," she said, smiling at him. "This is a pleasant surprise."

Ella Mae had met Noel and Kelly at the beginning of the summer when they'd graciously provided her with an alibi following her arrest on suspicion of murder. Since then, Kelly had taken Reba's place as Partridge Hill's housekeeper, and Noel often stopped by after work to share a meal with his wife and the LeFayes. He'd gotten a job in construction shortly after their June wedding, and Ella Mae had run into him inside her mother's house dozens of times, but only in the evening. After a long day at work, he'd stop off at the little bungalow he shared with his new bride, take a quick shower, and then drive to Partridge Hill smelling of soap and fulfillment. So Ella Mae found it strange that Noel was here at such an hour and stranger still that he was deadheading one of her mother's plants.

"I got laid off," Noel murmured after a long moment, his gaze fixed on the ground. "Things have slowed down and my boss had to let me go. Last hired, first fired."

Ella Mae sighed sympathetically. "I'm sorry, Noel. I know how much you loved building new homes."

"I've applied to other construction companies, but I'm not holding my breath." He stood up and gestured around the garden. "Your mom overheard me talking to Kelly about how I didn't think we could make our mortgage payment. She said I could take over the landscaping around here until I can find another job. Isn't she awesome?"

"Mom's lucky to have you, and I know Kelly will be thrilled to have you around," Ella Mae said. "We all will. We need a man's touch at Partridge Hill."

Noel's cheeks turned pink with pleasure. "I guess all those summers working in my mom's garden when I was a kid have paid off. Hers was nothing like this, but at least I can prune and weed and take care of the lawn." He glanced around doubtfully. "Though I don't know how your mom has kept up with all these plants and flowers on her own. Even with her special gifts."

"She's very dedicated to her craft," Ella Mae said. It was a relief not to have to speak in riddles around Noel. He and Kelly had stood in this garden early in the summer and the Luna rose had lit up like the moon for them, so they knew Adelaide LeFaye was an unusual woman. However, Ella Mae had no idea whether Kelly or Noel were of her kind or not, so she said nothing more.

After chatting for a few minutes more, Noel excused himself, saying that he needed to trim the boxwood bushes before lunchtime. With a smile, he headed for the garage, whistling as he walked.

He seems to be rebounding quickly after being fired, Ella Mae thought, turning down the narrow path leading to the Luna rosebush. As soon as she reached it, she released a gasp of dismay. Stepping closer, she whispered, "Oh, no."

For there was the brown bud clinging to the stalk,

unyielding as a closed fist—just as it had been since the last ceremony. The couple who'd come to the garden in hopes of discovering that their love would last a lifetime had been sent away without having been graced by the sight of a thousand fireflies or the magical glow of the Luna rose. They'd stood there, probably holding hands and hardly daring to breathe, and waited for a sign. And what they'd been given in return was silent rejection. Instead of a dream come true, they'd seen only a dark sky, a burnt umber moon, and a scattering of cold, unrelenting stars.

Ella Mae thought of Hugh. Would she ever dare to come to the rosebush with him?

"I think my chances of getting him here have dropped considerably," she mumbled and reached out to touch the bud. Hesitating, she withdrew her hand before she could make contact. There was something sacred about the hibernating flower, and she sensed it was best not to tarnish the bud with her own confused desires.

Hugh stayed on her mind all morning. As she stood in the pie shop's kitchen making ball after ball of pie dough for the freezer, his face kept appearing before her. Even above the pleasant din of country ballads playing on the radio or Chewy barking out hellos to passersby from his vantage point on the front porch, Ella Mae could hear Hugh's voice. She could hear his words of promise.

As if imagining how he looked and sounded wasn't enough, she could smell him too. The aroma of cold butter being blended into the floury dough should have kept her olfactory senses preoccupied, but she could still detect the lingering presence of Hugh's scent. In a room filled with the fragrance of dried herbs and fresh spices, she could detect dew-kissed grass and the cool, clear water of the swimming hole.

"He's not here," she reminded herself. "And you have other things to think about."

After all the dough had been made, Ella Mae loaded Chewy into her Jeep and drove several towns away to the closest butcher shop. She ordered fresh ground lamb and accepted a marrowbone on Chewy's behalf. She then stopped at Costco to restock her supplies of plain yogurt, sour cream, butter, and toilet paper.

By the time she put her purchases away at The Charmed Pie Shoppe and returned to Partridge Hill, she knew she wasn't going to stop thinking about Hugh. She couldn't stop. She wanted to hear his voice, to see his face, and to know that there might still be hope for them.

Ella Mae put on a fresh T-shirt, braided her hair, and spritzed her neck and wrists with a perfume that smelled of honeyed sunshine, and then jogged down the stairs of the guest cottage and looked around for her dog. Chewy was displeased over having to leave his bone, but when Ella Mae whistled and gestured at her bike basket, the little terrier leapt to his feet and allowed her to load him into his familiar seat.

Her legs pumped the pedals as she urged the bike faster and faster up and down the rolling hills. So much was resting on her performance during tomorrow's lunch at the pie shop, and the weight of it had her feeling reckless. She needed someone who could handle the wildness flowing through her now—someone who could meet the fire in her eyes with a fire of his own.

She arrived at the swimming hole breathless from her ride, but Hugh was not there. Ella Mae sat on the flat rock where she and Hugh had shared her container of succulent strawberries and took out her cell phone. She didn't call him right away, but tarried for a while throwing sticks for Chewy and skipping stones over the mirrorlike surface of the water. She desperately wanted to connect with Hugh, but she also had no idea how to undo the damage that had been done Saturday night.

Finally, after Chewy was completely tired out, she dialed Hugh's number.

"Ella Mae," he said flatly. It was the first time he didn't speak her name as though every letter were coated with sugar. He said it wearily, as if the very thought of her exhausted him. "What do you want?"

The words were stripped bare of all the tenderness and desire he'd recently shown her, and the brusqueness hurt. She flinched in the face of it and then gathered her courage. "I wanted to tell you that I didn't know Sloan was in Havenwood. I honestly never expected to see him again. Hugh . . . I was really looking forward to dancing with you."

"And now?" Again, his tone gave away nothing.

"I still want to have that dance," she whispered softly. "But I have to talk things out with Sloan. That's why I called you. I need a little time, if you're willing to give it to me. Time to sort this out. Time to become truly free. And I wanted you to know that my feelings for you haven't changed." She paused, remembering how closely she and Hugh had sat together on this rock. It had only been a handful of days since they'd kissed, standing waist-deep in the cool water, since they'd whispered their first tentative dreams of a future together.

If only he would appear now, she thought. If only he'd rise from the depths of the water like a merman, swim to the shore in a few, powerful strokes, and come to sit beside her. If only she could push a lock of dripping hair from his forehead and lose herself in his blue green eyes. She'd give anything to hear the yearning return to his voice. "Hugh," she said tremulously. "I still want you. I'll always want you."

Hugh was silent for a moment and Ella Mae dared to hope that she'd gotten through to him.

"When we're together, it's easy for me to forget that you're married," he said, shattering her hope like glass. "It was easy to believe that you'll be divorced in a few months, that we stood a chance, Ella Mae. I believed that right until the moment your husband showed up at the Shaws' house." He stopped and swallowed hard. "Even though I want to be with you, I refuse to be jerked around anymore. I've had more than my fair share of that with Loralyn. So there's really nothing for us to say to each other, Ella Mae. Not now. Not with the way things stand."

The tears filled Ella Mae's eyes, but she blinked them back. Hugh was right. Why should he wait in the wings while she worked things through with her husband? "I understand," she whispered. "But I'm not letting you go. The next time I stand before you, I will be free."

"Good luck, Ella Mae," he said and was gone.

Shoving the phone into her pocket, Ella Mae got to her feet and began picking up stones. She hurled one after another into the water, infusing each throw with her anger and heartache. Finally, she tilted her head back and yelled as loud as she could. Chewy immediately followed suit, raising his black nose to the sky and howling as if he were a fierce, wizened wolf and not a small, coddled terrier pup.

Back at Partridge Hill, she tried to distract herself by examining the books in her mother's library, but she was too restless to read.

"I wish tomorrow would just get here already," she told Chewy and closed an ancient tome describing how powerful her kind had been during the reign of the ancient Greeks. "Let's go find Reba. She'll know what I can do with this nervous energy."

And Reba did. "Adelaide, can you keep Chewy in the house for a spell? Ella Mae needs a little firepower to help her settle down."

"Are you going to the shooting range?" Ella Mae's mother asked, scooping Chewy into her arms and accepting a dozen kisses from the little dog.

"No," Reba said. "We're doin' things the old-fashioned

way. Soda cans in the woods." She turned to Ella Mae. "Bring your forty-five. I'm gonna grab some bigger guns from your daddy's cabinet. You need somethin' with a bit of kick. Somethin' that'll tire you out."

Ella Mae nodded. "Yes. Wear me down and then I'll crawl home, have some wine, a simple supper, and a hot bath before bed." She ran her hands through her hair. "Make that lots of wine."

"No booze unless you shoot well." Reba raised a warning finger. "Come on, help me pick out a nice rifle or two."

The sun was hovering close to the treetops by the time the two women reached a clearing in the forest west of Partridge Hill. With several acres separating their property from the closest neighbor, the LeFayes had never worried about having target practice in the woods, and Reba always kept a collection of soda cans on hand in case she felt like blowing off steam.

"Why do we always shoot at Dr Pepper?" Ella Mae asked as she loaded the Colt.

"I like the color," Reba said and popped a licorice twist in her mouth. She'd placed cans in a dozen trees, wedging them into tight nooks between branch and trunk. The aluminum winked in the autumn sunlight and seemed to taunt the two women as they raised their firearms and took aim.

Ella Mae quickly emptied her cartridge while Reba took her time with each shot, carefully aligning the sight on the old rifle to her target. With the licorice hanging from her mouth like a long red cigarette, she aimed at cans well beyond the Colt's reach. Every shot was deliberate and ridiculously accurate.

"If only we knew our enemy's identity," Ella Mae said, gazing at Reba in wonder. "They wouldn't stand a chance."

Reba shrugged. "We guardians have a code, girl. We're not allowed to burst in a place with our guns blazin'. We can only take out one of your kind if there's a clear and immediate threat. So far, the threats have all been invisible." She glanced down at her firearm and frowned. "This rifle's no good against microscopic bugs. I need a face. A name. Somethin' solid to attack. Somethin' that breathes, and plots, and can bleed."

"Tomorrow," Ella Mae promised. "We'll have answers then."

"You're that sure, eh?" Reba said and bit off the end of her licorice stick.

Ella Mae inhaled deeply, drawing strength from the forest. The scent of sticky tree sap, damp pinecones, and crisp, dry leaves clung to her like a shawl. Closing her eyes, she listened to the layers of sound enveloping her. Beneath the obvious chatter of squirrels and the chirping of birds, she heard more subtle noises. A sigh of wind, a leaf detaching from a twig and spiraling to the ground, a beetle crawling over a moss-covered rock. And then, in the stillness between the other sounds, she recognized the whisper of butterfly wings.

The tiny hairs on the back of her neck stood up and her head was filled with a sudden, overwhelming roar. It subsided as quickly as it had come, leaving her with the sensation of a hundred tiny heartbeats drumming inside her own heart.

Eyes still shut, she reached out for Reba's rifle. "Place a target for me, please."

She could feel Reba hesitate, but Ella Mae eventually heard footsteps moving away from where she stood.

Then, Ella Mae's senses sharpened even further and all the colors of the woods came to life behind the shutters of her eyelids. She saw the browns and grays of the tree bark, the rust-hued pine needles, the sun-dappled leaves, and far off in the distance, the wink of red. The Dr Pepper can.

She raised the rifle and aimed but didn't pull the trigger. Ella Mae waited for the picture in her mind to become

clearer still. She slowly breathed in through her nose and
out through her mouth, seeing the tiny fissures in the bark,
the spots of black and brown on the brittle leaves, and a line
of ants marching along the edge of a pine needle. Only then
did she focus on the soda can. Only then did she squeeze
the trigger.

She opened her eyes in time to watch the Dr Pepper can
disappear from a high branch over a hundred and fifty yards
away.

"Whoa," she whispered and instinctively looked up.
There, gathered above her in a cloud of black and blue or
black and gold wings, was a mass of swallowtail butterflies.

"Your totem," Reba said, her voice filled with awe.

Ella Mae gently laid the rifle on the ground and held out
her arms. Butterflies landed on her wrists, forearms, shoulders, and the palms of her hands. They formed a crown of
fluttering wings around her head. "My totem?"

"The butterflies formed the rainbow that led you to the
grove. I should have known as soon as you told me . . ."

"Known what?" Ella Mae said calmly. She felt a strange
mixture of power and peace flow through her body.

"Since they're your totem, you can command them,"
Reba said, wide-eyed. "Like your mama commands her
roses to grow. But this is rare. Havin' a livin', movin' creature respond to your thoughts." She gestured at the rifle.
"Did you ask the butterflies to show you how to hit that
can?" She jerked her thumb to where the Dr Pepper can lay
on a pile of dried leaves and twigs. A hole had pierced
straight through the loop of the letter *P*.

Ella Mae shook her head, smiling at the blue swallowtail
on her hand. "I just wanted to see the path the bullet should
take and they showed it to me."

Reba simply stared at her for a moment, but then recovered her usual aplomb. "Well, are you going to stand there

like a butterfly coat rack or are you going to help me pack up our guns before the sun goes down?"

Ella Mae had barely made it back to the guest cottage after helping Reba clean their firearms when the sky turned ominously dark. The storm front pushed to the northwest by the hurricane churning off Georgia's coast had arrived, and the rain began to fall just as Ella Mae pulled back her covers and climbed into bed with Chewy and a stack of cookbooks she'd picked up at a church rummage sale over the summer.

She flipped through a spiral-bound cookbook published in the fifties by the Junior League of Augusta. Ella Mae loved to read the vintage recipes and to study the black-and-white illustrations of women wearing aprons over flouncy dresses. With their pearls, pumps, and perfect hair, it came as no surprise that the drawings of their Sunday roasts and Thanksgiving turkeys were things of beauty. Ella Mae's favorite images showed mothers presenting their families with desserts like molded gelatin or Bundt cakes decorated with whipped cream and strawberries. The beaming children in these pictures were always immaculately groomed while the fathers wore tailored suits and expressions of smug satisfaction.

"There's no such thing as these Norman Rockefeller families," Ella Mae told Chewy. "Look at me. I was raised by five women and never knew my father." She showed the terrier the illustration of a glazed pound cake marking the cookbook's dessert section. "But this cake was real. You can't fake the taste of butter, flour, sugar, eggs, and spices. Food doesn't lie. It's either pure and delicious or it isn't." She glanced over the names of the women who'd contributed recipes. "Maud, Janet, Ruth, Iva, Shirley, Martha . . ." her voice trailed off and she closed the book and let it rest against her belly.

She thought of all the women who'd lovingly prepared the dishes listed in the table of contents, and for a moment, she wished she could cook for the single purpose of bringing delight to another. To bake without an agenda or any trace of enchantment.

"That's a thing of the past now," she said. "Just like this cookbook."

Setting the pile of books aside, Ella Mae turned off her lamp and snuggled up to Chewy. She listened to the steady patter of the rain and reviewed tomorrow's menu for the umpteenth time. Her last image before sleep was of Sloan, the Gaynors, and the Shermans seated around an enormous dining table covered by a cloud white linen cloth. Unlike the bright, happy faces peering from the pages of the Junior League cookbook, the assembled guests were tense, suspicious, or openly hostile.

At least Maurelle was a part of these drowsy imaginings. She stood serenely, ready to fill the guests' empty glasses with homebrewed iced tea. Reba was there too. Her order pad was in one hand, and when she dipped into her apron pocket with the other, Ella Mae wondered if she'd draw out a pencil or a pistol. That last vision of Reba, who'd been Ella Mae's friend and guardian since the day she was born, finally allowed Ella Mae to sink into sleep.

The rain had intensified by the time Ella Mae let herself into The Charmed Pie Shoppe. Her mother had volunteered to watch Chewy for the day, citing that the little terrier might be scared of the storm once it reached its fever pitch during the early afternoon hours.

As if proving her point, Chewy whimpered and then curled into a ball on the floral sofa in the sunroom. He hid his face beneath one of the plump pillows, but his tail gave away his lack of fear, and the women laughed as he thumped it against the cushions. And then, mother and daughter looked at each other. Their mirth immediately vanished.

"I know you'll do your best today," Ella Mae's mother said solemnly. "I wish I could be there, but my presence would only set the Gaynors on edge." She took her daughter's hand. "No matter what happens, I want you to know that I'm proud of you."

Ella Mae embraced her mother. "I won't let you down. Not you. Not my aunts. Not Reba. Or any of . . . our kind."

Hours later, she stood in pie shop's kitchen, inhaling the aroma of half a dozen lamb pies baking in the oven. Ella Mae had deliberated long and hard over what to serve but had finally decided upon the savory pie she'd planned on making for Sloan the night she'd caught him cheating on her.

As she'd blended the tender ground lamb with sautéed onions and garlic, she'd thought back to her girlhood. When she was eight, she'd stolen a pack of Reba's Twizzlers and had snuck down to the docks with a storybook and a Coke. She'd lain in the sun reading and snacking on licorice sticks until they were all gone. Later, when Reba had served her a supper of fried chicken, black-eyed peas, and okra, Ella Mae had felt too guilty to eat. Why had she taken Reba's candy? Why hadn't she just asked for it? Reba had never denied her anything.

Picking at her food, Ella Mae had remained silent. Hours later, she'd sat at the foot of her bed, too ashamed to sleep. The moon glared down at her from an ink black sky and, finally, she'd tiptoed downstairs, picked up the phone, and called Reba at home to confess her crime.

Clinging to the memory and to that overwhelming need to admit her wrongdoing, Ella Mae blended toasted pine nuts and yogurt into the lamb mixture. She then added lemon juice, cumin, and cinnamon, still focusing on that moment from her childhood. And, while pouring the filling into the piecrusts, she closed her eyes and concentrated on how she couldn't rest until she'd made her confession.

"There," she said, sliding the pies into the oven. "That should do it. But just in case, I'll add more of the same desire into the dessert."

The kitchen filled with the exotic scents of cumin and cinnamon, calling to mind a Middle Eastern food stand and the intense heat of a searing sun. Ella Mae was so focused on her cooking that she forgot about the storm beyond the pie shop's walls. Even a deafening crack of thunder was unable to penetrate the second memory she called to mind while crushing chocolate wafers over the bowl of her food processor.

Pouring sugar and melted butter over the chocolate cookie crumbs, Ella Mae became a teenager again. She pictured a gawky girl named Becky who'd just moved to town and had yet to make friends with anyone. Becky's face was covered with acne, she wore braces, and her clothes were dowdy and ill fitting. The popular crowd, led by Loralyn, instantly dismissed the new girl with sniggers of derision, but when Ella Mae had accidentally tripped Becky in the hallway, sending her books, ruler, and pencils skidding across the floor, she hadn't stopped to help her. She'd listened to the other kids laugh and had decided it was better to protect her own reputation than to be seen helping the most unpopular kid in the school.

That afternoon, Ella Mae's shame had twisted inside of her like a snake until she told Reba what she'd done.

"I'm not the one you need to be talkin' to about this," Reba had said, her face stern and unyielding. The next day, Ella Mae planned on apologizing to Becky, but she'd transferred to a school in another county and Ella Mae never got the chance.

"I still regret that day," she murmured over the pie filling—a light, fluffy, and decadent mousse made of creamy peanut butter, confectioners' sugar, whipping cream, and vanilla extract. When the mousse had been spooned over the chocolate crust, Ella Mae melted chocolate over a double boiler and drizzled the surface of several pies with its rich, brown sweetness. She then put the pies in the walk-in refrigerator.

"Almost ready," she said when Reba entered the kitchen.

"It's comin' down by the bucketful out there. Even the roses Maurelle's puttin' on the tables look like a storm. Only your mama could grow a blue gray rose."

Ella Mae glanced at the oven timer and wiped her hands on her apron. "I should have let Maurelle stay home. There's no telling what could happen today."

"As long as she keeps out of this kitchen, she should be fine and dandy. We'll have a few regular customers in the dinin' room, and that'll keep Maurelle busy and the rest of our guests on their best behavior."

Beyond the window above the sink, a sheet of lightning lit up the wet world. The kitchen lights flickered once but remained on.

"I've checked the guns," Reba whispered, moving over to the window. Her sharp gaze scanned the parking lot as if a nameless enemy were crouching behind the Dumpster or hiding behind a streetlamp.

"You've got to trust me," Ella Mae said, touching Reba on the arm. "No matter who comes back to talk to me or what you hear them say, you can't follow them. This will only work if I'm alone."

Reba frowned. "So you say." Her hand snaked around to the small of her back and Ella Mae knew she was making sure that whatever weapon she had tucked into her waistband was firmly in place. "I'll do it, but I don't have to like it. This goes against all of my trainin' and every bit of my common sense."

Maurelle pushed open the swing door and poked her pale face into the kitchen. "I didn't think anyone would come out in this weather, but a woman carrying a black-and-white umbrella is already at the door, Mr. and Mrs. Caswell are heading up the front path, and there's another couple right behind them. I think it might be the Shermans, but it's hard to tell in this rain."

"We'd best brew some coffee," Reba said, jerking her thumb at the window. "Anyone who's willin' to get soaked to the bone over a piece of pie deserves a free cup of coffee."

Ella Mae gave her a playful nudge. "Hey now, it's a damned good piece of pie."

Maurelle smiled at them and then left to get the coffee started.

After she was gone, Reba murmured gravely, "I'm hopin' and prayin' that it's your best yet." She then retied her apron strings and headed into the dining room to serve the first customers of the day.

Chapter 12

Reba reappeared in the kitchen with an order ticket for two slices of shepherd's pie for Mr. and Mrs. Caswell and wedges of chicken potpie for Verena and August Templeton.

"August braved the weather?" Ella Mae was surprised. August was the LeFaye family attorney and had carried a torch for Dee since the two had been in grade school together. A short, round, meatball of a man with a heart of gold, August had yet to win Dee's love, but he never ceased trying. He donated a great deal of money to area animal shelters in her name and was always prepared to aid any of her relatives. He'd certainly helped Ella Mae in the past and was currently working to secure her divorce from Sloan.

"August is sure to wonder why Sloan is here." She groaned.

"But he's too much of a gentleman to ask you in front of your other customers," Reba said. She'd always been fond of August. "He claims he was all set on eatin' the ham and cheese sandwich he brought from home for lunch when he got a powerful urge to pull on his boots, coat, and hat, and fight his way to our door. I reckon it's a good thing. Not many folks care to misbehave in front of a lawyer."

Ella Mae nodded and opened the oven door to make sure that the mashed potatoes covering the surface of the shepherd's pie had turned golden. A burst of warmth escaped from within, heating Ella Mae down to the bone and granting her a fresh dose of strength. The tendrils of air caressing her face reminded her of the touch of the butterflies. She slid her hands into her oven mitts and withdrew the pie. "Has everyone else arrived?"

"Verena's at a two-top pretendin' to be real interested in a newspaper article on the economy of China, and Loralyn and Opal have brought along another Gaynor harpy. The three of them are grumblin' about everythin' from the rain to the color of the walls to the flowers on the table." Reba arranged fresh greens tossed in champagne vinaigrette on two white plates.

Ella Mae cut generous slices of shepherd's pie and slid a steaming wedge alongside the salad. "Did Sloan come with them?"

Reba placed a sprig of parsley atop each piece of pie. "Yes, but the man's just sittin' there, all stern and tight-lipped. Hasn't said a word except to ask for coffee. Maurelle was right about the Shermans. They came in on the Caswells' heels and are now drip-dryin' by the front window."

"Any telling looks passing between them and the Gaynors?"

Reba shook her head. "Not even a polite how-do-you-do. The Gaynors are far too busy complainin' to acknowledge anyone else's presence."

"Okay. Let's serve Aunt Verena, August, and the Caswells, and then I'll start plating the lamb pie for our special guests. Give Maurelle some odd jobs in the dining room. I need her to stay out front."

Ella Mae gave herself over to the rhythm of the kitchen. The rush of running water, the thud of the oven door closing, the chop of a carving knife against the wood cutting board, the whisper of a wedge of pie shimmying from spatula to plate, and the subtle, upbeat sounds of soft jazz coming from the radio.

Maurelle and Reba served the lamb pies, and Ella Mae waited. She loaded utensils into the dishwasher, glanced out at the rain, and waited. A shimmering layer of water coated the asphalt of the parking lot. It rippled as the wind pushed the water this way and that, making the blacktop look like a dark lake. Ella Mae could almost imagine a monster hiding far below the surface—some coiling, serpentine creature waiting to rise through the blackness should the water become deep enough.

"Are you okay?" Maurelle asked from behind her.

Ella Mae jumped and then gave a nervous little laugh. "I just got lost in the storm for a moment." She studied Maurelle. "Have you talked to Candis?"

"Yeah. Just on the phone though." She shrugged self-consciously. "I'm not crazy about hospitals, so I didn't go sit with her and Mrs. Shaw. I feel really bad about that. What kind of friend am I if I can't be with Candis when she needs me most?"

Touching Maurelle on the arm, Ella Mae said, "She knows you're there for her. Sometimes the sound of a friend's voice is all we need. Besides, Rudy's at the hospital with her, right?"

Maurelle nodded, looking miserable. "I wish there was something I could do. None of this makes sense. How could Mrs. Shaw be fine one second and in a coma the next?"

"There's no obvious explanation as to how Freda was infected by *Listeria*. It's a mystery to us all," Ella Mae said, though she hoped she'd discover the reason soon enough. "I imagine you felt the same way when you were diagnosed."

Turning to the window, Maurelle's dark eyes grew pained. "When I learned how much my life was about to change, I couldn't breathe. It was like the color drained out of everything." She gestured at the rain-soaked world on the other side of the wet glass. "All I saw was gray, like now, except there wasn't a storm. It was totally quiet."

Ella Mae felt a sudden desire to protect Maurelle, to shield the pale, slim young woman from further hardship. "You beat cancer. You're a survivor. To me, that means you're due for a few rainbows." She smiled. "I know it sounds cheesy, but let's hope that Freda Shaw fights the way you fought. And when she comes through this, we'll have a big party for the both of you." Wagging her finger at Maurelle, she added, "You should be demanding more of life. You made it through a trial. Now's the time for you to laugh and dance and date a bunch of cute, unsuitable guys and drink too much and stay up way too late."

Maurelle gave a little smirk. "I know I'm too serious, but I've always been this way. Even before . . ." She plucked at the cuff of her long-sleeved shirt. "Still, I like the idea of dating lots of cute guys. And it's cool that you don't think I need to find Mr. Right straight off. What about you? Reba said that your husband's in town and that he wants to get back together."

Ella Mae jerked her thumb toward the dining room. "He's sitting out there as we speak."

"The good-looking guy in the black sweater?" Maurelle's mouth dropped open.

"That's him. He wants to talk things over with me, but I'm not sure that we have much left to say to each other."

Maurelle whistled. "Whoa. Heavy stuff. Was he Mr. Right once?"

"He was pretty close," Ella Mae said after a moment's hesitation and then turned away to pull open the door to the walk-in refrigerator. She paused in the threshold, letting the cool air steal some of the heat from her flushed cheeks. Maurelle had brought up the very question she'd been avoiding asking herself. But there it was. At one time, Ella Mae had loved Sloan Kitteridge. What she needed to know now was if she still did. Was there enough love left between them to give them reason to fight for their marriage?

Taking one of the peanut butter cup pies from the refrigerator, she carried it to the worktable. She did her best to clear her mind of all thoughts of Sloan, because those were not the emotions she needed to use when garnishing the pie.

Ella Mae was melting semisweet chocolate and a tablespoon of honey in the double boiler when Reba entered the kitchen burdened with a tray full of dirty dishes and glasses. She shot Maurelle a questioning look. "You takin' a break?"

"It's my fault she's back here. We got to talking," Ella Mae hurried to say. She dipped a teaspoon into the melted chocolate and drizzled it in a zigzag pattern across the surface of the pie. *Confess,* she whispered the command in her mind as her hand moved back and forth. *Tell me your secret.*

Reba scowled and jerked her thumb in the direction of the dining room. "They're ready for dessert. Except for Loralyn. Apparently she doesn't eat dessert. Ever."

Ella Mae hadn't seen this coming. "We'll bring her a slice anyway. This pie is irresistible."

Maurelle raised an inquisitive brow but accepted the plates of peanut butter cup pie and took them out to the dining room. Reba also collected several dishes and put them on her serving tray. "August is gonna want one of these, you know. Peanut butter with chocolate is his favorite."

"Don't worry, I made a pie free of enchantment," she said. "I'll have his and Verena's pieces ready by the time you get back."

Several minutes later, Reba returned, her mouth pinched in irritation. "While my back was turned, that little wench Loralyn gave her pie to August. I couldn't exactly rip the fork out of his hand or the whole jig would be up, so now what?"

"I guess we'll have to hope that Opal will feel like spilling her family's secret. Is she eating her dessert?"

"I saw her take a tiny nibble," Reba said with disapproval. "What a bunch of divas. It just goes to show. You can't trust folks who don't have a sweet tooth. It's simply unnatural to say no to anythin' made of chocolate."

Ella Mae couldn't agree more. "She won't be able to settle for one bite. The pie is too powerful. But what about the Shermans?"

"Maurelle served them first. I thought it would be a good idea to give you a little space between confessions, so I expect Lynn or Vaughn to be comin' back here in a minute or two, unless August beats them to it."

"That's no good," Ella Mae murmured to the saucepan of melted chocolate. Suddenly, she had an idea. "Have Maurelle wrap up some apple and cherry hand pies for him to take back to his office. On the house. She knows he's a friend of ours, so when he starts telling her how much he loves Aunt Dee, Maurelle will listen politely. You might even encourage her to steer August out onto the front porch. It's raining, but it's not cold."

Reba grinned. "And August will chew the poor girl's ear off goin' on and on about how sweet and lovely and gentle Dee is. Shoot, the hurricane will be in New England by the time he leaves."

Ella Mae had no idea whether her plan would work or not. All she knew was that within seconds of Reba's departure from the kitchen, Vaughn Sherman was pushing cautiously on the swing door, his wife trailing behind him.

"We're sorry to intrude," he said, sticking his hands into his pants pockets and gazing at the floor with a sheepish expression. He looked like a little boy caught filching apples from the neighbor's orchard. "If you're busy, we can leave, but—"

"We were hoping to have a quick word," Lynn said, cutting Vaughn off.

Wiping her hands on a dishtowel, Ella Mae pulled out the two stools tucked beneath the counter and smiled warmly. "Of course. Have a seat."

Because there were no other stools, she remained standing, the worktable separating her from the Shermans. Her Colt was hidden beneath a potholder, and she picked up a sharp carving knife and began to cut a fresh strawberry into paper-thin slices. She pushed the blade into the soft, red fruit very slowly and with infinite care, knowing that her rhythmic movements were hypnotic.

Lynn and Vaughn watched her intently, and then Vaughn began to speak.

"We're worried that our cheese might have been contaminated," he blurted, as if he needed to get the words out before losing his courage. Beside him, Lynn nodded wretchedly.

"Not on purpose. We'd never want to make someone sick," she added and wrung her hands together. "But we never had the soil or the water tested."

Husband and wife exchanged agonized glances.

"That's unfortunate." Ella Mae tried to sound sympathetic. "Did Freda Shaw ever buy or sample your products prior to the wedding?"

Lynn went pale. "On the day you came to the farm to test drive the Jeep, Candis and Rudy were visiting along with Maurelle and Rudy's parents. The Shaws both had work commitments and couldn't come. Vaughn and I sent a few varieties of cheese home with Candis for her parents to try."

Ella Mae frowned. "But no one else in that group was

infected with *Listeria*. Only Freda. So unless she ate a variety they didn't, it doesn't sound like your cheese was tainted." She stopped cutting the strawberry and gave the Shermans a steely stare. "What about Melissa Carlisle? Did she ever taste your cheese?"

The Shermans gazed back at her with blank expressions. "We don't know her," Vaughn said and then, hesitantly, turned to his wife. "Do we?"

She started to shake her head, stopped, and let out a little gasp. "Wait! I read about her in the paper. She died a few weeks ago, right? Not from . . . ?" She couldn't finish the question.

"Yes," Ella Mae said gravely. "She was infected with *Listeria*. Just like Freda."

Lynn ran her hands over her face. "Oh, Lord."

"The cheese found in Melissa's refrigerator was a soft white variety encrusted with chives. Does that sound familiar?"

"It does." Vaughn's voice was a hoarse croak. "We made a raw milk cheese with chives. It wasn't one of the cheeses we put out for Candis and Rudy to try, but I can't remember if we sent some home for Mr. and Mrs. Shaw or not."

Ella Mae studied Lynn. "Do you?"

She seemed to search her memory. "It's possible. I know I didn't serve any to Candis or Rudy because Candis told me that she didn't care for chives. However, I could have packed a wedge for her parents, to show them how many different varieties we had on hand. Vaughn and I were so proud of our fledgling business that we tended to go overboard. I know we brought you more varieties than you asked for too." She exhaled and Ella Mae could almost sense the invisible fear and distress riding the currents of Lynn's spent breath. The Shermans didn't appear to be hiding anything from her. Their secret was that their farm might be the source of the *Listeria* and that they may have unintentionally poisoned two women.

Was it an accident? Ella Mae wondered. And though it seemed cruel, she had to ask. "Did you have anything against Freda Shaw? Any reason to dislike her or wish her ill?"

The Shermans were taken aback. "Of course not," Vaughn said heatedly. "We've only spoken with her a time or two, but she's a lovely woman as far as I can tell."

"Yes," Lynn agreed. "Mrs. Shaw has only ever been friendly and polite to us. And she was so complimentary of our food at the wedding. Believe me, we're distraught over the very idea that she might be sick because of us. Because of our naiveté."

Sherman took his wife's hand. "We can't call it that, my sweet. We knew it was our responsibility to test the soil and water and we didn't do it. We assumed that as long as our equipment was clean and sanitized that our products would be safe."

Lynn's eyes grew moist as the truth of her husband's statement hit home. "You're right. We should never have taken visitors on tours around the farm. They tracked dirt into the area where we did our cheese making. Without realizing it, we may have invited that bacteria into the barn." She covered her mouth and let the tears spill down her cheeks. "Oh, Vaughn. What have we done?"

The couple held on to each other, and for an instant, Ella Mae knew that they weren't aware of her presence. Nothing existed outside the circle of their arms. She felt sorry for them, and she believed that they hadn't meant to hurt anyone. Still, they'd been negligent. By producing and selling their own cheese to members of the public, they were responsible for the quality of their product. Whether from ignorance or a casual disregard for the proper safety precautions, they'd failed to protect the consumer. Ella Mae was in the same business and, to her, that breach of protocol was inexcusable.

"You'll have to notify the health officials." Her tone was stern. "And shut down your operation until they can run the necessary tests. If your soil and water are clean, then you can rest easy, but if the contaminated cheese came from Sherman farms, then you'll have to face the consequences." Seeing their stricken faces, she softened her tone. "Please try to remember if you sold the cheese with chives to anyone else."

Lynn sighed heavily. "We only made it once and it doesn't keep long. That's why we took it off our menu. The one we gave you is probably the last menu to have it listed, and the only people who could have eaten it were those who came to the farm around the time Candis and Rudy did. I have no idea how Melissa Carlisle got a piece of that cheese, but I'm positive that we've never met."

Ella Mae knew her time with the Shermans was nearly up. She had to shoo them from the kitchen before Sloan and the Gaynor women finished their dessert. Coming around to where the unhappy couple sat, Ella Mae touched Lynn on the shoulder. "I'm sorry this happened, but you need to make it right. Will you?"

Husband and wife nodded solemnly and then left the room. Ella Mae watched them go. Their tread was heavy upon the floor but at least they were still holding hands. Ella Mae figured that whatever happened from this point onward, the Shermans would continue to hold on to each other, even as their dream of living out the rest of their days as artisan cheese makers came to an end.

The door hadn't had a chance to stop swinging before Opal Gaynor swept into the kitchen. She was trim and petite and had the same golden hair and blue eyes as her daughter. And like Loralyn, her eyes were bright and cold. They reminded Ella Mae of moonlight on snow. Opal kept her head titled at a haughty angle as she examined her surroundings.

She then feigned great interest in a loose thread protruding from the button of her tweed jacket. "You make a decent pie, Ms. LeFaye," she said. "Thank you for the invitation."

The Gaynors never forget their courtesies, Ella Mae thought. *Even if each word is covered with a sheen of frost.*

Aloud, she replied, "You're welcome. I hope you'll drop by again and be sure to bring your . . . I'm sorry, Reba said that you had a guest at your table but I'm afraid she didn't recognize her."

"No, she wouldn't. That's my cousin, Matilda." Opal took a step closer to the stool Lynn had vacated. "Tilda's visiting from Charlotte. She's on the city council there and is a very successful businesswoman. Loralyn and I have convinced her to relocate to Havenwood. We could use a woman with her intelligence and prowess to take up a leadership position in our own local . . . government."

Ella Mae knew why Opal was speaking so cryptically. The Gaynors were unaware that she'd been Awakened and Ella Mae wasn't about to give her own secret away, so she said, "Havenwood would certainly benefit from having such a smart, savvy woman as a resident. Especially since we might lose another woman with similar character traits." When Opal didn't say anything, she continued. "I'm talking about Freda Shaw. People say that she was a fair and honest judge. I'm assuming you know her, since Loralyn attended her stepdaughter's wedding."

Opal looked directly at Ella Mae without a trace of guile. "I've known Freda for years. What happened to her is terrible. And perplexing." Her eyes narrowed. "I heard she was infected with a food-borne bacteria. It wasn't from one of your pies, was it?"

"No," Ella Mae said, more than a little confused. If neither the Shermans nor the Gaynors had known that the cheese was contaminated with *Listeria*, then who was responsible for Melissa's death and Freda's grave illness?

Who deliberately gave the two women, both chosen to be the next Lady of the Ash, a piece of the soft white cheese filled with chives and a harmful bacteria?

The villain has to be one of our kind, she thought furiously and then focused on Opal once again. If she'd come into the kitchen to confess a secret, Ella Mae had yet to hear it.

"Was there something else I could help you with?" she asked sweetly.

Opal tugged at the thread hanging from her buttonhole again. "I'm sure you're aware that your mother and I don't exactly get along."

"So I've observed, though I'm not sure why," Ella Mae fibbed. Her mother had said that the Gaynors and LeFayes had been enemies since Arthurian times, and Ella Mae had read several accounts of the feud that had erupted between Guinevere and Morgan le Fay—a feud that had ended their friendship and had begun centuries of enmity between the two families.

"It's because of your daddy." Opal spoke so softly that Ella Mae could barely hear her. When the words finally registered, Ella Mae found she was too stunned to respond. "I loved Terran Heath long before Adelaide ever laid eyes on him," Opal continued. "He was mine and she stole him from me. And look how that turned out." Her mouth twisted in anger, but there was genuine sorrow in her cold, blue eyes.

Ella Mae was afraid to breathe, afraid to make a false move or say anything that might encourage Opal to stop talking. All her life she'd been trying to discover why her father was such a taboo subject. She knew that he'd been an archaeologist and had died during a cave-in. He'd been at the base of an Olmec tomb shaft when the supports above it had collapsed. With no means of escape, he'd either been crushed by rubble or had suffocated before rescuers could reach him. That same night, thousands of miles away, Ella Mae had been born.

And now this woman, whom her mother had been at odds with since Ella Mae could remember, was telling her that she knew Ella Mae's father? That she'd been in love with him? "I didn't know that you and my father were together once," she answered. "I don't know much about him at all."

"How typical of Adelaide. To keep him to herself even though he's long gone," Opal said with derision. "She wasn't always as hard as she is now, you know. His death changed her. And she was wrong about you. She kept you at a distance out of fear, thinking that you were meant to become . . . well, that's neither here nor there." She waved her hand around. "You became a pastry chef. And a fairly decent one at that." Clearing her throat, she forced her lips upward into a small, unpracticed smile. "All I wanted to say is that you and I are not enemies and I appreciate the invitation to lunch."

A boom of thunder startled Ella Mae, and the rain pounded against the roof with ruthless abandon. Opal glanced out the window and marched through the swing door before Ella Mae could question her further, and she had many, many questions. In fact, she was so busy reviewing everything Opal had said that she didn't notice Sloan entering the kitchen.

"I know that look." His voice was smooth as melted chocolate. Without hurrying, he crossed the room and came to stand beside her. "May I?" he asked, indicating the strawberry slices fanned across the cutting board.

She nodded, feeling wary. Neither the Shermans nor Opal Gaynor had seemed threatening, but Sloan did. He approached every challenge with the stealth and intensity of a stalking leopard, and Ella Mae knew that he saw her as a challenge, an obstacle to overcome, a prize to be won. He was a predator by nature, and seven years ago, Ella Mae had been the prey.

However, she was no longer the same woman he'd wooed

then. She was no longer the woman who'd shared his life in New York. She had become a new creature in Havenwood. Strong, willful, enchanted. Her senses had sharpened, and right now, they were warning her that Sloan Kitteridge was dangerous.

He smiled at her with a smile that didn't reach his eyes. "My beautiful Ella Mae. Here we are at last. Alone."

"Except for Reba and Maurelle and August," Ella Mae pointed out with an airiness she didn't feel.

Sloan reached out to push a tendril of hair away from her cheek, and she instinctively recoiled. His smile vanished. "That pale-as-death waitress went off with the little fat man. Apparently, he bought out half the store and needed help carrying all the pies to his office. Reba's the middle-aged pixie with the sharp tongue, right? She's out on the front porch talking to the big woman who could out-eat a troop of soldiers. They're both watching the storm. You should tell them to go on home. Hang the closed sign. I think you're done for the day, don't you?" His voice had grown lower and deeper as he spoke. It was nearly a growl by the time he uttered his last sentence.

Ella Mae put a hand on the potholder concealing her gun. "I'll worry about my own business, Sloan. Why don't we talk about us? Isn't that what you came here to do?"

He leaned against the cutting board and picked up her carving knife. Plunging the point of the blade into the center of a whole strawberry, he began to twirl the knife around and around, so that a hole appeared in the heart of the strawberry. It grew larger and larger as the knife spun in a circle, red juice seeping out from beneath the mangled piece of fruit.

"Stop that, please," Ella Mae commanded calmly. "I prefer my garnishes to be slightly more presentable."

Sloan dropped the knife with a thud and crossed his

arms like a petulant child. "I came back to this hick town because I'm angry. I've invested years in our marriage, Ella Mae. Years that I'll never have back. Years of sacrifice. You think I made a big mistake in the elevator with those women, but you don't know the half of it." He straightened up abruptly, as if he were surprised by his own speech.

"Why don't you tell me everything?" she purred, though inside she was raging. "I'm ready to listen."

He responded to her honeyed tone. Uncrossing his arms, he twisted the gold wedding band on his left ring finger and watched as it reflected the overhead lights. In the silence, the sound of the rain slapping against the windows intensified, and Ella Mae could almost imagine that the storm was trying to gain entry to her warm and cozy kitchen.

"Remember the day we met?" Sloan asked, his gaze distant and eerily blank.

"Of course," she said. "You drove your rental car into a ditch."

He grinned wolfishly. "I never could pass by a pretty girl without taking a second look. And you were pretty. Though not half as beautiful as you are now."

"And I'd never seen anyone like you. From your clothes, to your car, to the way that you talked. You were so fearless, so sure of yourself."

"I knew the right things to say to you, Ella Mae. And which secrets to keep from you."

This is it, Ella Mae thought. "Which secrets? Tell me now, Sloan, so you and I can move on."

"I don't have to hide the truth from you anymore. Or so I've been told." He scoffed. "And once you know, it'll be over between us for sure."

Lightning flashed, washing Sloan's face in a pure, white light. For a moment, Ella Mae saw the young man she'd fallen in love with, but then she blinked and he was gone.

She realized that she didn't know the person standing before her and that she'd never really known him. "Have I ever seen the real you?" she asked her husband.

He laughed derisively. "The real me was the guy in the elevator with that pair of frisky redheads. There've been lots of elevators and lots of other women, Ella Mae. I come from a long line of men and women with voracious appetites. I'm sorry, but I could never be satisfied by one woman." He touched his flat stomach. "At least you satisfied this appetite."

Ella Mae felt her anger rise, filling her blood with heat. She longed to pick up the carving knife and point it at him, wiping the smug expression from his face. Instead, she curled her hands into fists and willed her face to betray no emotions. "You said that you didn't have to hide the truth from me anymore. Who gave you permission to share your secret?"

"When I answer that question, you'll know my secret too," he said and tapped the tip of her nose with the pad of his index finger. It was all Ella Mae could do not to sink her teeth into that finger. "I'm done with this town and our sham of a marriage, so here it is. Drumroll, please." He gave her an expectant look and when she didn't move, he released an exasperated sigh. "Fine, be a spoil sport. Cousin Opal told me I was free to live my life as I saw fit. She talked me into marrying you seven years ago and I listened to her . . . advice. Now I don't have to listen anymore. My dues have been paid."

Ella Mae was flabbergasted. She stared at Sloan, trying to make sense of what he'd said. Finally, she managed a single question. "You're a Gaynor?"

"Mom's maiden name is Gaynor." He checked his watch, clearly growing restless. "You never guessed because I grew up in Connecticut. My folks didn't call our apartment and only visited us a few times. I'd never been down South until I moved to Atlanta. Can't say that I care for it much either."

A powerful crash of thunder shook the pans hanging from the ceiling rack, but Ella Mae was too stunned to notice. "I married a Gaynor?"

"You did. One whose gift is making lots of money by selling secrets." Sloan pulled off his wedding band and tossed it on the cutting board. "And now you can be divorced from a Gaynor. Good-bye, Ella Mae. Have a nice life."

Chapter 13

Ella Mae stood with her palms flat on the cutting board, the juice from the mangled strawberry oozing from beneath her palms.

Suddenly, Reba was beside her. She led her from the kitchen, through the dining room, and out the front door. Gently pushing Ella Mae into a rocking chair, she stood above her and stroked her whiskey-colored hair. "It's gonna be all right, sugar. Your aunt Verena's gone on home, but Reba's here. I'm right here."

Raindrops ricocheted off the flagstone path and sidewalk, and the sky had morphed from a pale pewter hue to an angry charcoal gray. The grass no longer looked solid, but had the watery, liquid appearance of a marshland. The wind was stripping the magnolia blossoms off the branches and hurling them into the air, and the battered petals fluttered to and fro like drunken butterflies, occasionally colliding with one of the hundred twigs torn from the trees and shrubs surrounding the pie shop.

"This'll be a fine mess to clean up," Reba grumbled to the storm. "As if we don't have enough goin' on already." She released Ella Mae and sat down in the other rocking chair. "I figured since no shots were fired and Sloan came out of that kitchen lookin' pleased as punch that you two were givin' your marriage a second chance. But then I saw your face and I knew that wasn't happenin'. If that man hurt you again, I swear by all that's good and holy that I'm gonna—"

"Sloan's a Gaynor," Ella Mae said, her voice strained and hoarse. "And apparently, he only married me because his cousin Opal told him to. He's never been faithful and now that he's been given permission to get a divorce, he wants out." She reached for Reba's hand. "He never loved me. Never. For seven years, I lived a lie."

Reba traced circles on Ella Mae's palm. "Some people wander through their whole lives like that, hon. At least your eyes have been opened and you can move on. You're young and beautiful and strong. Plenty of time to net another fish." She frowned. "But what's with Opal? Why would she give two figs about the man you chose to marry? Unless . . ."

"Unless what?"

Reba shrugged. "Sloan took you to a concrete jungle. You couldn't be Awakened there. The closest sacred grove is far upstate. As long as you stayed in Manhattan, you'd be a regular girl. No chance of any magic flowin' through you. It'd keep on sleepin' and, eventually, it'd fade away. Truth be told, most folks thought it already had."

Ella Mae nodded absently. "And because the Gaynors don't realize that I've been Awakened, they're letting Sloan cut me loose." She inhaled deeply, drawing the moist storm air into her lungs. The tiny molecules of rain and wind gave her strength. "At least I don't have to keep wondering. It's over and I'm glad to be rid of him."

"What about the other kitchen confessions?" Reba

wanted to know. "Opal's and the Shermans'? Please tell me that there's a killer for me to chase after. I'd like nothin' better than to sneak up on someone under the cover of thunder and lightnin'. It'd be like a Shakespearean play. A real tragedy of course. Like *Macbeth*."

Quickly recapping everything that the Shermans and Opal Gaynor had told her, Ella Mae tapped the pocket of Reba's apron. "You can disarm yourself for now. We still don't know who gave Melissa and Freda the contaminated cheese unless Aunt Verena heard something useful."

"She didn't," Reba said, clearly disappointed. She removed a small pistol from the apron, reached under her shirt and pulled another from a holster strapped against her right breast, and eased a small dagger from within a niche in her left cowboy boot.

"How are you able to wait on tables wearing that?" Ella Mae asked, unable to keep from smiling.

Reba pivoted the dagger so that its thin blade caught in the light, and grinned. "Girlie, this is nothin'. I've still got a throwing star taped to my lower back. That's why my posture's so damn good."

The two women laughed and all the tension that had been slowly building for the past few weeks shattered like broken glass. Ella Mae sighed and sank back into her chair. She began to rock, relishing the rhythmic creaks the curved runners made as they met the wood planks of the porch floor.

"My father and Opal," she whispered to the rain. "Who would have thought?"

"He was a charmer, that's for sure," Reba said. "I vowed never to talk about him, Ella Mae. Your mama made me promise and I'd never break my word to her."

Ella Mae shook her head in resignation. "I know, I know. You've been singing that same old song since I was in diapers. But why won't my mother share her memories with me? I want to know him. It might even help me understand why she kept me at a distance for so long."

"All I can say is that he and your mama weren't supposed to be together. The price they paid for goin' against the tide was a dear one." Reba stood up and collected her guns and dagger. "We've done all we can here today. Let's close up and hash this over with your mama and aunts, preferably over a bottle of whiskey and a big pot of my heart-warmin' beef stew."

Nodding, Ella Mae pushed herself out of the rocker, though she was loath to leave it. She felt utterly drained, and as she took a step forward, she nearly lost her balance. Reba's arm shot out and encircled Ella Mae's waist. "You put lots of energy into those pies. Magic doesn't happen without a cost," she reminded her. "Sometimes it just wipes you out for hours. That's why your mama sleeps half the day after one of her Luna rose ceremonies."

"But I've used enchantment in my pies before and I never felt like this."

"You didn't just bake them with a certain emotion this time, did you?" Reba asked.

Ella Mae thought about that for a moment. "I guess not. I was really focused on forcing the people who tasted my food to come back into the kitchen and tell me their secret. I mean, I put everything I had into bending them to my will." She shrugged wearily. "I couldn't be that strong or August would never have settled for talking to Maurelle."

Reba snorted. "Puh-lease. Once he started in on the subject of Dee, he couldn't stop if he wanted to. Her, you, me, the fire hydrant—the man's dam broke. Shoot, he's probably still singin' Dee's praises to—"

"Maurelle!" Ella Mae exclaimed. "I forgot all about that poor girl. I need to drive to August's office and pick her up. She can't be walking around in this storm. Will you take care of everything here?"

"Of course. I'll see you back at Partridge Hill," Reba said and escorted Ella Mae to her Jeep. They were both soaked by the time Ella Mae slid behind the wheel. "Where's the Colt?" Reba demanded before closing the door.

"Under a pot holder," Ella Mae said. "But don't go back for it. I'll be home soon enough."

Reba held up a warning finger. "Don't you move." She dashed back into the pie shop with the speed of an Olympic athlete and returned to the Jeep with a very heavy takeout container.

"Clever," Ella Mae said, and on impulse, threw her arms around Reba's neck. The two women held each other, water sneaking into the Jeep's interior and streaming down from Reba's face and hair onto Ella Mae's shoulders.

"I love you too, sugar," Reba murmured. She then broke away and raced up the front path again.

Maurelle was just jogging down the steps of August Templeton's law office when Ella Mae pulled up to the curb. Cracking her window, she yelled, "Hop in!" and then pivoted in her seat to grab a beach towel she kept in the back. Handing it to Maurelle, who'd gotten drenched in the space of a few seconds, Ella Mae glanced up at August's building. The red bricks were so wet that they'd turned a ruddy brown and the gutters had spit water into the flower beds until they'd turned into small pools, drowning the pretty pink asters and golden mums.

"I'm sorry you were stuck here," Ella Mae said as Maurelle rubbed her short, dark hair with the towel and wiped the moisture from her face. "August can be rather verbose."

"I'm not sure what that means, but if you're referring to the way he talks and talks without taking a breath, then he is that." Maurelle's tone had a sharp edge to it and she hastened to soften it. "I feel bad for him. He's got a major crush on your aunt."

Ella Mae checked for traffic before pulling away from

the curb, but downtown was nearly deserted. "He certainly does, and I don't think he has much hope. It's a shame, because we all love him. But we're not the ones who matter." She turned her windshield wipers on to their highest setting, and they fought furiously against the rain. "I wonder why he's staying at the office when the rest of Havenwood has packed up and gone home."

"He said that no storm would keep him from doing a full day's work." Maurelle turned to Ella Mae. "I'm with him. I'd rather wait tables than sit at home waiting for the wind to knock my trailer over."

This was the first time Maurelle had ever raised the subject of where she lived.

"Can you tell me how to get to your place?" Ella Mae asked. When Maurelle hesitated, she added, "Reba's closing the shop, so I'm taking you home. Are you in the trailer park on Leafwing Street or have you rented a place farther outside of town?"

Fidgeting, Maurelle muttered, "It's off Orion Road."

Ella Mae was stunned. That had to be at least seven miles from the pie shop. "You bike that far every day?"

"Yeah. I'm not as weak as I look."

Picking up the defensive note in her employee's voice, Ella Mae told Maurelle about the bike rides she'd taken as a kid, recalling how the distances had never seemed as long as they did now. She prattled on as she drove west, even though she didn't feel like talking. Eventually she tried to get Maurelle to open up a little about her past.

"My family isn't very close," she reluctantly mumbled as Ella Mae turned onto her street. "We're all loners," she said. "We talk on the phone and stuff, but not very often. It's cool though. We're just wired like this, I guess."

Despite the fact that Maurelle seemed untroubled by her solitude, Ella Mae felt sorry for her. When they reached a group of dilapidated mailboxes and Maurelle told her to turn right, Ella Mae paused. The narrow road ahead was littered with branches, and the unpaved surface was muddy and pocked by puddles.

"This will be a good test for my Jeep," Ella Mae said with forced cheerfulness. However, the first puddle she drove through was deceptively deep and the Jeep lurched roughly to the side. Maurelle thrust out an arm to steady herself against the dashboard and Ella Mae shot her a worried glance. Her gaze was attracted to a brown mark on Maurelle's right forearm, just above the wrist. It was thin and bent in the middle, like the jointed leg of an insect, and Ella Mae wondered if both of her arms were covered with similar scars. It was as if the flesh had been burned, leaving a brand seared into the skin.

"Watch out!" Maurelle shouted, and Ella Mae focused on the road again, swerving around a tree branch as wide and solid as a bodybuilder's leg.

"I feel like I'm in a video game," Ella Mae said once she had the Jeep back under control. She didn't speak again until a mobile home appeared from out of the gloom. Once, it had been white, but now it was a shade of sickly yellow mottled by bold patches of rust. The clearing surrounding the trailer had become overgrown with weeds and brambles. A broken lawn chair must have been toppled by the wind, for one of its metal arms was buried in the mud and its blue-and green-striped fabric was torn and faded.

"I'm guessing today was a lousy one for tips. Sorry about that," Ella Mae said as she pulled to a stop. She didn't know why she felt compelled to apologize to Maurelle, but she did. Perhaps it had to do with how little joy seemed to be in Maurelle's life. She'd battled cancer, didn't have any close family or friends except for Candis, and rented a beat-up trailer in the middle of nowhere.

Maurelle looked eager to escape. Her hand was already on the door handle. "Actually, I made out pretty well. Mr.

Templeton said that after all the talking he did, he owed me as much as he paid his therapist, plus extra for delivering all the hand pies to his office in the middle of a storm." She patted her hip pocket. "Trust me, I did okay."

Ella Mae sensed she was about to cross a line, but she forged ahead anyway. "Maurelle, why do you live here? Am I not paying you enough? Because if that's the case, we should definitely talk about your salary."

Flicking her eyes briefly at the dilapidated mobile home, Maurelle shook her head. "My wages are totally fair and the tips are above average. It's just that I have lots of debt. The rent here is dirt cheap and that's what I needed. Yeah, it looks like a dump, but it's quiet and the deer run through my yard at dawn and dusk, which is pretty cool. I'm not really an apartment kind of girl. I can't live in a box stacked up on a bunch of other boxes. I need to be around a few trees."

Recalling how difficult it had been to adjust to the Manhattan high-rise she'd shared with Sloan, Ella Mae nodded in understanding. "I get that. There's nothing like stepping out your front door and inhaling a deep breath of sun-drenched grass, pine, honeysuckle, and wild onion."

"Yeah," Maurelle agreed, and Ella Mae knew that it was time to let her go.

"Do you want me to pick you up tomorrow?" she asked.

Maurelle opened the door and jumped out into the rain. "No, thanks!" she shouted over the wind and water. "I'm all set!"

With Ella Mae's towel draped over her head and shoulders, the slim, dark-haired young woman dashed over the saturated ground, up a pair of rotted wooden stairs, and into the mobile home.

Ella Mae put the Jeep into reverse and prayed that she'd make it back to Partridge Hill alive. "I can just see me driving into a sinkhole. That would be the perfect way to end this insane day," she muttered, peering at the road in between the frenzied passes of her wiper blades. At the end of the tunnel of trees, a thin ribbon of lightning flashed across the gray sky. Ella Mae wasn't sure if it was a beacon beckoning her home or a warning that she was heading deeper into the storm.

That evening, Reba and the LeFayes gathered around the fireplace in Partridge Hill's library. On the other side of the large windows, the rain continued to fall. It had grown less violent as the afternoon gave way to night and no longer resembled a roaring lion. Now it merely scratched and whined at the door like a hungry tomcat, and the women were too focused on their conversation to pay it any mind.

Verena handed Ella Mae a glass of wine and sniffed the air. "Is that your beef stew, Reba? I hope so, because I'm famished!"

Reba nodded. "Sure is. Should be done in about thirty minutes. And I made a big pot of wild rice just for you. I know how you like to have somethin' to catch up all the gravy."

"You're a treasure!" Verena exclaimed. "Now, on to business. Earlier today, Buddy made a call to a friend at the Atlanta office of the Environmental Protection Agency. He'd had an aide drive the cheese from Melissa Carlisle's house straight to their lab as soon as Reba collected it for us, and the results are in. As we suspected, the cheese was contaminated with *Listeria*."

Sissy set her wineglass down and sighed theatrically. "But we *still* don't know if Freda ate the same cheese."

"No, we don't," Dee agreed. "Adelaide asked Peter and Candis, but neither of them can remember what became of the cheese sampler the Shermans prepared for the Shaws."

Ella Mae, who was wrapped in a luxurious silk blanket

embroidered with wild roses, shook her head in astonishment. "That's kind of odd, don't you think? Either the Shermans are lying or Peter and Candis are lying. And I don't think the Shermans could have lied to me if they wanted to. The confession pie was really potent."

"That's for certain, judging from what Opal divulged!" Verena cried, shooting a meaningful glance at Ella Mae's mother.

"I'm more interested in why Opal Gaynor wanted Sloan to take me away from Havenwood seven years ago," Ella Mae said quickly, hoping to save her mother further discomfort.

Reba took a sip of whiskey from a red Solo cup. "Guess you can ask her Saturday night." She grinned gleefully. "I can't wait to see the look on their faces when you show up in the sacred grove, my girl."

Ella Mae's mother studied her with a worried expression. "No more enchantments for you until you recover from today's labors. You can ask Maurelle if she remembers seeing Candis take a box of cheese home with her from the Shermans' farm. Other than that, no more magic. You need to rest up for the harvest."

Relaxing her tired body against the soft cushions of the couch, Ella Mae murmured her assent. Her aunts began to discuss whether Tilda Gaynor would ever make a good Lady of the Ash. Ella Mae listened for a few moments, but then her focus shifted to the dancing orange and yellow flames in the fireplace. The fire's warmth coaxed the tension from her muscles, and the soft crackle of wood allowed her mind and body to slowly relax. Her eyelids began to grow heavy, and she decided to close them just for a second.

Before she knew it, Reba was shaking her gently on the shoulder with one hand while balancing a bowl of steaming beef stew in the other.

"Eat up. You need your protein. I added extra carrots just

like I used to when you were little." Reba smiled as Ella Mae cupped the bowl between her palms. "You were so wild about carrots. Remember how I'd call you Flopsy every time you wanted them for a snack?"

"I remember asking you not to call me that at the bus stop," Ella Mae murmured groggily and raised a forkful of stew to her mouth. The blend of garlic, onion, paprika, beer, and a healthy splash of Worcestershire was as comforting as the blanket around her shoulders.

Sissy dabbed her lips with a napkin and pointed a finger at Ella Mae. "You had *such* a terrible sweet tooth when you were a girl. We were certain you'd have a mouth full of cavities before you graduated high school. That's why Reba took to chewing licorice sticks, you know. You never really liked them, so it was the *one* candy she could keep around."

"I stole one of her packs once," Ella Mae admitted solemnly. "Ate the whole thing even though I didn't really want them. That's one of the memories I used to make the confession pies. I can still remember how terrible I felt about taking something Reba loved without asking her first."

"Oh, sugar. You were such a good girl," Reba said, her nut brown eyes growing moist. "You shouldn't be feelin' bad over somethin' so small and unimportant."

Ella Mae looked around at her family. They sat in a semicircle with her in the center, as if even here, in the only house she'd ever known, she needed protecting. She searched their dear faces and felt such a powerful rush of affection for each of them that she longed to jump out of her chair and embrace them all. Instead, in a thick voice, she said, "This is why I can't understand why someone would volunteer to be the Lady. If I lost any of you to that awful sacrifice, I'd never recover."

"People do it to protect and serve our kind, but also to elevate their own family," Dee explained. "The Lady is our ultimate authority and she speaks through a living relative. A translator of sorts. Let's say I became the Lady—"

"Heaven forbid!" Verena interrupted. "You're too gentle, Sister. The Lady needs to make difficult decisions. And we could never be separated! It's always been the four of us."

"I'm just using myself as an example." Dee gave Verena a reassuring pat and turned back to Ella Mae. "One of my sisters would speak for me, earning a revered position in our community. People bring gifts to the Lady's family and see them through hardships. Her relatives become wealthy, influential, and protected. No one is allowed to deliberately hurt someone who shares the Lady's blood."

"The punishment for that offense is truly *awful*," Sissy whispered. "You're taken to the grove and stripped of your gifts. The old tales say that the pain is like being burned alive."

Ella Mae finished her stew and put the bowl aside. Ignoring Sissy's dramatic statement, she frowned. "Money and power, huh? I can see why the Gaynors want someone in their clan to volunteer. I assumed that because Melissa didn't have any family, she wanted to become the Lady for the greater good, but what about Freda? She doesn't strike me as someone who's completely willing to give up the rest of her life for any of the reasons you've mentioned."

"It's a calling," Dee said. "Some people hear it and some don't. Freda told the elders she felt the urge to volunteer the moment she heard about Melissa Carlisle's death."

Verena shook her head. "I wish I knew how to wake her up! If Freda keeps sleeping, we'll have to agree to Tilda Gaynor as our next Lady, and Havenwood will not be the same. For one thing, Buddy won't be mayor much longer!"

"Change comes with *every* new Lady," Sissy said, directing her statement at Ella Mae. "I can remember our grandmother telling us how the Lady of her time insisted that we pool our money to purchase large tracts of land. The land was donated back to the town and was quickly turned into wildlife sanctuaries and parks. Without that Lady's guidance, we'd have housing developments instead of nature trails. But some families fought the movement tooth and nail. They thought they could leave the preservation of the parks, the island in the middle of Lake Havenwood, and the forests surrounding the town to the *next* generation."

Dee turned down Reba's offer of more wine and leaned forward in her seat. "It's all right to be frightened of this ritual, Ella Mae. Life is totally different after you've been Awakened, and you've had so little time to adjust. Hopefully, you'll see how beautiful and moving the transfer ceremony is come Saturday. When the Lady is reborn, we'll celebrate our uniqueness with food and dancing and song. Two times each year, we are all one family. It sounds cliché to say that it's magical, but it is. It's one of the most enchanting nights you'll ever know."

Ella Mae liked the sound of that. "When's the second occasion?"

"The spring equinox," her mother said. "Your birthday."

A log collapsed in the fireplace, sending a burst of sparks up the flume.

"And the anniversary of my father's death," Ella Mae added softly, looking directly at her mother.

The room filled with a weighted silence. The lick of flames and the snap of kindling were the only sounds. Ella Mae's mother turned to stare at the fire, and for a long moment, she became lost in its light.

"I told you that our kind was cursed," she said in a low voice tinged with anger. "We can't have children without paying a horrible price. Your father was not of our kind, but he wasn't like other people either. He was . . . a man of the earth. We were foolish. We thought that we could trick the curse, but we were wrong. Terran paid for our mistake with his life."

Ella Mae swallowed hard. "And I was the mistake."

"No!" her mother shouted, startling everyone. "But I've always been afraid to love you. I've always been afraid that the curse wasn't done—that it would take you from me too. I thought that if I kept you at a distance, then you'd be safe." Her hazel eyes grew watery. "That was my second mistake."

Adelaide LeFaye never cried, and so Ella Mae was unsettled to see tears spill onto her cheeks. She rushed to her mother, throwing her arms around her. Ella Mae whispered, "I'm here, Mom. I'm right here. And we have years and years ahead of us." She ran a hand over her mother's black hair, reveling in the silkiness of her thick tresses and the scent of roses, fertile soil, and moonlight clinging to each strand. "I'm sorry you lost the man you loved," she said, drawing back to look at her mother's face. "But at least that love was true. No one can take that from you."

Her mother nodded and touched Ella Mae's cheek. "You'll find that too. I promise you." She wiped away her tears and smiled. "And you're right, we have all the time in the world to build new memories together."

A buzzing noise sounded from the corner of the room and Verena jumped up to pull her cell phone from her purse. She examined the screen and her face instantly turned wan. "No!" she cried. The hand holding the phone began to tremble violently.

"What is it?" Dee asked, rushing to Verena's side, with Sissy on her heel. Instinctively, Ella Mae reached out to grasp her mother's hands. Behind them, Reba adopted her gunfighter's stance, her fingers poised over the holster on her hip, her eyes dark and wary.

Verena glanced around the room, her eyes falling on each of them, but they were wide and glazed with shock and could focus on nothing. "Buddy sent me a text," she said in an uncommonly soft voice. "I asked him to check on Freda while I was here."

There was a long pause in which they all waited for someone to ask the question no one wanted to ask. Finally, Reba squared her shoulders, exhaled, and said, "And?"

"She passed on a few minutes ago. Oh, Lord help us all. Freda Shaw is dead."

Chapter 14

It took a moment for Verena to come out of her daze.

"I need to call Buddy and find out what happened," she said and half stumbled from the room, leaving the rest of the women to sit in stunned silence. They were so quiet that Ella Mae could hear the sound of the antique mantel clock ticking. She'd always loved the pretty old clock. Its white porcelain case was decorated with pink peonies and golden buttercups and reminded her of a wedding cake. Ella Mae used to beg Reba to let her open the glass door so she could gently wind the clock with its tiny metal key.

Now, as the hour struck eight, the chorus of high-pitched chimes was not a welcome sound. They were too merry, too rich and sweet, like an oversugared dessert. When Ella Mae had been a girl, she used to stretch out on the sofa and wait for the tiny bells to ring. The airy music would make her think of carousels and ballet dancers and the song of the ice cream man's truck.

In the face of Freda's death, however, the sound was

mocking and cruel, and Ella Mae was half tempted to cover her ears. Glancing around, she could see Reba and her aunts staring at the clock with clenched jaws and vacant eyes. Only her mother seemed unaware of the chiming. Sitting ramrod straight, her gaze was fixed on the fire. With flames dancing in her eyes and the filaments of silver in her black hair set aglow by the firelight, her mother looked like a deeply troubled queen.

"Mom?" Ella Mae whispered into the heavy silence. She wanted her mother to speak, to tell her what she was thinking, feeling.

Just then, Verena came back into the room. "What a tragedy!" she cried and collapsed onto the sofa. "Freda just slipped away. Like that!" She snapped her fingers and shook her head in dismay. "Like a candle flame blown out by the wind."

"Was Peter with her?" Dee asked.

"No. He got a call from Candis an hour ago. It seems that on her way home from the hospital, she hydroplaned and ended up in a ditch. She tried to reach Rudy at his parents' house first—he was taking a much-needed break from the constant bedside vigil he and Candis have been keeping—but no one answered. Assuming they'd lost power because of the storm, she called Peter's cell phone."

Ella Mae thought of how dark it had been driving back through Havenwood after she'd dropped Maurelle off. The strong winds had downed trees and knocked the power out across most of the region, plunging the town into blackness. It had been restored at Partridge Hill fairly quickly, but the majority of Havenwood's residents were still in the dark.

"Candis must have felt so scared and alone," she said mostly to herself. "Sitting there in the rain, trying to contact her husband, only to hear the phone ringing on and on."

"Poor Rudy. He's going to feel terrible about not being with Candis when she needed him," Dee said.

An ugly thought wormed its way into Ella Mae's mind. "What do we know about the Lurdings?"

Sissy gave her a quizzical look. "They're not of our kind, but they seem like good, decent people. Why?"

"Well, since we can't seem to figure out who wanted Melissa and Freda dead, maybe we need to think about the possibility that one of our kind hired a third party to do their dirty work." Ella Mae spoke tentatively, knowing that she hadn't had the chance to consider the flaws in her theory. "The Lurdings have been to the Shermans' farm. Any one of them could have given Freda the tainted cheese."

Reba pulled a licorice twist from her pocket and wound it around her finger. "She has a point. What do we know about these folks?" She turned to Sissy. "Lots of people seem good and decent, when right below the surface they're as rotten as a fallen peach."

Sissy nodded in agreement. "Do you have any confession pie left, Ella Mae?"

"One. Are you going to take it to the Lurdings?"

Verena answered instead of Sissy. "We both will. If they've got nothing to hide, then we'll simply have brought them a delicious meal as a show of sympathy. Our visit won't seem strange. After all, Rudy just lost his mother-in-law. The only way we Southern ladies know how to deal with grief is to eat too much rich food, drink too much whiskey, and wear big hats to the funeral!" She rubbed her temples and sighed. "Though I don't think any of those things will comfort Peter and Candis."

"There's something else to consider," Ella Mae's mother said quietly. "Now that Tilda Gaynor's at the top of the volunteer list, she's probably in danger."

Reba scowled and continued to wind and unwind her candy around her finger. "I can't believe the Gaynors aren't involved in this somehow. Maybe they had someone else handle the details, since that's what they always do. Makes more sense viewin' them as the culprits, considerin' they had a relative lined up and ready to step in the second Freda got sick."

"Tilda applied to be a candidate months ago," Dee argued softly. "She wasn't chosen at the time because her company has a track record of hostile takeovers and the elders felt we needed someone with a more balanced approach. Both Melissa and Freda were interested in preserving the status quo, while the Gaynors have been arguing for a more aggressive leader since the current Lady began to show signs of fading."

Ella Mae put a hand over her heart. "I never imagined I'd be defending that family, but I don't think Opal is involved in the deaths of the other two candidates. If she had a more recent, a more pressing secret, then it would have come out today."

"What do you think, Adelaide? Should we bring the Gaynors in on what we know? Call a truce in the name of the harvest and the future of our people and find the culprit together?" Verena demanded solemnly.

Rising, Ella Mae's mother moved closer to the fire. She picked up the brass-handled poker from the stand next to the fireplace and began to jab at the burning wood. "I'll speak with Opal tomorrow." Keeping her back to the rest of the room, she prodded the logs until the yellow sparks looked like a mass of agitated bees. "There is another possibility none of us have spoken aloud." She stopped moving, the metal tool hovering over the flames. "The killer could be one of the Shadow Children."

Sissy gasped. "*No.* It can't be. There hasn't been an assassin in Havenwood for years and years."

The word assassin gave Ella Mae the chills. Neither the fire, nor the soft blanket, nor the presence of her family could stave off the fear. "I remember hearing about them that night in the library," she said. "After my Awakening."

Her mother pivoted away from the fire and stood holding the poker in front of her like a spear. "Yes, I explained how we're related to Morgan le Fay, the Gaynors to Guinevere, and the Shadow Children to the wizard, Merlin. What of it?"

"I'm wondering what chance we have against this creature," Ella Mae said. "Even if we all join forces and protect Tilda until Saturday night, this assassin could still attack her in the sacred grove, right?"

"They cannot enter our sanctuary!" Verena boomed in a resonating voice.

Dee pulled on her long braid of auburn hair and nodded. "It's true. They are too twisted inside to gain entry into our sanctuary. They have become something other than our kind."

"I think the Gaynors are pretty slimy too, and it's never stopped them from sneakin' in," Reba grumbled.

"How would I recognize one?" Ella Mae wanted to know. "An assassin?"

Reba snorted. "If you turn around and find yourself face-to-face with a silent person with crazy eyes wieldin' a knife, gun, Taser, baseball bat, or a big rock, then you know you're lookin' at a Shadow Child."

"Unfortunately, they look just like the rest of us," Sissy said. "They've learned to blend in and hide the ugliness of their twisted souls. But *most* of them are old. You see, the things they do exact a toll on their bodies. A twenty-year-old Shadow Child can look like a sixty-year-old human. Depends on how many lives they've taken."

Ella Mae was horrified. "How could someone deliberately lead that kind of existence?"

"It's in their blood," her mother said blandly. "Very few of them can resist their nature. They were born to hunt us."

Reba held out her hands. "Don't terrify the girl. At least tell her that there aren't many Children left. Their lives are nothin' but evil, but they're also as short as my great-aunt

Helga. And assassins don't make the best parents. Most of their newborns are dumped at the church door in a dirty cardboard box. And those are the lucky ones."

"That's true," Sissy said. "There are very few of their kind and they're all loners. And we haven't seen one in Havenwood for decades."

Sighing in weary exasperation, Ella Mae looked from woman to woman, her gaze coming to rest on her mother's lovely, anxious face. "What can we do?"

"Keep Tilda Gaynor alive," she said. "She's our only hope, as scary as that thought may be."

Verena crossed the room, took the poker from her sister's hands, and slid it back among the other tools. It fell into place with a loud clang. "Dee. Sissy. You should move in with Adelaide until after the harvest. We need to close ranks."

Dee stared out the window and shuddered. "I've never been afraid of the dark before," she whispered and then edged closer to the fire. "But now it feels like the darkness has become invisible. We can't see it coming or going, but it's taken two of us with it into the night."

Verena put an arm around her youngest sibling. "The night doesn't last forever, Delia. You'll feel better in the morning. Until then, I'm driving you and Sissy to pick up your things. No one would dare try to breach Partridge Hill. Not even a Shadow Child."

Ella Mae's mother gestured at the fire poker. "I almost wish they would. My powers might be growing weaker, but there are more weapons in this house than even an assassin could defend against."

"Like Reba?" Ella Mae asked, imagining Reba arming herself using the arsenal of guns and knives locked in cabinets in the study.

"And you," her mother surprised her by saying. "Everyone else's gifts will continue to fade until there's a new Lady, but yours seem undiminished. In fact, they're growing stronger. Reba told me about the appearance of the butterflies during your target practice. And look at what you did with the lamb pies today. There's no telling what you're capable of once you fully tap into your powers."

Ella Mae tossed her blanket aside and stood up. "Then I'd better figure out what those are. I don't think an enchanted pie is going to save Tilda Gaynor. Or anyone else."

The next day, Ella Mae was so distracted that she had trouble making her simplest recipes. Reba kept scolding her for charring the crusts or not whipping the meringue into the perfect peaks.

"Focus, girl!" Reba waved a Twizzlers at her during the middle of the lunch service. "Ms. Palmer asked for no onions on her salad and you made a mountain of onion rings on her plate." She thrust the dish under Ella Mae's nose.

"I can't help it," Ella Mae complained. "I keep wondering what kind of confessions Aunt Verena's getting out of the Lurdings, how Mom's talk is going with Opal Gaynor, and how Candis is holding up."

Reba jerked her thumb toward the swing door. "Maurelle will be back any second to fetch a slice of coconut cream pie for Mr. Copperman, so ask her."

Ella Mae was almost afraid to talk to Maurelle. She was so pale that her skin was nearly gray, and her eyes were bloodshot. If she looked this fragile and haggard over worry for her friend, then Ella Mae hated to raise the subject and make her feel even worse.

Unfortunately, Maurelle caught her staring.

"I know I look like a vampire," Maurelle said quietly and managed a weak smile. "But you've seen me eat normal food, so your jugular vein is totally safe."

Laughing awkwardly, Ella Mae dropped her gaze to the

coconut cream pie. "I'm sorry. I'm just concerned about you. You have a long commute to work, you're on your feet all day, and now you're bearing the burden of Candis's grief. If you need to just call it a day, then feel free to go home. A few hours of extra rest might do you the world of good."

Maurelle shook her head. "I like being here." She picked up a stray mint leaf from the counter and rubbed it between her fingers. "Unless how I look is freaking people out. I don't want to run your customers off."

"Oh, you're not!" Ella Mae exclaimed, abashed.

"A couple of them have joked that I need more vitamin D," she said playfully and collected Mr. Copperman's dessert. Then, she hesitated. "I do feel really bad for Candis though. Really, really bad. And for Mr. Shaw too. They've been so nice to me and to everyone else they meet. They don't deserve to suffer like this. It's not fair."

"No one deserves that kind of pain," Ella Mae said gently.

Maurelle nodded and pushed the swing door open with her bony elbow.

After the lunch rush was over and the dining room had been reset for afternoon tea, Ella Mae turned the dishwasher on, untied her apron, and sat on the back steps. Inviting the sun to warm her face and the crown of her head, she sipped a glass of iced tea flavored with orange slices and checked for voice mails on her cell phone.

Her mother had called and told her to get back to her as soon as she was free.

"Is everything all right?" was the first thing Ella Mae asked.

"Yes," her mother answered. "I just wanted to fill you in on your aunts' visit to the Lurdings. They're not involved, Ella Mae. Mr. and Mrs. Lurding confessed to being envious of the Shaws' lovely house and the fact that they bought Candis and Rudy a horse as a wedding gift, but other than that, they are genuinely good people."

Ella Mae was relieved. She liked the Lurdings.

"What about Rudy?"

"As you predicted, he's utterly guilt-ridden over not being with Candis when her car went off the road. It wasn't much of a secret. I think he would have told us about it without eating a piece of your pie." She uttered a small sigh. "He's a sweet boy. He even said that he would regret not being able to get to know Freda more and that he'd give anything to take his wife's grief away."

Ella Mae felt a stab of sorrow. "I can't even imagine what Peter and Candis are going through."

"They're going through hell," her mother said. "Believe me, I've been there. The pain will be less intense as the years pass, but it never truly disappears. Despite what people say, time doesn't heal all wounds. We take some of them with us to the grave."

"Mom . . ." Ella Mae began. She wanted to comfort her mother, but she didn't know what to say.

"Sorry, I didn't mean to turn maudlin." Her mother's tone became flat and businesslike. "I've been busy too. Opal and I managed to meet for coffee without trading a single insult. According to her, the Gaynor clan has been guarding Tilda twenty-four-seven since she got to Havenwood. They have their own version of Reba, you know."

Picturing a tall, haughty blonde with a rifle slung over one shoulder, Ella Mae grimaced. "That's an unpleasant thought. Can't Loralyn just turn her siren powers on and convince the killer to give himself up to the authorities?"

"Her gift only works on men, and there's no proof that our killer is male. Even if he were, all of us are weak right now. Loralyn couldn't talk a guy into opening a door for her until after the harvest."

"So the LeFayes and the Gaynors have become allies?" Ella Mae couldn't keep the doubt from her voice.

"For now," her mother said and rang off.

Amazed, Ella Mae went back inside. She stepped into the walk-in to make sure she had enough lemon and triple berry tarts lined up for afternoon tea. The chocolate chess pies were depleted, but she didn't feel like making more. After all, she'd already ruined half a dozen orders between breakfast and lunch and didn't want to bake a fresh round of imperfect pies. However, she had to prep a fresh batch of whipped cream, as her regular customers would expect a generous dollop atop their teatime dessert.

Placing the stainless steel bowl from her commercial mixer in the refrigerator to chill, Ella Mae took a tub of sugar down from the shelf and searched for an upbeat song on the radio. She then slipped her apron over her head and began making the whipped cream.

By the time her dessert garnishes were prepared and stored in the refrigerator, it occurred to Ella Mae that she hadn't seen Reba or Maurelle for over half an hour.

"I hope they're both taking a well-deserved break on the front porch," she said to the tall vase filled with bright orange gladiolus perched next to the sink. After another five minutes had passed, Ella Mae decided to head into the dining room to look for her waitresses when Maurelle burst through the swing doors, her dark eyes round with terror.

"Something's wrong with Reba!" she cried, her face eggshell white. "She's on the floor and she can't breathe!"

Pulling her phone from her apron pocket, Ella Mae barreled through the doors, dread making her movements agile and quick.

Reba was sprawled on the black-and-white tiles, feet bucking wildly and hands clutching at her throat. Her eyes bulged in panic and her tongue hung from her mouth, as if she was desperately trying to suck in even the tiniest molecule of air. She looked like a hooked fish thrown into a pail, left to flop and gasp until it died.

Ella Mae thrust the phone at Maurelle. "Call nine-one-

one!" she shouted and lifted Reba's head off the ground, peering into the cavern of her mouth in search of an obstruction, but Reba's airway appeared to be free of foreign objects. Ella Mae murmured, "Let me look at you, let me look at you," while trying to examine Reba's neck. She had to pry Reba's hands away, and when she succeeded, she saw an angry red mark a few inches above the soft hollow between the collarbones. The small, swollen circle resembled an insect bite.

"Did something sting you?" she asked.

Reba managed an agonized nod.

Maurelle was begging the emergency operator to hurry, and Ella Mae felt a rush of blinding rage course through her. She'd never felt so inept, so utterly useless and helpless. The world spun around her and the only thing keeping her from losing the last shreds of her sanity was the weight of Reba's head on her lap. She stroked the familiar nut brown hair, whispering for Reba to stay calm, to relax so that the oxygen could make its way into her straining lungs.

"Close your eyes," she said. "Picture us in the forest when the butterflies came. There was a breeze, remember? The sun was going down, but there was still enough light to see them drift down from the sky. Can you see the Dr Pepper cans in the trees? Remember how you taught me to let go of all my thoughts before I squeezed the trigger? Do that now, Reba. Let go of your fear. Go back to the forest. Relax. Let the air in. Relax. Let go." Ella Mae repeated her mantra over and over again, unaware that she was crying until her tears fell onto Reba's cheek.

The scene was nightmarishly similar to that of Candis's wedding when Freda had so suddenly taken ill, and Ella Mae forced the thought from her mind.

This isn't the same thing, she convinced herself. *Reba's having an allergic reaction or something. She's not sick. She won't die.*

Taking her eyes from Reba, who seemed to be drawing in just enough breath to hold on to consciousness, Ella Mae glanced at Maurelle for a single, intense second, "Did you see what happened?"

Maurelle's voice quavered as her words tumbled out. "N-No. She was outside watering the plants on the front porch. I didn't hear anything weird, but then she came in with her hands on her neck and dropped to her knees. Sh-she looked . . . surprised."

"That's all? What about before that? Who was in here? Who was on the patio?" Ella Mae's questions were curt and sharp. Fear and anger made her sound cruelly abrupt, but she couldn't spare the time or energy on kindness at the moment.

"I'm sorry," Maurelle said miserably. "I don't know anything else. We haven't had a customer since Mr. Copperman left. I was cleaning the fingerprints off the display cases, so my back was to the windows. I'm so sorry."

Ella Mae took another precious second to scan the closest tiles for evidence, but she saw nothing. "It's not your fault," she whispered to Maurelle, and then she shouted, "Damn it all! Where's that ambulance?" She tried not to tense her body. The last thing she wanted was to have Reba's throat tighten up again.

"Can you go out front?" she asked Maurelle. "Look around for what could have bitten her or—" The sound of an approaching siren interrupted her. "*Go!* Tell those paramedics to hustle their asses!"

Maurelle dashed outside like a shot.

"Reba, help is coming," she murmured, bending over her beloved friend. "They're right outside the door, so don't you dare leave me. You stay in our forest and breathe that beautiful, fresh air. You stay there, you hear me? Stay and watch the butterflies. Stay with me, Reba. Stay with me. Stay with me."

When the paramedics entered, Ella Mae was rocking Reba like a mother rocks a sick child. She resisted being pulled from her at first, but then relented and scooted backward to allow the EMTs to do their job. Glancing from the middle-aged man who put an oxygen mask over Reba's mouth and nose to the young woman who had placed the flat disc of a stethoscope under Reba's T-shirt, Ella Mae tried to interpret their expressions, but their faces were unreadable.

"I'm not leaving her side," she told the male paramedic as he and his partner loaded Reba onto a collapsed gurney. "So if you're going to tell me to follow you in my own car, you can save your breath. I'm not leaving her."

For a moment, she thought they'd argue, but the male gave her a brief nod.

"Can I do anything?" Maurelle asked as the paramedics raised the gurney to its full height. She was leaning heavily against the counter, looking paler than Reba.

The female EMT paused. "Are you okay, miss?"

"Yeah, I'm fine," Maurelle answered in a thin voice and pointed at Reba. "Just take good care of her." Her dark eyes found Ella Mae's. "Do you want me to come?"

"No, just lock up and go on home." Ella Mae hurried past her, close on the heels of the paramedics.

Inside the ambulance, she put her hand over Reba's, taking comfort in the warmth of her skin. Closing her eyes, Ella Mae pictured the forest near Partridge Hill. The sound of the siren lost its shrill edge and slowly faded away as if Ella Mae had gone underwater. The rocking sensation of being in a moving vehicle disappeared. All she could sense was the feel of the afternoon sun falling upon her shoulders and the whisper of butterfly wings.

Find out what did this to her, she commanded. She repeated her orders over and over until the hum of wings turned into a roar inside her head.

Still holding on to Reba's hand, she opened her eyes and turned to look out the window in the rear doors of the ambulance. Her heart swelled with hope and she felt a powerful surge of strength when she saw an enormous cloud of multihued butterflies rise into the sky.

"It's going to be all right," she told an unresponsive Reba. And for the first time, she truly believed that she was capable of controlling fate. The magic was exploding inside her. She was riding in the ambulance, but she was also floating on an air current. And then, she fluttered over grass blades and parted the shadows until she could see the source of Reba's wound.

"It's a spider bite," she told the female paramedic. "A brown recluse. Will that help you treat her?"

The paramedic gave her a dubious glance. "I thought you said you didn't know what happened."

"I didn't then," Ella Mae said, her mind's eye cluttered by images of the flowers bordering the pie shop's front walk. "But I do now. Everything's become so clear."

Chapter 15

Ella Mae paced the hospital hallway, too restless to sit in the waiting room. Every few minutes, she'd stop by the nurses' station to check on Reba's status, but there was still no word.

Finally, a physician in sea blue scrubs tracked her down in the corridor. "Ms. LeFaye?"

"Yes." She searched his face for clues and found none. "How's Reba?"

The doctor explained that because Reba's throat swelled so dramatically in response to the spider venom, she couldn't get enough air into her lungs. As a result, she'd been quickly sedated and intubated.

"Now that her breathing's been regulated, she's out of immediate danger," he told Ella Mae in such an even, confident voice that she could have kissed him. "This is the first time I've seen a brown recluse bite to the neck. Usually, they occur on arms and legs. A person will accidentally press against the spider, triggering its defense system. Ordinarily, they're shy creatures." He glanced at the notes he'd scrawled on Reba's chart. "Brown recluse bites aren't typically a cause for concern unless they happen to young children. The smaller the patient's body, the more damage the poison can inflict."

The doctor's insinuation wasn't lost on Ella Mae. "And Reba's petite. Nearly as small as a child."

He nodded. "That's right. Her recovery may not be as swift as that of an adult female of average height and weight. And the location of the bite may cause complications as well. The venom produces enzymes that break down human tissue. The necrosis has occurred around your friend's windpipe, causing the entire throat to swell. We've given her antitoxins to counteract the venom and are pumping her full of antibiotics, but so far, the swelling isn't abating."

"What does that mean?" Ella Mae asked, a trickle of fear running through her.

"She needs to be kept sedated until we can get that swelling down. Having a breathing tube isn't comfortable, so we've put her in a medically induced coma. She'll have to remain in this state until her throat has returned to its normal size."

Hearing the word coma, Ella Mae grew cold all over. Crossing her arms over her chest, she felt all the power that had flowed through her in the ambulance ebb away like melting snow.

"Can I see her?" she asked, hating how her voice had become as thin and fragile as a dragonfly wing.

He nodded. "Come with me."

When they reached the ICU room, Ella Mae's first thought was that Reba didn't look like Reba. A breathing tube poked from her mouth, IV tubes ran from her arm, and beeping monitors and screens filled with moving lines or pulsating waves flanked her head. Ella Mae glanced at the machines with dread. She couldn't begin to decipher what their blinking lights, hums, or ever-changing readouts meant, but she hated them all the same. She knew this was illogical, for they were keeping Reba alive, but someone like Reba wasn't meant to be attached to such devices. She was a warrior. She was supposed to be invulnerable.

She would hate this, Ella Mae thought and swallowed a sob. Coiling her hands into fists, she told herself to be strong. Reba needed her and she had to be clearheaded and sharp-eyed. Tears and anxiety were useless, so Ella Mae fought them both until her emotions were under control.

Turning to the nurse attending to one of Reba's IV drip bags, Ella Mae asked, "Is she responding to the medication?"

The nurse shook her head. "Not yet. Right now, her body is reacting to the toxins by fighting it the only way it knows how. It's releasing inflammatory agents, which creates the swelling. We're trying to get rid of the venom, but so far, our antitoxins aren't working as well as we'd like."

Ella Mae nodded. "She's a fighter. Normally, that would be a good thing, but I guess in this case, it's a detriment."

"No, no. It's always better for us to work on a strong, healthy patient," the nurse assured her. "Your friend has the physique of a woman twenty years her junior."

"Yeah, she's pretty special," Ella Mae murmured and squeezed Reba's hand.

When the nurse kindly told her she had to go, she leaned over and whispered in Reba's ear, repeating what she'd said in the back of the ambulance. "Let go," she begged. "Stop fighting. Just let go."

The moment she left the room, Ella Mae rushed outside and called her mother. Within thirty minutes, the LeFayes were all gathered in the ICU's waiting room. Verena questioned anyone wearing a hospital ID, but the answers were all the same. "We can only wait and see."

"I'm not a fan of wait and see!" Verena bellowed and

then drew a notebook from her voluminous hot pink bag. Smoothing her black pants, she sat in one of the room's plastic chairs and did her best to lower her voice. "This spider bite is probably a freak accident, but with the harvest only three days away, I'm not sure I can wholly believe that. We're going to take turns watching Reba's room. She must never be left alone. Not for an instant!"

"Then we should guard her in pairs," Sissy said. "One of us could miss something. Nothing can get past *two* LeFayes."

They decided on four-hour shifts, beginning with Dee and Sissy. Ella Mae and her mother would go next. Verena would partner with Buddy, and then they'd start all over again. Buddy didn't know of his wife's magical abilities, but he was so devoted to Verena that he'd sit in the hospital all night if she asked him to.

Verena tapped on her notebook. "This won't do. We have to rearrange Ella Mae's schedule so she can get to the pie shop in time tomorrow."

"I'm not leaving Reba," Ella Mae protested. "I don't care who else comes or goes. I'm staying here."

"She wouldn't want that," her mother said. "What about the shop?"

Ella Mae's face darkened. "I'm not baking pies while Reba's in the ICU! The shop will stay closed until after the harvest."

Dee touched her on the shoulder. "Yesterday, you told us how sorry you felt for Maurelle—how you wished she didn't have to live in that junky trailer. Can she afford to miss three days' worth of tips?" She looked into Ella Mae's eyes. "I'm not trying to make you feel guilty, but your mother's right. Reba would want you to keep the pie shop open. This schedule will be hard enough on you as it is, seeing as you'll be losing sleep guarding her at night."

In the end, Ella Mae relented. "But only if you promise to call me if there's any change in her condition. Good or bad."

Her mother and aunts gave her their word.

"I'm going to the shop now," she told them. "To find that spider. Maurelle saw Reba on the front porch earlier this afternoon. If it's still there, I need to get rid of it."

"That spider likes porches," Dee said. "Barns, basements, attics, woodpiles. Someplace safe and dry and warm, but with a nice, dark corner. You'll recognize it by the violin shape on its body, on the part near the head where the legs attach."

"Thanks," Ella Mae said to Dee and then turned to her mother. "Can you drive me? I came in the ambulance with Reba."

"Of course." Her mother's jaw was tight with anger. "I'd like to get my hands on that damned spider."

Verena wagged a finger. "Not literally! Stick the thing in a bag and bring it back to Dee. She needs to make sure the docs are giving Reba the right medicine."

At the pie shop, Ella Mae and her mother searched the ground for the spider but couldn't find it, dead or alive. Ella Mae had seen it through the eyes of butterflies during the ambulance ride, but she couldn't find the exact spot now.

Sitting in a rocking chair, she closed her eyes. She allowed her body to relax and focused on the sugared vanilla scent of the roses climbing up the columns and onto the roof. She listened to the birds twittering to each other from the branches of the magnolia tree and felt the slightest sigh of wind. And then, she heard the hushed murmur of butterfly wings.

Show me the spider, she commanded and instantly felt

the ground drop away. In her mind's eye, she rose into the sky and then darted downward again, her flight path jarring and bumpy. She saw the body of a brown spider lying belly up on a patch of dirt next to an ochre-colored chrysanthemum.

Opening her eyes, she jumped up and searched the yard. The butterflies were clustered along the flagstone path, hovering over one of the dozens of chrysanthemums she and her mother had planted prior to Candis's wedding. Hurrying down the path, she squatted next to the plant and immediately spotted the spider. Using a twig, she pushed it out of the dirt and into the light.

"Dead," she told her mother.

"Get a bag. Dee will want to see it."

Ella Mae unlocked the pie shop and returned half a minute later with a baggie and a pair of small tongs. As she picked up the spider by one of its legs and examined its brown body and violin-shaped markings, she looked up at the butterflies. She silently thanked them and they quickly dispersed.

Watching them flit away, Ella Mae was struck by an ominous thought. "If I can command butterflies, is it possible that someone could have . . . told this spider to bite Reba?" She dropped the lifeless arachnid into the bag, sealed it, and stepped back onto the porch.

Her mother paled. "Yes. With magic, anything is possible. But why would someone go after Reba? Unless . . ."

"They wanted to get to me," Ella Mae finished for her. "But why? I have nothing to do with the Lady of the Ash."

"I don't know what's going on, but I'm not taking any chances. I'm going to give Maurelle a week's worth of tip money," her mother stated firmly. "Hang a note on the door. You're officially on vacation. Starting now."

Ella Mae examined the spider in its cocoon of plastic. "After this month, I could really use one."

* * *

Ella Mae dropped her mother off at the hospital and then drove over to Canine to Five to collect Chewy. Hugh met her at the door, his face filled with concern.

"I just talked to one of my EMT buddies. He told me he responded to a call at the pie shop. Is everything okay?"

"No," Ella Mae said in a leaden voice. "Reba was stung by a brown recluse. On the neck. She can't breathe on her own."

Hugh raised his hand and touched his own neck. "God, that's terrible. Can I do anything? Take care of Chewy? Help you out at work?"

"You can hold me," she blurted without thinking. It was what she wanted from him more than anything else. The feel of his strong arms encircling her body would make her feel sturdy and safe, if only for a small measure of time.

Without hesitating, he closed the distance between them and crushed her to him. Drinking in his familiar scent of dew-covered grass and the cool, deep water of the swimming hole, she clung to him.

"Sloan and I are finished," she whispered into his shoulder. "He's played me for a fool for our entire marriage. He . . . he . . ." She trailed off. Not because telling Hugh how Sloan had deceived her would hurt too much, but because her mind had involuntarily taken her back to Reba's hospital room. The pain of her husband's duplicity was instantly overshadowed by her fear of losing Reba. A sob welled up in her throat.

"Shhhhh," Hugh said. "I've got you. I won't let go."

A cacophony of dog noises—barks, yips, whines, growls, and snorts—came from the main room behind them, but Ella Mae didn't hear a thing. Hugh's words were the only sounds she registered.

"I've got you," he repeated, murmuring into her whiskey-colored curls. He kissed the crown of her head, her brow, her cheek, and her chin before his lips brushed against her lips. He'd barely made contact before he pulled away, but not so far as to detach from her embrace. He gazed down at her, his blue eyes shimmering with tenderness. "Sorry, I can't help myself. Whenever I'm around you, I want to kiss you in the worst way."

She smiled. "The feeling's mutual. And everything about you makes me feel stronger, more steady. So kiss me all you like."

He did, giving her another kiss, light as air, before tucking a strand of hair behind her ear. His fingers lingered at the base of her neck, tracing little spirals on her skin. "I'll hold you for the rest of the day if that's what you need. All night too." He gave her a little grin. "Believe me, I'd like nothing better. But I imagine you want to be with Reba."

Nodding, she told him about the shifts Verena had created. She didn't explain that their bedside vigils were part guard duty. Until the harvest, she wouldn't know whether Hugh was one of her kind or not.

"I'll come with you," he offered. "Or I could swing by in an hour or so and bring supper for you and your mom. Trust me, you don't want to eat hospital food."

Ella Mae grew slightly stiff in his arms. Did she trust him? She wanted him, yes. But did she know him enough to trust him? She'd trusted Sloan, and look where that had gotten her. And Hugh could be manipulated by Loralyn at any given opportunity. He could turn on Ella Mae and her family at Loralyn's command.

Except now, Ella Mae thought, feeling a thrill of hope. *She's too weak to enthrall him. This is the only time I can truly know if he wants to be with me or not.*

"Supper would be really nice," she said. "So would your company."

He gave her a boyish smile and gently released her from his embrace. "Let's get Chewy then. He's been acting kind of funny all day, like he has separation anxiety or something. I wonder if he knew you were distressed. Sometimes our animals can sense stuff like that, even when they're not with us."

"I can believe that," Ella Mae said, following him through the doorway into the central play area. *I wouldn't be surprised if Chewy wakes up one day and speaks in complete sentences,* she thought, remembering what her mother had said. *With magic, anything is possible.*

Upon seeing her adorable terrier, Ella Mae sank to her knees, laughing as her little dog raced toward her, barking happily. "I missed you!" she cried as Chewy leapt onto her lap. His tail wagged furiously as he covered her face with a dozen wet, sloppy kisses.

Ella Mae drove home to Partridge Hill and took Chewy on a quick walk down to the dock. She played a brief game of catch with him on the slope of soft grass leading to the water's edge, and when he was tired out, she let him rest in her mother's garden while she prepared to return to the hospital. Verena had called to report that there had been no change in Reba's condition and no suspicious activity or visitors either.

"Were you able to reach Maurelle?" Ella Mae's mother asked as they climbed into her Suburban.

"No. I left a message on her cell phone. It's the only number I have for her." Envisioning Maurelle's trailer, Ella Mae assumed that her employee didn't have a home phone. "I told her I was closing the shop for a week and that she was getting a paid vacation. I've already put a check in the mail, and it should get to her by tomorrow afternoon at the latest."

Ella Mae's mother gestured at her daughter's handbag. "You brought the spider?"

"Yes, it's in here. I'll give it to Dee as soon as she and Sissy show up." She glanced out at the woods. The trees passed by the window in a blur of green and brown and deepening shadow. "Hugh asked if he could bring us supper and I told him he could. It's just a friendly gesture," she added quickly. "Let's not get into why he isn't right for me and all that, okay?"

"Suit yourself." There was a chill to her mother's voice. "But this is hardly the time to encourage him. Things are complicated enough."

It was impossible to argue with that statement, so Ella Mae kept quiet.

As it turned out, Hugh was so courteous and obliging that he managed to charm the doctors, nurses, and Ella Mae's mother. He brought trays of chicken salad sandwiches, homemade slaw, big bags of kettle chips, and rich chocolate brownies. When he presented Ella Mae with a plate, she protested that she wasn't hungry, but he coaxed her into eating, saying that Reba needed her to maintain her strength. He stayed with them for hours, and before he left, he kissed Ella Mae's hand and told her mother that should she need anything, he was only a phone call away.

The next day brought another round of shifts and worrying and waiting. The LeFayes watched over Reba, studying her swollen throat, the lines on the monitors, and the nurses' expressions for the slightest indication of improvement in Reba's condition, but there was no change to observe.

Hugh reappeared during Ella Mae's shift. He read aloud to Reba from a worn, leather-bound copy of *Robin Hood* that he'd had since he was a boy, his strong, deep voice filling the room with vitality. Dee thought Hugh had struck upon a wonderful idea and showed up at her next shift carrying a copy of *All Creatures Great and Small*.

On Friday afternoon, Ella Mae ran into Suzy Bacchus in

the lobby. Suzy was carrying two grocery bags filled with books, but as soon as Ella Mae told her that she was visiting Reba in the ICU, Suzy dropped the bags on the floor and threw her arms around her friend.

"Are you visiting someone too?" Ella Mae asked.

"No, nothing like that." Suzy pulled out an old paperback from the nearest bag. "I have a box in my store where people can donate gently used books. When the box fills up, I bring them here. One of the hospital volunteers told me that the patient library had been closed due to lack of funds and manpower, so she and I created our own. Only with our library, the patients can keep the books they like."

It warmed Ella Mae's heart to hear this. "That's so sweet."

Suzy shrugged. "It's the least I can do. I feel like I got a clean slate coming to Havenwood—that my future is a blank book waiting to be written. That's a good feeling." She hugged Ella Mae again. "Call me if I can do anything for you. I mean it. I'd like to help. That's what friends are for."

"Well, I could use some advice," Ella Mae said and, over a cup of vending machine coffee, asked Suzy what to do about Maurelle. "She's not returning my calls, and that has me a little concerned. Still, she's a really private person, so I don't think I should just drop by her place unannounced, do you?"

After considering the question, Suzy shook her head. "You told her to take a vacation and you sent her a check. Was the check cashed?"

Ella Mae nodded. "This morning."

"Then she took you at your word. She's dashed off to the beach or to Atlanta for a long weekend. She's your employee, remember? She doesn't have to tell you her plans. Really, Ella Mae, there's nothing to worry about."

If only I could believe that about everything, Ella Mae thought, thanked her friend, and headed up to Reba's room.

* * *

On Saturday morning, eight hours before the harvest ceremony was to begin, Ella Mae sat in her mother's kitchen
drinking coffee with Sissy and Dee. Chewy had wolfed
down his breakfast and was snoozing in a patch of sunlight
near the back door. When the phone rang, he was so startled
that he leapt to his feet and raced around the room, looking
for the source of the clamor that had interrupted his first nap
of the day.

Ella Mae's mother rushed to answer the phone, and when
she did, the lines of worry on her forehead turned smooth
and her face lit up with happiness.

"The swelling's going down!" she cried jubilantly.
"Reba's responding to the medication!"

All four women whooped and hollered. They danced
around the kitchen, embracing each other and taking turns
scooping Chewy off the floor to cover his black nose with
joyful kisses. He grinned in delight as the sunlight streamed
through the windows and covered all of them with a warm,
golden glow.

"We'll still need to maintain our shifts," Sissy said.
"Right up until we have to leave for the harvest."

Dee fished a pack of Twizzlers out of the pocket of her
denim overalls. "Look what I've been keeping ready for
Reba."

Seeing the licorice twists, Ella Mae's smile vanished. "If
she doesn't get released today—and I doubt she will—what
happens to her powers?"

"Reba doesn't need to replenish like we do," her mother
explained. "Unlike us, her gifts are more about innate skills
and years of devoted training and less about magic. The
harvest keeps her body youthful and agile, so she'll slow
down over the winter. But when the spring equinox arrives,
her vigor will be restored."

"I wish she didn't have to wait. After all, there's a killer out there," Ella Mae pointed out.

"Once we have a new Lady, Havenwood should be safe," Sissy said. "With all of us walking out of that grove tonight with renewed powers, it's the *murderer's* turn to be afraid."

At the hospital, the LeFayes were told that the swelling in Reba's neck was completely gone and the doctors were bringing her out of her medically induced coma.

"It'll take a few hours until she's fully awake, but you should be able to talk to her later tonight," a nurse told them.

Ella Mae kissed Reba on the forehead and promised to return as soon as the ceremony was over.

Before she knew it, she was standing at the wall of boulders that separated the normal world from the enchanted one. She was both exhilarated and terrified. In a few moments, she'd lay eyes on all the magical folk of Havenwood. There'd be no more guessing. Ella Mae was looking forward to that, but she wasn't eager to bear witness to the Lady of the Ash ritual, no matter how moving Dee said it was.

"Go on, Ella Mae!" Verena ordered. "I want to be right on your heels when the Gaynors realize that you've been Awakened! I bet their mouths will hang so far open you could throw a tennis ball inside." She laughed heartily and her sisters joined in.

Influenced by her family's merriment, Ella Mae closed her eyes and stepped through the rock.

She immediately heard music. Sweet, magical music that played in time to her own heartbeat. The feathery notes of a harp entwined with those of an Irish flute. Underlying these airy sounds was a more subtle melody—the soft, high ringing of tiny bells and something else that Ella Mae couldn't identify. It was a humming, a slow, steady throb of energy. It washed over Ella Mae like a wave of pure light.

Looking down, she noticed that she was dressed in a clingy slip of a dress, made entirely of a shimmering silver fabric. Stars seemed to wink from every crease and fold, and her bare skin glimmered and sparkled. Turning to look at her mother and aunts, Ella Mae gasped. All four were clad in shining silver and were as radiant as brides.

"We've got nothing on *you*," Sissy said. "You look like a Greek goddess. There's not a man alive who won't fall in love with you this night."

This comment propelled Ella Mae deeper into the grove. Wanting to know whether Hugh was of their kind, she hurried through the apple trees, marveling at the gold and silver fruit hanging from the boughs.

Coming upon the clearing, she exclaimed in amazement. Women in silver dresses and men in silver togas stood barefoot in the soft grass, holding unadorned goblets made of clay. Most of the celebrants were gathered around an enormous banquet table covered with hundreds of platters of fruit. Clusters of deep purple grapes were tucked alongside mounds of ripe mangoes. Pears, peaches, and plums were piled next to dates, kumquats, star fruits, kiwis, and pomegranates. Small trees bearing bright oranges bloomed at each end of the table, and dozens of pottery wine jugs were grouped at the center.

"This whole scene feels ancient." Ella Mae stared at the wooden dishes and clay cups.

"Our origins are just that. Ancient," her mother replied, pouring two cups of wine. "A toast. To your first harvest."

The two women clinked rims and then Ella Mae drank. The wine was like nothing she'd ever tasted before. It was as smooth and sweet as honey, but also tasted of the forest—earthy and rich and very, very old. The drink came to life in her belly, sending tendrils of warmth all over her body. For an instant, she could see silvery orbs of light hovering about the heads of the people in the clearing. They looked like half moons. But when she blinked, they were gone.

Everywhere she turned, there were familiar faces. She saw people she regularly bumped into at the grocery store, the farmer's market, the post office, or the bank. She saw neighbors, customers, and fellow churchgoers. There were lots of strangers too. She knew that people had traveled from distant parts of Georgia to attend the harvest, but she was in awe of how many of her kind were present.

"Long time no see!" a woman said from behind her, and Ella Mae swiveled to find Suzy smiling at her. Her pale hair glowed in the moonlight, looking as silver as her dress, and her eyes shone like a sea reflecting a sky full of stars.

"Oh! I am so glad you're here." Ella Mae hugged her friend. "Now I don't have to keep any secrets from you."

Suzy offered her an apricot. "Then I should start off by telling you that our grove in North Carolina was turned into a subdivision called Ashtree Commons. That's the main reason I moved to Havenwood. The stuff about getting away from a guy was true too."

"I'd have to guess that your talents have something to do with books."

"Yes, though it's not obvious because Suzanne's my middle name and means 'lily,' like the flower. But my first name is Mneme. In ancient Greece, she was the muse of memory. I can remember anything I've read in a book and I try to use my knowledge to help women. Lilies are the flowers of motherhood and childbirth and all that good, girly stuff, so when you put the two names together, I'm kind of like a female fount of knowledge."

Ella Mae was impressed. "Wow. That is so cool. And useful. I'd love to figure out how I could do more to change people's lives for the better."

"Word is that you've just been Awakened. It'll take some time for you to know the extent of your powers. Besides, it's no small gift to be able to make enchanted food." She waved her hand around the grove. "No one's been Awakened at our age, so you're all anyone can talk about tonight. Other than wondering where the new Lady is."

At the mention of the new Lady, the silvery wash of light lost its sparkle for a moment. Ella Mae turned, seeking the ash tree at the heart of the glade. The Lady of the Ash was more stooped than before, and there were only a handful of leaves on her branches. Several people were standing in a ring around her trunk. They had one hand placed against her peeling bark and were holding on to each other with their free hands.

Suzy followed her gaze. "They're saying good-bye. The Lady can talk to them now. Her voice will be really strong and clear in their minds right before she passes. It's really beautiful. She tells them all the things they've done to make her proud and what they need to do to continue to serve our kind. Then she'll sing them an ancient song of parting, which takes away their sorrow, and she'll be gone."

Ella Mae searched the crowd for the Gaynors but didn't see Opal, Loralyn, or Tilda anywhere. "Where are they?" she asked aloud, scanning the faces as a feeling of alarm began to take root in the pit of her belly.

Suddenly, her mother was there by her side. "Tilda Gaynor's been bitten by a black widow spider. She'll live, but she won't be coming to the grove. We have no Lady." She shot a fearful look at the fragile ash tree. A haunting song floated from its branches and drifted over the grove. Everyone fell silent.

"This is the end," her mother whispered.

Ella Mae knew that she wasn't talking about the last minutes of the Lady's life. This was the end of their magic too. The end of everything. And just when Ella Mae had been hoping for a new beginning.

Chapter 16

Ella Mae knew that she'd look back on the next few moments for the rest of her life. She'd constantly wonder if she could have done something to change the outcome. If she could have spoken powerful words or clung to her mother's arm to prevent her from moving. Had she known what was to happen, would she have had the courage to sacrifice herself? To put herself in her mother's place?

But Ella Mae did nothing. She stood still, watching in mute dread as the Gaynors pushed their way through the crowd of magical beings. Already, the silver coronas Ella Mae had seen around every head were becoming dim. The sweet and haunting melodies drifting through the glade were growing faint, and the platters of plump, ripe fruit on the banquet table had lost their luster.

"*YOU!*" Opal Gaynor shrieked upon seeing Ella Mae. Her eyes were wild with fear and desperation. Like everyone around them, she could feel her magic ebbing away. But she was clearly shocked by Ella Mae's presence in the sacred grove as well.

Ella Mae's mother took a step closer to her, as if to shield her daughter from Opal's crazed glare.

"It can't be!" Loralyn shoved past a couple holding hands. Ella Mae barely registered that it was Kelly and Noel before Loralyn began shouting. "You? You're not one of us! You're nothing!" She wore a look of naked hatred.

"The Lady!" someone cried. "She's about to leave us!"

Opal swung around to stare in horror at the shriveled tree. "Ella Mae LeFaye should take her place!" she yelled loud enough for everyone to hear. It was easy enough to do because the grove was eerily silent. Only the low murmur of the Lady's song drifted through the crowd, spellbinding many into a hypnotic state. Ella Mae realized that most of her kind didn't realize that their powers were about to disappear forever. The Lady's song was supposed to fill those around her with peace, and that's exactly what it was doing.

But Ella Mae didn't feel tranquil at all. And Opal's words tore through her like a lightning bolt. "What?" she asked, stunned. "Me?"

"No!" Her mother thrust out an arm as if to protect Ella Mae.

Opal strode forward, her cold and desperate gaze never leaving Ella Mae's face. "She could be the Clover Queen!" she declared at the top of her lungs. "She comes to her gifts late in life. She was born the night of the spring equinox and is the child of two magical parents! She might be the one we've been waiting for! She should accept her fate and serve us! She should become the Lady and save us!"

People began to stir from their stupor. Murmuring broke out around the table, and Ella Mae felt eyes on her. Too many eyes. Silently wondering. Hoping.

Her mother turned her back on all of them and took Ella Mae's face in her hands.

"Look at me, Daughter. See only me."

Ella Mae wanted to ask what Opal Gaynor was talking about, but she responded to the gentle command in her mother's tone and met her eyes.

"I am so proud of you, Ella Mae. You have been my greatest achievement. Your father would have loved you dearly. As I do." Her hands moved over Ella Mae's hair, her fingers passing through the silky locks, moving downward until they came to rest on Ella Mae's shoulders. "I love you so much. I need you to believe that. Your coming home allowed my heart to open and bloom like a rose. You taught me about hope and joy and the true meaning of family. I will always be with you, Ella Mae. Do not despair. I will always be here when you need me." Her hands fell away. "I love you, my sweet girl. Always."

And then she kissed Ella Mae's cheek, her lips as soft and cool as a snowflake, and began to run.

"NO!" Opal shrieked again.

Ella Mae's entire body felt leaden. By the time she realized what her mother intended to do, she was too far away to stop her. A guttural cry welled up inside her, and she ran toward the dying ash tree. The song had ceased and the Lady's family had broken their chain. They moved out of the way so that Ella Mae's mother could press her back against the peeling bark and spread her arms wide. She lifted her proud chin, and her long hair came loose from the clasp at the nape of her neck and cascaded down her shoulders, the black woven with strands of silver snagging on the rough pieces of bark.

There was such a profound stillness in the grove that time seemed to have frozen.

"Accept me, my brothers and sisters. Accept my offer of service. I vow to be worthy. I vow to keep you strong and lead you down the straightest path. I pledge my body and my future to you. Take me if you will."

"We accept!" a dozen voices replied in unison.

Ella Mae shouted "NO!" at the same time, but her protest was lost in the din.

A white light shot up from the ground and washed over Adelaide LeFaye. It was so intensely bright that Ella Mae instinctively threw up a hand to shield her face. Alongside her, her aunts did the same.

"Stop her!" Ella Mae sobbed. She saw the tears streaming down her aunts' cheeks. She saw the despair in their eyes. *"Save her!"*

Verena just shook her head and wept.

The light lost its searing edge. Ella Mae lowered her hand and watched in horrified fascination as the trunk of the ash tree absorbed her mother's body. It happened quickly and gracefully. One moment, her mother was suspended on top of the bark, and the next, she went under its surface as if she were sinking into a pool of water.

The tree immediately lost its aged appearance. It grew taller before their eyes, and leaves sprouted along every branch. The bark turned smooth and the limbs straight and strong. And then, without warning, thousands of fireflies descended from the sky and covered every inch of the tree with their ethereal glow.

"NO!" Ella Mae called out. Before the fireflies landed, she could still see the outline of her mother's figure. Now, the moving, glowing swarm obscured her view, and panic gripped her heart like a vise.

This can't be happening! she thought, unable to push the words out. There was no breath in her lungs. There was only the luminescent ash tree and the empty place beside her where her mother had once stood. *This can't be happening!*

She stumbled over to the tree, and when she reached out to touch it, the fireflies parted.

"Mom," she whimpered. "Not you. Please. Not you."

The tip of a slender branch brushed against her cheek.

"I'm here," a voice whispered inside Ella Mae's head. *"I am transformed, but I am still your mother."*

The fireflies began to alight from the twigs and leaflets, gradually revealing the new Lady of the Ash. The trunk had curved hips and the swell of breasts, and there, carved into the bark, was the face of Adelaide LeFaye. Her eyes were closed, but Ella Mae could see her within the tree.

Ella Mae threw her arms around the firm, warm trunk, and her mother tried to soothe her. To the others, her words sounded like the rustle of wind, but to Ella Mae, her mother's voice murmured, *"Hush now. It's all right. You will have the life I dreamed for you."*

"I don't want it without you," she cried into the bark.

"You are worth any sacrifice. You're my daughter. The light of my heart."

En masse, the fireflies lifted into the air. They hovered just above where the people had gathered in front of their new Lady, and then the insects unfurled their legs and dropped silver rose petals onto the magical men and women. The petals shimmered like spun moonlight and everyone cupped their hands to receive them.

"Hail to the Lady!" Verena called out, her eyes shining with tears.

The entire assembly dropped to one knee and bowed their heads in homage. "Hail to the Lady!" they shouted.

With her palms flat against the trunk, Ella Mae turned to look at the gathering. The moment the rose petals made contact, the people looked like they were burning. An orb of light grew outward from the center of their chests until their entire bodies were engulfed in a pure white radiance. It was like watching a hundred stars being born. It was the most beautiful thing Ella Mae had ever seen.

"The renewal," her mother explained.

"I don't want magic. I want you back." Ella Mae's voice was hoarse from heartbreak.

"You'll speak for me. For all of our kind. You will be the most important woman in Havenwood. I am tired now, my sweet girl. It takes great strength to communicate with you like this. Go join the others. Do not be sad. Continue to hone your gift. Find love. Live fully."

And then her mother fell silent. Ella Mae couldn't sense her in her head anymore. She glanced around. People had begun to laugh, to feast, and to dance. Music had sprung out of nowhere and it was no longer the soft, lulling songs she'd heard upon first entering the glade. This was fiddle, fife, and drum music. The music of the carefree.

The fireflies were drifting away. The handful that remained formed a circle around Ella Mae's head. She felt the blinking creatures place something in her hair before disappearing into the silver and lilac sky.

Dee came up to her, her face red and mottled from crying. "It's a wreath of roses."

"No," Sissy said, joining her sister. "It's a crown."

Ella Mae touched the velvety roses and the petals released a burst of fragrance that smelled of her mother. Her throat tightened, but she was too spent to cry another tear.

Verena, who'd been a pace behind Sissy, put her arms around the slim waists of her younger siblings and drew them close. She fixed her gaze on the Lady. "You fool, Adelaide! You were always so headstrong!"

"And the bravest of us all," Sissy added. "I should have *known*. You wouldn't let our magic fade. And you'd never let Ella Mae go back to being the girl she was before. You wanted to show her how much she meant to you."

The LeFayes each put a hand on the Lady's trunk. They stood like sentinels as the rest of their people celebrated. Most of the others came close to pay their respects. When Kelly and Noel approached, Ella Mae had to turn away. Seeing the young couple made her think of Partridge Hill and how someone else would have to tend to her mother's roses.

Only the Gaynors kept their distance, and though Ella Mae searched every face, she didn't see Hugh Dylan among her people. Somehow, this disappointment mattered little now. She couldn't imagine seeking him out after this. What would she have to say to him?

Here, in the midst of her kind, she felt destroyed by loneliness. Magic had taken everything from her. All she had left now was sorrow. And anger. And yet, there was one person she desperately wanted to see.

"If Tilda was attacked, there's still a threat out there. Beyond this grove," Ella Mae said quietly. "I feel like I've been torn in two. I don't want to leave my mom, but I need to make sure Reba's okay." She examined her aunts' faces beseechingly. "I'm going back to the hospital. I've had enough of this place." She gestured around the grove. "This is what an enchanted life means? It doesn't feel like a gift. More like a curse. A burden."

Dee hugged her tightly. "You made an unwilling sacrifice tonight, sweetheart. We all did. But she's not gone. She's not lost to us. She's just . . . changed."

Ella Mae pulled away. "She won't ever come back to Partridge Hill! It'll be empty! What about the roses? The Luna ceremonies? What about *me*?" Tears pricked her eyes. "I need to get out of here. I can't sit here with all this pain and watch people eat grapes and dance!"

Sissy was about to protest but Verena stopped her with a look. "Let her go."

The only person who tried to speak to her as she fled the grove was Suzy, but Ella Mae couldn't talk to anyone. She could see the concern and sympathy on her friend's face as she hurried past. It was a relief to step through the wall of boulders into the real night.

The first thing that struck her was the darkness. It was thick and impenetrable—layers of black shadows stacked from ground to sky. If there was a moon, a bank of smoky clouds had blotted it out. There wasn't so much as a single star to light Ella Mae's way to the parking area.

She could feel the path under her feet easily enough however, and she was unafraid of the spiky silhouettes of the bushes and pine trees. Too numb to feel much of anything, she walked in a stupor down the curving slope of the mountain, concentrating on one thing: getting to Reba.

When she reached the parking lot, she walked over to her mother's Suburban and slumped against the hood. Letting out a groan, she cursed in the darkness. She didn't have the keys.

"You're an idiot," she mumbled aloud.

"I couldn't agree more," said a voice from behind her.

Ella Mae whirled. The shadowy figure of a woman appeared around the rear of the SUV. The whites of her eyes glittered, and Ella Mae caught the flash of teeth as she smiled. The woman's outline was strangely familiar.

As she drew closer, Ella Mae instinctively retreated.

The woman paused and leaned casually against the Suburban's side. Suddenly, the flame from a lighter blazed through the darkness, and Maurelle put the flame to the cigarette dangling from her mouth. She had threads of gray in her hair and lines etched into the skin around her mouth and the corner of her eyes. Ella Mae gasped.

"You're . . ."

"Older?" Maurelle scoffed. "Yep. And I've got about ten more years to add before the night is through." She inhaled deeply and then blew a stream of smoke into the air, all the while studying Ella Mae with the cold, predatory gaze of a serpent. "You don't look so hot yourself."

Ella Mae couldn't take her eyes from Maurelle's middle-aged face. "You're a Shadow Child. You're the killer we've been trying to find."

Tucking her cigarette between her first two fingers, Maurelle clapped once, twice. "Took you long enough." She snorted. "And they say you're special. I don't know why. I don't see anything remarkable about you."

A fiery rage took hold of Ella Mae. It pulsed through her, as if her blood ran white-hot beneath her skin. "You failed. Even though you killed Melissa and Freda and poisoned Reba and Tilda, you failed. There's a new Lady, and she's stronger, wiser, and more powerful than you could have expected."

Maurelle arched her thin brows. "Must be a LeFaye for you to be acting so high and mighty. I'd say it hurt you pretty bad too, seeing as you look like someone just died. I mean, it's not like you can have a deep, meaningful relationship with a tree."

Ella Mae's rage grew. If not for Maurelle, Melissa Carlisle would be the Lady of the Ash and Ella Mae's mother wouldn't have needed to sacrifice herself. Ella Mae wanted nothing more than to curl her hands around Maurelle's throat and squeeze the breath out of her, but she couldn't fight an assassin one-on-one. She had to find another way.

I've got to keep her talking until the others come out of the grove.

"Go on," Maurelle said as if she'd heard Ella Mae's thought. "Ask what you want to ask while you can still talk. You're my last mark. After tonight, I retire in style."

"Someone's paying you to do this?"

Maurelle shrugged. "The Children have money. We pool our resources to finance our operations. When they're successful, we're rewarded very nicely. If your kind could stop squabbling long enough to work together, you'd be as well off as we are. But you're as shallow and petty as you've always been."

Ella Mae glared at her. "And you're evil. Not only did you kill two good women, but you also ruined the lives of innocent people."

"No one's innocent." Maurelle tossed her spent butt on the ground and crushed it with the toe of her black boot.

"Candis is," Ella Mae shot back. "And what about the Shermans? Was the soil of their farm contaminated when they starting the cheese-making venture or did you just happen to see to that?"

Lighting another cigarette, Maurelle moved toward Ella Mae until they were only a foot apart. Ella Mae didn't step back this time, but Maurelle didn't even look at her. She pulled herself onto the Suburban's hood and sat cross-legged, as if she and Ella Mae were two friends having a chat over coffee and scones. "Ah, that's better. I've been on my feet way too much lately. I don't see how people can wait tables. What a crap job."

"The Shermans?" Ella Mae prompted irritably. Maurelle's relaxed detachment incensed her more and more with every passing second.

"Lynn and Vaughn Sherman could have had it worse. I injected *Listeria* into *one* batch of cheese. If I'd had my way, I would have infected the entire water supply. Sure, some regular people, the ones I call sheep, would've gotten sick, but a few of your pathetic kind might have been wiped out too. Kids and old folks mostly, and what good are they to anyone? I always think the death of a few sheep is worth the risk if it means I can kill some of your people. Unfortunately, my brethren disagreed." She made a noise of derision. "They are way too paranoid about the media."

Ella Mae remembered what she'd been told about the Shadow Children. "You can't afford to strike at us like that. There are too few of you. Isn't that right?" She let her anger take control. "So you sneak around in the darkness. You stick syringes into cheese and make sure the tainted food gets on the right plates. If you ask me, that's far more pathetic than anything my kind does. It's downright cowardly."

Maurelle was off the hood in a heartbeat. "You must be really eager to die," she growled, standing on her tiptoes and pointing her finger within an inch of Ella Mae's throat. Then, she suddenly smiled. "Oh, I get it now. It was your mama, wasn't it? She jumped on the grenade when no one else would. That's why you're so mad." She began to laugh. "Man, that is rich. She probably did it to protect you. Did someone call you the Clover Queen? One of the glorious Gaynors perhaps?"

Though she said nothing, the answer must have shown on Ella Mae's face.

"Ha! They did call you queen!" Maurelle cried triumphantly. Her voice sounded older than it had before, but everything about Maurelle was now unfamiliar. Ella Mae had known her as a quiet, reserved, and private young woman. Now she stood in front of a mature and confident killer.

"I don't even know what the Clover Queen is." Ella Mae tried to feign indifference. "And it doesn't matter. We have a Lady and our magic's been renewed."

Repositioning herself on the hood of the SUV, Maurelle flicked the remainder of her cigarette onto the windshield of another car. "It totally matters. You're the second part of my mission." She raised two fingers. "First, eliminate all known candidates for the next Lady of the Ash." She dropped her middle finger. "Second, if there's any sign that Ella Mae LeFaye has come into her powers, eliminate her."

The anger seeped out of Ella Mae. A hard knot of fear took its place, lodging itself in the pit of her stomach. "Well, I'm not going to voluntarily eat a hunk of contaminated cheese, so your last assignment won't be easy."

Maurelle laughed heartily. "Good for you! I like it when my victims show a little spunk. And I don't have any cheese. Just like I don't have and have never had cancer."

"You just pretended to be sick so you could befriend

Candis?" Ella Mae asked in revulsion. "How long were you planning this . . . mission?"

"For a year. And it wasn't any cakewalk either. Do you think I enjoyed sitting through those cancer meetings? What a downer. I only made it through because I knew half of the people in there would die before I'd have to listen to their griping again." She released another twisted laugh.

"But why Candis? Freda hadn't even volunteered to be the Lady at that point."

Maurelle shrugged. "Candis was my in with you people. She was my age. She was moving back to Havenwood and invited me to come along. She even asked if I wanted to live with her and Rudy until I found my own place. Gross." She shuddered. "And most important of all, she wasn't magical. She was the perfect little sheep. I knew I could use my fake cancer to get her to trust me, want to help me, and to listen to me when I made subtle little suggestions like visiting Sherman Farms to sample cheese on the same day you were coming to the farm to buy that dumb old Jeep." She held up her hand. "I knew you were going. I bugged your phone while you were at work."

Despite this disturbing revelation, Ella Mae was relieved to hear that the Shermans were truly innocent. No matter what else happened, at least two people could continue to live their dream. "So you delivered the tainted cheese to Freda?"

"I sure did. That's why Candis doesn't remember giving it to her. And I delivered a little gift box to Melissa Carlisle too. Wrote a note from the Shermans saying they wanted to compliment her for producing such fine honey. A few days later, I stopped by to pay her a visit. Good thing too, since she was writing a thank-you note for the cheese. You people are too damn polite."

"But Melissa was perfectly healthy. How could the bacteria kill her? Unless . . ." An image of the brown recluse lying dead in the pie shop's front yard surfaced in Ella Mae's mind.

"Yessssss?" Maurelle hissed. "Would you like to see what my skin disease really looks like? The real reason I keep my arms covered is to hide my beautiful weapons." She unzipped her black sweatshirt with agonizing slowness, her mouth curved into a crooked smile. "Of course, I'm missing a few of my pets. I had to send them out into the world. I needed them to weaken Melissa, Reba, and Tilda. Freda got sick without my help. All that wedding stress did her in. That was so thoughtful of her. She kept me from aging for a little while longer."

And then, the sweatshirt was off. Maurelle balled it up and threw it on the ground. From a pocket in her jeans, she withdrew a slim flashlight and switched it on. Propping it under one of the Suburban's wiper blades, she aimed the beam at her torso and held her right arm close to the yellow light. From wrist to bicep, the skin was covered with tattoos of spiders. Specifically, black widow spiders. She then turned to show off her left arm, which showcased half a dozen brown recluse spiders.

"You can see where I've lost three of my little darlings," she said ruefully, pointing to a blank spot near her elbow on one arm and a larger patch of bare skin near the wrist of her other arm. "And now, I'll have to say good-bye to two more. I can't take any chances with you, Clover Queen."

Ella Mae tried to fuel herself with anger once more. She felt sparks of it inside her and tried to fan them into a fire. Fear couldn't save her now, but fury just might. "Why didn't you just kill me at the shop? Why all the drama?"

"I had to do things in order. Knock off the volunteers for the Lady first so that a weaker person would take their place. Then, find the location of the sacred grove. We might not be able to enter, but my brethren can damage it all the same. We'd just love to see a new housing development right here.

Kind of like the one we built in North Carolina." She sighed in satisfaction. "You were my last objective, and I had to get Reba out of the way before taking you out. She's old and small, but very skilled. I only got to her because she'd let her guard down around me."

A spider tattoo on Maurelle's left arm began to move. At first, it was just the twitch of a leg, but then another leg shifted, and another. And then, one of the black widows stirred, its abdomen swelling until it became a living, three-dimensional creature.

"Jesus," Ella Mae breathed in terror. "Is that your magic?"

"Every Shadow Child has a unique weapon," Maurelle answered, grinning at the spiders as they transformed from flat ink drawings to gruesome, wriggling threats. "These are mine."

Ella Mae knew she should run, but she was too spellbound to move. She also suspected Maurelle was anticipating her escape and that the moment she made to flee, the end would come quickly. First, Maurelle would deliver a chop to the windpipe or some other debilitating blow followed by dual spider bites on her neck. No one would come down from the grove in time to save her. For all Ella Mae knew, the revelers would stay there until daybreak.

"What's this Clover Queen stuff?" she asked while trying to think of a way to defend herself against imminent attack.

"It's a prophecy about a woman who can undo Myrddin's curse. I think it's a load of crap, but I was told to kill you just in case it's not, and I've got no problem with that." The brown recluse crawled down her forearm and onto the back of her hand.

Pointing at her enemy's face, Ella Mae said, "You'll be sixty if you do this. Are you seriously willing to trade all that time away for money?"

Maurelle nodded. "Hell, yeah. This is as good as it gets

for one of the Children. We get one major assignment, and if we blow it . . ." She drew her finger across her neck. "If we succeed, we get a pile of money and anonymity. That's all I want. We're not like your kind. We don't want families or kids or long walks on the beach. We're born with a craving to use our weapons, and once they're spent, we want to live out the rest of our time alone."

"What a miserable existence," Ella Mae remarked.

"I think the same of yours. At least your dull, insignificant life is about to come to an end."

By this time, the black widow had made its way onto Maurelle's other hand. Cooing at the arachnids, Maurelle carefully combined both spiders into the bowl of her left hand. In a blur of movement, she pulled an object from her front pocket. In the pale glow of the flashlight beam, Ella Mae recognized it as a Taser.

That's why no one runs, she thought despondently. And as hopelessness began to wash over her, she shoved it aside and sent out a silent call to the butterflies and moths. Her eyes were open, transfixed on the spiders, but her mind had become calm and clear.

"Go ahead," she taunted Maurelle; her voice sounded far away to her own ears.

Swarm her, she commanded. Though she couldn't see anything, she instantly heard the whisper of hundreds of wings. They were rushing in her direction, propelled by an enchanted wind.

"They're coming for you," she told Maurelle with absolute confidence.

Maurelle closed her fingers protectively around her spiders and glanced to her right and left. "Don't try to play me. It's way too late for that. Try to die with some dignity. After all, you could have been a queen. You might have been the one to change the fate of all those you love. But not now."

"They're coming," Ella Mae repeated and felt a surge of

power flow through her. Maurelle must have sensed it too, for the lustful glimmer in her dark eyes wavered.

She looked up and saw a mass of butterflies and moths descending toward her. The insects were packed into a dense cloud and were spinning like a tornado. Sparks flew from their wings and tiny lightning bolts shot into the black sky.

"If I'm going down, then you're coming with me," Maurelle said and raised the Taser. Before she could use it, Ella Mae struck out with her right leg, kicking Maurelle's hand as hard as she could. The weapon dropped to the ground and skittered under the Suburban.

Maurelle hissed in anger. Quick as a blink, she reached around to the small of her back and withdrew a knife from the waistband of her jeans. Its blade shone menacingly in the narrow circle of light. Adjusting her grip, she shifted her weight in order to plunge the blade into Ella Mae's heart.

But she never got the chance. A rock cracked against the back of her head and she crumpled to the ground as if her bones had turned to water.

Tossing the rock aside, Reba saluted the storm of butterflies and moths swirling above her. "Thanks, y'all. I'll take it from here."

Chapter 17

Ella Mae stepped over Maurelle's inert form and lifted Reba right off her feet. She hugged her so tightly that Reba squirmed in her arms the same way Chewy did.

"You're squeezin' me like you're tryin' to juice an orange, girl! You need to be more careful with someone in my delicate condition."

Instantly letting her go, Ella Mae stepped back and gestured at Reba's attire. "Did you mug a doctor?"

Smoothing a crease in her blue scrubs, Reba grinned. "I had to bust out of there. They weren't gonna let me go until tomorrow, and that simply would not do. First of all, I'd seen the killer and I knew she'd go after you next." She nudged Maurelle with the heel of her foot. "I was mighty woozy from the blow to the head she gave me, but I had enough brainpower to recognize a poisonous spider. I tried to get away, but my legs gave out real quick." Squatting, she examined the ink spiders on Maurelle's arms. The ones that had been moving a few seconds ago had returned to their two-dimensional shapes.

"I used to like spiders," Ella Mae murmured.

"Maurelle's are special. The venom of her little pets works three times faster than that of your run-of-the-mill poisonous spider." She shrugged. "Guess I should be right glad she wasn't covered with snake tattoos."

Ella Mae shuddered at the thought. "What do we do now? Bring her to the police?" But she immediately realized how impossible that idea was. "No. We can't explain this. Tattoos that come to life. An assassin who contaminated cheese with *Listeria* and ages by a decade with every person she kills. They'd lock *us* in a cell."

"We'll take her to the grove," Reba said. "I need to go there anyhow. I'm up and around, but I won't be my feisty self unless I get a dose of fresh magic."

"Oh, Lord." Ella Mae took Reba's hand. Gathering her strength, she said, "Maurelle got to Tilda. There was no one to take the Lady's place and she was fading fast. Mom . . . She . . ."

Ella Mae didn't need to finish. Reba could see the terrible truth written on her face.

"Adelaide?" she said, thunderstruck. "Adelaide?" She stared into the darkness for a long moment. "I need to see her. Come on, give me a hand with this bag of bones."

Bending down, Ella Mae slid an arm under Maurelle's back. Together, she and Reba half dragged the unconscious killer up the path leading to the wall of boulders. When they finally reached the rock barrier, Ella Mae was breathing hard.

"I thought Shadow Children weren't able to enter," she said, putting her palm against a cool boulder.

"They're not." Reba shifted Maurelle, taking on her full weight, and gestured for Ella Mae to proceed. "You go ahead. This moment is between her and me."

Too weary to argue, Ella Mae closed her eyes and entered

the grove once more. The music of celebration was still being played, and she could detect a new and familiar perfume in the air. "Roses," Ella Mae whispered.

An instant later, Reba appeared behind her. In a flash of light, Ella Mae saw the outline of Maurelle's body. It was only there for a second and then it was gone. A pile of ash lay at Reba's feet. After giving it a dispassionate glance, she began to disperse it with the toe of her shoe.

"Was she just . . . vaporized?" Ella Mae asked.

"It's the only way to deal with one of them," Reba answered and then shut her eyes and inhaled the pure, clean air of the grove. "Wait here, hon. You've been through enough tonight, and I'm gonna take you home. But I've gotta see your mama first. I failed her, and if she wants to assign a new protector, then it's her right to do just that."

Ella Mae was horrified. "*No!* I don't want anyone else. You're my family, Reba. I just lost my mom. You can't leave me too."

"I never thought the day would come, but Maurelle bested me. I mistrusted the girl from day one, but I told myself I was bein' silly. Told myself she was too weak to be a threat. Look what my mistake cost us. Look what it cost you—the person I love most in this world."

"Mom will never send you away," Ella Mae said. "She knows that I can't handle this change without you. I couldn't make it through tomorrow, let alone the future, which stretches out in front of me like a long, dark tunnel. I can't go into that tunnel without you."

Reba gave her a quick hug. "Oh, darlin'. There's plenty of light up ahead, you'll see. Now get comfy on a patch of nice, soft grass and try to rest. You're safe now and I'll be right back."

Obeying, Ella Mae walked a short distance away from the mound of ashes that was once Maurelle. She sat on the ground with her back supported by the trunk of an apple tree and allowed her eyelids to droop closed. Slowly, she was lulled to sleep by the gentle caress of a breeze.

When Reba shook her awake, she felt oddly refreshed, as if she'd slumbered for days and not minutes.

"I feel so much better," she said guiltily. "Not so sad. How can that be?"

"It's your mama." Reba smiled. "She'll heal you whenever you come here. Her magic runs through every blade of grass, every leaf, and every flower in this place. She *is* this place. When she told you she'd always be with you, that's what she meant. And you'll be her voice. When she has somethin' to say, she'll speak to you." Reba was unable to hide the touch of sorrow in her eyes. "Until then, it's you and me, kid. For some crazy reason, she wants me to stick around, so let's go home."

Jiggling the keys to the Suburban, Reba held out her hand and helped Ella Mae to her feet. As they slowly made their way back to the parking lot, Ella Mae asked, "How did you get here anyway?"

"I hotwired a motorcycle from the physician's lot." Reba's teeth shone white in the darkness as she gave Ella Mae an impish grin. "There's nothin' like the feel of a powerful engine between your legs when you're chasin' after an assassin."

"How are you going to return the bike?"

Reba waved the question off. "I ran into my favorite mechanic at the grove. In exchange for a movie date, he's gonna load it on his tow truck and drive it back to the hospital. Let's just hope that doctor is workin' the night shift."

The ride home was quiet. It was only when Reba turned into the driveway of Partridge Hill that Ella Mae realized the full impact of her mother's sacrifice. A few lights were burning downstairs but otherwise, the house was shadowy and quiet.

"Your aunts are sleepin' here tonight," Reba said. "As for

tomorrow night and the ones after that, you and I will manage. As long as we're together, we can make it through this."

Ella Mae didn't reply. She got out of the car and hurried to the guest cottage to see Chewy. After she hugged and kissed him until he wriggled in protest, she led him into her mother's garden.

She knew sleep would evade her, so she and Chewy aimlessly wandered the garden's gravel paths. Everywhere Ella Mae turned, she saw roses encased in a shining layer of silver. They looked like small moons, glowing softly on dark branches. Ella Mae's hand strayed to her head. She was still wearing the wreath of roses. Hers remained velvety to the touch and were as sweet smelling as a bridal bouquet. They had not turned hard and brittle like her mother's had.

When she came upon the Luna rosebush, Ella Mae took one look at the tight bud nestled amid the thorns and felt tears pool in her eyes. Dropping onto the stone lovers' bench, she lay down in the fetal position and wept. Chewy whined and licked her hand a few times, but he was soon distracted by a low-flying bug and trotted off to pursue it.

Chilled, Ella Mae curled herself into a tight ball. The whole garden felt frozen, as if winter had come early and covered every plant and blossom in a sheen of ice. Her mother's absence had robbed the garden of its magic, and it was no longer a place of riotous beauty, but a mausoleum of flowers and memories.

Ella Mae whispered for her mother to come home. She repeated her entreaty over and over again until sleep came and coaxed her into silence.

Sunlight woke her. It warmed the heavy wool blanket someone had laid over her and burnished her hair a fiery auburn when she lifted her head off a pillow. Wondering who had made her so comfortable in the night, she looked around, feeling groggy and slightly hung over even though she had had only one cup of wine.

Hearing the sound of footsteps on the gravel, Ella Mae tensed, but then Chewy appeared around the corner of a boxwood bush and barked out a cheerful greeting.

He was followed not by Reban or one of Ella Mae's aunts, but surprisingly by Suzy Bacchus. She carried two large mugs and wore a tentative smile.

"Hi," she said. "I thought you might want some coffee. It's oil-spill strong."

Ella Mae let out a laugh. "Sounds like Reba's. I call hers the Exxon brew." She accepted the mug and invited Suzy to sit on the bench beside her.

"Your aunts told me you slept out here," Suzy said after a long moment of silence in which both women sipped their coffee and watched Chewy paw at a beetle scuttling over the dirt. "I can see why. It's beautiful."

Confused, Ella Mae looked at her. "Beautiful? The roses are frozen. All the colors have leaked out. It's totally depressing."

Suzy shook her head. "Really, they're glorious. Come and see."

Ella Mae followed her friend to another section of the garden and gasped. The roses were as bright and vibrant as a kindergartner's finger painting. Hovering above the plump, robust flowers were hundreds of butterflies. The garden was populated by a dozen species, and at once, Ella Mae knew that her creatures had been tending to her mother's roses since dawn. She sent them a silent thank-you; her aching heart healed a fraction by the sight of the restored garden.

"Can you get over the scents?" Suzy inhaled deeply. "Vanilla, honey, caramelized sugar, a summer rain, the first frost. Everywhere I walk I smell something different."

Bending over a cluster of flowers in a cheerful yellow hue, Ella Mae drew in a breath and smiled. "These remind me of the beach. Hot sand under my feet, the sun on my shoulders, and a wind carrying salt from the ocean." She brushed a petal with her fingertips. "My mother isn't gone. She's still here."

Suzy nodded. "I'm glad you're feeling better about what happened. I don't think I could be as strong." She turned away to examine a lilac-colored rose.

"It was really nice of you to check on me," Ella Mae said.

"Hey, I'm your friend and you've been through hell. Your mother became the Lady, and a Shadow Child's been plotting to kill you for months. Just the thought of it gives me the chills." She rubbed her arms. "Reba told everyone about the murders last night. How Maurelle gave Melissa and Freda contaminated cheese to throw suspicion on the Shermans. How she used her spider tattoos to poison her victims, making them more susceptible to the *Listeria*. And she nearly succeeded in murdering Reba and Tilda."

Ella Mae shook her head. "It's been a nightmare, but at least I can talk to you about everything. Who else would believe that a pie shop waitress was an assassin pretending to have skin cancer in order to keep her enchanted spider tattoos covered?"

The two women began to laugh. Standing under the warm sun amid her mother's roses, Ella Mae knew that she would endure. Perhaps, she'd even learn to flourish like this garden. Life would never be the same, but she would not surrender to grief. Her mother wouldn't want that for her.

"I wonder if they'll send another Shadow Child," Ella Mae said as she and Suzy passed a rosebush covered with crimson blooms. "Maurelle made it pretty clear that her kind was out to destroy our sacred groves. She claimed responsibility for having a North Carolina grove turned into a subdivision."

Suzy's green eyes grew dark with anger. "That was ours." Clenching her fists, she kicked a large chunk of gravel, sending it scuttling across the path. "This is awful. As if things

weren't tough enough for us already. We can't have kids
without some earth-shattering sacrifice, we need to renew
our magic every year, and we have to keep our identities
and abilities secret. On top of all that, the Shadow Children
want to obliterate the few sanctuaries we have left." Her
hand flew over her mouth. "I'm sorry, Ella Mae. The last
thing you need to hear is my griping."

"Actually, it's refreshing," Ella Mae said. "And I feel the
same way. Sometimes I think what we are is a rare and
wonderful gift. Other times, it seems like a curse. Right
now, I'd trade every ounce of magic I have to get my mother
back. Since that's not possible, I plan to do something else
to change our future for the better. I'm going to be my mother's voice, and I refuse to let anything happen to our grove
or to our people. My days of being a victim are over."

Raising her coffee cup, Suzy said, "I'll drink to that."

Ella Mae and Suzy gently touched the rims of their mugs
together and then drank down the last of Reba's strong brew.
Afterward, they continued walking toward the house. Occasionally, a butterfly would land on the wreath of roses on
Ella Mae's head, and Suzy would identify it by name. "A
zebra swallowtail is hitching a ride and a tawny emperor is
coming in for a landing. Glad I flipped through that book
on the moths and butterflies of North America a few months
ago. It could prove useful, since I'm going to be hanging out
with the Queen of the Butterflies."

The word "queen" resonated in Ella Mae's memory.
"Both Maurelle and Opal Gaynor called me the Clover
Queen. Have you ever heard that before?"

Suzy furrowed her brow. "No. Did they say anything else?"

"A woman of our kind is supposed to be able to break
Merlin's curse. She's supposed to be born on the spring
equinox and to come to magic later in life."

"You've got the second requirement down. What about
the first?"

Ella Mae pointed at a large rosebush forming a semi-circle around a birdbath. Its flowers had a cotton candy pink in the center and its edges were trimmed with a translucent white. "This bush was planted right before my mom went into labor and bloomed right after I was born. It's called the Ella Mae rose, but my mother also referred to it as the First Blush of Spring rose."

"Because you were born on the spring equinox," Suzy said, her gaze locked on the roses. "Boy, I wish I could tell you more about this Clover Queen business. And yet, I hear you have quite a remarkable library in your house." Her eyes were glinting. "I'd bring you coffee every morning if I could take a peek at those books."

Ella Mae smiled. "You don't have to bring me a thing. I'd be grateful for your help. I need to find out more about this queen. It might save our kind. I don't want us to be victims again. Any of us." She touched Suzy on the arm. "Let's start tonight. We could share a bottle of wine, order a pizza, and do some research? What do you say?"

Again, Suzy seemed to hesitate. "Do you remember what I told you about my gift? That I remember anything I've read?"

Sensing that Suzy had something important to tell her, Ella Mae stopped under a wrought-iron trellis covered by a tangle of mango-colored roses releasing a sweet, citrusy scent. "Sure."

"The reason I came here this morning was to tell you that I once read about an object that would supposedly release the Lady of the Ash forever. In other words, we wouldn't need a Lady anymore. The elders could work together to make decisions for our people and no one would have to sacrifice themselves to keep us magically charged." She touched the point of a thorn with her index finger and a bright bead of red blood appeared on her skin. She examined it thoughtfully. "I'm too much of a newcomer to have raised the subject with the elders, and honestly, the whole thing sounds pretty insane, even to me. But after I saw your face last night, I knew I had to at least tell you about the legend."

Ella Mae grabbed Suzy by the hand. "Oh, please! I'd do anything to set her free!"

"I only read about a reference to it, unfortunately. The legend says that the spell can be broken using a powerful object called the Flower of Life. It's supposed to grow at the bottom of an enchanted lake and can only be reached after surviving great peril. That's all I know." Suzy sounded deeply disappointed. "While we're looking for info on the Clover Queen, we should keep an eye out for allusions to this magic flower."

Hope bloomed inside Ella Mae. She could feel it chasing away the cold despair she'd felt the night before. "You and I are going to be spending a lot of time together," she told Suzy with a smile and released her hand.

"That's fine by me," Suzy said. "I'll bring Jasmine to hang out with Chewy, and you and I will sit around eating and drinking and reading until we've either saved the world or turned into reclusive, overweight alcoholics."

Ella Mae shook her head. "Can't do that. In fact, after I say good morning to Reba and my aunts, I'm heading out for a long run. If I'm going to take on the Shadow Children and face untold perils trying to set free my mother from the ash tree, then I need to be in the best shape of my life."

"I'll be the bookish sidekick, if you don't mind. I only run when I hear an ice cream truck," Suzy said and linked her arm through Ella Mae's. "I have one more question for you."

"Yes?"

"Does Reba cook when she's upset?"

Nodding, Ella Mae sniffed the air. Now that they were so close to the main house, she could detect the scents of bacon, toast, buttery biscuits, and fried eggs overpowering the perfume of the roses. "I hope you're hungry. She's probably made enough food for an entire football team. In fact, she may have invited an entire football team for breakfast. Reba has all kinds of healthy appetites."

Suzy looked amused. "She and I are going to get along splendidly."

After her run, Ella Mae tidied the guest cottage and then took Chewy down to the lake for a game of catch. When he finally grew tired and settled down under a bush for a nap, Ella Mae walked to the end of the dock and sat with her feet dangling in the cool water.

Autumn had painted the trees surrounding the lake in gold, orange, and cranberry. The hues reflected in the water's flat surface, creating an ocean of color. Ella Mae drank in the sight and planned to describe it to her mother when she visited the grove after lunch. She could work on the week's menu while telling her mother what she'd learned from Suzy.

The figure of a man suddenly appeared on the path descending to the lake, and Ella Mae immediately put aside thoughts of her mother, Clover Queens, and magical flowers. Hugh waved and, tucking a small basket under his arm, jogged down the slope.

Ella Mae watched his approach with a pang of bittersweet longing. He was not of her kind. She could never reveal her true self to him. And yet, she couldn't picture a future without him. Somehow, they were tied together.

"How's the water?" Hugh called from the other end of the dock. Chewy darted over to say hello, and Hugh scratched the little terrier behind the ears and then patted him on the flank. Chewy's tail wagged feverishly, and he licked Hugh's hand before returning to his place in the shade.

"The water's perfect," Ella Mae beckoned for him to join her. "Come on in."

She was dazzled by the brightness of his smile and the glint of gold in his hair. As he strode toward her with the easy confidence of a warrior, she was once again struck by how magnificent he was. How Beautiful. A chiseled marble statue of a Greek god come to life. But even Hugh's powerful arms and strong shoulders couldn't endure the weight of her secret burdens.

"This is a nice surprise," she said as he sat down.

Kicking off his shoes, he rolled up his jeans and plunged his feet into the lake. Tilting his face up to the sun, he sighed in contentment. "I went to the hospital before I came here," he said. "Rumor has it that Reba checked herself out last night. Hope she wasn't wearing one of those gowns that don't cover your backside."

Ella Mae laughed. "She wasn't, though I don't think it would have bothered her much. Her doctor wanted her to stay another day and she wouldn't hear of it, so she swiped some scrubs and took off."

"The billing department will find her easily enough," Hugh said, opening his eyes and looking at her. "But I'm glad she's okay. I know how close you two are."

Ella Mae nodded. "She's like a second mother to me." Instantly regretting her choice of words, she fished around for a change of subject. She didn't want Hugh to know that her mother wasn't around, and she wasn't ready to spread the tale she and her aunts had concocted over breakfast. Come Monday, they'd let it be known that Adelaide LeFaye had embarked on a lengthy tour of the world's most memorable gardens. She was traveling alone and planned to spend a considerable time away from Havenwood.

"Give me a year to search for this flower," Ella Mae had pleaded over her untouched plate of bacon and eggs. "After that, you can make up whatever story you want to explain why she doesn't come home. If I fail, that's what we'll be forced to do, right? Pretend that she's died?"

Verena had nodded glumly.

"We won't need to create a fictional skiing accident or car crash. I'm going to bring her back," Ella Mae vowed. "You'll see."

"Hey," Hugh said, pulling her into the present by laying his hand lightly over hers. "You drifted away for a bit."

She smiled at him. "Sorry. I'm really worn out."

With his free hand, he placed the small basket on her lap. "These are for you. They're the last of the season. I thought you could make a few pies that'll taste like summer."

Ella Mae folded a checkered dishtowel back to reveal the round curves of a dozen peaches. The aroma of sunlight and sweetness curled around her, warming her like a shawl draped over her shoulders. She rubbed her thumb across their silky skins. "They're lovely," she said. "And I have enough for two or three pies."

"Don't bake one for me," he said. "Don't do anything for me. Let me spoil you a little. I'd still like to take you on that date we never got to go on. You're done with Sloan. I'm done with Loralyn. The world makes more sense when I'm with you. Everything's better. Anything's possible. Let's give it a shot. Say yes, Ella Mae. Be with me." He squeezed her hand and looked at her with his bright blue eyes. His stare was so intense that she felt he could see right into her heart.

Powerless to say anything else, she whispered yes. He leaned over and kissed her. It was a soft and tender kiss that spoke of more than just desire. It was a kiss promising long walks and shared meals and endless hours curled up together on the sofa watching old movies. Ella Mae believed in the kiss. She believed in Hugh.

Tracing his jaw with her fingertip, she said, "Can we keep things rated PG until I'm officially divorced? I'd like to do this right."

He nuzzled her neck, planting a featherlight kiss on the

soft skin just below her ear. "Make it PG-thirteen and you have a deal."

She gently pushed him away. "And we have to protect what we're trying to build. You need to avoid Loralyn and I need to stay as far away from Sloan as possible. They're a part of our past. Let's leave them there." Ella Mae didn't mention the stunning floral arrangement she'd received from Opal and Loralyn Gaynor. According to the note, the bouquet of star-of-Bethlehem flowers was meant to symbolize reconciliation between the two families. Now that the Lady of the Ash was a LeFaye, even the Gaynors were forced to be respectful and courteous. Ella Mae had read the note, written in Loralyn's elegant script, over and over again, hoping that the sentiment was genuine. She'd like to have the discord between the two families become nothing more than a bad memory.

Hugh slid his arm around Ella Mae, making her forget all about Loralyn. "I agree," he said. "From this moment on, we only look ahead."

With their fingers entwined, Hugh and Ella Mae watched a pair of mallards skim over the surface of the lake. The male and female ducks coasted above the water in perfect unison, strong and graceful as two dancers moving in time to the same music. As the ducks approached the shore, they veered to the south and abruptly rose higher into the sky. They quacked once and flew off toward the cloudless blue horizon.

Hugh looked at Ella Mae, his eyes glimmering with happiness. "It's like they're saying, 'Here we go.'"

"Yes." Smiling, she cupped his face in her palms and drew his lips down to meet hers. "Here we go."

Chapter 18

Ella Mae spent the afternoon in the grove, nestled at the foot of the ash tree that was her mother.

There were no signs of last night's celebration, and the silvery glow had given way to a soft yellow light. The clearing below the rise where Ella Mae sat was no longer a circle of tidy grass, but an entanglement of wildflowers. Bees and butterflies darted in and out of the sea of blooms while hummingbirds hovered over the brightest petals. Reba had been right when she said that her mother was in every part of the grove.

It had felt strange at first—to rest her back against the ash tree's bark and start talking, as if her mother could engage in normal conversation. But after a while, Ella Mae got used to speaking without expecting a reply. She knew her mother was listening, so she told her about Suzy's visit and how she and her friend planned to research the Clover Queen and the Flower of Life.

After that, she took out a notebook and a pile of the latest food magazines and created a menu for the week ahead. "It's apple season," she said. "Apple caramel pie, apple ginger crumble pie, apple cheesecake pie, apple pie with a cheddar cheese crust . . ." she trailed off, thinking of the golden peaches Hugh had brought her.

Guard your heart, her mother whispered, and Ella Mae wondered if she could now read her mind.

"I'm going to be very careful this time around," she promised. "When I think about what my life would have been like had I stayed in New York . . ." She pushed away the anger that bubbled up inside. "Those redhead twins did me a favor. If not for them, I wouldn't have known that I was living a lie—that my real life had yet to begin." Glancing upward, she studied the bits of clear blue sky peeking through the tree leaves. "I need to be smarter too. I hired a Shadow Child to work in my pie shop, for crying out loud. But I'm not innocent anymore, and I think that these things have happened for a reason, no matter how much they've hurt me. I've got to believe that I'm going to grow and blossom like one of your roses—that it'll all be okay in the end."

A leaf detached from one of the lower branches and floated downward, brushing against Ella Mae's cheek like a kiss.

Don't come to me too often. Go discover your destiny.

"Yes. That's the word." Ella Mae pressed the side of her face against the ash tree's trunk. "Destiny." She could hear a muted hum inside the bark. It sounded like a distant heartbeat. Ella Mae liked its steady, comforting rhythm. "I won't fail you, Mom. I'm going to change things for all of us."

Other than the rustle of the wind through the leaves, the grove was silent. Ella Mae knew it was time to get started on the promises she'd made, so she drew in a deep breath of her mother's scent of moonlight and roses, and said good-bye.

* * *

The days passed. Ella Mae continued to bake pies and Reba continued to serve them. The shop was busier than ever, but Ella Mae refrained from placing an ad in the *Daily*. She and Reba simply let it be known to their regular customers that Maurelle had suddenly quit and The Charmed Pie Shoppe needed a new waitress. By the end of the week, people Ella Mae barely knew began to show at first light, volunteering to take Maurelle's shifts for a day or two.

"To express our gratitude," they'd whisper, and she knew they were referring to her mother's sacrifice.

She accepted their offers. Not only did she need the help, but Ella Mae also enjoyed growing closer to more of her kind. None of them behaved differently from the non-magical folk of Havenwood, and yet she felt a connection to those who'd been at the harvest. It was as if they were joined by invisible threads—wispy and delicate as dragon-fly wings. She liked the idea of being a member of this secret society. It lessened her loneliness and assuaged her grief.

Her aunts didn't give her many opportunities to mope. They were constant visitors at both The Charmed Pie Shoppe and Partridge Hill, and Suzy would often show up at Ella Mae's guest cottage after her workday was over, Jasmine in tow. The poodle would romp through Adelaide's gardens, Chewy trotting happily at her side, while Suzy and Ella Mae sat in the sunroom, poring over books, scrolls, and old documents.

And then there was Hugh. He took Ella Mae on Sunday afternoon hikes, to quiet, casual dinners, or to the movies on Saturday nights. He'd show up unannounced on weekday evenings too, bearing a bottle of wine and Chinese takeout. After building a fire in the guest cottage's tiny living room, he'd pour the wine and hand Ella Mae a plate loaded with kung pao chicken, ginger beef, spring rolls, and steamed broccoli. They'd eat on the sofa, Ella Mae's legs thrown over his, and talk about the day.

Despite all the company and attention, Ella Mae missed her mother. She went to the grove when she could, but there were days when her mother didn't speak to her at all.

"It's as if she's asleep," she told her aunts one evening as they supped on Reba's spaghetti Bolognese. "I can sense her in there, but she can't respond. It's like she's dreaming or something."

Dee gave her a sympathetic look. "You have to remember that she is part of the tree now. Who knows what it means to be an enchanted tree?"

"I think Ella Mae has it right," Sissy said and put her hands over her heart in a typically theatrical gesture. "Adelaide *is* dreaming."

"It's not like she has to be on a schedule!" Verena bellowed. "The rhythms of nature are not the same as ours. Adelaide's tuned into primeval things we can't even begin to imagine!"

Passing a basket of garlic bread to Reba, Dee said, "I wonder what she sees, what she's experiencing."

"It must be a bit like Ella Mae's butterfly vision, don't ya think?" Reba said and motioned for Sissy to hand over the carafe of red wine. "How far could you travel through their eyes?"

Ella Mae shrugged. "I have no idea. I haven't needed to see beyond Havenwood yet, but with the way things have been going, I wouldn't be surprised if I needed to fly to all kinds of strange places in the future."

The women talked about the foreign countries they hoped to visit one day, until they heard the rumble of a familiar engine. Ella Mae wiped her mouth with a napkin and stood up.

"That must be my Jeep," she said. "I dropped it off to be

serviced this morning, and Noel and Kelly told me they'd
drive it back for me. They went out to celebrate the new
business Noel reeled in from a huge garden center in
Atlanta."

"The boy's doin' a fine job," Reba added. "Adelaide will
be pleased to know that her darlin' plants are in good hands."

Ella Mae nodded. "I'll ask them to join us for dessert. I
made two pear and almond tarts."

Verena put her fork down. "Just two?"

Ella Mae paused on her way to the back door and called
to Verena over her shoulder. "Don't worry! I bought two
gallons of vanilla ice cream to go with the tarts."

Stepping into the lavender twilight, Ella Mae walked
through the fragrant herb garden and crossed the lawn divid-
ing the main house from the guest cottage. When she
reached the driveway, she rushed over to her Jeep, shouting
in delight.

"Wow!" she cried. "Look at you!"

The faded white paint had been replaced by a pink raspberry hue that matched The Charmed Pie Shoppe's front
door. Across the side, the name, location, and phone number
of the shop had been written in curly, butter yellow font.
Ella Mae's favorite detail was the luscious cherry pie occu-
pying the Jeep's rear panel. The pie had a golden lattice crust
from which sugar crystals glistened like tiny pieces of ice
and looked good enough to eat.

Kelly opened the passenger door and hopped out.
"Ta-da!" she shouted, throwing her arms out. "Isn't she gorgeous?"

Noel came around from the driver's side and handed Ella
Mae the keys.

She couldn't take her eyes off the Jeep. "This is the most
beautiful car I've ever seen."

"There's a peach pie on the other side," Dee said from
the edge of the driveway. "After all, we are in Georgia. And

if you look closely, you'll see little silver stars here and there. For those rare few who don't already know that your pies are charmed."

Ella Mae swung around. "Is this your doing? I thought I was just getting a tune-up."

Dee smiled and moved to her side. "One of my artist friends wanted to do something special for you. Well, for all of us."

"Another token of gratitude?"

"Yes." Dee slid an arm around Ella Mae's waist. "People need to do this. They're grateful to your mother for renewing their magic. Some of them depend on their abilities to feed their families. It would be wrong to deny them the chance to thank us for that."

"But this is just for me," Ella Mae protested. "And all the help I've been getting at the pie shop? I'm feeling a little too appreciated."

"So should we have your Jeep painted white again?" Dee quipped.

Ella Mae ran her fingers along the glossy paint, noticing the silver stars for the first time. They winkled and sparkled just like the real ones coming to life in the night sky. "No way. But I would like to bake a few pies for the person who did this. I have to do something to show how happy I am with my beautiful billboard on wheels."

"I'm sure that would be fine," Dee said. "Now let's show this baby off to Reba and my sisters."

Every morning, Ella Mae would leave her guest cottage before sunrise and walk through the brisk, end-of-September air to the garage. She'd raise the door, take one look at her pink Jeep, and smile.

The bright, cheerful hues had the same effect on other motorists. No matter where Ella Mae went, people would honk and wave or give her a thumbs-up.

"I love your car, lassie!" an old woman leaning heavily on a walker shouted one afternoon while Ella Mae paused at a red light. "It makes me feel young and happy."

Even though she was worn out from a long day at the pie shop, Ella Mae had immediately pulled over and offered the woman a ride. "I know you're not gonna rob me or kill me or have your way with me," she teased in a thick Scottish burr. "You're a LeFaye. You're good folk."

The woman's name was Mrs. Drever, but she pronounced it "Dreever." She lived in a tidy, moss green cottage overlooking the lake. She invited Ella Mae in for a cup of tea and the best shortbread Ella Mae had ever tasted.

"My people are all bakers," Mrs. Drever explained. "Bakers and fishermen."

"Where are you from?"

Mrs. Drever gestured at the framed map of Scotland hanging above the mantel. "Find Inverness and keep going to the northeast until you hit the sea. The Orkneys are just there. Nothing else nearby but ocean. My daughter, Carol, lives in the same village where I grew up. She's coming to visit tomorrow."

"Please bring her to the pie shop. I'd love to treat both of you to lunch."

Two days later, Reba marched into the kitchen and informed Ella Mae that her Scottish guests had arrived. Ella Mae dusted off her apron and pushed through the swing door in time to see a woman with ash-blond hair and gray green eyes help Mrs. Drever to her seat.

"You must be Carol." Ella Mae smiled and introduced herself. "Your mother's a delight. We had such a nice visit."

"That was very kind of you to bring her home," Carol said. "I don't get to Havenwood as often as I'd like and I worry about her."

Carol's burr wasn't as pronounced as her mother's, and Ella Mae was about to ask where else she'd lived when she noticed a glass pie dish on the table. It was covered with tin foil so Ella Mae couldn't identify it. Neither could she conceal her curiosity.

"What do we have here?"

Peeling back the foil to reveal a cloudy layer of whipped topping speckled with chocolate shavings, Carol said, "Ma told me about your customer-of-the-week pie, so we made you our favorite. Banoffee pie. I've tasted modernized versions, but I think our old family recipe puts them all to shame." She handed Ella Mae an index card listing the ingredients and instructions.

"This is a real treat. People have given me recipes before, but this is the first time anyone's made me a pie." She brought the dish close to her nose and inhaled the sweet aroma of ripe bananas, melted toffee, and crispy gingersnaps.

Ella Mae thanked Carol. She gestured at the pie and smiled. "Ma always said that a baker's hands were especially beautiful. Even though they were covered with knife cuts, burns, and scars, they spoke of all the things the baker had made to warm the bellies and the spirits of the folks he or she served."

"That's lovely." Ella Mae put the pie on the table and glanced down at her palms. "I have a few marks."

"You'd best get back in the kitchen and get some more," Mrs. Drever said with a wink, and she and Carol began to laugh. Ella Mae wished she could linger with them for hours, chatting and listening to Scottish tales, but her apple ginger crumble pies would be scorched if she didn't get them out of the oven within the next minute or two.

She picked up the banoffee pie and thanked the Drevers once again.

"I believe you'll be marked soon enough," Carol predicted, her gray green eyes glowing with warmth and wisdom. "You're going to do great things. I'm certain of it."

The comment made Ella Mae pause. Was Carol one of her kind? Was there a sacred grove in the Orkneys? Mrs. Drever had said that the LeFayes were good folk. Could she teach Ella Mae something new about her family?

Unfortunately, she couldn't tarry or her pies would be ruined, so Ella Mae smiled and told the two women to order anything they wanted, on the house, of course.

She barely got to the apple pies in time, but when they were safely positioned on the cooling racks, Reba burst into the kitchen.

"Guess who's here? Lynn and Sherman Vaughn. They wanna come on back. That all right with you?"

Ella Mae nodded and took a quick peek at the second round of dessert pies baking in the second commercial oven. These were apple pies too, but these had been mixed with cranberries and walnuts and topped with a cinnamon spice crust.

Lynn Sherman came in first. She carried a rustic basket stuffed with a variety of cheeses. "We promise this will be the last time we'll invade your kitchen and interrupt your work."

"We just had to thank you," Vaughn said. "We had our soil and water tested and it's clean. Thank the Lord. It's clean."

"But the cheese with chives was contaminated," Lynn reminded him gently. "We don't know how and we were very straightforward with the health inspectors. They couldn't find any traces of *Listeria* on our equipment, and we're allowed to continue making cheese."

Vaughn took the basket from his wife and placed it on the worktable. "You made us aware of how important food safety is to people in our line of work, and we're grateful that you cared enough to talk to us."

"And to trust us to do the right thing," Lynn added.

Ella Mae already knew that the Shermans weren't

responsible for the *Listeria* contamination. Maurelle was. But since she couldn't tell the Shermans the truth, she congratulated them heartily instead. "Someone brought me a pie," she said. "Pull up a stool and we'll share it."

The kitchen was perfumed by the scent of apples and cinnamon. Ella Mae grabbed the coffee carafe from the dining room and poured three cups before slicing the banoffee pie. At the first taste, she moaned in pleasure. The blend of sweet bananas, silky toffee, and airy whipped cream contrasted perfectly with the buttery crunchiness of the gingersnap cookie crust.

"Heaven," she murmured and then blushed as a slice of banana fell off her fork and onto the floor.

"We didn't see that," Vaughn teased.

Having finished their coffee and pie, the Shermans chitchatted for a few more minutes and then left Ella Mae to her work. The lunch rush was over, and Reba informed her that the dining room was nearly empty.

"I'm goin' outside for a Twizzlers break," Reba said. "The garbage truck is due anytime now, and there's a fine, strappin' young stallion who rides on the back. I like to watch that boy in action."

Grinning, Ella Mae turned off the oven timer and grabbed a potholder. With her left hand, she pulled the first of the apple-cranberry-walnut pies from the hot oven. She placed it on the worktable, took a step back, and reached for the next pie.

And then she lost her footing.

Careening off balance, she pivoted her body away from the oven door, her left hand still closed around the apple pie. As she fell, she released her hold on the pie dish in order to free both hands to help break her fall.

She landed hard on her right hip, and the glass pie plate crashed against her open palm. She cried out in pain as it burned her flesh, and yanked her hand from beneath it, but not fast enough.

"Ella Mae?" Reba was suddenly at her side. She glanced at the raw, angry wound and quickly helped Ella Mae to her feet. "Come on, hon. Let's put that hand under cool water."

With her hip aching and her hand throbbing, Ella Mae hobbled over to the sink and leaned against the counter as Reba held her palm under a gentle rush of water. She then snapped a stalk from the aloe plant on the windowsill and, pulling Ella Mae's hand out of the water stream, squeezed the fresh juice onto the red burn.

"Oh, that's better." Ella Mae could feel the pain receding a little.

Reba broke off another aloe leaf and cut it lengthways. Digging out the clear sap and pulp with a spoon, she mashed the contents in a bowl until it resembled a thick paste. She gently smeared it over the burn.

"I'm so glad Mom gave me that plant," Ella Mae said.

Even though the burn was covered in paste, Reba continued to study Ella Mae's hand.

"I slipped on a banana slice, of all things," Ella Mae explained, and when Reba still didn't respond, she said, "It doesn't hurt much anymore. I don't think it's that bad, is it?"

"It's gonna leave a scar," Reba said, and when she looked at Ella Mae, her eyes were as round as moons. "A real special scar."

Ella Mae brought her palm closer to her face. "What are you . . . ?" And then she saw it.

There, burned deep into the tender, soft skin, was a four-leaf clover.

A thrill of fear and exhilaration coursed through her. "I think it's me, Reba. The Clover Queen," she whispered. "I don't know why and I don't know what this means for me or for any of us, but I'm ready to find out."

Reba exhaled and bit off the end of her licorice stick. She chewed mechanically, her astonished gaze fixed on the puckered, red shamrock.

Finally, she looked at Ella Mae and smirked. "Well, just don't go expectin' me to call you Your Highness."

Ella Mae threw back her head and laughed. The sound mingled with the scent of aloe oil and baking apples. It floated through curls of warm steam and wisps of pale sunshine. It rang like bells from a high turret—loud and strong and magical.

Recipes

Charmed Piecrust

2½ cups all-purpose flour, plus extra for rolling
(place in freezer for 15 minutes before use)
1 teaspoon salt
1 teaspoon sugar
1 cup (2 sticks) unsalted butter, very cold, cut into ½-inch
  cubes (to make the butter cold enough, put into 6 to 8
  tablespoons of very cold water)

Combine flour, salt, and sugar in a food processor; pulse to mix. Add butter and pulse until mixture resembles coarse meal and you have pea-sized pieces of butter. Add ice water 1 tablespoon at a time, pulsing until mixture begins to clump together. Put some dough between your fingers. If it holds together, it's ready. If it falls apart, you need a little more water. You'll see bits of butter in the dough. This is a good thing, as it will give you a nice, flaky crust.

Mound dough and place on a clean surface. Gently shape into 2 discs of equal size. Do not overknead. Sprinkle a little flour around the discs. Wrap each disc in plastic wrap and refrigerate at least 1 hour.

Remove first crust disk from the refrigerator. Let sit at room temperature for 5 minutes or until soft enough to roll. Roll out with a rolling pin on a lightly floured surface to a 12-inch circle (Ella Mae uses a pie mat to help with measurements). Gently transfer into a 9-inch pie plate. Carefully press the pie dough down so that it lines the bottom and sides of the pie plate. Use kitchen scissors to trim the dough to within ½ inch of the edge of the pie dish.

Roll out second disk of dough and place on top of the pie filling. Pinch top and bottom of dough firmly together. Trim excess dough with kitchen shears, leaving about an inch of overhang. Fold the edge of the top piece of dough over and under the edge of the bottom piece of dough, pressing together. Flute edges by pinching with thumb and forefinger. Remember to score the center of the top crust with a few small cuts so that steam can escape.

Charmed Egg Wash

To achieve a golden brown color for your crust, brush the surface with this egg wash before placing the pie in the oven.

  1 tablespoon half-and-half
  1 large egg yolk

Note—if you're short on time and decide to use the premade piecrusts found in your grocery store's dairy section, then use the egg wash on the crusts to give them a homemade flavor.

Charmed Georgia Peach Pie

1 Charmed Piecrust
12 fresh, ripe peaches
½ cup firmly packed dark brown sugar
⅓ cup granulated sugar
1 teaspoon ground cinnamon
¼ cup all-purpose flour
2 tablespoons butter, cut into pieces
1 large egg, beaten
2 tablespoons turbinado sugar (sugar in the raw)

Prepare Charmed Piecrust.

Peel peaches and cut into slices. Stir together brown sugar, next 2 ingredients, and ¼ cup flour in a bowl; add peaches, stirring to coat. Immediately spoon peach mixture into piecrust in pie plate, and dot with pieces of butter.

Carefully place remaining piecrust over filling; press edges of crusts together to seal. Cut off excess crust and crimp edges of pie. Brush top of pie with beaten egg; sprinkle with 2 tablespoons granulated sugar and a dusting of cinnamon if desired. Cut 5 slits in top of pie for steam to escape. Or, create a lattice top by cutting dough disk into strips using a fluted pastry wheel. Place on top of filling and follow the egg/sugar/cinnamon finishing touches. Protect edges of crust with foil or pie shield.

Freeze pie 15 minutes. Meanwhile, heat a cookie sheet covered with a sheet of parchment paper in oven 10 minutes. Place pie on hot cookie sheet.

Bake at 425 degrees on lower oven rack 15 minutes. Reduce oven temperature to 375 degrees; bake 40 minutes. Cover loosely with aluminum foil to prevent overbrowning, and bake 25 more minutes or until juices are thick and bubbly (juices will bubble through top but parchment paper will protect your tray). Transfer to a wire rack; cool 2 hours before serving.

Charmed Apple Ginger Maple Crumble Pie

1 Charmed Pie Crust (if you don't want to make your dough from scratch, use Charmed Egg Wash on a refrigerated Pillsbury crust)

6 cups peeled and chopped apples (pick your favorites or substitute the apples for Bartlett pears)

1½ tablespoons cornstarch

½ teaspoon salt

¼ cup packed brown sugar

¼ cup pure Grade A maple syrup

1 tablespoon lemon juice

1 teaspoon lemon zest

½ teaspoon ground ginger

CRUMBLE TOPPING

⅔ cup flour

½ cup old-fashioned oats

½ cup packed dark brown sugar

⅓ cup cold butter, cut into small pieces

Roll out pie dough and place in a 9½-inch deep-dish pie dish. Put in the freezer to set.

Preheat the oven to 400 degrees. Place the chopped apples in a large bowl with the cornstarch, salt, brown sugar, maple syrup, lemon juice, lemon zest, and ginger. Toss well using your fingers.

Place the apple mixture into the pie dish. Place the pie into the center oven rack and bake for 45 minutes.

While baking, take all the crumble topping ingredients and place them in a bowl. Use your hands and mix the ingredients until large crumbs form. Refrigerate until use.

After the 45 minutes are up, remove pie and reduce heat to 375 degrees. Sprinkle the crumb topping evenly over the pie and bake for another 15 minutes. Cool on a wire rack for at least one hour. Serve with a scoop of vanilla ice cream.

Charmed Peanut Butter Cup Pie

CRUST

Store-bought Oreo or chocolate cookie crust
(Or for homemade chocolate cookie crust):
1 ¾ cups chocolate cookie crumbs
¼ cup sugar
½ cup butter, melted

FILLING

1 ⅓ cups semisweet chocolate chips (about 8 ounces)
⅔ cup plus 1 ¾ cups chilled whipping cream, divided
1 tablespoon honey
2 teaspoons pure vanilla extract, divided
1 cup creamy peanut butter
½ cup confectioners' sugar

If making homemade crust, preheat oven to 350 degrees. Spray 9-inch glass pie dish with cooking spray. Blend chocolate cookie crumbs, sugar, and butter in food processor and press mixture over bottom and sides of pie dish. Bake crust for 15 minutes. Let cool.

Combine chocolate chips, ⅔ cup whipping cream, honey, and 1 teaspoon vanilla in microwave dish and microwave until chocolate melts (2 to 3 minutes, depending on strength of your microwave). Whisk until smooth and spread majority of chocolate mixture over bottom of crust, leaving a few tablespoons of the chocolate to drizzle on top of the finished pie later on. Freeze crust for 10 minutes.

Whisk peanut butter and 1 teaspoon vanilla in small bowl. In medium bowl, beat 1 ¾ cups whipping cream and ½ cup sugar until very thick (don't beat until peaks form, however). Fold into peanut butter in parts. Spoon peanut butter mousse over chocolate layer and chill for 1 hour to 1 day. Garnish with drizzles of leftover chocolate mixture.

Charmed Mini Lemon Tarts

   5 ounces cream cheese at room temperature
   ¾ cup granulated sugar
   2 large eggs
   ½ cup freshly squeezed lemon juice (requires 3 large lemons)
   1 tablespoon grated lemon zest
   2 packages mini graham cracker tart crusts (for a total of 12
       mini tarts)

Preheat oven to 350 degrees.

Using a stand mixer or food processor, blend cream cheese until smooth. Add the sugar. Once the sugar is completely mixed into the cream cheese, add the eggs. Next, add the lemon juice and zest, and process until completely blended and smooth. Spoon the mixture into the individual tarts, filling to the top. Bake the mini tarts approximately 15 minutes or until filling is set.

Let cool and top with berries, whipped cream, a sprig of mint, or a piece of lemon cut into a small triangle.

Mrs. Drever's Charmed "Customer of the Week" Banoffee Pie

CRUST

1 stick butter, melted
1 tablespoon brown sugar
10 ounces ginger snaps, crushed fine

FILLING

1 14-ounce can sweetened condensed milk
3 ripe bananas, sliced
2 tablespoons lemon juice
1½ cups chilled heavy whipping cream
1 teaspoon pure vanilla extract
1 tablespoon confectioners' sugar
Hunk of milk chocolate candy bar for garnish (Ms. Drever prefers Cadbury Dairy Milk)

Prepare ginger snap crust: In medium bowl, mix melted butter with brown sugar. Add crushed ginger snaps. Mix well. Press mixture into 9-inch pan. Bake at 350 degrees for 5–8 minutes. Cool.

Put can of sweetened condensed milk in large saucepan and cover with water. Boil for 2 hours (adding water when necessary). Cool. Open and stir with fork to remove any lumps. (It will be brown in color.) Spread on top of the ginger snap crust.

Slice three bananas and sprinkle with lemon juice. Arrange over the toffee.

Put large mixing bowl and electric mixer beaters in freezer for ten minutes. Remove and add heavy whipping cream. Whip until peaks are just about to form and then add in vanilla extract and sugar. Continue whipping until stiff and spread on top of banana layer. Grate milk chocolate over the top. Chill until serving.

Charmed Lamb Pie

1 cup pine nuts
1 tablespoon olive oil
1 large onion, chopped
1 clove garlic, minced
2 pounds ground lamb
2 teaspoons salt
½ teaspoon pepper
2 tablespoons mint, finely shredded
2 teaspoons cumin
1 teaspoon cinnamon
2 tablespoons lemon juice
1 cup plain yogurt
1 Charmed Piecrust

Preheat oven to 350 degrees. Spread pine nuts on cookie sheet and toast for ten minutes. While nuts are toasting, sauté onion and minced garlic in olive oil (1 to 2 minutes) and then add lamb. Cook until lamb is nicely browned (about 5 minutes) and then drain excess liquid. In large mixing bowl, combine lamb mixture with spices, pine nuts, lemon juice, and yogurt. Pour filling into piecrust. Bake for 25 to 30 minutes at 400 degrees.

Dear Reader,

Thank for you spending time with Ella Mae and the colorful cast of characters of Havenwood, Georgia. The next book in the Charmed Pie Shoppe Mysteries is due out in January 2014.

Until then, I'd like to invite you to pay a visit to another charming and intriguing small town. Oyster Bay, the fictional hamlet featured in my Books by the Bay Mysteries, is located on North Carolina's Crystal Coast. Home to heroine Olivia Limoges, a budding novelist and successful restaurateur, Oyster Bay is filled with quaint shops, sunburnt tourists, and a host of unforgettable residents. And while Olivia and her friends, and the Bayside Book Writers, aren't enchanted like the folks of Havenwood, they too believe in the magical power of family and friendship.

So take a trip to the beach and experience a seaside paradise known not only for its serene beauty, but also for the unusual amount of mayhem and murder occurring within its limits. To whet your appetite, turn the page to enjoy a chapter from the forthcoming Books by the Bay Mystery: *Poisoned Prose*.

Happy reading,
Ellery Adams

> Words—so innocent and powerless as they are,
> as standing in the dictionary, how potent for
> good and evil they become in the hands of one
> who knows how to combine them.
>
> —Nathaniel Hawthorne

"Death by chocolate. That's what the coroner's report will read," Olivia Limoges said to the woman sitting next to her. She pushed away a plate still laden with a caramel brownie, a hazelnut petit four, and a square of peanut butter fudge. "I'll have to be rolled home in a wheelbarrow."

"That's why this place is called Decadence." Laurel Hobbs, local reporter and mother to twin boys, bit off the end of a strawberry dipped in white chocolate and moaned. "How can you resist the many, many temptations being offered to us? Here we are, two of the lucky few invited to this exclusive event, and you're showing restraint. Seriously, Olivia, try this one. Just take a bite."

Olivia glanced at the Amaretto cream puff and shook her head. "I think it was a mistake to drink multiple martinis during the cocktail hour. I could hardly refuse the chocolate martini I was given for the initial toast, and then Shelley pressed something called a Snickertini into my hand and stood there while I drank it. I didn't want to offend her on her big night, and Michel would poison me at work tomorrow if I did anything to upset his beloved chocolatier, so down the hatch it went."

Laurel held up her hands. "No more talk of poisoning, strangling, or any other form of murder, please. I think we've had enough violence to last us several lifetimes. Besides, Michel would never turn on you. He's the head chef in the most celebrated restaurant on the North Carolina coast and you own the place."

Gesturing around the desserterie, which was filled with Oyster Bay's most influential townsfolk along with a dozen journalists and television personalities from out of state, Olivia shrugged. "The Boot Top can't compete with an establishment serving every guest a dark chocolate shopping bag filled with white chocolate mousse. And did you see what Shelley used as a garnish? Sugared raspberries and a Decadence business card made of fondant. Incredible."

"No, you probably can't compete with that. I guess you should be happy that Shelley doesn't serve seafood or the Bayside Crab House would be in trouble too."

"Speaking of the Crab House, I should pick up some treats for my niece. I saw some starfish lollipops on the counter. Each one is made of raspberry-filled chocolate and costs more than an entire Happy Meal, but she's worth it."

Laurel grinned. "It's a good thing you're an heiress. You could buy every last piece of candy in here if it took your fancy."

Olivia bristled. "Hey, I work as hard as the next person."

"You do. You spend all those hours between two restaurants and yet you stay so thin." Laurel shook her head in disbelief. "How can you be around such exquisite food all day long and not weigh a million pounds? If I weren't your friend, I'd really hate you. I still haven't worked off the rest of my baby weight and the twins are almost four! Oh well, now's not the time to count calories." She popped a truffle into her mouth. "Look at Shelley. She's sweet, beautiful, and clearly isn't shy about sampling her wares. A woman with Shirley Temple dimples and Marilyn Monroe curves. No wonder Michel fell for her. Ah, here he comes now."

Michel was glowing. Olivia barely recognized him out of his white chef's coat, but he cut a nice figure in his rented tux. "Can you get over my Shelley?" he asked, sitting next to Olivia and giving her a brotherly kiss on the cheek. "If I weren't madly in love with her, I'd be desperately jealous. She's got everyone under her spell. I told you she was an enchantress."

Olivia rolled her eyes. "Spare me, Michel. I've overindulged on tarts and cakes and bonbons and I can't stand another ounce of sugary sweetness."

"Then you should try the spicy chile chocolate," Michel suggested. "Or the bacon flavored." Olivia gave him a dark look, but he was too jovial to notice. He and Laurel began to compare notes on their favorite treats, going into endless detail about the perfect balance between sea salt and bittersweet chocolate.

"I'm going outside for some air." Olivia took her water glass and headed for the kitchen. Without asking permission, she breezed through the swing doors into the narrow space, surprised to find it empty of both wait and cooking staff. Shelley had hired servers from a local catering company for her grand opening and they were all busy in the main room, but where was the dishwasher? An assistant pastry chef or sous chef?

The kitchen was a mess. The sink was full of stainless steel bowls coated in dried caramel, jam, buttercream, and chocolate in every shade of brown. The remnants of crushed nuts, chopped fruit, and mint sprigs were strewn across the cutting board and every burner on the commercial stove was obscured by a dirty pot or sauté pan.

"Shelley's going to be up very late tonight," she said, unable to stop herself from picking up a bag of flour that had toppled from the counter onto the floor. "She's got to hire some full-time help."

Like many of the stores lining the streets of downtown Oyster Bay, Decadence had a small concrete patio out back where the merchants and their employees would take smoke or lunch breaks. Shelley had placed a pair of Adirondack chairs, a picnic table, and a potted fern on hers. The fern didn't look like it had long to live, but Olivia decided to prolong its existence by dumping the contents of her water glass into its bone-dry soil.

She went into the kitchen, refilled the glass, and repeated the process three times before the soil was moist to the touch.

"I think it's a hopeless cause," a voice said from the alley-way behind the shop.

Olivia jumped.

"Damn it, Flynn." She scowled at the handsome, middle-aged owner of Oyster Bay's only bookstore. "Is this how you spend your evenings? Creeping among the town's garbage bins?"

"Only when beautiful women are nearby," he replied nonchalantly and sat down at the picnic table. "Is this how you spend yours? Dressing to the nines and watering half-dead plants?"

Olivia studied the man who'd once been her lover. He was as carefree and confident as usual. His mouth was always on the verge of curving into a smile, and there was an ever-present gleam of mischief in his gull-gray eyes. A textbook extrovert, Flynn loved to swap gossip with his customers and play with their children in the bookstore's puppet theater. He was lively and friendly and fun. Everyone liked him. He was everything Olivia was not and that's what had initially drawn her to him. However, their strong physical attraction hadn't been enough to hold them together and they'd both moved on to form more meaningful relationships with other partners.

"What are you thinking about right now?" Flynn asked. "You've got this look on your face. Like you've gone back in time and want to linger there a moment. Perhaps you are reminiscing about us?" He raised his brows and smiled a little. "We had some electric moments, didn't we?"

Trying not to let him see the accuracy of his guess, Olivia joined him at the picnic table. "Where's Diane? It's a Saturday night in June. The stars are shining, the ocean breeze is blowing, and the town is stuffed to the gills with tourists. So why aren't you out wining and dining your girlfriend?"

"Because we had a big fight," he said without the slightest trace of emotion. "And because I wanted the chance to talk to you."

"Oh?" Olivia's tone was guarded. "In the middle of Shelley's event? How did you know I'd be here?"

Flynn shrugged. "It was a sure bet that she'd invite you. Any small business owner with half a brain would. Do you know how many new customers I've gotten because you recommended me?"

"I love Through the Wardrobe." Olivia was careful to praise the store, not its proprietor. "I'd do anything to see it flourish. A town without a bookstore is an empty shell of a place."

Beaming, Flynn leaned toward her. "I'm so glad you said that. It makes it easier to ask you for a big favor."

Olivia gestured for him to continue.

"*The Gazette* and I are partnering to sponsor a storyteller's retreat next month. It's for people all over the region who make their living performing folktales. I'm going to schedule some children's programs at the shop, and the paper will arrange for adult performances at the library. If there's enough interest, we'll use the high school's auditorium."

"That sounds wonderful, Flynn," she said sincerely. "But where do I come in?"

Olivia had to give her former lover credit. He didn't dance around the point or try to soften her up with compliments. He simply opened his hands so that his palms formed a bowl and said, "I need help funding the event. The expenses were supposed be covered by the *Gazette*, a grant, and me. Well, the grant's fallen through. But we have to go on. Things have been set in motion. Hotel rooms have been booked. Ads placed. Invitations sent and accepted. But we don't have enough money to pay for it all. We need a philanthropist, Olivia. The storytellers need you."

"Don't lay it on too thick," she warned. "How much are we talking about?"

Eyes flashing in premature triumph, Flynn reached into his shirt pocket and withdrew a slip of paper. "I've itemized all the costs for you. This way, you'll have proof that I'm not heading out on a Caribbean cruise at your expense."

Olivia didn't unfold the paper. She tucked it into her Chanel evening bag and promised to look it over in the morning. "I never make decisions when my belly is stuffed with chocolate."

Flynn laughed. "An excellent motto. After all, chocolate stimulates the mind's opioid production, creating feelings of pleasure that will eventually wear off. But if you'd like to prolong the sensation of euphoria, I'd be glad to assist with that." He stood and held out his hand to her. She took it, allowing him to pull her to her feet. He studied her pale, silvery blond hair, which was swept off her brow in a modern wave, and then lowered his eyes to her necklace of moonstones and black pearls. His gaze drifted down the curves of her body, taking in the formfitting, vintage-style cocktail dress made of black lace with satin trim and Olivia's long, tan legs.

"I'd try to kiss you, but your police chief boyfriend would probably hit me with his baton."

Olivia pulled her hand away. "I don't need him to defend my honor. I can clout you all by myself, thank you very much." She smiled to take the sting from the words and wished Flynn a pleasant rest of the evening.

Once Flynn had gone, she hesitated for a moment at the kitchen door and then decided not to return to the party. She walked down the alley and stepped onto the main sidewalk, heading for the public lot where her Range Rover was parked.

In order to reach her car, she had to pass by Fish Nets, the bar where her writer friend, Millay, worked. It was not an establishment Olivia regularly frequented, as it reeked of tobacco, body odor, and stale beer. The music was too loud; the entertainment was limited to a stained pool table and decrepit dartboard; and the floor was covered in spilled liquor, discarded chewing gum, and chewing tobacco spittle. And yet, Olivia had grown up among its clientele. Her father had been a fisherman, and most of the old timers within had known her since she was a skinny, towheaded girl with the shy, sea-blue eyes.

Pausing at the door, she considered how ridiculous she'd look drinking whiskey with a group of work-worn men and women. She'd walk in wearing her cocktail dress and heels while Millay's patrons would be dressed in soiled and tattered jeans, frayed denim shorts or skirts, and T-shirts that had been washed so often than their logos and designs were no longer decipherable. Their skin would be bronzed by the sun and weathered by wind and worry. Their hands were scarred and dirty and their language coarse, but they knew her. They knew her story. They knew her mother had died in a tragic accident, that her drunkard of a father had abandoned her when she was only ten, and that she'd come back to Oyster Bay after a long absence in order to reconnect with the past and strive for a new and better future.

They've accepted me all along, she thought with a rush of gratitude and entered the bar. *These are my people.*

For a moment, her appearance stunned the crowd into silence, but it only lasted a heartbeat. Men and women warmly greeted her with catcalls and raucous shouts. Millay waved her over to the bar and polished a tumbler with a dish towel.

"Don't give me the stink eye. This one's clean," Millay said before pouring a finger's worth of her best whiskey into the glass. "It's the only thing in here that is, besides you. Aren't you supposed to be down the street with the rest of the snobs?"

"Why would I want to sip champagne and devour plates of sumptuous desserts with Oyster Bay's elite when I could be here, sitting on a wobbly stool and breathing in toxic air?" Olivia gestured at the taps. "Buy you a beer?"

Millay grinned. "Absolutely. But I prefer the King of Beers."

She reached into the refrigerator behind her and pulled out a bottle of Budweiser. Popping the cap off with a neat flourish, she clinked the neck against Olivia's tumbler. "In the immortal words of Minna Antrim, 'To be loved is to be fortunate, but to be hated is to achieve distinction.'"

Olivia laughed. "Despite your best efforts, I believe you are genuinely adored."

"In this place, yeah. Beyond these walls, I'm that girl the old biddies point and frown at in disapproval. I use too much makeup, my skirts are way too short, and I wear black boots all year long. I'm the scourge of the Junior Leaguers and I take pride in knowing they're afraid to look me in the eye." She pretended to claw at the air with her left hand, causing the feathers hanging from her black hair to swing back and forth. Millay's blend of several races had lent her an exotic beauty, but she preferred to celebrate her artistic nature by piercing her eyebrows, wearing rows of hoops in her ears, and dying the tips of her jet strands neon pink, orange, or green. Lately, she'd taken to adding accessories to her textured bob. Tonight, she wore crimson feathers, but at the last meeting of the Bayside Book Writers, the twentysomething barkeep celebrated the final round of edits on her young adult fantasy novel by decorating her hair with glittery Hello Kitty clips.

"That's why you're such a talented writer," Olivia said. "You're fearless in life and on paper. You have the courage to be you, but you're also willing to be vulnerable. That's hard when you're used to wearing armor. Believe me, I know."

Millay shook her head in disgust. "What kind of crack was in that chocolate you ate? Don't go all fortune cookie philosopher on me, damn it. Hurry up and finish that whiskey. You need to wash that sugar out of your system."

Olivia complied. Millay immediately refilled her glass while a man sat down on the vacant stool to Olivia's right.

He lifted the faded John Deere cap from his head and said, "Evenin', ma'am."

"Good evening, Captain Fergusson." She gestured at her tumbler. "Would you join me?"

"Reckon I will. Thank you, kindly."

When Millay had poured two fingers of whiskey, he turned to Olivia and she raised her glass. " ' May the holes in your net be no bigger than the fish in it,' " she said, reciting one of the fishermen's traditional toasts.

He nodded and replied with one of his own. "May your troubles be as few as my granny's teeth."

Sipping their whiskey, they fell into easy conversation about the commercial fishing industry. Captain Fergusson supplied both of Olivia's restaurants with shrimp and had recently expanded his operation. He was now her primary source for blue crab and flounder as well, and she often met his trawlers at the dock when they returned with full cargo holds. Olivia would chat with the captain and his crew as she made selections for the restaurants. She liked Fergusson and, more important, she trusted him.

Fergusson had cast off from the dock while it was still dark to fish the waters off the North Carolina coast for the past forty years. And it showed. He was grizzled, his pewter-colored beard was wiry, and his eyes were sharp from decades of gazing into the horizon. He was gruff, blunt, hardworking, and fair, and Olivia had grown quite fond of him.

As they spoke, other fishermen drifted over and inserted themselves into the conversation. Olivia bought clams, oysters, mussels, scallops, and a dozen different fish from many of them. Before long, she called for shots of whiskey for the entire motley crew. In between swallows, Olivia praised everyone she recognized for the quality of their seafood while the men and their wives shared predictions about the summer harvest. This naturally led to a discussion about the weather, and Olivia realized that to a bar filled with fishermen, construction workers, farmers, and yardmen, each day's forecast had a direct effect on their livelihood.

"You'd best get ready for a hot, dry summer," one of the women told Olivia.

Another woman, clad in a lace-trimmed tank top that was several sizes too small for her generous chest, pointed a cherry-red acrylic nail at a man chalking the end of his pool cue. "Boyd said his pigs have been lying in the mud for weeks." She cocked her head at Olivia. "Do you know about pigs?"

"Only that I like bacon." Olivia smiled. "But I didn't think it was unusual for them to roll around in the mud. I thought that's how they kept cool."

"Sure is," a second woman agreed. "But it ain't normal

for them to do it all the time. See, when they carry somethin' around in their mouths—a stick or a bone or somethin'—then you know it's gonna rain. When they just lie there in the dirt for days on end, a dry season's comin'."

A man wearing a black NASCAR shirt elbowed his way into the group. "The ants are all scattered too." He looked at Olivia. "When they walk in a nice, neat line like little soldiers, then we're gonna have a storm. I got a big nest right outside my front door and they haven't lined up in ages. It's no good."

"Woodpeckers aren't hammerin' neither," another man added, and someone else mentioned how the robins had left his yard weeks ago and that he was certain they'd gone west into the mountains. "The animals know things we don't."

Everyone nodded in agreement and then one of the women turned to Captain Fergusson. "What's the sea been tellin' you?"

"She keeps her secrets close, but the moon says plenty." He put his whiskey down. Cupping his left hand, he raised it into the air, palm up. "We got a crescent moon right now, and she's lyin' on her back like she's waitin' for her man to come to bed. We won't see a drop of rain until she gets up again. Mark my words."

The women tut-tutted and murmured about summers gone by. Summers of unrelenting heat. Long days of dry wind and parched ground. They talked of how the land had gone thirsty even though the ocean was close enough to touch. The salt had clung to people's skin, making them sticky, short-tempered, and lethargic.

Olivia spotted a local farmer, Lou Huckabee, on the fringes of the group. He'd been listening to the exchange closely. "I'll still get you all your produce, Miss Olivia," he said above the music. "Don't you fret."

"I know you will, Lou. And every piece of fruit will taste like it was plucked from the richest soil on earth, washed and delivered straight to my kitchens. That's why I won't serve my customers anything else. You have a feel for growing things like no one I've ever met."

He dipped his head at the compliment, flushing from neck to forehead. "It's a callin', to be sure."

"To farmers," Olivia said, and held up her glass.

"To farmers!" The men and women around her echoed.

Next, they toasted fishermen, fishermen's wives, an array of different types of laborers, Millay, Olivia's mother, and on and on until Olivia was dangerously close to being drunk. Despite the close air and the way the whiskey made her feel overheated, she was too content to leave. And when Captain Fergusson began to tell a tale about a pod of dolphins changing into mermaids, she became as instantly enraptured as the rest of his inebriated audience.

While the old man spoke in a voice as weathered and worn as his face, Olivia thought about the note Flynn had given her. She glanced around at the people in the bar, reflecting on how each and every one of them had grown up listening to the stories of their parents and grandparents. Their elders passed down folklore on the weather, animal husbandry, treating ailments, courting, raising children, and more. And here they were now, sharing those same stories. Old, well-loved, and oft-repeated stories.

They are as much a part of us as our DNA, she thought. She knew that in the small, coastal town of Oyster Bay, the local legends focused mainly on the sea. She'd heard them over and over since she was little, but now she was suddenly curious to hear what tales Flynn's storytellers would bring to share with them.

A burst of laughter erupted as Captain Fergusson reached the end of his story. The woman in the tank top took a long pull from her beer and said, "Them mermaids might not be real, but my daddy saw the flaming ghost ship last September. Said it came out of the fog like somethin' sneakin' through the gates of hell. He was supposed to bring his catch into Okracoke that night so it'd be fresh for the mornin' market, but he sailed home with it instead."

No one laughed at her. Millay wiped off the bar and poured another round. "I've heard about that ship before. Would you tell me the whole story?"

The woman nodded solemnly, but there was a gleam of excitement in her eyes. Olivia saw it and smiled to herself. She'd seen the same spark in her mother's eyes every night at bedtime. Without fail, Olivia was sent to sleep with a spectrum of wonderful images and words floating through her mind. And though her childhood was long gone, a good story was no less magical to her now.

"A long time ago, a ship full of folks from England sailed to Okracoke," the woman began.

Olivia turned away from the storyteller so that she wouldn't see her take out her phone. She quickly sent a text to Flynn, telling him she'd be glad to help defray the costs of the retreat, and then turned the phone off and put it back in her purse.

When the woman was done with her tale of murder, robbery, and revenge, the talk returned to the weather, as it so often did at Fish Nets.

"It's hard to prepare for a dry season," Lou Huckabee told one of the fishermen. "I can irrigate, but nothin's the same as real rain."

"That's true enough," the other man agreed. "Much easier to get ready for a storm. You know they're comin' and you know that, by and by, they'll pass on through."

Olivia sighed. "Still, we've had enough storms to last us a lifetime. I hope the big ones pass us over this year."

Captain Fergusson covered her hand with his, and Olivia sensed that he knew she wasn't referring to hurricanes, but to the number of violent deaths that had occurred in Oyster Bay over the past few years.

She squeezed his hand. "I could use a season of peace and quiet."

"It's all right, my girl," he said as tenderly as possible. "Life ain't always easy and it ain't always fair, but there's beauty in every day. You just gotta know where to look."

Olivia considered this. She looked around the room and decided that he was right. Tonight, the beauty had been in this rough place filled with rough people. It had been in their lore and their legends and the way in which their stories bound them all together, weaving a spell of binding that could never be broken.

On impulse, Olivia told the captain about the storyteller's retreat. "They'll bring energy and tranquility and a little bit of magic to our town," she said, smiling widely.

For a long moment, the old fisherman didn't respond. Then he rubbed his bristly beard and slurred into his cup, "Outsiders tend to bring us things that we don't want. Sure, stories can be like a fire on a cold night. But they can burn too. There ain't nothin' can cut deeper or sting with more poison than words can. You'd best keep that in mind, Miss Olivia. Words have power, and all things of power are dangerous."

And with that, he tossed back the last swallow of whiskey, slipped off his stool, and stumbled out into the night.